A
Rogue
About
Town

Also by
Rebecca Connolly

The Arrangements:
An Arrangement of Sorts
Married to the Marquess
Secrets of a Spinster
The Dangers of Doing Good
The Burdens of a Bachelor
A Bride Worth Taking
A Wager Worth Making
A Gerrard Family Christmas

The London League:
The Lady and the Gent

Coming Soon:
A Tip of the Cap

The Spinster Chronicles:
The Merry Lives of Spinsters

A Rogue About Town

Rebecca Connolly

PHASE

Phase Publishing, LLC
Seattle

Text copyright © 2018 by Rebecca Connolly
Cover art copyright © 2018 by Rebecca Connolly

Cover art by Tugboat Design
http://www.tugboatdesign.net

Phase Publishing, LLC first paperback edition
August 2018

ISBN 978-1-943048-57-1
Library of Congress Control Number 2018951689
Cataloging-in-Publication Data on file.

*A*cknowledgements

To the incomparable and marvelous Jeremy Irons, whose voice, talents, and brilliant depth inspired the mentor of all my spies, and whose magnificence in representation is a glorious addition to the cast of this book.

And to my bed, who has never once let me down, is always there for me, and knows exactly what I need. This is truly an affair of the heart.

Want to hear about future releases and upcoming events for Rebecca Connolly?

Sign up for the monthly Wit and Whimsy at:

www.rebeccaconnolly.com

Chapter One
London, 1824

"*Thank* you so much, Rogue. You don't know how much it means to me."

Gabriel Statler barely avoided snorting as he tipped his hat to the teary woman whose name he couldn't actually remember and tried to get away as fast as he could.

"Fank you, Wogue!" called the little boy whose stupid folly had caused Gabe this trouble in the first place.

Gabe glanced back at them, nodding once more, then striding away before a crowd could gather. It wasn't the time of day for people to mill about this part of London, but stranger things had happened, and crowds had formed for him for less.

He'd never had this trouble before last month, and he would have vanished underground for a few months to escape his newfound fame, but Cap, Eagle, and the Shopkeepers thought his exposure could help their work for the Crown. After all, Gent was a popular fellow, and he accomplished a great deal because of it.

Gabe had never found the need to point out that Gent was actually a congenial chap, whereas he would rather eat glass than socialize with anyone at all, but now it was something that ought to be mentioned.

It made no difference. Apparently, Gabe's reticence was perceived as a hindrance to his performance, and an area upon which he needed to improve.

Also, as Cap pointed out none-too-gently, his popularity had been his own fault, and he could be the one to deal with the fallout.

There was really no arguing with that. Not that he generally argued with Cap anyway, being his superior and a coldly terrifying man, but he had been mightily tempted.

Even Weaver had something to say on the subject. The second-in-command for all the spies in England was a former operative that had accomplished an unbelievable amount in his prime. He now served as a diplomat to various nations on the Crown's business, while still serving in her covert operations.

He also happened to be an old friend of Gabe's.

Being one of the Shopkeepers earned him a certain level of respect and authority, in theory, though Gabe found that level of respect waning as the years went on. He listened to Weaver's opinions and jabs, promptly ignored every single one of them, and moved on with his life. Unfortunately, Weaver was his superior, higher even than Cap, and therefore he had enough power to affect them all. He liked that power, and it was more of an affliction for Gabe than anything else.

Particularly with Gabe's recent misfortune.

He hadn't meant to start a fire. He was generally a very careful operative and would never do anything so drastic as to set fire to an entire building. But the meeting with Gaspar had not gone according to plan, and when the idiot had tried to kill Gabe rather than deliver the information he had been paid for, Gabe had no recourse but to respond in kind. And after he'd finished with him, as Gaspar was no fighter, there wasn't much to do with the body. It wasn't going to work to drag him down three flights of stairs to toss him in the river, and he couldn't move the large man by himself anyway. He could not leave the corpse for Gaspar's associates to discover, as they might make connections. Therefore, the body needed to disappear.

So, Gabe had put out his cheroot cigar in the pile of papers the abandoned building had collected as various vagrants had used it for housing over the years. The lack of rain lately had aided the fire by keeping the wood of the building dry, as had the flask of alcohol that Gaspar had kept on his person.

No one would miss the building, and none of London's fire brigades would rush to its aid. He'd have to write it up in the report, but given the situation, there would be no repercussions from his actions.

He'd been out of the stairwell and headed back into the shadows of the night when he'd heard the only thing that could have stopped him in his tracks.

A woman's scream.

Now, it ought to be stated that Gabe was no Gent. He did not grow anxious at the thought of a woman's tears or swoons, and he saw no reason to incorporate polite manners into his everyday life. He did not open carriage doors, aid women crossing the streets, or dance with wallflowers. He found most women to be ridiculous, ignorant, and altogether useless.

But he did draw the line at having them die by fire, especially when he had caused it.

So, he'd done an uncharacteristically heroic thing, and gone back into the burning building to save the woman, who happened to have a small child. When they had been seen to safety, he'd vanished.

If only he'd never told the woman his name was Rogue when she'd asked.

If only that damned reporter Emmett Barnes hadn't somehow gotten wind of the rescue associated with an abandoned building burning to the ground in the Seven Dials and managed to track down that woman and get the details.

If only the account given, published, and circulated throughout all of London's papers hadn't made him seem so heroic.

He was still bristling that someone had told Barnes that he was an investigator of sorts, and strongly suspected Rook was part of that. Rook was an insufferable peacock and enjoyed causing mischief for his colleagues. Gabe had been strongly tempted to put in a request for Rook's demotion back to his simple Foreign Office position, but they were short-staffed with the League, and Rook was a damned good operative.

Plus, Gent had up and married the only worthwhile woman of their generation Gabe had ever met. He was currently taking an unprecedented leave to romance her into oblivion, or whatever it was that one did on a marriage trip. So, they really did need the help.

It was an irritating turn of events in his life to suddenly be sought after. Gossip on the streets carried well, and various rumors about the Rogue and his associates grew like wildfire. Their office was not easy to find, but enough managed that they'd hired a maid and an extra clerk to give the place a better feel.

Granted, the maid was a spy-in-training, and the clerk was another clueless candidate from the Home Office who would never be suited for fieldwork, but since they provided another set of hands for their previously lone clerk to work with, no one was about to complain.

The tasks they brought to Rogue were simple enough.

"Find my husband." He was being unfaithful with her sister.

"I've lost my mother's jewels." Her husband had a gambling problem.

"I think the King is my father!" He wasn't.

And the task he had finished just now. "I can't find my son! He's been gone for two days, and I've looked everywhere!"

This one Gabe had begged to push off on someone else. Children made him uneasy. Even Gent's minion children left him at ends with himself, and they were some of their most useful informants. In fact, he'd used them to track down the wayward child when he'd been told that he had to take the case.

It had all worked out well enough, as the child had been hiding out in the back of a local bakery for two days eating all the scraps. He had not been pleased to have Gabe discover him there, but after a stern lecture that was probably not best suited for a lad of such a young age, he was rather keen to return to his mother. The tearful reunion would have made several hearts warm.

Not Gabe's, but several others.

He lowered his cap over his eyes as he passed a few other people, cursing the fact that now his face had also been too accurately sketched and published, which wreaked havoc with his precious anonymity. He was going to have to resort to better disguises when he went out. Gent managed it, and Tilda was always willing to offer assistance.

He didn't trust Tilda not to make him genuinely ridiculous, but she was talented in the art of costuming and prosthetics, and her actresses were often unrecognizable after she was done with them. He could do worse for an ally.

Plus, Tilda never asked questions. Well, rarely anyway.

Once, he would have had some concern for his personal safety at being so easily recognized. The idea of people wanting to harm him, or kill him, was not a new one. He'd developed that particularly regrettable tendency long before he had willfully engaged in spycraft. His temperament, mingled with his unfortunate past, and his penchant for gambling, had often put him into situations that had flirted on the border of villainy. He'd been ruined so many times it had become a habit, and, title or no title, he had thrived in not thriving.

He hated being titled. Everybody knew that Lord Wharton was a rapscallion and worthless card sharp, or had been, and if he ever went out in society, he was avoided as much as Lord Blackmoor ever was, if not more. It seemed that a ruthless gambler with a skewed sense of morality was just as wicked as a suspected murderer, and everyone knew that gossip was truth in the eyes of the highly-opinionated.

And yet, he was still pursued by matchmaking mothers for his title, lowly as it was, and worthless as he was.

What did that say of the value of London's daughters?

Gabe was under no illusions about himself. He was not handsome, and he was not charming. He had nothing to recommend him except a temper and tenacity, and when he felt like using it, a bit of cleverness. He had done well in school without much effort, and he had caused enough trouble to warrant several harsh punishments, none of which had taught him any sort of lesson. Gabe had also evaded a good deal of trouble by sheer wit and stratagem, and if his current employers knew half of what he had done, or nearly done, they might have placed him on the other side of the spectrum.

Of course, knowing the Shopkeepers, and Eagle, they might already know.

He'd never quite figured out why exactly he'd been brought into the London League. He had no honor, so they could not appeal to his sense of king and country or any sort of positive views on humanity. Oh, he liked England well enough and would sing "God Save The King" when he had to, and he'd endured his usual responsibilities with Parliament, but he was not naïve enough to believe England's emerald shores were as pure as everyone else seemed to think. He had no family, except for his aunt, so they could not ask him to consider them and their safety. He was not a sportsman, gentleman, noble man, or nice man.

Yet they had convinced him. To risk his life for something worthwhile rather than for nothing in particular. To claim a cause as his own and give over to it wholeheartedly. To have the world never know what deeds he had done and how many times he had saved them. To never be truly seen.

They'd appealed to his recklessness and his desire to be withdrawn. He'd only considered it for a few hours before reporting in, and he had not looked back since.

Nobody knew what he really did, and nobody cared.

His aunt, however, was one of the most tenacious women on the planet, and she, unfortunately, did not fit with that previous statement. She cared. And she wanted to bestow her inheritance on him.

The trouble with that was that he was not exactly worthy of it, and he did not meet the qualifications necessary to do so. Only one thing held him back.

Bachelorhood.

He shuddered. Much as Aunt Geraldine had helped him over the years, her focus on his marital state drove him to the edge of his sanity. Against any sort of precedent, she claimed to love him and to wish for his happiness.

Only his mother had ever claimed the same, and as he'd not had her since he was eight, he could not be sure his memories were not tinted with the rosy color of the past. His father had died shortly after his birth, due to the same recklessness that ran through Gabe's blood. Left to his own devices, Gabe had formed his own moral compass.

It didn't work, but it was there all the same.

So, how he had become a valued spy in the highest realms of England's ranks was beyond him. But it was better than wasting away in the Seven Dials drowning in debt and running from death threats.

Part of his terms for entering this world had been for his prior debts to be satisfied, and they had been so. At the time, he'd thought that condition would be rejected, and he could go back to putting himself into an early grave. When Eagle hadn't blinked at the suggestion, even when Gabe had emphasized the astonishing amount, he'd sensed there was something particular they wanted him for.

As of yet, he hadn't figured it out, but having a purpose for his life had changed him. Now, he only risked himself when he had to, and his gambling had much improved, as had his ability to fight. He thrived on having a focus, and the thrill of adventure had never gotten old.

Being a strange sort of sideshow for the lower classes of London was not exactly giving him that thrill. It made him want to strangle something on occasion, and it was not the satisfying work he had been used to.

He nodded at one of Gent's older minions, a boy of thirteen or so, who pulled at his ear nonchalantly as if to scratch. Gabe knew better. The boy had information.

Gabe moved closer to him and pretended to search for a coin. "What?"

"People askin' about ye, Rogue," the lad said with a brush of a sleeve across his nose.

Gabe snorted. "That's not unusual, give me something I can work with."

"People willing to pay."

That sparked his interest. Most of the people who sought him out were of such low means that he could maybe earn bread or some intangible IOU that was unlikely to ever be paid, but money was never heard of.

"How do you know they are willing to pay?" he asked, folding his arms.

The lad shrugged and nudged the ground with his filthy boot. "They said so. Made no secret of looking for you or that there would be money."

Gabe shook his head, restraining a sigh. That was a sure way to get false information and be played for a fool. London's lower classes had no qualms about dishonesty, nor of taking advantage of naïveté when there was money involved.

"Probably idiots looking for lost trinkets," Gabe muttered,

wondering how long his superiors would make him live out this farce.

"Don't think so," came the thoughtful reply.

Gabe looked at the young man with a raised brow. "No?"

He shook his head pursing his lips. "They got cheated about information once... just once, and now the blighter's missing."

Gabe whistled low, shaking his head. That was most certainly not normal. "All to find me?"

His response was another shrug that told him nothing.

"Where?" he asked, holding out the coin, waiting for the answer.

"Office," the boy replied, offering his hand. "Watch yourself, Rogue, I've 'eard it's dodgy."

Gabe snorted and dropped the coin into the waiting palm. "My entire life is dodgy. Might as well tell me it's Tuesday."

"It's Thursday," the lad quipped.

Gabe frowned at him but found the sharp wit amusing all the same. "Back to your station and be quick about it."

The boy dashed off, whistled sharply, and vanished around a corner.

Gabe exhaled slowly, unwittingly curious about this rather determined customer who sought him. It could be anything, and he would need to proceed with caution. His mind whirled with possibilities. There were people who would love to find him and thrash him, but those individuals did not know him as the Rogue. It was highly unlikely that anyone would be able to connect him as Lord Wharton, sketch or no sketch. Whoever had drawn it was not that talented, and certainly not as accurate as Hal would have been. But Hal was unusual with her eye for detail, which was why she was an asset to the League.

No one in high Society would have looked at the drawing of him and been able to identify Lord Wharton in it, thanks in part to his reclusive nature, so it was not likely to come from that corner of his life.

Which could make this infinitely more dangerous.

As bewildering as it sounded, the danger he had once known in his life was nothing compared with what the London League had brought him. Joining the conglomeration between the Home and Foreign Offices had seemed like a prudent idea at the time. They could be outside of any pure jurisdiction and somewhat beyond the law. Yet the challenges had been harrowing at times and cost them quite a bit. Not that anybody in England would have any idea, as most of their work had prevented disastrous events that could have set the country on its ear. But the Shopkeepers, England's highest political powers and most influential men, knew all, and had extended their gratitude.

Even if the London League had done something truly outrageous, he suspected they would still keep them on. It was proving valuable to have a spy network centralized in their largest and most popular city.

The thought gave Gabe some comfort as he made his way towards the quiet section of London where their offices sat. He could act with his own limited conscience and instinct and probably maintain his position. Or, at least, not be shot for his actions.

He was rather averse to being shot. Having experienced it once or twice, he was not inclined to repeat the experience.

Now, being shot *at* was something he could not avoid, and was happening with alarming frequency now, but that was neither here nor there.

Gabe shook his head as he turned into the familiar, narrow cobblestone alley. He needed to focus if he were to deal with a customer who wanted him so badly they got rid of a lying informant to get to him. Who knows what other extremes they had gone to for the same?

Oddly enough, he found that flattering.

Unless, of course, they wanted to kill him. Then again…

He pushed open the door to the office and didn't even blink at the sight of Callie arguing with the new clerk. The two did not get on at all, and the clerk, who was as nameless as his counterpart for the time being, did not approve of Callie's dabbling in their employers' work.

Of course, neither of the clerks knew the full extent of what the London League did, and that Callie was invaluable to them, least of all because of her ability to keep house and order for them. She'd make a damned fine addition to the Tailor's arsenal of spies if they could manage to get her into the Convent. What all of England saw as the prominent Miss Masters finishing school, which had turned out several well-educated and well-finished misses, was also the finest training ground for female spies that had ever existed. In fact, it was officially the only one built for that exact purpose.

Gabe nodded at the silent clerk, looking just as wiry as ever, and patted Callie on the shoulder as he passed her.

"Client in the waiting area, Rogue," the clerk said, adjusting his spectacles.

Gabe nodded. Then he nodded at the others. "Shut them up, will you, Matthews? Before Callie kills Thomas."

"That is not my name!" the other clerk cried in dismay. "Matthews isn't his name, either."

"I do not care," Gabe told him, only briefly glancing at him as he moved into the area between offices. It had recently been designated for their customers to wait for one of them to take up their case.

Sitting on the bench within was a woman, plainly dressed, but not cheaply, and she gave no indication that the argument in the next room had been overheard. Her boots were worn and dirty, her hem uneven, and her gloves bore a dark stain near the left thumb. She was slight in frame, and her bonnet hid her hair and face, but Gabe didn't care about any of that. There was no way this was the person who had been hunting him.

Which meant it was just another boring case like all the rest.

Gabe barely restrained a groan and leaned against the wall, folding his arms. "What can I do for you?" he asked, not bothering for the politeness his colleagues had mastered.

The woman looked up at him, revealing vibrant, wide-set, blue eyes, a strong jaw, and a willful demeanor that belied her delicate stature. "Are you the Rogue?" she asked in a low voice.

"I am."

She rose with surprising grace and clasped her hands in front of her. "Then yes, there is something you can do."

He was really not in the mood for being toyed with and gestured impatiently for her to continue.

She raised a brow, her mouth tightening. "Shouldn't we discuss this privately?"

10

"Tell me what you want, and I'll decide where we discuss it," he snapped.

"I don't see how you can dictate so much when I will be the one paying you," she replied in a sharp tone.

Gabe rolled his eyes and gave her the most withering glare he could muster, which happened to be rather impressive. "Might I remind you that you are here because you need me, and not the other way around?"

Something in her eyes flashed, and she tilted her chin down ever so slightly, which, oddly enough, made the hair on the back of his neck stand on end. "I do need you, Rogue, and I have gone to extraordinary lengths to find you. I will pay you two hundred pounds simply for taking on my case. I expect, under such conditions, that when I suggest that we speak in private, you accommodate me by providing that privacy."

Gabe blinked at her, half-startled, half-impressed. It was rare that people were not intimidated by him, and even rarer that said person be a woman. In fact, he had never met a woman under the age of fifty who could stand in the face of his harshness and not become teary or begin trembling. Not only was this chit not put off by it, but she was giving as good as she received.

Now that he looked at her again, perhaps she was capable of making a man disappear.

He pushed off the wall with a grunt, glowering still. "You'd better step in my office then, Miss…?"

She lifted her chin once more, no trace of embarrassment, modesty, or nerves. "Amelia Berger. And before we get into the details, you should know that I will be fully involved in this investigation, so you may want to tell the clerks out front to let me in without question next time."

Gabe did not try to hide his look of derision, suspicion unfurling in his stomach as she swept proudly past him towards his office. She thought she would control him, did she? Well, she could think again, and he would be only too glad to inform her so.

Chapter Two

*A*melia took in the shabby, but surprisingly organized office as she entered, praying she could keep her face composed.

He was not at all what she expected.

For one, she expected a handsome man. Anyone named Rogue certainly ought to be fine-looking. She had prepared to deal with a handsome man, one who might view her with sympathy and interest.

The scowling, brooding man with little manners and no respect was a bit of a shock, and while not altogether unattractive, she certainly would not have called him handsome. He had the sort of manners that made one wonder if his mother was disappointed in him, and when he had lashed out, she had reacted in kind.

Her mother had warned her about her temper, and her tendency to strike first and beg apologies later. If ever.

Now, it seemed, she would have to see the truth of it.

But Rogue had not sent her from the building and was apparently willing to listen, despite his obvious apathy, so perhaps her prickly side would come in handy. She'd come too far and suffered too much to go back, and she would put up with a good deal to see her goal achieved.

For another thing, Rogue had all the warmth of a blizzard in Northumberland. She had expected sternness based on the description of him she'd received, but never in her life had she dealt with someone so utterly unapproachable. It didn't make any difference to her. She was long past being intimidated by anyone, but she could not deny that it was off-putting.

She'd heard the way he'd spoken to the others in the front, and the brusque tone suggested authority and low tolerance. This was a man who would not be moved by emotional stories or pitiful circumstances. She doubted he had emotions that extended beyond disapproval and irritation, but one could never tell on first impressions. After all, she was a sharp-tongued shrew more often than not, but she had cried herself to sleep more times than she cared to recall.

Not recently, but she had done. Tears had long become a thing of the past.

Amelia turned as she heard the door close behind her, waiting to see what Rogue would do. He was a puzzle, speaking in proper tones without an accent, yet dressing as though he were a dock worker on a good day. He was clean-shaven, though his jaw was dotted with dark stubble, and his eyes were an almost eerie pale shade. And when they fixed on a person, as they did now, they had a tendency to steal one's breath. And not in a fluttery sense.

Rather as if one were frozen.

Rogue sat down in the chair behind the desk and gave her an appraising look. "Well," he said after a moment, "you have your blessed privacy, so tell me what you want."

Amelia blinked in surprise, taken aback by the rudeness of this stranger, and she sank down into a chair near her. But Amelia Tribbett, not Berger, was most certainly not the sort of woman to take that in stride, and her brows snapped down. "If you're going to speak to me like that, we are going to have quite a hard time of it."

Rogue snorted and leaned one elbow on the arm of his chair. "I don't particularly care what kind of time *we* have with this, Miss Berger, as I have not agreed to do anything yet. You have said that you will pay me at least two hundred pounds for doing whatever it is that you have come for, yet I would be willing to wager that two hundred pounds that you have less than five in your tatty reticule at this moment."

Amelia's jaw dropped, and she clutched the aforementioned reticule tightly.

Rogue lifted a dark eyebrow, one corner of his mouth pulling as if he would smile but did not. "Am I wrong?" he taunted.

Amelia slammed her mouth shut, grinding her teeth. "If you

want to discuss payment," she forced out, "I can assure you, I have all that…"

"I don't care about the bloody payment," Rogue interrupted with a wave of his hand. "Money is money, and I'll take it."

She was not surprised in the least. Her opinion of him was rapidly forming, and it was not exactly favorable. "A gentleman would never accept as much as I'm offering."

That could not have had less of an effect on him. "If you're looking for Gent, he'll be back in a week or so. Until then, you've got me. I am not a gentleman, and I have never claimed to be." He shrugged a shoulder. "I will take your money because I will earn it, and if the number is exorbitant, that is your problem, not mine."

Amelia chewed her lip a little, nodding slowly. "Well, then. I appreciate your candor."

"Brutal honesty is what I can promise you, Miss Berger."

She tilted her head a little. "Not success?"

Rogue snorted. "Until you tell me what the hell I am doing, I cannot bloody well promise anything."

That was true, but there was no need to say it like that. Not that his vulgarity offended her, but really, it wasn't called for. Apparently, he really was no gentleman.

It made no difference to her. She'd not dealt with gentlemen often in her life, so she could undoubtedly manage this situation. Rogue might be rough and disapproving and irascible, but he would have to do far worse to get to her.

"Fine," she said simply, untying her bonnet and removing it, setting it down beside her, and patting her hair.

She delayed as long as she possibly could, enjoying the tension emanating from the man across from her. The longer she took, the more his tension grew. If she played her cards right, he would snap at her for wasting time, and then she could have the cool upper hand. But when she was starting to irritate herself without more than a tightening of his fist as a response, she gave in.

"I need you to help me find my father," she admitted, sitting up as tall as she could without stretching.

There was a faint exhale that ought to have come with a dramatic eye roll but did not. "Is he missing?" he asked in the most patronizing tone she had ever heard in her life.

Amelia gave him a hard look. "In a manner of speaking. I don't know him. I never have."

Rogue rested his head on his hand, leaning more fully into the chair. "Trying to collect an inheritance, are we? Gain a title? Will you be paying me out of the proceeds from your newly-devoted father?"

She smiled bitterly at him. "My reasons are my own. And what I intend to do with the information is as well. Your job is to find my father, not judge me."

"I judge everyone," Rogue replied, straightening. "No one is excluded."

"All the more reason to keep it to myself," Amelia returned. "No sense in giving you additional fodder for poorly conceived impressions and incorrect assumptions."

Rogue's brow furrowed, and he now gripped both armrests, though not tightly. "Who says I would be incorrect?"

Amelia only smiled.

Rogue drummed his fingers against the chair, once, twice, staring at her in the silence. Then he exhaled sharply. "I am going to need more information than that to determine if finding your father is even feasible, Miss Berger."

Amelia shrugged and allowed herself to relax a little. If he was not going to press her motives, she really did not have much to hide. Her own identity, admittedly, but this wasn't about her. It was about her father. "I will tell you what I know."

"Everything?" he asked sharply.

"As you said," she replied with a nod. "Brutal honesty. If you do not have a care for my feelings, I will not have a care for yours. Sentiment is wasted on the emotionally inept."

Rogue scoffed. "Steady on, you might truly damage my feelings. All three of them."

Amelia rolled her eyes and scratched her forehead where her bonnet had rubbed. They had never felt comfortable on her, and she would undoubtedly never adjust. "Where would you like me to start, oh sensitive one?"

"The part where you get to the point."

Amelia shook her head with a snort. "It's a miracle your

colleagues haven't killed you."

"They try." He shrugged again. "No one has succeeded yet."

"More's the pity."

Rogue's exasperation was growing louder with every breath. "I will start charging you for wasting my time if you don't get on with it."

Amelia glared at him, which earned her a warning raise of one eyebrow, and then she sat back and tucked a strand of hair behind her ear. "I never knew my father. My mother never spoke of him, so I presumed I never had one. Not in the way that matters, that is. We lived in circumstances decent enough until I was eight, and then suddenly there was no money. We were forced out of our home and into a village nearby, sharing a home with another family. Mother was never in high spirits, but that seemed to weigh her down further. I never saw her smile again."

Her tone had been even, unaffected, and calm, but suddenly memories were flashing through her mind, and her throat constricted. She would never forget the horror of watching her mother waste away before her eyes; how she had gone from being a vibrant, beautiful, although somewhat cold woman, to a lifeless imitation of one; the sunken, hollow look that never left her and the almost confused expression etched on her face; watching her shrink into a tiny, feeble frame that could barely sustain her own weight.

No child should have to witness that.

No child should have to raise her mother.

Amelia would never have made it but for her child-like determination to make her mother smile again. And after that naïveté passed, all that was left was sheer determination and willpower, and that had sustained them for a few years, but no more.

"And then?" the impossible man across from her prodded.

"And then," she snapped, "she died."

He held up his hands in a sort of apology or surrender, but his expression had not changed from the bored and displeased countenance he had borne so well before.

"When I was ten," she went on, "she became ill. Everything became a trial for her. She was always weak and exhausted, and I went to work in her stead. This lasted perhaps two years. When she could no longer rise from her bed, I stayed to nurse her. She was rambling nonsense, trapped somewhere between asleep and awake, and it was rare that I could get her to recognize me. The family we lived with became irritated that we were so burdensome without funds to aid them, so we were sent to the poorhouse, even with Mother in her condition." Her throat tightened, and the taste of bile filled her mouth. She glanced up at the man watching her. "Have you ever seen a poorhouse, Rogue?"

He had the good sense to look more humane at her tone and nodded once.

"There are no doctors there," Amelia recalled bitterly. "Everything smells of death and disease, waste and rodents. There was no one to tend her but me, and I knew nothing. It did not take long for her to stop eating, to speak only nonsense, and to look the part of a corpse. All I could do was stay by her side and pretend my ministrations would make any difference. Then I began to realize that her nonsense ramblings were nothing of the sort." She shook her head, the familiar fury rising within her. "She was pining for a man. For her love. Speaking to him, declaring herself, begging him to stay. She told him about me, reminisced about some courtship, and sobbed with all the agony a broken heart has known."

"She was delusional," Rogue muttered without sympathy.

Amelia nodded, not rising to his bait. "And hysterical, despite her weakness. But it was the most clarity I had seen from her in months. When I prodded her, tried to break through and ask about him, she would only weep further and say how he was gone and could not return."

"And you believe her."

She nodded once more. "I do. If you had seen her, the change in her when she spoke of him, you would have too."

Rogue scoffed loudly. "Doubtful."

Amelia gripped her skirt tightly in her fist, directing her fury at him now. "Listen to me, Rogue. I am not a romantic. I am the furthest thing from it. I have lived in the real world, and I do not have a single sentimental bone in my body. I am telling you, my mother loved this man so much that a life without him drove her to her death. She died of a broken heart."

17

His expression did not change, but he did not refute it.

"She died calling for him," Amelia said quietly, looking away. "It was the last thing she said. Never mind me, she had long since forgotten me. But not him." She ground her teeth briefly, then forced a calming breath. "I left the poorhouse as soon as I could sneak away. I would be much better on my own than trapped there with the helpless and hopeless."

"Where did you go?"

"Away," she replied vaguely with a sniff and a shrug. "I collected our things and left that godforsaken village behind me. I worked and scraped, vowing that as soon as I could manage to raise the funds, I would find the man that abandoned my mother and left her to die."

Her vehemence did not seem to impress him. "And now you have the funds?" he asked dubiously.

She met his icy gaze evenly. "And now I have the funds."

He made a noise she could not interpret and leaned forward on the desk. "You do realize that the most likely outcome is that he is dead."

"Of course, I do," she returned with what was probably too much bite, "but I still want to know who he is."

"What will you do if that is the case?" Rogue pressed, his eyes fixed on her.

She shrugged. "Enjoy the prospect of him suffering in hell for all eternity."

"And if he lives?"

Amelia smiled tightly. "As I said, what I do with the information is my own business."

Rogue watched her for another long moment, then grunted and sat back once more. "How did you hear about me?"

Amelia nearly sighed with relief. She was not willing to discuss details, particularly with what she had planned, not to mention what she had done. She had learned well that outright lying was not safe, but neglecting to provide all the information was less of an issue. And something about Rogue warned her to tread very, very carefully.

She tried for an easy manner. "I long ago learned that I did not have the skills to manage something like this myself. I asked anyone I could for the name of a capable investigator." She managed a smile.

"You would be surprised at how far your reputation extends."

"I doubt it," he muttered.

That seemed odd, but she did not think he was speaking to her just then. The dark shade that had drawn over his eyes was unexpected and certainly uncalled for, considering he should be thrilled with additional cases and funds.

Yet he was surly and miserable and seemed to wish her gone, even with her exorbitant offer.

Curious mystery, this one.

"And what did these random individuals say about me?" he asked reluctantly, rubbing his brow, which did nothing for the furrows there.

Amelia tilted her head, a strand of her chestnut hair falling free of her ear. "That you are a man who will see the task done, no matter what. That you are dangerous, reckless, and not to be trusted. A man without honor or restraint. That you once rushed into a burning building to save a mother and child who were…"

Rogue suddenly swore colorfully and slammed a hand down on his desk, startling her.

"What in the world?" she snapped, adjusting her hair and putting a hand over her suddenly racing heart.

"I hate that rumor," he grumbled, avoiding her eyes. "It makes me seem like a bloody hero, and I am not."

Amelia almost smiled. Almost. "I never said you were a hero."

He glared more darkly at her. "It was implied."

She shook her head slowly, now letting herself smile a little. "I never imply. Far too much effort involved." She considered him for a long moment. "Are you saying the story isn't true?"

"Did you hear any other stories about me?" he asked, sitting back once more.

Amelia nodded and glanced out of the remarkably filthy window, considering the tidy state of the room. "Several. I don't believe half of them."

"So, why believe that?"

She sighed heavily and looked back at him, taking in the oddly disheveled dark curls that were too long for polite society. Yet his speech was perfect, no common accent or limited vocabulary.

Between his dress, his accent, and his manner, she could not get a proper idea of him. He belonged nowhere, it seemed.

Like her.

She shook herself of that vein of thinking and returned to the conversation at hand. "Because it is the only thing I've heard that leads me to believe you are human," she told him. "You are not a criminal, you are not honorable, and you get the job done. I did not care about much else."

"There are many such others," he insisted, shaking his head. "Why me?"

"I am not about to flatter you or let you turn this interview into a sermon on your virtues or lack thereof," Amelia declared in irritation. "I picked you because it was repeatedly stated that you are the best, and I will not settle for less. Now, will you do it? Or am I to waste both of our time a bit longer?"

"Are you done with your tragic tale yet?" Rogue asked, his tone suddenly that of boredom as one of his hands scratched his chin.

Sensing she was being toyed with, Amelia clenched her jaw and nodded once.

Rogue nodded slowly, his fingers now moving absently along his jaw, his eyes fixed on her.

She willed herself not to blink as she stared just as boldly back.

"This seems fairly straightforward," he mused quietly. "Why the extremes?"

She had expected the question and smirked. "I have spent long enough waiting, Mr. Rogue. And I fear it will be more complicated than either of us believe."

He straightened up in his chair, observing her carefully, as if her secrets were laid out on her face for him to read.

Unfortunately for him, Amelia had spent her entire life keeping secrets, and not a soul alive knew them. "Well?" she prodded.

Rogue slowly exhaled, closed his eyes, and shook his head.

"No?" she cried, nearly coming out of her seat. "Why not?"

He exhaled again noisily and gave her a hard look. "Miss Berger, that was a sigh of resignation and shaking my head at the sheer idiocy of what I am about to do."

She held her breath. "Which is?"

"Find your father, take your money, and do all of it very quickly," he answered, pushing to his feet and brushing off his filthy trousers. "Because if I do anything else, you are going to plague me to death and ruin my tolerably uncomplicated life."

"Too right," she quipped, beaming with relief.

He frowned at once. "Don't smile like that. I have not done you any favors. If you are determined to be as involved as you say, foolhardy as it is, then you will obey my orders and directives, everything I say with exactness. I don't care that you are funding the venture, it is my skills that you have come for."

Amelia got to her feet, bonnet and reticule in hand. "Surely not *everything* you say," she protested. "I've been trying my hand at this for years, I know more than you think."

"And a marvelous job you have done, I am sure," he drawled with a dismissive wave of his hand. "Tomorrow, you will come back to this office at ten minutes past twelve with a list of everything you know and all of the documents in your possession. You will be prepared to tell me everything relating to your past, and if I find that you are lying, I will toss you from this building without a word and without a care for how it offends you."

Instinct stiffened Amelia's spine, and she lifted her chin defiantly. He was not that much taller than her, and she could undoubtedly swing for his jaw without any difficulty and probably knock him to the ground. But she needed him on her side, despite the bristling she was feeling and against her desire to blacken his eye. So, she bit her tongue and nodded once.

"And I want fifty of those pounds upfront," he added, motioning to the door.

She snorted and gave him a hard look. "And if I refuse that?"

Rogue smiled or made an attempt at one that actually frightened her. "Then we will consider your offer a lie, Miss Berger, and the aforementioned statement stands."

She returned his smile with a sickeningly sweet one of her own. "Then it is lucky for me that I am able to do so."

He inclined his head. "Indeed, it is."

She shook her head, her jaw aching from the tension there. If she managed to survive this venture without murdering him, it would be a miracle. She was a strong-willed woman with nothing to lose, but he was a stubborn man without manners. It would be a battle every step of the way, and she had absolutely no intention of losing. She had earned the right to know who her worthless waste of a father was, or had been, and she deserved the justice that her mother would never have.

She marched passed Rogue out into the waiting area and turned for the front, where the clerks were quietly working, the maid now gone. The sooner she left here, the less likely she would say something she might regret.

"*Attention à la marche,*" Rogue called from behind her.

She looked down at her feet automatically, moving out of the way, and realized too late that he had meant to catch her off guard. A girl in her situation should not know French, and yet she had not only understood but had reacted, just as he had wanted her to.

He was testing her.

She stopped and exhaled slowly through her nose, then turned to face him. He stood in the doorway between the waiting area and the front, smiling smugly.

"*Diable vous emporte,*" she spat, clenching her fists at her sides.

Rogue raised a brow and bowed mockingly. "*Merci.*"

Amelia bit back a screech and whirled back to the door, let herself out, and slammed it behind her. The man was the most insufferable creature she had ever met on the planet, and if she were not desperate, she would never have put herself through this. But revenge would be sweet when they achieved their goal, and she would thank him profusely when that day came.

She stormed out of the narrow street where his office stood and made her way towards the boarding house where she had left her scarce belongings. Her uncle had refused to do any more for her than that, which she was wise enough to be grateful for. Since he was not her uncle after all, and since she had been delighted to leave their judgmental and impossible hovel of a home, she did not expect more. She had been on her own for almost ten years and spending the last two with them had been some of the worst, impossible as it seemed.

But what was a girl to do without known relations? Making up a connection seemed the most sensible decision, and they were just honorable enough to take in family.

They'd never be able to locate her if they ever discovered the truth, and she was grateful for that.

She put her bonnet on her head and quickly tied a knot, wishing she could give up her pretense of finery. She'd never had to manage this much of a fuss before, it seemed ridiculous to start now. But she would do what she had to do now that she was back in London.

Even suffer the Rogue and his foul temper and fouler glares.

As long as she could remember her mother crying for Daniel, whoever Daniel was, she could suffer it. She smiled grimly to herself. Whatever came of this, she was confident that she would at last find satisfaction in her life.

She crossed the busy street and eyed a small child watching her curiously. The girl could not have been more than seven, and her wide eyes knew the worldliness that Amelia's had known.

Amelia smiled a little and tossed a coin at the girl, her smile growing further at the toothy grin she received in return.

London, for all its horrors in her past, was still a fine place. Even better for the ending that would come with it.

Chapter Three

*G*abe rubbed at his eyes and shut the ledger on his desk, waving away the cloud of dust that rose with the force. No matter how he pored over the accounts from day to day, there always seemed to be more questions than dust, and the dust was always prevalent.

It ought to be cleaner, as they now had Callie about, but Callie was not comfortable with the offices yet, and he couldn't blame her. With all that they contained, no matter how coded they were, secrets were rampant within. The more one knew about the nature of their work, the more one was likely to jump at shadows. And the more danger one was likely to be in.

He did not find fault with Callie's disinterest in the offices. Once she was bolder and had survived a few scrapes, she would be more inclined to become more deeply involved. Of course, it was entirely probable that she would not wish to remain a maid at that point.

That was the trouble with training the maids and street urchins of England. They all became so accomplished and could blend in so well that very few wished to remain in the lower station. Oh, they would help out when it was called for, but it took a great deal of persuasion to have someone genuinely dedicated to the benefits of service.

Gabe groaned and stretched in his chair. It had been a hellish day, what with the hoyden wreaking havoc upon his plans, and then trying to catch up after her extraordinary interview, only to be distracted by thoughts of her story the entire time.

Miss Berger was lying.

About what, he could not say, but it was an absolute certainty.

He was almost positive she had given him a false name from the careful way she had said it, and her clothing told a story of meticulous care, which a dress of that sort was not generally given. Either it did not belong to her, or it was her best one. From the state of her coat and shoes, he suspected the latter.

It was not uncommon for those seeking assistance to portray the best and most respectable version of themselves when doing so. Of course, had Miss Berger truly wished to present that picture, she would have behaved with far more gentility. That betrayed her more than anything else. No refined woman was so direct and impertinent unless they were so ancient it was excusable or so hated that they did not care.

Her story had so many gaps in it that he could have danced a reel through them all, though he avoided dancing like a plague. Did she honestly think that they would be able to discover the identity of her so-called father with the obviously limited details she had?

He did not believe the man she sought really *was* her father.

Something, and he was not entirely sure what, prodded him to give her a bit of French for effect, and she reacted perfectly in line with his suspicions. Based on her story, she was from a poor and unfortunate family, probably with limited education, and no possible reason to know French, let alone to translate something as obscure as "mind your step". Her fury at his catching her was truly something to behold indeed. He was quite proud of that.

Provoking people was always so enjoyable, particularly when their ire rose so spectacularly.

He did not trust Miss Amelia Berger, or whatever her name was. He knew she was driven, stubborn, willful, and remarkably quick-witted; intelligent, bold, and not easily intimidated; secretive, hard, and in possession of a temper. She was, in fact, just the sort of person that would make a dangerous and unpredictable opponent. There was no reason, none whatsoever, that she should have two hundred pounds to give him. He did not like this combination, which was why he had taken her on. Better to draw her in and risk it than let her alone and be ignorant.

He hated being ignorant. There was too much at stake.

Only earlier this year they'd been investigating a circle of relatively influential British men who were supporters of a renegade French faction determined to overturn all that had happened since the downfall of Napoleon, and there were far too many loose ends for their comfort. The last five years or so had grown particularly uncomfortable because of the group, whose trouble was relatively minor, but the potential was unknown. The Shopkeepers had everyone on the alert, and Gent's turn with rooting out select members and tracking funds had gone reasonably well.

Of course, there had been the added inducement of one supporter trying to gain a significant amount of money through marriage to the woman Gent loved, and all of that through means most nefarious. But as the plot had been very neatly thwarted, Sir Vincent Castleton was now no more than a faint itch in the grander scheme.

Gabe felt a perverse pleasure wondering what the blackguard had suffered when he'd had to report back to the others that his grand plan had failed.

Whatever it had been, they had been remarkably quiet of late. With Gent away, Rook had taken up the task of minding the traitors. It was a bizarre twist to see the peacock suddenly become an imitation of Gent, but he did a reasonably good job at it. He was a skilled operative and while not as invisible as Gent tended to be, he was not far behind.

Of course, neither of them had ever matched what Trace had been able to do when he'd been with them, but he had been a rare operative.

Gabe leaned his head back against the chair with a wince. It had been over three years since that night on the docks, and still, the pain of it lanced his heart. Trace, known to the world as Alexander Sommerville, had been almost a brother to him, as well as his cousin. His deep-seated investigations into the underworld of London's shipping industry had been deemed too dangerous for any of them to take on. But Alex had insisted and gone ahead with it anyway. He was always taking the most impossible assignments and somehow made them less impossible.

Had he seen the dangers that night before the rest of them had? Did he have a sense that he might not survive the skirmish?

Whatever it was, they had all been caught unawares, and Gabe, for one, had never let it go. He doubted Gent or Cap had either, and certainly Eagle and those above him were still looking, but with all that England had to contend with, the death of one operative, no matter how it came about, was really not that shocking. Never mind that Trace had saved the lives of every Shopkeeper singlehandedly at least once. Never mind that Trace had never been caught until the day he died. Never mind that…

Well, Gabe's temper was his weakness, and nothing like reliving that night could ignite it.

Ever since then, he avoided any situations that did not feel right. His instincts had been well-honed, and danger would not dissuade him. But neither was he as reckless as he had been when they'd all seemed invincible.

They now had proof that they were no such thing.

Nothing scared a man so completely as proof of his own mortality.

Nevertheless, it was now Gabe who saw to the darker sides of London, and well did it suit him. His ledgers of various gambling losses and debts were growing more and more complicated, though how he would explain that to Coin when he required additional funding for his efforts, he had no clue.

Coin was meticulous with his budgetary allowances, and Gabe's reckless ways had earned him more than one lecture on the subject. But as he had not heard any reprimand from the superiors, he was not inclined to change his behavior.

As they had no answers for why Trace had met his end the way he had, Gabe was not satisfied with anything surrounding those events, or that investigation. At times, he was literally itching with the need to go over every aspect of the events, the investigation that led to it, and his cousin's personal life. Anything that could help them find the closure they lacked.

He would much rather be doing that than sorting out long-lost fathers, who probably did not exist, and entertaining high and mighty misses with misplaced indignation. But instinct told him to watch her closely, and he would not have been surprised if she might have several ulterior motives to working with him and with their task.

A knock at his office door shook him from his reverie, and he glanced up in surprise. Eagle leaned against the doorframe easily, his lined face looking stark and aged against the faint light of the candles.

Gabe jumped to his feet in surprise. "Sir."

Eagle smiled a little, inclining his silver head and gesturing at him as he pushed off and entered the room. "Sit, sit, Rogue, for heaven's sake."

Gabe did so a bit awkwardly. Eagle rarely came to the offices anymore unless they sent for him, and their meetings with him elsewhere were never in the same place.

Come to think of it, Gabe had no idea where Eagle spent most of his time or what exactly he did.

That was probably the point.

"What can I do for you, sir?" he asked as he observed the older man respectfully.

Eagle snorted softly. "Am I the only man on this earth that you refer to as 'sir'?"

"Yes," Gabe said with marked frankness.

"Why?"

He shrugged. "You're the only one who deserves it. Is there something you need?"

One side of Eagle's mouth lifted, tugging at the faintest scar there. "No, nothing. I merely came by to see how things were progressing. I am surprised to find anyone here at all, given the late hour."

Gabe glanced out of the window briefly. "I hadn't even noticed."

Eagle made a noncommittal noise. "Busy, are you?"

"I suppose," he answered slowly. He looked up at his mentor, and then managed a sheepish smile. "The cover of my being an investigator is becoming a thriving business in and of itself."

That drew a wry chuckle from the older man. "I wondered about that."

"I'm just too sought after," Gabe said with a heavy sigh. "Most of the tasks are simple enough, but all are time-consuming, and I find I am always attempting to catch up on the more important matters."

"To the mother that has lost him, the missing child is the more important matter," Eagle replied, his tone off-hand, but his expression severe. "Even if he is in a bakery."

Gabe barely managed to avoid rolling his eyes. "Yes, sir. But if I am to keep an eye on the usual gambling rings and somehow infiltrate the ones near the docks, I need time and preparation to do so. At present, I have neither."

Eagle crossed an ankle over his knee and tilted his head. "Feeling at odds, are you, Rogue?"

"A bit," he admitted, scratching the back of his head. "I think one of my contacts might have information on the guns for the faction, but it has been difficult to have much contact of late."

Eagle nodded slowly, watching him, but making no reply. He did that quite often, somehow managing to draw out the information he desired with just a look. That was a skill that Gabe could use, but it would probably only come when he'd had the years of experience that Eagle had accumulated. He'd seen the revolution and several skirmishes, that much everybody knew, but what exactly Eagle had been or done when he'd been in the field himself was completely unknown.

Gabe had even snuck into the dossier files to see what lay within, and Eagle's file had been suspiciously devoid of detail.

Maddening life, spycraft.

"I think, Rogue," Eagle finally said with a sigh, "that you have learned your lesson. You may cease to be such a popular figure now."

That caught his attention. "Truly?"

There came a sage nod and a faint smile. "Finish up whatever your case-load happens to be at present, and then turn your attention to the 'more important matters', as you called them."

Gabe winced a little, wondering if he would be hearing that phrase regularly from now on. "I didn't mean…"

"Oh, please, Rogue," Eagle interrupted with a laugh. "I know you well enough to know that family ties barely exist for you, and you'd sever what you could if you were not so secretly fond of your aunt."

That, at least, was true and made him smile. "I would like to see you try to cut ties with Aunt Geraldine, sir."

There was a brief flash of a devious grin that made Gabe widen his eyes and his stomach clench. Could the Eagle, with all his past and everything he had done, know his aunt personally?

That was startling on far too many levels to contemplate further.

"All I meant, sir," he said quickly, desperate to move away from that particular topic, "is that I am a spy, and I should like to get back to what it is I was trained for."

"I understand, Rogue." He smiled for a second, then let it fade, his eyes clouding in thought. "On the other hand..."

"Don't say it," Gabe groaned, putting his face into one hand.

"The cover must remain intact, and it is difficult to pose as a group of investigators when there are no investigations." Eagle continued, musing.

Gabe put his head down on his desk. "Please, no..."

"Maybe we should keep you on." There was a long pause that Gabe did not acknowledge, keeping his face pressed into the wood. "But..."

Gabe raised his head at the small word, drawn out as it was.

Eagle seemed amused by his distress. "We can take everything through your clerks, now that you have two, and anything truly requiring the skills of you four can be brought to you. Otherwise, Hobbs and Doyle can handle it."

Gabe sat back, sighing heavily. "Thank you." Then he frowned. "Wait, are those their names?"

Eagle looked surprised. "You don't know?"

He shook his head, not bothering to pretend at guilt that he did not feel. "We don't use names here, so we haven't learned theirs. Unless you've told them to me just now."

"I haven't."

"Are you sure?"

"Yes."

"So, if I wanted to call them One and Two...?" Gabe asked slowly.

Eagle folded his arms, shrugging. "Just do it by seniority to avoid confusion. Do they mind not having names?"

Gabe grinned freely. "One doesn't. Two very much does. But he is new, he'll figure it out."

Eagle nodded, then shook his head with a smile. "I envy you all down here."

Gabe snorted and laced his fingers behind his head. "Why?"

"Freedom and ignorance," Eagle said, his smile fading. "You think you know the evils of the world, the burdens that it bears, but your view is so limited. Wider than the average person, I grant you," he allowed when Gabe made a noise, "but limited all the same. And you all have such energy, your wits are sharp, and the adventure still calls."

Gabe did not like the sudden melancholy turn of this conversation, and he straightened. "Eagle, is there something that I need to…"

Eagle shook his head quickly. "No, no, my boy, not at all. I am merely feeling my age. That happens when you retire from the field. Even in the administration, the work is just as taxing. And I am tired."

That did not make him feel any better. Eagle had somehow taken an interest in Gabe from the first, and he was quite sure that no one else could have convinced him to come into the life of a spy, let alone work in the London League. Talk of his leaving, or any other unpleasant topic surrounding him, made him very uneasy.

"Maybe you should take Two with you, then," Gabe suggested, trying to lighten the moment. "You could call him by his proper name, whatever it is, and he could take some of the burdens from your shoulders. Lord knows you've done enough for your country to earn a reprieve."

Eagle laughed knowingly. "If you knew all that I had done, Rogue, you would not send someone as inexperienced as Two to me. Give him your tasks, not mine. Far simpler and easier to manage."

"As it happens," Gabe protested, "I have just one task right now."

"Two will be much relieved by so light an assignment," Eagle said as he pushed to his feet.

Gabe rose as well, his brow furrowing. "Actually, I think I will keep that one."

Eagle paused. "Indeed? Something of interest?"

"I don't know yet," Gabe admitted. "It could be. It doesn't add up, and the client… Well, she could be more than what she seems. I don't trust her."

Eagle clapped a hand on his shoulder. "Then keep it, by all

means. And perhaps bring Rook in on it. He'll need something to do."

"Where is Rook, anyway?" Gabe asked, more curious than caring. "I haven't seen him in at least a week, and it's not even my birthday."

"Tending the flowers," Eagle replied with a sober air, even as he smiled. "It was his turn. He'll be here in the morning."

Gabe's curiosity vanished, as did any sense of teasing. There was one assignment in the League they all shared and did so without complaint, protest, or thinking. When they had lost Trace, and it became clear they were not going to get him back, his last will and testament had been brought out. The real version, rather than the official one his solicitor would have, instructed his brothers to be sure to tend the flowers.

Cryptic, even in official documentation, but Alex had trusted no one. It had been clear to them, however, what his wishes were.

Off in a quiet corner of Cheshire was a young woman by the name of Poppy Edgewood, and she had lost as much as they had on that night, if not more, in a way. She had been the heart that beat within Alex's chest, and it was very like him to assign her care to them in his absence, to see that she was looked after, even if he could not do it himself.

So, every other month, or thereabouts, one of them would vanish for a small portion of time to 'tend the flowers', and though none of them had met Poppy face to face, they knew quite a lot about her, her dealings, and how things fared with her. She was the most well-protected woman in England, Gabe had no doubt.

And she had no idea.

"Stay close to your instincts, Rogue," Eagle said, bringing him back to the present. "They will do you credit." Then he patted his shoulder once. "Except for the time with the fire."

"Once!" Gabe protested as Eagle left the room. "One time!"

"Never again, Rogue!" Eagle called, laughing.

"It's not funny," Gabe muttered, shaking his head. He moved back to his desk and gathered the materials he would need to look over before returning in the morning. Some men, like Cap, never took their work home with them. But Cap had a family, and Gabe had no one. His work was his life, and what was more, he enjoyed it.

What would Aunt Geraldine say should she discover that Gabe enjoyed anything at all?

He grunted to himself as he shrugged into his jacket. He was due at her house for dinner soon, and that would mean dress clothes. Houser would not appreciate that. He rather enjoyed being more of a butler and less of a valet. But as he was also a footman and had never been trained in any of the duties of anything he did, he was mostly grateful to be earning a respectable wage. It had taken years to pull Houser up to snuff, but there was not much else to do when the reformed criminal owed Gabe his life. Gabe had told him ages ago that there was no debt owed, secretly wishing to be rid of anyone who thought well of him, but Houser insisted that what honor he did have he meant to keep.

Gabe hadn't been able to shake him for six years, and now he was rather used to the scraggly old fool. He had a limited enough staff as it was, and simple bachelor quarters did not require more.

Now, if he were to ever take up residence at Whitleigh, his family home on Oxfordshire, he would have a great deal more to contend with. The place was a mausoleum, and it would take a sizable staff just to run it. As it was now, there was nothing and no one within. Unless some stray creatures had taken up residence, or local vagabonds found a hidden entrance.

The entail on it was too tight to break, but as Gabe had no use for it, there was no sense in spending the money he did not have on a place he did not need.

Much to Aunt Geraldine's dismay.

The soft knock on the back door brought him up, and he gathered his things, blew out the candles, and made his way in the dark for it.

A small girl with dark eyes and tattered clothing sat on the step and beamed up at him when he exited.

"Daisy," he greeted, smiling against his will. "Ready to go home?"

She nodded and rose, stepping back to let him lock up. Then she took his proffered hand and let him lead.

"How was your mark today?" Gabe asked, shaking her hand a

little.

"All right," she replied, clicking her tongue against her teeth. "'e don't do much, and nobody's been to visit for ages excepting the bat, but 'e don't ever see 'er. She cursed somefink horrid today. I watched the 'orses mostly. Fink Gent'll let someone jus' watch the street soon? It's boring, now Miss Margaret's safe."

Gabe chuckled, amused by the dramatic tone she had taken. "Perhaps. Anything exciting happen?"

Daisy shrugged, rubbing a grubby hand across her nose. "Robbie thrashed Frank again, but Jamie put a stop to it. Molly weaseled a luncheon out of ol' Mrs. Lynch wif some tears, and I got a sixpence."

"Sixpence?" Gabe asked with a smile. "How did you manage that?"

"Pretty lady came down the street an' smiled at me. Then she gave me sixpence and a wink." Daisy looked up at him with a frown. "She came this way, come to fink. You see a lady in a brown coat and stained glove?"

Gabe barely managed not to jerk the small hand in his surprise. "Chestnut hair? Cheap boots?"

"Tha's the one." Daisy reached into her pocket and held up the coin. "Sixpence."

Gabe smiled, despite his now rampant curiosity. Miss Berger must have lodgings in this direction. Well, well, he could certainly do something with that.

"Hide that from your father, Mouse," Gabe warned. "You know what he'll do if he finds it."

Daisy shoved it back into her pocket. "Aye, same as 'e'd do if 'e found the rest. But 'e won't find 'em. 'e's too drunk to see 'is toes."

Gabe felt a jolt of pain in his gut. No girl of seven should have to have such a harsh understanding of the world, nor of her father, the only parent she had. Daisy was being raised by her associates in Gent's passel of children, and by the London League themselves, if he were to be honest. He hadn't meant to take an interest in any of the urchins, but somehow Daisy had managed to become something to him. Just what, he couldn't say.

But a few nights a week he walked her home, and they had fallen into a comfortable routine that was their own little secret.

Well, Gent probably knew, but he hadn't said anything. He suspected he might have a great deal to say once the glow of love and new marriage faded.

They approached the docks and the residences nearby, only for loud and unmistakably intoxicated shouts to meet their ears. Daisy moaned softly and moved a little closer to Gabe, her eyes somber.

Gabe looked towards the closest rooms, lit within despite the filth on the windows and the shape of a man pacing could be seen.

He might be a rogue with no honor and a man without manners, but even he was not heartless.

"Tell you what, Mouse," he said, turning away and tugging her along. "You stay elsewhere tonight. Tilda or me?"

Daisy did not bother to hide her relief as she grinned up at him. "Anywhere!" she gushed. "Fanks, Rogue!"

He couldn't help it; he smiled back at her. "My pleasure, Mouse. How about staying with me tonight? Tilda has her hands full with the rest, and Houser wants a rematch."

Daisy sniffed as she shuffled along beside him. "Fine, but 'e cheats, and badly."

"Don't tell him that, he thinks he's a cardsharp, and we must let him have his pride."

Daisy's giggles lit the London night, and Gabe found far too much delight in it, but he couldn't bring himself to live up to his name or his nature.

Just this once.

Chapter Four

"That's ten pounds, Miss Berger."

Amelia glared at the coarse-faced woman holding out her hand. "Mrs. Jenkins, when I began lodging here two weeks ago, you clearly told me five."

"Mayhap I've changed me mind."

Amelia made a soft tutting noise as she turned to check her hair in the mirror. "That would be very poor business. And when my uncle, Lord Farley, returns from his time in the Indies and inquires as to my venture into London's temporary lodgings and the report for the Housing Board, I shall have far more to tell him than I thought." She quirked her brows and waited as the woman started sputtering, her already red face turning a more frightening shade.

"Four pounds, Miss Berger," Mrs. Jenkins said quickly, backing out of the room. "For my mistaken calculations. At your convenience, of course."

She closed the door with just as much efficacy as she had escaped, and Amelia smiled to herself as she finished preparing for the day. She'd become so adept at lying, it was a bit shameful. But ever so much fun.

She glanced at her reflection in the small and poorly-cleaned mirror, made a face at how drawn she looked, and then collected her borrowed valise of belongings and materials. It was reasonably light, but there was far too much for the small reticule she had. She shifted her grip on it, made her way out of the boarding house, and down the busy street.

It was earlier than she'd been told to arrive, but she was not about to dally around with nothing to do but wait, and she was anxious to see what Rogue could make of her lists.

And she wanted to know what he did when confronted with the unexpected and complete defiance of his dictates. She wanted to rile him. Typically, she was not so inclined, but something about him just made her want to poke and prod and see what would happen.

She'd been awake much of the night as she went over her own notes of the situation, everything she knew, which was not much, and what little belonged to her that might offer some indication of a direction, at least.

She did not have much to lose but time. And her lodgings. Mrs. Jenkins' boarding house was not exactly ideal, but Amelia had seen far worse, and she would stay as long as she could. She had not lied to Rogue, she did have the funds to pay him. But she did not have much more than that. She had his fifty, as he had ordered, and the rest was safely hidden away, as she did not trust Mrs. Jenkins to not have the room thoroughly searched and put back together during her absence. She only hoped that Rogue was not going to charge her additional measures on top of the two hundred pounds for whatever expenses they might accrue from this mad venture. She could never manage it.

It had been hard enough to raise decent funds to employ anybody.

She shivered as she recalled her more harrowing moments while earning money. It was astonishing that she was still alive and sentient this day.

But she was beyond that now, and she was not about to consider herself a victim of anything but the man who could have saved them both. She did not want sympathy, she wanted retribution. She wanted to know, for herself, if her life could have been more than what it was. If there was a chance of that, she wanted the man who had rid her of that chance to pay for it.

Her mother was another complaint, but one that grew more dim and distant with time, as much as she hated to admit it. She had very few pleasant memories of her mother and even fewer that she could remember clearly. All she had in her past was hardship, depression, and wondering if this was the day she would be an orphan. In truth, she had been an orphan since that day they'd left the cottage in Surrey.

Amelia Tribbett had been on her own since the age of eight, mother or no mother.

She glanced around the busy street, wondering if any of her old comrades were still about. London's children were a unique blend, and she had learned much from her time among them. It was how she had survived, and she would not be the woman she was today without them, for good or evil. She also would not have at least a third of her vocabulary if not for them.

That made her smile.

The streets of London were easy to navigate if one knew them well enough, which, thankfully, she did, although she had never been to the small side street that Rogue and his associates worked out of. It seemed strange to admit that, given how much she had traipsed about, but it was the truth.

And she had never heard of him before the other day. Gent, she had heard of, as had everyone with ears in the last decade or so, but never Rogue.

But then, she had never been one for gossip anyway.

She entered the narrow street with a smile on her face, despite the dismal prospect before her. It was a sunny day in London, which did not happen enough for it to not feel new every time, and something about Rogue's surliness and reputation for success gave her hope.

Of all impossible things.

She knocked on the innocuous door to the office, and it was quick to open, with the dark-haired, easily-distressed young man greeting her with a simple nod.

"Come in, Miss Berger," he said in a clipped tone, stepping back.

She inclined her head as she stepped past him and took in their almost cramped front room. The other clerk, a scrawny, ginger-haired man with spectacles, looked irritated beyond belief as he sat at his desk, furiously scribbling away.

There was no sign of the pretty blonde maid from the day before, and Amelia could not tell if that was a good thing or bad.

The dark clerk gestured towards the hall and then glared at his colleague with such venom that Amelia nearly laughed.

"Thank you," she told him with a smile. "I know the way."

He nodded and turned back to his desk.

"Rogue's not expecting you yet," the other said in a surprisingly polite tone, not looking up. "Perhaps you would care to wait?"

"No, I wouldn't," she replied, continuing on towards the offices.

The scratching pen stopped, and she glanced over her shoulder to see both men staring at her in a sort of horror.

She gave them a small smile and a half wink. "Gentlemen."

They began whispering to each other the moment she moved again, their previous trouble apparently forgotten.

Amelia paused before the closed door and tilted her head at it, wondering if she was feeling polite enough to knock.

She was not.

She pushed open the door to his office with a flourish. "Mr. Rogue, I have come for my appointment."

Rogue was bending over his desk, poring over documents with a gentleman with hair the color of aged gold. Nearby was another man, one who actually looked like a rogue, despite his equally common clothing, with his finely chiseled Roman features and dark hair. She imagined many going weak at whatever smile he might possess.

He and the other two stared at her in surprise, and she simply folded her hands before her, waiting.

Rogue dropped his head, exhaling sharply. "Miss Berger, did I not say ten after twelve?"

"You did," she confirmed with a prim nod.

He looked back at her, his features tightening. "Then why the devil are you here almost an hour before that appointed time?"

Amelia fought a smile, and she knew that he saw. "I felt we would both be anxious to begin."

"You were wrong," he snapped, straightening to his full height. "And what in hell gives you the presumption to barge in here, and…"

"Rogue," the taller man next to him said in a low voice, his gaze on Amelia.

Rogue instantly closed his mouth, though she had no doubt he was still railing inside his head, as his throat remained taut and his eyes spoke of his fury.

The handsome one apart from them looked between Rogue and Amelia with interest. "Friend of yours, Rogue?" he finally asked in a would-be innocent tone.

Rogue flicked a seething glance at him that drew forth a grin.

The man pushed off from the wall and came to Amelia. "Miss Berger, was it?"

Amelia nodded, holding out her hand.

He took it and bent to kiss it with some gallantry, turning that grin of his up at her. "A pleasure. You may call me Rook." He kissed her hand again, then stepped back, watching her with a certain measure of amusement.

Amelia raised a brow, unable to resist smiling back. "Are you sure your name shouldn't be Rogue?"

Rook laughed warmly and winked at her. "If only, Miss Berger." He turned a little and nodded at Rogue. "Him you already know, but the rather respectable and somber one over there currently wondering why he ever brought me on is Cap."

Cap exhaled with a measure of exaggerated patience that confirmed Rook's claim and inclined his head. "Miss Berger." He looked at Rogue briefly, then back at her. "I trust Rogue is meeting your needs adequately."

Amelia had a sense that she ought not to tease this one as she had Rook, nor should she provoke him as she would Rogue. "He is thus far, yes, Cap. Sir."

He almost seemed to smile but did not manage it. "No need to 'sir' me, Miss Berger."

"Is there not?" she murmured, her eyes flicking to Rogue automatically.

Rogue said nothing.

Amelia looked back to Cap, raising her chin a little. "I have only just begun my association with Rogue, sir, and so I cannot honestly say if my needs are being met adequately. But I have no reason to doubt they will be."

Cap inclined his head, then clapped Rogue on the back. "Thank you for the update, Rogue. I will leave you to get started with Miss Berger."

Rogue murmured something that sounded suspiciously like

"Must you?" as Cap nodded at Rook and the two moved to exit the room.

Amelia threw a frown at Rogue, which made Rook chuckle and wink at her.

"No eavesdropping, Rook!" Rogue yelled as they closed the door. "I mean it!"

Rook replied with something in another language that made Rogue snarl, and he flung himself into the chair by his desk, shaking his head.

Amelia took a seat herself, allowing a small smile to grace her lips. "Shall we begin?"

He gave her a look. "By all means, begin."

"Such politeness," Amelia commented with a soft clucking as she reached for her valise. "And after I've met your pleasant colleagues?"

"If you want to work with them, be my guest," he snapped. "In the meantime, stop wasting my time."

Amelia was not about to shift her case to the others, not when she had heard so much to Rogue's credit. No one had ever said he would be respectful or pleasant, so she did not have much to complain about. Beggars could not be choosers, after all.

She nodded firmly and opened the valise, reaching within. "First things first."

She put the requested fifty pounds on his desk with a bit of force, meeting his eyes. "Money, as requested."

He inclined his head and pulled the notes from beneath her hand pointedly. He shuffled through them, made a face of satisfaction, then folded them and shoved them into his trousers. "Good. Next."

That was all she was to expect? Well, this was going to prove a fascinating venture, if she was the only one that would be doing anything.

Amelia exhaled. "You asked for a list."

Rogue nodded. "I did."

She waited to see if he would tell her more, give her some indication of what he wanted her to do with it, but there was nothing in his gaze except expectation and growing impatience.

She produced the two full sheets that made up every person of significance she had ever met in her entire life and any information she had with regards to her parents' past.

It was not much, but it represented her life, so there was undoubtedly some hidden significance with that irony.

Rogue snapped his fingers and held out his hand, flexing his fingers.

Amelia had already been in the process of handing the papers over, but now she held them back. "Excuse me," she said slowly, blinking as if she had missed something. "Did you just... snap at me?"

Rogue only looked mildly sardonic. "I might have done."

Amelia frowned and narrowed her eyes. "I am not a dog. You will not do that again."

He shrugged. "I might, if I think it will accomplish what I wish. I live by no rules, Miss Berger, except those of self-preservation and self-interest."

Amelia watched him for a moment, waiting for him to change his statement, to give her some sign that he might actually possess some sort of a heart.

The evidence did not present itself.

"Well," she replied with a sniff, holding the papers just out of his reach, "in the interest of self-preservation, do not snap at me. Ever."

Impossibly, that seemed to amuse him. "Duly noted, Miss Berger. Now, the list, if you please."

She gave it to him and waited for the criticism to start.

It did not take long.

"Why have you not listed any of your family on here?" he asked, brow furrowed as he scanned the paper.

"I have," she told him, rising and coming around the desk. She leaned over and pointed. "Here."

"Mary Palmer?" He glanced up at her. "And yet your name is Berger?"

Amelia shrugged. "I adopted my uncle's surname when he took me in, but my mother's name was Palmer."

He sat back, nodding as he looked at the list. "Before or after she married your father?"

"I don't think there ever was a marriage."

That brought Rogue's head up, and he shook it slowly. "Do you have any idea how complicated this will be without a marriage?"

Amelia gave him a tight smile. "Why do you think I raised two hundred pounds for the effort?"

He shook his head again. "We will need every bit of it."

Amelia said nothing but smiled.

"I can hear you smiling," he muttered. "Stop."

"I can't," she said, shrugging again. "You said 'we'. It's the first time you've said as much."

Rogue exhaled noisily and set the paper down. "Miss Berger, for someone who claimed to be without sentiment, that is a remarkably sentimental observation. If you continue to behave that way, you will not only put me in a foul temper but make this entire venture a much more painful process."

"A foul temper," Amelia mused. "What would that be like?"

Rogue gave her a telling look. "You do not want to know." He looked back at the list and hummed softly. "Why is your uncle not on here?"

"My uncle?" she asked, frowning as she looked over his shoulder.

"Your uncle whose name you took when he took you in," he recited with more than a touch of condescension. "By your account, his last name should be Berger."

Amelia swallowed, closing her eyes at her blunder. "My uncle is married to my mother's sister and has a very poor memory. His wife has little recollection of her sister, and so there is not much use there. As such, I did not think they would be of much use to us."

"Convenient," Rogue mumbled under his breath. He sat forward and ran his finger down the list. "Surrey and London? You've not gone far in your life."

"Far enough," Amelia said in a dark tone before she could stop herself.

Rogue looked up, and she met his eyes coolly.

He turned back to the paper, then sighed. "You do realize, Miss Berger, that your being illegitimate significantly decreases the benefit you could receive from this venture if we find the man you seek, don't you?"

Amelia moved back to her chair and sat, taking the time to formulate a careful answer. "That would be true if I sought actual benefit. I am not looking for an inheritance or even a family name."

"So, what do you seek?" he asked, his tone surprisingly devoid of the sarcasm and derision she had learned to expect as his usual manner.

"The truth," she said simply, keeping her voice emotionless. "Identity. Answers."

"Revenge?" he prodded.

She looked up at him slowly. His voice had remained the same, no hint of suggestion or judgment in it, but she did not trust him. His eyes were both assessing and comprehending, and she suspected he knew far too much about her already.

She glanced away and leaned her chin on her hand. "That will depend on what we find with the rest."

"I see."

Amelia turned back to him, her temper flaring. "Do you? Do you see, Rogue? Because all I have received from you is judgment and criticism, and a decidedly pessimistic view of absolutely everything. I know what a wild venture this is, but I am willing to risk it because the chance for answers is worth it to me. If I can but understand even a portion of why my situation is what it is, to know even some of who I am, then perhaps my life might make the smallest bit of sense."

Rogue stared at her for a long moment, his brow slightly furrowed. "Very well, then," he finally said. He picked up the papers and held them out. "Take these out to the clerks and work with them to assemble a list of resources we might use to reach them. Organize it by location. When that is done, we will have a workable plan."

She took the papers, nodding. "And what will you do?"

He stood up from his desk and gave her a look. "I will start investigating, Miss Berger. It is what I do." He smiled blandly. "And what you're paying me for."

Chapter Five

$\mathcal{I}$t was going to be the worst possible assignment he had ever been given, and he'd once been assigned to infiltrate Bow Street and impersonate a Runner. It was much easier to work with criminals than legitimate law enforcement, as the criminals did not take much convincing of one's dissolute behavior and never trusted you even if you were one of them. The honest ones were harder to convince of anything, let alone of being someone worthy of their trust. Once you were accepted by them, however, you were not easily let out.

He could have still gone back into that world, so safely had he gotten out.

But he much preferred the criminals.

He would rather take the criminals now than this ridiculous scheme. The list Miss Berger had given him was a poor representation of anything, but he supposed that, if she were telling the truth, her past did not have much to offer them. He'd looked over it carefully, and it was too neat, too tidy, which meant there were holes in her story. He had many, many questions for her, none of which would be pertinent to the case that he had been hired to do, but all of which would aid him in rooting out what her purposes were and whether or not she could be trusted.

The trouble seemed to lay with the fact that he could not manage to speak to her without provoking her. It was too easy to nettle her, and she fought back with such surprising sharpness that it was far too tempting to set aside.

He'd left the office shortly after setting her to work with the clerks, instructing her to only work with One as Two was still learning what was useful and what was not. He might have imagined it, but he thought she was amused by his names for them. He hoped she would not form attachments to them. It would be rather disagreeable to have her around all the time just for their amusement.

After two days of scouring the streets, he had to admit that he could find nothing on the identity of Amelia Berger, saving her lodging in the cheapest boarding house that could still be categorized as strictly such. It only confirmed what he already knew. She was not what she seemed.

He'd found her uncle easily enough, and the story there was even less convincing than hers had been.

The dingy living quarters of the overpopulated and over-pious Berger family had not encouraged him, nor had it when the dimwitted uncle claimed he'd had no idea that his "Margie" had a niece, as he hadn't known she'd had a sister. But a short conversation with Mrs. Berger had confirmed that she did, in fact, have a sister, and she had severed ties with her when her shameful life had become too offensive to bear.

Gabe had faintly wondered what horrifying lifestyle had caused such strife and suspected it could have been an overly frivolous hair ribbon, as the pair before him had been the most colorless and formless shapes of humans he had ever come across.

No wonder Amelia had left them.

He would have fled the first night.

It came as no surprise to him that Amelia had simply shown up on their doorstep one day and claimed to be a relation in desperate need of support. The Bergers claimed she had never asked them for a farthing, only a place to stay. She had worked as a maid for them as well as doing some work in the local shops and homes, most of which would make any respectable person's skin crawl. Apparently, she had never once complained about the conditions. They had not felt right about turning away a family member so desperately in need, and as she had shown none of the willfulness of her late mother, they saw fit to keep her.

It had apparently been quite moving when Amelia had asked if she might take on the family name, forsaking completely that of her disgraced mother, and they had only been too delighted to allow it.

When he'd asked why she'd left, they both looked troubled. "Her mother's spirit must have turned her," Mrs. Berger had said. "She was suddenly filled with discontent, thinking herself too good for the circumstances we offered her, and she began filling the children's heads with all sorts of dangerous talk. Imagine our little girls thinking for themselves and not doing what we say!"

"Imagine," Gabe had muttered.

They'd told her to go and had given her the address of the boarding house but would not do more for her until she repented and came to herself.

Gabe suspected they would wait several lifetimes for that.

He hadn't actually set out to investigate Amelia while looking into some of the groundwork for her case, but it just happened to pan out that way. He wasn't convinced of her innocence, but the more he knew her, the more he suspected something else lay at the root of her intentions. She was driven, he could honestly say that, and far more than her initial impression had led him to believe. She had not only completed the tasks he had assigned her and One, but she had done such a thorough job with them that he had been convinced that One had done it all.

He'd been stunned when the truth had come out.

He'd expected that work to keep her occupied and out if his way for a few days, but they had finished it in the single day he'd been about the streets. Today, he'd told them to keep going, to proceed with analyzing the most likely ways to get information on each person, tasks they would need to complete, and an overall plan. It was another item to take up time, as Gabe already knew what he was going to do, but until he had set everything in motion, he needed a distraction for her.

If they accomplished this as quickly as they had the last, he would have to think of something else for tomorrow. And if Amelia was this efficient, he might actually have to take her along with him.

That was a terrifying thought.

And when, exactly, had he started thinking of her as Amelia?

That made him frown more than anything else. Familiarity was not something he was in favor of. It tended to produce a bond that did not exist and encourage further familiarity, and he could not maintain his distance once things became personal without everything becoming utterly mangled between the parties.

Although, if this madness took as long as he thought it would, he would be forced to have Amelia around for quite some time. He could never be polite, or pretend at it, for so long. Formality was sometimes worse than familiarity.

He could not win.

One thing was certain, however. None of Gabe's contacts had ever heard of Amelia Berger, none of his respectable inquiries had turned up anything on Mary Palmer, and there was absolutely no way in hell that he was in possession of the facts that he would need to even make success plausible.

It should also be noted that Mr. Berger was, in fact, married to Marjorie King, not Palmer, and her sister had been named Dorinda.

Lies and false names.

Not at all suspicious.

He smirked to himself as he approached the office. He wouldn't tell Amelia that he knew. He'd let her think him naïve enough to believe her, then sit back and wait for all hell to break loose when her case completely crumbled.

Besides, he wanted to know the real story. He might be a rogue with no honor, but he did have a tendency toward curiosity.

He pushed into the office to find Callie and Amelia on one side of the room, glaring at One and Two as if war had been declared. One and Two, for their parts, looked utterly terrified as they attempted to stand their ground.

Gabe looked between the two sides, then shook his head and walked directly between them and headed for his office.

Perhaps he was not so curious.

He sank into his chair and began rifling through the papers on his desk, scanning his notes and matching them with the ones in his head.

Barely two minutes later, Amelia entered, without knocking, and stood at his desk, arms folded, and tapping her foot.

Gabe could not have been less interested in what she had to say and continued to read his notes with the same focus he had before.

Amelia tapped louder and louder, and just when Gabe thought

she would start stomping her feet, she cleared her throat.

He glanced up at her, his face perfectly composed. "Yes?"

Amelia's pale eyes skewered him, and her lip curled a little. "Are you going to tell me what you found?"

Gabe frowned and sat back. "Why would I?"

"Because it is my case."

He shook his head at once and held up a finger. "It is *my* case, Miss Berger. I am the one investigating, and it is my skills that are being employed. You happened to present it, and that is all that can be said for you."

Amelia placed her hands on his desk and leaned forward. "Let me make one thing perfectly clear, Rogue. I meant it when I said I would be involved in this investigation. I will not let you shut me out, and I will not be given mundane tasks to keep me occupied anymore. Your clerks can do that very well; they do not need me. When you return from your investigative efforts, I expect to be informed of your progress. Is that clear?"

Gabe stared at her for a long moment, his heart pounding a bit oddly as he noticed for the first time how her cheeks flushed when she was indignant.

Then his rational mind took over, and his own indignation rose, prodding him to rise from his seat and match her pose on the desk. "Let me make something clear to you, Miss Berger. I do not report my progress to anyone but Cap, certainly not to my clients, and certainly not to you. If I have something to tell you, I will do so. I have no intention of shutting you out, I had you do those tasks because they needed to be done, and I do not believe that One and Two could manage a passable job on their own, considering the information you could provide them."

Amelia's jaw tightened, and she met his gaze for a long moment, then she swallowed. "You could at least take me with you on your investigations."

Gabe almost smiled. "Not all of them, Miss Berger. There are parts of London I must frequent that would frighten even you."

She *did* smile, though it was a cold, chilling sort of smile. "No, I don't think they would."

Something about her tone unsettled him, but he was quick to

shake it off, and he pushed away from the desk, returning his gaze to the papers before him. "As it is, my investigations thus far have been unproductive."

"Really?" Amelia asked without any trace of irony. "Why? What happened?"

Gabe looked back at her. "Nobody knows who Mary Palmer is."

Amelia's brow furrowed. "How is that possible? She's from London, I know she is."

Gabe sat back down in his chair and gave her a thoughtful look. "How?"

She leaned against his desk, tilting her head. "How what?"

"How do you know?" he prodded, gesturing with his hand a little. "How exactly do you know she was from London?"

She lowered her gaze, her brow furrowing further in thought. Her folded arms tightened against her, and her lower lip pulled as if she was gnawing the inside of it. "She always spoke of London. And in great detail, things I confirmed when I finally came here myself. Even when she was nonsensical, she always spoke of London."

"That could mean anything."

Amelia shook her head. "No, she was from London, I'm sure of it. She could not speak of it in such a way without having lived here. She knew shops and streets, people who worked there and proprietors to visit. I assure you, she knew London very well."

Gabe frowned, processing the information. Even so, it could still mean anything. She could have visited London often, could have lived here for part of her life but not all, or even, he supposed, could have been a girl from a high Society family who came to London for the Season.

Whatever the truth was, someone ought to have known of her.

Unless that name was also false.

He turned a harsh eye to Amelia, who reared back a little in confusion.

"What?" she asked.

"It is going to be remarkably difficult," he said slowly, "more difficult than it already is, to accomplish anything without complete honesty between us."

Her eyes widened. "I've been honest with you."

"Have you?"

"Yes."

"Then what is your mother's name?" he demanded.

"Mary Palmer," she recited, looking bewildered. "I was Amelia Palmer before I changed my name."

He sneered a little. "Then why does no one in London know her name?"

"I don't know," she snapped. "Did you ask all of London?"

Gabe glared, then pushed off his chair. "Come with me."

She followed at once, her drab grey skirts swishing against the floor, being too long for her and collecting all manner of dust and crumbs in their length.

"Where are we going?" she asked, keeping pace with his long strides as they entered the front room.

"Bonnet," he said shortly.

She grabbed hers and jammed it on her head. "Where are we going?" she asked again.

He nodded at Callie, sweeping near the door. She opened it for them and offered a confused look that he did not respond to.

"Rogue!" Amelia demanded, grabbing his arm. "Where are we going?"

"You don't know your mother's story," he told her as they walked. "London does not know her name. That leaves us with few options, aside from your list, which does not appear to be worth our time as things are. So, I am taking you to someone who can give us another alternative."

"Who?"

He smiled grimly. "An artist. One who only needs a description to begin and is very accurate."

Amelia groaned and shuffled a little beside him. "An artist? We don't have time for that."

Gabe gave her a hard look. "Do you have a particularly pressing deadline that I do not know about? Trust me, we have time for Hal."

She obviously did not believe him, but she would see.

He'd never met anyone as talented as Hal, and there was no one else he trusted with this task. But he'd never tell Amelia that.

Hal did not live far from their office, so it was a short walk, which was merciful, as Amelia plagued him with questions he quite simply refused to answer. What did he think their next step ought to be; how did he expect to discover her mother's identity; where should they look for answers…

She rambled on and on, and her voice began to grate in his ears. He tried to keep his stride as per usual, which was long and efficient, but the more she peeved him, the faster he walked. Unfortunately, she matched him stride for stride and had not become winded in the least.

It was the first time in his life he could recall actually being pleased to see Hal's temperamental butler, bodyguard, manservant, and Lord knew what else. Tad was a reformed criminal, though the level of his reformation was in question. Gabe had been the one to recommend him, given his penchant for loyalty, an uncommon trait in a man with his past, but a deuced useful one.

Tad nodded at him, had no expression for Amelia, and gestured up the stairs before disappearing.

"Well," Amelia muttered, "that's the most honest man I have ever met. Quite a pleasure to receive my due by way of greeting."

Gabe coughed a laugh, shaking his head as they mounted the stairs. "Tad has never managed politeness, and I fear he never will."

"Oh, and have you managed it?" she asked, smiling a little.

"Only on Wednesdays and only if the weather is fair."

Amelia chuckled a low laugh that oddly charmed him, which laughter rarely did. But hers was honest and raw, and he suspected she did not laugh often.

Why that should be significant, he couldn't say.

They quickly moved into Hal's library, which was the studio these days, and Hal, never one for propriety, scared the wits out of him by teetering on the top of a ladder, trying for a book out of reach.

Gabe bit back a coarse expletive and moved to the ladder quickly. "Damnation, Hal, are you trying to fall to your death?"

Hal snorted and tossed him a wry look, her blonde locks tumbling around her shoulders. "Of course not, Rogue. If I fell, which would be a very faint if, I would only manage to injure myself, perhaps break something. Don't be a hero, it doesn't suit."

Gabe groaned his disgruntlement and shook the ladder lightly.

"Get down, Hal, or I'll topple you on purpose."

Hal leaned out further, snatched the book she'd sought, then gripped the ladder once more. "On my way. Don't look up my skirts."

He snorted and averted his head. "As if I were even remotely tempted."

"I can't tell you how delighted I am to know you treat everyone this way and not just me," Amelia said from somewhere behind him.

"That is enough from you, thank you," he grunted, helping Hal down the last few rungs.

Hal hopped down and tilted her head up at him. "I didn't know you knew that phrase. Wonders never cease." She turned to consider Amelia, folding her tartan shawl around her more tightly. "How do you do?" She curtseyed then approached. "They call me Hal."

Amelia grinned without reservation, which was a bewildering sight as it made her entire face brighten. "They call me Amelia. It is very nice to meet you." She glanced at Gabe, then back to Hal. "I think you and I will get along splendidly."

Hal snorted and tilted her head towards some chairs. "I doubt that. I don't get along with anybody. That's why I'm a spinster living alone with a practically mute former criminal for my companion."

Gabe rolled his eyes and sank into a chair near her. "You never complained before, Hal."

She sniffed and gave him a look. "You never listen, so I might have, and you'd never know." Then she sighed, and her expression became more pleasant. "What can I do for you, Rogue? I presume this is not a social call."

"You know very well I never make social calls," he reminded her dryly. "No, I need you to make a sketch."

"Yes, that much I had figured." Hal looked at Amelia with seemingly infinite patience. "They never call on me for anything else, so I really am never expecting to be asked about popular fashions or the like."

Amelia snorted and covered her mouth, her eyes flicking to Gabe.

"Miss Berger here," Gabe said, barely managing to reply without sounding overly irritable, "is going to describe a person for you from memory. And then, I think, you should make one of her as well."

Amelia looked startled. "Of me? Why?"

"Comparison," he said simply. "And it is entirely possible you resemble her more than you realize, so on the off chance that Hal gets it wrong…"

"I'll forget you said that," Hal muttered as she gathered her supplies.

"…then we have a second picture, should it be needed," he finished without pausing, ignoring Hal, as he usually did.

Amelia frowned a little, not quite comprehending. "I suppose that makes sense… I've never been particularly fond of having my likeness taken."

"And who might have asked?" Gabe returned.

She glowered at him. "Wouldn't you like to know?" Then she turned her attention to Hal, who nodded, and Amelia began to describe her mother.

Gabe watched as Hal somehow managed to translate the description into a detailed drawing, and he marveled at her skill. He had his own motives for the picture of Amelia, but there was no way he could manage it now that she knew there would be one.

He moved behind Hal to watch more closely, then leaned down and murmured, "Make a copy of your sketch of Amelia for me, Hal."

"Personal?" she hinted with a smile, her tone as low as his.

His throat tightened in protest. "No," he managed. "No, it's for an investigation."

"Aren't they all?"

"A different one. Secret. And important."

Hal's jaw tightened and her gaze on Amelia hardened, not that Amelia noticed, lost as she was in her description. Hal nodded once. "I'll send it to your office later. Send one of Gent's children to me."

Gabe patted her shoulder. "Thank you." He moved back to his chair and sat down, listening to the description, and forming a mental picture in his head.

Amelia Berger might not know it, but she was being investigated just as thoroughly as her mother.

He would find out the truth, and he would use any means necessary.

He always did.

Chapter Six

"*It* is unnerving, to say the least, Rogue."

"I don't see why. It's only your mother."

Amelia sighed and averted her eyes yet again. "Yes, and she's dead. I don't particularly enjoy seeing her face when I look over there."

Rogue shrugged. "Then don't look over there." He put the paper he had been perusing down and went into his office, leaving her out in front once more.

He was missing the point entirely. There was nothing she wanted less than to stare at the likeness of her mother as it sat propped against the shelf. Why it was there, she had no idea, but it bothered her. The last time she had seen that face, it had been gaunt and haggard, a mask of death, and it had haunted her dreams for years.

They'd had the picture for a few days, and Rogue had gone out with it but hadn't yet taken Amelia with him, despite her endless complaints and reminders.

His excuses were unending, and each as legitimate as the next. She could not question him, as every time he could explain and defend his reasoning. She could not even accuse him of leaving her out, not when every time he returned he brought her into his office and gave her a full report.

It was maddening, wanting to complain but having nothing to complain about.

Eventually, he would see that he could accomplish more with her at his side than he could by leaving her out.

He had to.

Unless he was far more skilled than she'd thought, and he was already on track to finding her father, in which case she would never say another word about it.

But considering he had said nothing of the sort, she doubted that very much.

He was a difficult man to understand. Years of studying people had given Amelia a bit of a knack for getting a feel for the manners and personality, and sometimes morality, of an individual, and usually quite quickly. But Rogue was the most complicated man she'd ever come across. Oh, she'd had a fairly accurate first impression, that he was ill-mannered and closed-off and did not care about reputation or appearances. But the more she got to know him, the more she felt that his first impression was intentional.

The rumors about him had all been the same, except for his saving of the woman and her child. By every other account of him, he ought to have left them to their fate. He did not save bystanders from runaway carriages, or anything a sensible man with morals of any sort would. He ought to have only done a passable job of his investigation until she tempted him with more funds. And yet he was ruthlessly driven, remarkably quick, and she had seen with her own eyes the loyalty and respect for his colleagues as they came through. Rook to a much lesser degree than Cap, but she had still seen it.

There was something admirable about him, and she wasn't sure what it was. He had shown genuine care and concern for Hal, and their relationship had been something akin to siblings, if one actually liked their siblings. She would never have expected Rogue to be capable of any emotional relationships of any kind, but the evidence was before her eyes. He might not be able to stand One and Two, but he did not mistreat them, either. Callie was another story, but Callie was sharp, and Amelia suspected she had a more significant role in the office than met the eye.

The irascible Rogue had a soft spot for women? And a potentially honorable one? That seemed highly unlikely. But something was off here, and she was going to figure it out.

Assuming she ever got away from this damned desk and the papers that seemed to come at her intentionally.

Poor One. He'd cleared off a corner of his desk for her, and he'd never complained once. But going through files for every Palmer born within a decade of when she thought her mother was within a twenty-five-mile radius of London proper was not exactly something that Amelia had the patience for. She had no idea how the clerks managed to accomplish such tedious tasks without wanting to screech like a bedlamite.

Amelia understood the need for the task to be done. She did.

But why did she have to be the one to do it?

"Berger!"

Amelia rolled her eyes to the ceiling. He'd long since lost propriety, and now she was just another member of the staff, and the only one with a proper name. "What?" she called back.

Two snorted a laugh across the room, and she gave him a quick grin. Two was young and annoying with lofty expectations, so whenever she could amuse him, she claimed it as a victory. He could learn to be less pompous and pretentious, and enough time with this crew would give him ample opportunity.

"He's going to come out here, now," One muttered, hiding a smile as he ducked his face closer to the desk and his own work.

"Good," Amelia said simply, making another mark in her ledger. "Because I was not about to go in there for him to tell me nothing again."

"He might have found something this time," Two suggested, his doubt bordering on the blatant.

Amelia gave him a look rife with her own sentiments on that point, and he chuckled again.

"Get in here!" Rogue bellowed from his office.

"Better do it," One suggested with a nudge.

Amelia shook her head firmly. "No, thank you," she called back.

One and Two were not laughing now. They looked between the doorway to the offices and Amelia repeatedly, their faces a mix of anticipation and worry.

Brisk footsteps caught their attention, and the two clerks straightened up. Amelia continued to work on her mindless task, pretending she was not the least bit curious.

The footsteps stopped near her. There was not a sound in the room but the scratching of her pen.

"Miss Berger," Rogue said in a barely controlled voice that almost hid his anger.

She knew enough not to prod him too far. She finished her notation, then looked up at him politely. "Yes, Rogue?"

His expression was thunderous, and she wondered if she might possibly have irked him one too many times. She couldn't help it; it was just too tempting to provoke him, to defy his unspoken orders, to deny him command. He gave her the most entertaining look, something between distraction and rage, and his own confusion at the dissonance within him was evident.

He became disheveled, agitated, and lost some of his blessed control.

He became... actually quite attractive.

The errant thought caught her off-guard, and she looked at him in a bit of a different light. His features weren't so harsh as she'd once thought, his eyes were really quite astonishing when they weren't so cold, and his rugged roughness was enough to raise a bit of warmth in her cheeks. And his lips were...

Goodness sakes, was she examining Rogue to find attractiveness?

That was quite enough of that.

She cleared her throat a little. "You bellowed?"

One side of his lips quirked. "So did you."

She paused to acknowledge that with a dip of her chin. "Was there a purpose to our mutual bellowing?"

Rogue folded his arms and gave her a look. "I thought you might want to get out of this office and venture into London's depths to follow a potential lead regarding your mother."

Amelia stared at him, eyes wide. "What?" she eventually managed.

"Unless, of course, you would rather stay." He lifted a brow at her.

Amelia was to the door in an instant, snatching her bonnet and frantically tying the ribbons as the clerks laughed to themselves.

Rogue sauntered over, smirking a little. "Subtle, Miss Berger. One would think you've been held prisoner here."

"And one would not be wrong," she returned, flinging the door open.

Rogue chuckled as he followed, stuffing some papers into his jacket pocket, and shutting the door. "You ought to perhaps revise your opinions of prison, Amelia. Our offices are nothing of the sort."

Amelia looked up at him, clasping her hands behind her as they walked. "Have you been in prison then?"

He shrugged a shoulder. "Once or twice. I don't recommend it."

She smiled a little, amused that he was so cavalier about the whole thing. That was the sort of past one usually had regrets about and felt some degree of shame. But he admitted it freely and almost in passing.

"What were you in for?" she asked with more curiosity than she ought to have done.

Rogue smirked again, shaking his head. "Nothing worth repeating."

"Or regretting, apparently," she mused, smiling more broadly.

"Regrets are a waste of energy," he said easily. "I learned a lesson, it proved a point, and I did not make the same mistake again. Until the next time I was arrested."

"For the same crime?" Amelia laughed.

He shook his head. "No, a different one. I make the same mistakes in different ways. Variety, you know."

She laughed and shook her head, far more amused than she should have been. "Well, thank the Lord you weren't hanged for your crimes, Rogue. Imagine the trouble I would have if I had to have someone else take on my case. What if I had to go with Rook?"

Rogue snorted as he took her arm and led her down a different path than the one she'd started on. "You'd not find anything with Rook except for gossip and fops. Gent would be much of the same, but fewer fops, and more poor females in need of saving."

"Saving?" Amelia asked with a surprised laugh. "What, does the Gent have a hero problem?"

"Gent is everything a hero should be," Rogue told her, his tone sounding too derisive for what should have been praise. "Enough honor for two toffs. He protects reputations, he saves women from runaway carriages, he is the protective elder brother of every woman in London, and if I did not know better, I'd think him a monk."

Amelia laughed heartily at his descriptions, his tone still disgusted. "He sounds rather ideal."

"If you like the honorable sort, I am sure he is." Rogue nodded at two unsavory looking men who kept their distance. "Otherwise, you will find him rather insufferable."

She smirked a little. "I don't recall saying anything about liking or disliking, it was a simple observation. You must allow that today's ideal man is all honor."

"Alas for the lost art of villainy."

He was apparently determined to maintain his dubious character, and she was more curious about that than anything else. "Is honor such a terrible flaw?" she asked, prodding a little.

He considered that for a moment. "I suppose not, if I must be brutally honest, but I've always found it terribly inconvenient, particularly for our line of work. I make it a point to avoid honor at all cost. Less expectation allows me far more freedom."

"So, you are a dishonorable bottom-dweller who loathes all politeness and clings to the vain hope that he won't be corrupted by the light?" she asked, laughing to herself.

Rogue glanced down at her, seeming amused himself. "More or less, yes."

Amelia made a soft noise of acknowledgement. "You keep saying you have no honor, but rushing into a burning building to save a mother and child seems fairly honorable. Heroic, even."

Rogue's glower was swift and potent. "Don't do that, Amelia. Don't pretend I'm something I am not."

His defensive tone was surprising, despite what she already knew of him. The first time she'd mentioned hearing that story, he'd reacted similarly. That alone had convinced her of its reality, and the more she learned of him, the less surprised she was by his actions that night. He claimed no honor, but he took great care with his work. He claimed villainy, but he'd never behaved beyond the level of curmudgeon and certainly had never truly behaved badly.

In short, Rogue, in spite of his name, was nothing of the sort.

He was simply cantankerous.

Then why the act? And why the hatred of such a daring and honorable deed? "So why did you save them at such peril to yourself?"

He shrugged, his jaw tight. "Collateral damage makes for a lot of paperwork."

Amelia frowned and shook her head. "I don't believe you really feel that way."

He gave her a sardonic look. "You don't know me, Miss Berger, and don't let any amount of time in my presence let you believe that you do." He strode ahead of her, making no effort to ensure that she followed.

Amelia stared at him in confusion and not a small amount of irritation. For a man of no manners, he certainly had his own offended quite easily. He was determined to remain aloof and distant from any relationships beyond brief acquaintances, and heaven forbid that he should open himself enough to give an honest answer about anything at all. She hadn't asked him to bare his soul, only to ask why he saved the woman and child when he seemed so bitter about it. Surely a man with no morals, manners, or honor would not have cared one way or the other.

Then again, if the story was true, the screams had been what had brought him back, and she supposed one would have to be utterly without heart or soul to ignore such a sound.

So why was Rogue determined to be considered such a vile creature when it was plain he was not?

Amelia had never been one for riddles, but suddenly she had a fierce desire to solve this one. Why he had to be at the root of it irked her, but one did not get to choose the riddles that intrigued them. She only hoped that she would not get bitten in her attempt to solve it, but the danger could not be helped.

She smiled to herself, wondering how much goading it would take to dissipate his anger enough for him to be witty and surly again.

And then she had it.

Grinning, she scampered ahead and linked her arm with his. "You cannot call me Miss Berger once you've decided to call me Amelia."

He jerked and tried to yank his arm away. "What are you doing? Get off."

She shook her head. "You called me Amelia. Twice, if I recall.

This, I believe, makes us friends."

"And there you would be wrong, Miss Berger," he said through gritted teeth, pulling his arm out of her grasp. "I have no friends, least of all you."

Amelia snorted and rolled her eyes. "You have friends, Rogue. Cap and Rook, surely…"

"Associates," he said firmly. "Brothers-in-arms, perhaps, but we do not meet socially."

"You don't meet anyone socially," she pointed out, folding her arms.

"That makes it very easy to avoid the inconvenience of friends."

She couldn't help it; she laughed out loud. Thankfully, there were not too many people milling about where they were, so her amusement at the expense of the mysterious Rogue was not going to be remarked on. He would be relieved by that knowledge, she was sure.

Rogue was looking at her as if she had gone mad, but he smiled all the same, which was a sight she would likely never become accustomed to. It literally changed his entire demeanor, and she rather liked it.

"Oh, all right then," Amelia managed, once her laughter faded. "We do not have to be friends if the thought distresses you so. But please, can you call me Amelia? I promise not to have any thoughts of friendliness on your part. It's just that formality makes me uneasy."

"What gives you the idea that I would wish you to be anything but uneasy?" Rogue countered, raising a brow. "What if I don't care about your personal comfort?"

"Oh, for heaven's sake," Amelia muttered, throwing up her hands and marching ahead, turning down the cobblestone road. "You are the most impossible, intolerable, insufferable, in…"

He suddenly grabbed her arm and pulled her the other way down the street, obviously the path least travelled. It led through narrow alleys with leaning buildings, dark stone that had never seen the light of day and was unquestionably the sort of place that girls like Amelia ought to be particularly apprehensive about treading through. But as there were no girls like Amelia, she did not have such fears.

"Before you can come up with yet another word that means the same thing, Amelia," Rogue said rather pointedly, leading her down the dank and filthy road, "you ought to consider not going ahead of me when you have no idea where we are going."

"Well, where are we…" she started with venom, then stopped when she realized what he had said and looked up at him sharply. "Did you just call me Amelia?"

He tilted his head at her, his face suddenly filled with apparent concern. "That is your name, isn't it? Ought I to call you something else?"

She beamed up at him and dipped her chin. "Amelia it is, thank you, Rogue."

"Don't thank me for forgoing politeness," he replied, snorting softly, his expression returning to its normal state. "I can't abide it myself, so it is no sacrifice on my part. And stop smiling like that, it makes you look like a child."

Amelia shrugged, falling into step beside him again. "I've gotten my way. That brings out the child in all of us."

"God help me," Rogue muttered.

"So where are we going, then?" she asked him, granting him a reprieve from her eagerness.

He inclined his head down another side street, and she turned with him. "Do you know where we are?"

Amelia frowned, looking around her, not seeing anything particularly distinct about the rather unremarkable street or the buildings nearby. Nothing notable that would have separated it from any other part of London's less-than-elegant side. She thought back, mentally retracing their steps, but shook her head.

"No, not really," she admitted, wincing a little. "We've gone further east than I know. We must be nearly to Mayfair."

Rogue looked surprised at that. "Very good."

"We're in Mayfair?" Amelia squeaked, feeling a bit slack-jawed and looking around with new appreciation. She'd never even come close to Mayfair, it was too far and too grand for her to attempt entrance, despite her excellent skills with impersonation. Besides, she'd never had a reason to.

He chuckled, shaking his head. "No, we are not. Welcome to Covent Garden."

That surprised her as much as if he'd said Mayfair. Everybody went to Covent Garden for the theater, it was wildly popular. But when it looked like this, she wondered why.

Rogue saw her look and smirked. "This is the back side, Amelia. You ought to know I would never take the fashionable way."

That made her laugh, and she followed him down another side alley. "Of course, why would anybody do that?" She shook her head, smiling. "Why are we in Covent Garden? Do you know someone here who could help us?"

"Oh, yes," he said with a sage nod that she was instantly suspicious of. "Someone here will help us a great deal."

Amelia narrowed her eyes. "How?" she asked slowly.

He smiled congenially. "In many ways."

Now she was genuinely nervous. "Who are we seeing, Rogue?"

"Tilda."

Amelia rolled her eyes. "As if that helped me at all. Who is Tilda?"

Rogue opened a door that probably ought not to have been unlocked and gestured for Amelia to precede him. "Tilda is a former actress of the stage, and now a gifted costumer with her own troupe of actresses. She works with us quite frequently and has never once let me down."

"High praise, I am sure," Amelia snorted softly. "Why are we seeing Tilda? Will she know something?"

"No," Rogue said simply, "but she can do something."

Do something? That didn't make sense, how was a costumer supposed to help them with their investigation? Unless they were going in disguise, but that did not seem likely considering nobody knew Amelia, and Rogue was… well, Rogue was himself. What else could they need her for?

Rogue was looking at her with a sneaky little smirk, and Amelia stilled. "You wouldn't dare…" she breathed, hoping he was not suggesting what she feared he was suggesting.

He was nodding before she finished. "Oh yes, Amelia Berger. You are going to be seeing Tilda to see what she can make of you, because I refuse to take you to any sort of modiste. Costs way too much money, and Tilda we can get for free."

"Oh, can you?" chimed in a dry voice from nearby.

Amelia turned to see a tall, dark-haired woman who was dressed simply, but with an air of refinement that many women would spend their entire lives attempting to cultivate. She wasn't looking at her, as her attention was entirely devoted to Rogue in a manner that positively begged for an explanation, her expression some mixture of derision and delight. She could only presume this was Tilda, from the measuring tape around her neck and the hint of paint on her eyelids, making her somehow exotic despite her simplicity.

Rogue plucked Tilda's hand from her hip and kissed it warmly. "Help me, Tilda, won't you?"

Tilda chuckled and patted his cheek. "You know I can't resist you when you use manners."

He grinned raffishly. "You know I only use them for you."

"I'm feeling rather uncomfortable," Amelia announced without ceremony, wondering with a stroke of horror if the two were lovers.

They turned to look at her with the same assessing look, startling her.

"Yes," Tilda murmured, nodding slowly. "Yes, I see what you need. Easy."

"What?" Amelia cried, looking down at herself. "What do I need?"

"What don't you need would be the better question," Rogue said with infinite patience.

She glowered at him, making Tilda laugh again. "Why are we wasting time with this?" she demanded. Then, realizing she might offend this rather terrifying woman, she winced and looked at her. "No offense?"

Tilda waved that off with a smile. "None taken. Follow me." She crooked a finger as she turned to continue down the hall.

Amelia made a face and looked back at Rogue. "Why?" she hissed.

Rogue lifted a brow at her. "Because there is no way in hell I am going anywhere with you looking like that."

He put a hand on her back and pushed hard, forcing her ahead of him, and leaving absolutely no way for her to escape her fate.

She would never forgive him for this.

Chapter Seven

*W*ell, there was no hope for it now.

He had delayed her for as long as was humanly possible.

Now he had to take Amelia out with him.

He shook his head as he pushed back from his breakfast and headed out of the dining room. He didn't want to go anywhere with her, let alone take time to do it, but there were no other excuses he could possibly give. He'd expected Tilda to be able to distract her sufficiently for a time, and he'd even planned on their forming some sort of friendship, much as that might plague him later. But neither had happened, and his plans were no further along than before.

Amelia had been livid, which had surprised him, as surely all women enjoyed the opportunity to dress up and parade around in new things. Yet she had been surprisingly feral and had actually gnashed her teeth at him, though she was pleasant enough with Tilda. Tilda, shockingly enough, had found the whole thing quite amusing.

Actually, that was not surprising at all. Tilda had an appreciation for irony and enjoyed making his life difficult.

By the end of their interminably long interview and task, Amelia had not only met most of the actresses of Rogue's acquaintance but had found herself stocked with several gowns much better suited for their mission. They would help her look the part far better than any of her rags might have done. It was better for his investigation, but worse for his personal preference, as he would now be forced to have her come along with him. All he'd wanted was for her to not look as though she were his servant, not to give her some sort of high hand over him.

He should have thought this through a little more carefully.

But at least now Tilda and her girls knew who Amelia was, and they could track her for him, should the need arise.

And provided they would agree to it.

He was not comfortable with this situation. Something was not right, and he could not place it. He'd spent his evenings showing Amelia's picture around to some of his contacts, but no one seemed to recognize her. He had eyes on her at all times, but no one reported anything suspicious.

He'd even tried to distract himself by attempting to get information about the weapons he'd heard the faction was trying to move, but that, too, was surprisingly silent. Nothing about guns, traitors, smuggling, or even anything that sounded remotely French. Either he was losing his touch with his craft, or there truly was nothing to report. He doubted that. There was always something to report. Which meant either he needed to dig deeper, or the silence was the telling.

He hated silence. It was too unnerving.

Gabe rolled his eyes and tugged at his collar, wondering why Houser had starched his cravat, knowing he was not going to wear it for long. He never did, unless he was in character, and today was not one of those days.

"Going somewhere, sir?" Houser's deep, gravelly voice asked.

Gabe barely managed to avoid jumping and turned to the hulking man, who had somehow appeared without him knowing.

If Houser ever decided to turn against him and return to a life of crime, Gabe would die a swift and silent death.

"Yes," Gabe told his scruffy servant, currently surveying him through expressionless eyes.

"Your aunt is in the green room."

He might as well have said it was Wednesday for all the emotion those words held, and yet Gabe tensed with a hiss.

"Aunt Geraldine?"

Houser raised his scarred brow. "Do you have another?"

That earned him a scowl, which, as usual, had no effect. Gabe looked towards the aforementioned room. "What does she want?"

Houser snorted softly. "I didn't ask, and she didn't say."

Gabe pursed his lips in thought, his brow furrowing. "She didn't send word ahead of time, and it's early in the day... That isn't good."

"Probably not."

Really, it was as if Houser were trying to be less help than usual.

Gabe loved his aunt, he honestly did, though he would never admit that to anyone. But that did not mean he wanted to see her as often as she wanted to see him. She wanted him to live with her, for pity's sake, and that was not going to happen no matter how pitifully she begged.

But in order to keep the peace, and save her feelings, and not actually blacken his soul to the extent the world thought it, he never refused to see her.

He sighed heavily. "Tell Daisy to eat in the kitchen and then wait for me. Aunt Geraldine would never recover if she thought I had a child in this house."

"Does Daisy count as a child?" Houser asked thoughtfully, though he smiled.

Gabe could not help smiling himself. "You know better than that. What's more, you like the child."

Houser grimaced. "Like is a strong word..." he muttered.

Gabe clapped his servant on the arm. "Houser, you would deliver her a tea service on a gold tray if she asked you nicely enough."

"She would do it, too," Houser said with a small chuckle, making no attempt to deny it. "She cheats at cards, though."

Gabe shook his head as he headed towards the green room. "So do you, my friend. She just does it better."

Houser's hoarse laugh echoed in the hallway as Gabe left him.

Gabe paused outside of the green room, steeling himself. Aunt Geraldine was a formidable opponent, and he would need all his wits to avoid being trapped into something he'd detest. Some of his associates had relations that were ridiculous and simple-minded, and they were able to outmaneuver them easily.

He was not so fortunate.

Aunt Geraldine was sharp and witty, not nearly as hardened as he would have been in her position, and in possession of a generous heart, which made him question their being related at all. She was the furthest person from ridiculous he had ever come across, and she would not be persuaded or distracted from her purpose. Early on in their renewed relationship, he had tried. He'd put on the most cultivated character portrayal he had ever managed in his life, and any slightly less sensible woman would have been completely swayed by it.

Aunt Geraldine had not even batted an eyelash.

Usually, he could anticipate her maneuvers, but this one was completely unexpected.

And suddenly, he was terrified.

He cleared his throat softly, then entered the room. His aunt turned at the opening of the door and raised a thin brow in the sort of look that seven-year-old boys receive regularly.

"Gabriel," she said simply.

He bowed politely, then went to her side and kissed her hand. "Aunt. To what do I owe the pleasure?"

Geraldine snorted softly. "To what do I owe your politeness?" she asked, her Northern accent ringing proudly out, as it always had done.

"I'm not being polite," he replied as he sank into a chair. "I speak in irony."

"You always speak in irony, and I never understand why," she muttered as she also sat, her crepe skirts rustling as she did so.

Gabe made a face and shook his head. "Why would you intentionally wear crepe, Aunt? You are not in mourning, as evidenced by that... unusual shade of green. Surely you would wish to wear something more comfortable."

"If I wished for your opinion on fashion, Gabriel," Geraldine snapped with a flick of the fan in her hand, "I would have asked you for it." Then she tilted her head, her lips spreading into a smile. "And I had no idea you knew what crepe was. Are you interested in fashion after all?"

He shuddered and waved his hand. "Not a bit. I know what any other man knows, and what we know is that crepe is damned uncomfortable, and you shouldn't enjoy wearing it."

She frowned at his choice of word but said nothing of it. "Yes, well, when you've had your heart broken as I have, Gabriel, you might choose to remind yourself of it by wearing the uncomfortable fabric of mourning clothes without the sacrifice of limiting one's wardrobe to black."

Gabe rolled his eyes and put a hand to his brow. "Yes, yes, you've told me. I still don't believe you, since you've never told me when or where your heart was broken, let alone by whom."

"And what good would that do?"

He gave her a serious look. "It makes it rather difficult to avenge you, my dear."

She looked surprised for a moment, then smiled with genuine affection. "Why, that may be the sweetest thing anyone has ever said to me."

"Don't tell anyone," he muttered, shifting his gaze to the window. "And surely whomever broke your heart said sweeter things, or else your heart would not be broken over him."

Geraldine laughed softly. "Oh, he did, but without your sincerity."

Gabe looked back at her and folded his hands. "So, tell me who he is so I might be equally sincere with him."

She smirked and shook her head. "No, my dear, I rather like you out of prison."

"You didn't say the same ten years ago."

"You were a wastrel ten years ago."

"I'm a wastrel now," he suggested with a nonchalant shrug. "I simply behave better."

Geraldine somehow managed to roll her eyes without actually rolling her eyes, then sighed softly. "Doesn't your servant know to bring a tea service?"

Gabe snorted and glanced towards the door. "Of course, he does. Whether he chooses to act on such proprieties is another matter entirely."

On cue, Houser entered with the tea tray, somehow looking the proper manservant despite scruff and lack of livery. He set the tray down, nodded to Geraldine, then to Gabe, and then exited, all without a word.

Geraldine shook her head as she helped herself to tea. "Gabriel, how can you possibly manage a proper household with one servant and a cook? You need a housekeeper, maids…"

"I thought you told me I could never survive a houseful of women," Gabe interrupted smugly.

"…footmen, a driver, a valet," she continued smoothly, only pausing briefly during his outburst. "You are a lord, and you ought to live like one."

He groaned at the familiar argument and pinched the bridge of his nose. "I am only technically a lord, and barely even that. There is no point in putting on a show for people who do not care." He gave her a dubious look. "As you well know."

Geraldine matched his expression nearly perfectly. "They might care if you had a bit of a show."

He gave a reluctant chuckle and took a biscuit from the tea tray. "Why should I care, Aunt?"

"You know why," she grumbled, sipping her tea.

Gabe flashed her a grin. "No, I know why *you* care. Why should I?"

Geraldine set down her tea firmly, the china clinking loudly. "Because you will never manage a wife if you cannot even be seen as a polite member of society."

He glanced up at the ceiling thoughtfully, making a face.

His aunt made a sound of amusement. "Are you truly considering my words, or are you planning a witty response?"

"Neither," he said easily. "I'm trying to decide which part of your answer requires my response first; the inane idea that I somehow want a wife or the equally ridiculous assertion that I wish to be seen as a polite member of society."

As he predicted, it elicited his aunt's version of a screech, which was more of a harrumph mixed with an impatient sigh. "Gabriel, if you don't marry, you'll be cut off without a penny."

He smiled at her. "I haven't got a penny now."

Now she emitted the same sort of screech anyone else would give. "Gabriel! I want to name you my heir!"

Just to irritate her, he shrugged and folded his arms. "Go ahead."

Geraldine's look was scolding. "You'll waste it if I give it to you now."

He almost smiled. "I'll waste it no matter when you give it to me," he informed her quietly.

She threw her hands up and picked up her tea again. "Why do I bother?"

"I haven't the faintest idea."

Geraldine looked at him through narrowed eyes, sipped her tea, and finally hummed softly.

Gabe waited, smirked, rubbed his fingers together, then tilted his head. "Something else you would like to say, Aunt?"

"So many things," she quipped, sighing finally. "So many things."

He grinned and crossed a leg over his knee. "Say them, then. You've never exhibited restraint with me before."

Geraldine lifted her chin with a sniff and shifted her legs beneath her green skirts. "I will not say anything of the kind, Gabriel. I am above that."

Gabe tossed his head back and hooted a laugh. "Since when?"

"Oh, really," Geraldine protested, coloring slightly, "you will make me sound quite odious. As if I would ever admit to anything less than perfectly ladylike behavior."

He snorted and took another biscuit.

His aunt observed him carefully, then gradually leaned back against her chair in an uncharacteristic lapse of propriety, her eyes still on him.

Gabe raised his brows but said nothing.

Then Geraldine smirked a smug little smirk.

Gabe's stomach dropped, and his eyes widened. "You did something."

His maddening aunt only sipped her tea again.

He set both feet firmly on the floor and leaned forward, no longer amused. "Geraldine, what did you do?"

"Nothing," she murmured behind her teacup, her smile just barely visible.

"I have ceased to find this funny, Aunt," he growled.

Geraldine set her cup back on its saucer. "I haven't."

If his aunt had ever peeved him more in his life, he couldn't recall the instance. "What did you do?" he asked again, keeping his voice controlled.

"What was necessary," she replied.

"Meaning…?"

"You refuse to do what you must to meet the qualifications for legally inheriting what is mine, so I am taking the choice away from you." She straightened up and folded her hands neatly in her lap. "You will attend a ball in two weeks that is being held for the express purpose of finding you a bride."

His jaw dropped. "The hell I will!"

"Once you have found a woman to your tastes," she continued as if he had not protested, "we will proceed with your courtship, which I will, of course, assist you with. I know your limits. But you know that I have the authority to disinherit you, and you know that you need my money."

"But…"

"You do not have a say in this matter," Geraldine snapped, somehow still smiling. "Lord Wharton needs a wife, and if he waits too long, he will not have the means to restore his family's heritage."

Gabe sat back roughly. "You assume that Lord Wharton wishes for such a thing."

Geraldine raised a brow, her smile just as maddening as before. "What Lord Wharton wants is mattering less and less to this particularly benevolent aunt who wishes to give him patronage."

He knew that tone, and he knew it all too well. She was not going to be moved, and he was not going to get his way.

There was nothing else to do.

"Fine," he muttered grudgingly. "We'll have the ball."

"I do apologize," Geraldine said with an imperious tilt of her head. "It seems I have given you the impression that you have any say in the matter."

Gabe stared at her for a moment, then had to laugh, and laugh heartily. He'd always wondered where his more candid nature had come from, and it seemed he finally had the answer.

He looked over at his maddening relation and smiled. "Am I allowed a condition?"

She folded her arms. "One. And it will depend on the condition."

"I only have the one," he assured her.

She raised a brow, which he took to be an indication to proceed.

"A masquerade." He spread his hands out. "That is all I ask."

Geraldine's brow furrowed. "Masks will defeat the purpose. How is anyone supposed to fall in love with you that way?"

"The way that is allegedly supposed to happen," Gabe drawled, settling more fully into his chair. "Someone who wants me for me and not for my irresistibly attractive visage, would not that be ideal?"

"On second thought," she replied with a sniff, "let us cover your face. No sense in terrifying the poor, desperate creatures."

Gabe rolled his eyes and shook his head. "So delicate with my feelings, Aunt."

"You have no feelings, and you know it." She rose and brushed off her dress. "Very well, a masquerade. And my condition for *you* is that I let it be known what Lord Wharton is wearing so that those with a sincere interest may seek you out."

"That should amount to roughly zero women," he answered, rising himself. "I can live with that."

Geraldine moved to him and put a hand to his face. "Don't underestimate your charms, my dear. You will be flocked by females eager for your attention."

Gabe chuckled softly, took her hand from his face, and kissed it. "I never underestimate my charms. I only have three of them, so it is quite simple to keep them where they belong."

She shook her head and swept past him towards the door. "I will send you an invitation to the ball when I can."

"What a relief," he called after her. "I should hate to not be invited to my own ball."

"You are not that fortunate, Gabriel!"

He drummed his fingers on his chair, processing the idea of a masquerade ball to help him find a wife. Find a wife... If he wanted to find a wife, he would do so. Despite what everyone, including his aunt, thought of him, he was capable of charming a woman. He was.

That did not mean, however, that he wanted to marry one.

And yet, he was not entirely opposed to the idea in general.

He got to his feet quickly, the shock of that thought acting like a bucket of cold water dumped over him. Since when had he actually considered marriage?

The masquerade was the only thing that would save him here. He could be charming and warm, or withdrawn and brooding, and no one would quite know if he really was Lord Wharton or not. The misses would come and go, try in vain to rouse his interest, and he could enjoy giving each one a very different version of himself to confuse the accounts.

It would be the most entertainment he'd had in years. Provided none of the poor deluded females actually thought they had a chance with him.

Because unless his aunt dragged his unconscious body to a church and somehow coerced that unconscious body to agree to the insanity of the marriage vows, not even her scheme of a ball would get him to an altar.

And yes, he did need her money to restore his family heritage, but he didn't care about that, so he really had no incentive to act on her wishes. He was paid well enough by his superiors for what he did, and his living situation was perfect for him as it was.

Marriage. Why was the entire world obsessed with the idea?

He strode down the hall, and when he couldn't find Houser, continued to the kitchen.

A remarkably adorable child with wide, dark eyes and the hair to match sat in a dirty, worn dress on a bench, wiping the crumbs from her mouth. Mrs. Lucas, his termagant of a cook, looked almost congenial as she smiled at the little girl. That alone was enough to stop the idea of marriage and family. He did not need his cook looking like that.

"All done, love?" Mrs. Lucas asked Daisy, still not seeing Gabe.

"Yes, ma'am," Daisy replied with a bare hint of a lisp.

"Good," Gabe grunted as he pushed further in. "Because we have to go."

Mrs. Lucas frowned at him, which he undoubtedly deserved due to his tone, but as it was the usual way she looked, he felt marginally better.

Daisy, however, did not frown but beamed at him. Which showed her true naiveté and innocence and made him question her place in the harsh world they both lived in.

She jumped off the bench and skipped to his side, taking his hand. "Off we go, then!"

He smiled a little and shook his head, leading her out the back door. "You're going to keep a close eye on your new mark, Daisy."

She looked up at him, confused. "Why?"

He sighed heavily, looking up at the dismal grey skies. "Because I'm going to take her somewhere tomorrow, and when we get back, she might act irrationally."

"Where are you going?" the little girl asked, almost bouncing in her excitement.

"Surrey. To the house she once lived in." He winced and squeezed Daisy's hand. "And she might hate me for it."

Chapter Eight

$\mathcal{A}$melia was a complete bundle of nerves sitting in the carriage across from Rogue. They had left London early this morning, and he had said little about their destination. She was dressed as a proper country woman, and he was her equal in appearance. It was unsettling how normal he looked, and how attractive.

There was that disastrous thought again!

He was not that attractive. In fact, he was barely passable. Amelia had seen several men in her life that could be considered ridiculously attractive, and Rogue would not even be able to stand in the same room with them. Nobody would notice him while those sorts of men were around.

But those men were not around now.

Only Rogue was.

And considering that she somehow found him attractive despite his lack of attractiveness, that was no comfort at all.

It was a blessing that he was surlier than a goat with a toothache.

They had been travelling for several hours, and his glower had been the only companion she had known as yet. He rode in complete silence. He'd not said a word about luncheon, and despite Mrs. Jenkins' current fear of Amelia's connections and the future of her establishment, she was adamantly unwilling to provide any sort of breakfast before her usual hours.

Amelia was used to not having regular meals, but she had never been pleasant about it.

And despite the fact that they had changed horses once already, Rogue had not gotten out of the carriage, so neither had she. Given his reluctance to take her anywhere, she was not about to complain, lest he toss her out and force her to walk back to London.

It seemed rather a far-fetched worry, but considering Rogue was unpredictable, did not like her, and had no manners, it might not have been so very outlandish.

He was currently glaring out of the window, exactly as he had been doing for hours. For all his attention, she might not have even been in the carriage with him. When it was early, she did not mind, as she was not particularly loquacious in the mornings and Rogue was not loquacious at all. Now that it was daylight and the day was surely half gone, the silence was utterly deafening.

And it was doing nothing for her nerves.

What if she had finally pushed Rogue too far, and he was getting rid of her?

That seemed unlikely; he would never have done so personally. He undoubtedly had other lowlife, skulking individuals for such tasks.

What if he had uncovered something about her past and was getting her out of London for her safety?

She snorted aloud at that. Imagine Rogue rushing her out of London to save her. And with the horses at a trot at that. Daring rescue from a burning building or not, Rogue was no hero. Especially not for her.

She did briefly consider the idea that it could be nothing more than an investigative venture. However, considering the length of time they had been travelling, that also seemed far-fetched.

What sort of person got into a coach with someone they could not stand without knowing why they were doing so or where they were going?

Apparently, Amelia Tribbett did.

The carriage turned onto a somehow less travelled path than the jolting road they had been on, and Amelia let out a pained sound as a dip in the road led to her slamming her head against the ceiling.

Rogue looked over at her finally, and she hated herself for making a sound at all. He seemed to consider her for a moment, then one side of his mouth quirked.

"What?" she grumbled, rubbing her head.

He checked a pocket watch he wore in his vest and looked back up at her. "Nearly six hours in a carriage in complete silence, and it takes you ramming your head into the ceiling for a single sound to be emitted. Well done."

Amelia gaped at him and barely resisted the urge to kick his shins. "You've been testing me?"

Rogue scoffed and replaced his pocket watch. "Not at all. I see no need to converse uselessly, but I did anticipate you would need to fill the silence."

She tilted her head a little, narrowing her eyes. "Are you admitting that you were wrong?"

He shrugged nonchalantly. "Freely and without restraint."

That was shocking, and she did not bother hiding it. "You are?"

"Would I admit to such if I were not?"

"I haven't the faintest idea," she admitted bluntly. "You constantly surprise me."

He grinned outright at that, which nearly blinded her with its brilliance. "That, my dear Miss Berger, is part of my charm."

Her sight restored, she chortled and sat back rather inelegantly. "Is that what we are calling it?"

"I am the Rogue, am I not?"

"For all I know, it could be a self-proclaimed title." She folded her arms and raised a brow. "Is it?"

Rogue gave her a crooked, smug smirk. "It is not."

Amelia wasn't sure she believed him, but she suspected that he would react more strongly to the idea of being proclaimed a liar, if for no other reason than because he had insisted on honesty from her. She could hardly call him honorable, but she could not exactly call him the opposite either. And even between villains and blackguards, there had to be some level of honesty and trust.

For a little while, at least. While it served their purposes.

"Where are we going, Rogue?" she asked, venturing into the anxieties that surrounded her. "If we keep driving, we'll be in France before long."

"Before or after we drown in the Channel?" he replied, crossing his ankle over a knee.

Amelia gave him a hard look, fighting the instinct to be amused at his quip.

He sighed in response and shook his head. "Use your deductive reasoning, Amelia. You are not unintelligent and are quite capable of drawing your own conclusions. Tell me what you know."

She hadn't expected that, and suddenly felt a bit ill at ease. Her few years in school had left her with a fear of sudden and direct attention in situations where she was not in possession of the necessary information. She became quite dumbfounded and on occasion even stammered like an idiot.

It was why she avoided situations like these as often as possible.

Still, she could not let Rogue in on a weakness of hers. He would pounce on it and exploit it whenever he fancied.

She thought back and focused on the journey thus far. "Out of London, followed the river, turned south, a couple of turns, the sun is on you, not me… Surrey, no doubt, as we are west as well."

"Very good," Rogue said with a nod, only slightly mocking.

"Surrey is a big county," she informed him, as she might have an irritating child. "We could be anywhere."

Rogue snorted. "Why would I want to be just anywhere in Surrey? I'm not asking you to draw me a bloody map, Amelia."

"No need to be so rude, I am not intentionally obtuse," she snapped.

"No, it just comes with your person." He shook his head and looked out of the window. "And I am always rude. Nothing personal."

Amelia stared at him for a long moment, trying to find the meaning behind his words. "Is that your version of an apology?"

He glanced over with a raised brow. "Not at all. An explanation. Apologies are useless when no remorse is felt."

She really shouldn't have been surprised. Rogue did not have the usual spread of emotions that an ordinary human possesses, so it only followed that his awareness of his own insolence was minimal at best.

The carriage slowed, and Amelia looked out the window.

A small village was down the road, but they were not headed in that direction. They were stopping, pulling off onto a narrow, overgrown path, and to one side was a tiny, ramshackle cottage with an equally wild garden and a sinking roof on one side. The windows were filthy and broken, vines had almost entirely taken over the front of the house, and the door hung askew and open. It was plain to see that nobody was inhabiting the place, and no one had for quite some time.

But none of those things registered significantly with Amelia. She could not take her gaze off the place, and her eyes began to burn, not with tears but with fury.

"What is this?" she managed to say through tight lips and gritted teeth.

"Self-explanatory," Rogue replied gruffly, exiting the carriage.

Amelia did not move, staring at the cottage with a dozen emotions coursing through her.

"Amelia."

She blinked and shifted her gaze to Rogue, standing outside the door and looking at her with a vague expression, his eyes somehow less frosty than usual.

There was absolutely no way she could get out of this carriage and go into that place.

"Do you know what this is?" Amelia asked, her voice breaking, embarrassing her.

"Yes," came the stiff response.

She met his eyes again and saw firm resolution there, which did nothing for her own convictions, as they were currently in complete disarray. She gripped her seat with white knuckles, her nails biting into the fabric, and she felt a slight tremor coursing through her.

This had been her house. The house that they had been forced out of because there was no more money. The only good memories she had in her life had been here.

She barely recalled them. She'd intentionally buried them because it was just too painful to dwell on. Going back in there… That was utterly out of the question. And if the heartless man staring from outside the carriage had any sort of decency, he would never have brought her here.

But he had. And he still stared.

And then, to her surprise, he extended a hand to her.

Amelia stared at it for a moment, then looked up at him again. Gone was the vacant look, and in its place was understanding, concern, encouragement… It was the look of a man whose hand one would take when it was offered.

And despite her desire to slap it, and him, she found herself taking his hand instead and letting him help her from the carriage.

"That's it," he murmured, without any hint of patronization.

Amelia brushed off her skirts, the burning in her eyes intensifying. "I hate you," she hissed.

"That's all right," Rogue replied, putting a surprisingly gentle hand on her back and pushing her forward. "I'll get over it."

If he hadn't sounded so unaffected by it, she wouldn't have laughed. She'd have been well enough off with a callous "I hate you, too," or a "Thank you". Even a blunt "I know," would have been safe. But the complete lack of concern or emotion was unexpected, and laugh she did.

It gave her a little satisfaction to see Rogue looking at her as if she had taken leave of her senses, despite wondering what he must think of her. There was something to be said for taking people by surprise and finding new ways to do so.

"Are you done?" Rogue asked mildly when her laughter subsided.

She nodded, placing a hand on her chest. "Forgive me."

"For laughing?" He snorted. "If that requires forgiveness, the entire world is damned to hell."

Amelia smiled a little at him, then took in the sight of the house again. "I don't want to be here, Rogue."

He exhaled noisily beside her, clasping his hands behind his back as he walked. "And if we cared about what you want in this venture, that would be taken into consideration. As it is, here we are."

She gave him a rough scowl, even though she appreciated his response. It was oddly comforting to have him return to his usual nature. She knew how to combat this version of him.

"Then explain to me why I must endure this," she muttered stubbornly. "What can we possibly gain from a place that I have not lived in for close to fifteen years?"

"Can you think of anything but your own discomfort right now?" he asked in return, stepping around a puddle and finding the almost indistinguishable stone path.

Amelia growled and followed, shaking her head. "Why are you

answering my question with a question?"

He looked over his shoulder at her. "Why are you?"

There were not enough obscenities in existence to adequately bombard him with, but she ran through all the ones she knew in her mind, and when she had exhausted her list, she felt marginally better.

Rogue pushed open the rickety door and stepped into the dim and dusty building, coughing a little as he did so.

Amelia hung back, looking into the cottage but keeping her feet firmly planted on the path outside. She glanced at the ground beneath her, images of a small girl sitting just there with her dolls flashing through her mind.

And that bush, now wild and taking over the place, used to be a perfect hiding spot.

And there, she had buried treasures beneath the front window just behind her mother's flowers.

"Amelia."

She looked up and into the cottage again. Rogue stood in the middle of the room, hands on his hips, tilting his head at her.

"What?" she eventually said after several swallows.

He took two steps in her direction, his mouth twisting in thought. "I need you to get out of yourself right now. I realize this is difficult, but we need answers, and this place could give them to us. Can you set aside your personal feelings and investigate with me?"

She pressed her tongue to her teeth hard, thinking over his words. Then she wet her lips and said, "Are you saying you need my help to do your job?"

Rogue smirked a little and folded his arms. "Not at all. I need you to get into the small and dusty places that I am too delicate to venture into. And if we stay too long, this drafty place is going to give me a cold, and I am rather peevish when ill."

She nodded soberly, wrapping the borrowed shawl around her tightly, despite the warmth of the morning. "I can only imagine. Well, I do aim to be of service. Where would you like me to begin crawling?"

For some inexplicable reason, his almost smile nearly set her to tears. "Over there," he indicated with a faint flick of his hand. "You should be able to find all sorts of cobwebs and dust and dead insects in that area."

Amelia snorted, took a short breath, and stepped into the cottage purposefully, striding over to her assigned portion without thinking about it. "For heaven's sake, Rogue, I'm not a dog."

"Of course not. Dogs are pleasant."

"Clearly you have been associating with the wrong sorts of dogs."

"I have never met a dog I do not like."

"As I said…"

"Dogs also do not talk."

Amelia glanced over at him as he ventured into another room, shaking her head. "They do talk," she said to herself. "You just don't know what they are saying, you dolt."

"Don't talk to yourself," Rogue called from wherever he was. "I refuse to work with a madwoman."

She sighed as she walked around the tiny kitchen, everything encased in dust, but just as they had left it fifteen years before. "At least you're admitting that you work with me, now!" she called back, her voice wavering as she spotted an old apron.

She picked it up and shook it out, wincing and sneezing as the dust flew everywhere.

"Against my will, I can assure you!" he responded, more faintly than before to her ears.

The apron was filled with holes, faded and filthy with age and neglect, she could still see it around her mother's waist, sprinkled with the same flour that would also be on the floor. Her mother had never been particularly skilled in the kitchen, and never clean about it.

Amelia shook her head, forcing the memories and emotions back. She wadded up the apron and tossed it into the corner. She needed to focus, not dwell where she ought not. There wasn't time for this.

"Did you fall into a hole?" Rogue bellowed. "I haven't heard you say anything in minutes."

She closed her eyes with a weak smile. "No, just waiting for something intelligent to respond to!"

There was nothing else to find in the kitchen, and she dared not venture into the bedrooms, where memory would be strongest, so she turned her attention to the parlor. It had always been shabby, and time, not to mention the roof falling in, had only highlighted that.

"Was your mother always this terrible at keeping house, or only for special occasions?"

Amelia threw a hard look towards the sound of Rogue's voice. "I'd hate to see what the state of your home would look like after fifteen years of neglect."

"My home has had twenty-five years of neglect, thank you very much," came the response from the bedrooms. "It still has a roof that functions as such. And I cannot write my name in the dust on furniture there."

She frowned and exhaled shortly through her nose. "Well, if you had the ability to write your name at all, perhaps you could!"

She might have imagined it, but she thought she heard him chuckle, which surely had to be impossible.

A worn chest to one side of the room caught her eye, and she went to it, sinking to the stained and warped floors. The lid lifted easily, and the contents within were relatively clean and dust free, considering the disastrous state of the exterior. There was a shawl that Amelia couldn't place, some mending that had never been finished, and stacks of old letters.

She picked up the letters and found them to be mostly business-related, and the signature was impossible to make out. No help there, but perhaps Rogue would find them useful anyway.

Setting them aside, she went back to the chest, ignoring laundry lists, mercantile orders from the village, and sketches of various household articles. She had forgotten that her mother had tried to improve her artistic talents. They had been poor to begin with and had only gotten worse with practice. Even as a child, Amelia had been able to see that. She pulled all the papers out and set them aside, wondering just what Rogue would find useful in all of this.

At the bottom of the chest lay a stack of books, all bound in the same black cloth, and well worn. Amelia reached for the top two and flipped one open, then gasped.

It was her mother's handwriting. Pages and pages of it, detailing her activities and her thoughts from day to day, and even cataloguing

Amelia's accomplishments in childhood. The date at the top of the page dated this one as being when Amelia was four, and she had just informed her mother that she wished to dance so she might be as pretty and talented as the blacksmith's daughters.

Amelia had no memory of any of the people in this village, save for the landowner who had forced them out.

Dancing? She blanched at the thought. She certainly had learned to dance since then, but hardly for entertainment. It was a matter of survival and finding out information, all in the pursuit of answers to the questions in her life.

She turned a few more pages in the journal and found a new entry.

"Dearest love," she read aloud, frowning. Why would her mother begin an entry in such a way?

"Did you say something, Amelia?" Rogue called from somewhere behind her.

"Not to you!" she responded, her face flushing. Imagine if he'd heard her! She returned to the book and turned to more entries, finding them all addressed to "my love" or "dearest love" or something of the sort.

She put that volume aside and took the other, opening it and scanning quickly. More of the same headings to each entry, and there was an entry for nearly every day. Inside the chest, there were at least six more volumes, and Amelia pulled them all out and into her lap, staring at them.

Her mother had been writing to the same man Amelia had been seeking. Her father. These journals were for him, letters detailing the parts of his life that he was not witnessing.

What sort of answers and memories would lie within them?

For the first time in her life, Amelia wasn't sure this was what she wanted at all.

"What did you find?"

She spun in her place, gasping a little.

Rogue raised a questioning brow. "You forgot I was here? I've been bellowing at you all afternoon, so either you are losing your hearing, or your mental status is far more deteriorated than I expected."

Amelia couldn't manage a quip in response and handed one of the journals to him. He took it gingerly and flipped it open. His eyes widened as he scanned a page, then turned it over to the next.

"Journals," he said unnecessarily.

She nodded. "I had no idea she kept them. I expect she wrote them when I was not about."

"Or she did, and you didn't notice." He shrugged and handed it back to her. "You were a child, you can hardly expect to remember every detail."

Amelia caressed the cover, chewing the inside of her cheek. "But I've been over my past several dozen times. It feels like something I ought to have known."

"Well," Rogue sighed, picking up the stack, "perhaps you were hopelessly dim-witted and easily distracted. It is not much of a stretch."

She looked up at him, then grabbed a nearby shard of fallen roof and rapped him sharply across the shins, the wood snapping against the leather of his boots.

He jumped back with a grunt, squinting at her even as his mouth quirked. "Down, girl. Don't you want to see what I found?"

"That is a rather difficult question to answer," Amelia muttered. "Do I? I can hardly say."

Rogue snorted and handed her a small doll made of cloth, missing an eye, and somehow dirtier than the rest of the cottage.

Amelia stared at the toy, her fingers grazing the fabric with familiarity. "Dolly," she whispered.

"Oh, that's original," Rogue teased, his tone oddly without scorn.

She smiled at her forgotten friend. "I took her everywhere. Buried her as a treasure more times than I can recall."

"I can see that, yes."

Amelia shook her head and tucked Dolly into the pocket of her gown, then looked around the room. "Why is this place exactly as we left it?"

"You left it with a gaping hole in the ceiling? Not very considerate of you, I doubt anyone wanted it in that condition."

She gave him a would-be patient look, and he scratched the back of his neck.

"Not sure," he admitted. "If it was seized, by rights the landowner could have taken another tenant. My man is checking with him while we are here, so we should have answers soon. It does seem a bit odd, doesn't it?"

Amelia nodded, picking herself up off the floor. "The village is not a prosperous one. Perhaps he could not find anyone who wished to take it."

Rogue shook his head in thought. "There are always those who are looking for a place like this, especially if the owner is in a bargaining mood." He shrugged again and pulled an old book from the back of his trousers. "Here, this was in the bedroom. The only book here, I'm afraid."

"We didn't have many." She opened it and smiled at the ink splotches inside the cover. "I tried to write my own story in this one. Mother was not at all pleased."

"Please tell me you were walloped."

She chuckled and adjusted her hold on the book, whose spine was falling apart. "I believe I was, but not very forcefully."

"Which explains your lack of stamina and discipline." He shook his head with a frown. "No wonder you are so unruly."

"One more word out of you, Rogue," she said as menacingly as she could while smiling. But the threat went unfinished as she found a corner of the paper inside the cover to be loose. That could merely indicate a poor attempt at rebinding... But why? She pulled it back gently and found another beneath.

It was inscribed.

"Rogue..." Amelia breathed, holding it out for him to see, though he had stepped closer as soon as he had seen her pull the paper.

Mary Clairbourne.

"Does that name mean anything to you?" he asked, all teasing and lightness gone.

Amelia shook her head slowly, her heart sinking into her stomach. "No, not a thing. I don't know anything about this." She swallowed harshly, her throat tight. "But that is my mother's handwriting." She looked up at him, hardly able to breathe. "What does this mean?"

He did not speak for a long moment. "It means, Amelia," Rogue said slowly, seeming to choose his words with care, "that we have more questions, and more chance for answers, some of which you may not like, and all of which you will be unprepared for. This is no longer straightforward and simple, and everything we know is now useless. I am willing to keep going, to pursue this to the end, as promised, no matter how convoluted this past of yours is. The question is do you still want to know everything?"

His look was penetrating and intense, and Amelia suddenly had the sense that he was asking a more profound question than what it seemed. There was an energy to him now that was missing before, and she could now see exactly why he was rumored to be so skilled. He was focused and determined and ready to proceed down a now-wildly unknown path if she was.

"Are you asking in sincerity or as a courtesy?" she asked quietly, her voice unsteady.

"Amelia..."

He'd never said her name like that. It sent a ripple down her spine with its firmness, its low timbre feeling like a caress despite the serious nature its speaker had. He was not mocking her or teasing her, he was not derogatory or spiteful. This was Rogue in all his sincerity.

And suddenly his name suited him.

"Yes," she replied, trying to make her voice as firm as his had been. "Yes, I want to know everything."

Chapter Nine

*G*abe's mind was whirling with the new revelations as they arrived back in London that evening. He and Amelia had talked almost nonstop on the trip back, exchanging theories and concocting strategies, and he found her insight to be both intelligent and astute. She would have made an excellent spy if she recognized authority at all, and if she weren't so reckless.

Then again, he was as reckless as they came. And he was a damned fine spy if he did say so himself.

He didn't like the way Amelia's face had looked when they walked up to the cottage. She was a vibrant woman, even if she did plague him to death, and no one should have looked so stricken. He'd known it was going to be a struggle for her, but nothing could have prepared him for that.

Gabe wasn't usually affected by the emotions and expressions of women, but this time he could not ignore it. He'd done his best to taunt her out of her mood, raise her ire so she would be distracted from memories, and he thought he'd done a decent enough job. She'd given him some biting quips in return, some of which he was rather impressed with, and the hollow look eventually faded into a mild discomfort. Until they'd found the secret of the book, she'd been doing quite well.

Why that should have satisfied him, why his ability to investigate suddenly hinged on her emotional stability, he was afraid to identify. But he knew himself well enough to not even attempt to deny that was exactly what the stakes had been. He could not have done anything had she been morose and haunted, or, heaven forbid, if she had shed tears.

He hated tears. There were many things about women that he detested, vocally and privately, and many typical feminine qualities that annoyed the sense out of him. Above everything and anything, tears were the worst. But if Amelia had shed them…

For some reason that would have been significant.

It was another reason he had kept her talking the entire ride back and had spent more money than he'd meant to on food for the return trip to London.

He needed the distraction now.

And it was leaving him feeling shaken.

Amelia was still rambling on about something to do with the village that she had remembered, as she had been doing for a while. It seemed that setting foot in her childhood home had unlocked stored-away memories, and he had stopped listening ages ago. They were almost back to the offices, and he needed her gone while he processed everything.

"Did you want to take the chest with you, or should I keep it?" he asked, interrupting some tale about a dog and a blacksmith.

She stopped and looked at him, her brow furrowed. "You are… asking me?"

"Yes…" he drawled slowly, starting to feel hesitation creeping in. "The chest belongs to you, so it only follows to ask what you wish to do with it."

Her brows knitted further. "You're not going to seize it for your investigation regardless of what I want?"

He tilted his head at her and folded his arms. "My investigation? Are you under the deluded impression that I am some sort of law enforcement taking on your case for the honor and protection of kingdom, country, and neighborly concern? You hired me, Amelia, which means that, whether I like it or not, you are tied to it, and, on occasion, I must consult with you. And allow you some leniency."

Amelia scoffed loudly, which he pointedly ignored.

"Look," he growled, "do you want the damned chest or not?"

"You take it," she insisted, shaking her head, grinning at him. "Perhaps you can find something useful in it, and I would only wallow in memories, no doubt. It would be a shame to waste your concentrated efforts to goad me out of melancholy today just for sentimentality, which you abhor."

Gabe stilled, staring at her hard. Then he exhaled roughly. "You knew what I was doing?"

Amelia's smile turned wry. "I knew. It wasn't hard to notice. You delivered your barbs almost jovially."

He grunted and looked away. "I can see I need to work on my level of enthusiasm for well-placed insults and derision."

"Why'd you do it?" she asked, her voice curious but soft.

He didn't like that tone. It made him feel vulnerable somehow.

"Because you would have been emotional and weepy and useless, and I didn't need another reason to regret bringing you along." He made his tone as sharp as he could while still sounding indifferent, fighting for his old manner with her.

He didn't even know his manner had changed until that moment.

"Would not," she murmured, and he could hear the smile in her tone.

"Yes, you would," he insisted, watching the buildings of London pass them by. "It would have been a waste of a day if you hadn't been dragged out of that cesspool of feminine impulse, and the only way to do that was to prod you."

"So, you're telling me that you cared enough to keep me out of the dark places."

He shook his head. "Not at all. I have a low tolerance for wallowing in despair when there's a task to be done. Nothing more."

There was silence for a long moment, and then there was a hand on his knee. He looked over to see her smiling at him far too gently.

"Thank you," she said softly.

He stared at her for far too long, gaze fixed on the blue of her eyes, almost smoky in their shade, and the tender regard she seemed to be offering him. The lock of hair that hung loosely near her ear, the barely palpable weight of her small hand on his knee, and the somehow perfectly sculpted cheekbones that were now tinged with an alluring shade of pink. It was madness. It was sheer and utter madness…

She was stunning.

He immediately shifted and returned his gaze out the window.

"For doing my job? You're quite welcome. I always do my job."

Her hand left his knee, and he could breathe again.

"Of course you do," she said with a substantial measure of irony. He could hear her shaking her head and the faint sound of laughter being muffled.

He ignored her completely.

The carriage pulled to a stop, and Amelia did not wait for him. "I'll start asking questions about Mary Clairbourne tonight," she called over her shoulder. "I know some people in London now."

He stared after her for a few heartbeats, processing the insanity that had come out of her mouth, then scrambled out of the carriage. "Whoa, whoa, come back here."

She did no such thing. She held her head high and strode forward as proudly as if she owned the city.

He groaned and grabbed her arm. "Stop, Amelia."

She stopped and turned to face him expectantly.

"Are you completely mad?" he asked, keeping his voice down as there were several people about. "You want to go out about London at night by yourself and ask questions about your mother?"

"I do, yes," she replied simply, not at all concerned. "There's a lot of work to do, and I know just where to start."

He shook his head and gripped her arm harder. "You don't know anything, Amelia. You don't know a blasted thing about any of this. You have names, you have your own bias, and you have whatever vendetta you refused to tell me about. That is all. You don't know anything. That's why we went to Surrey, to get answers. And we have some now, and this chest could give us the information we need. We need to be smart about this, not go risking everything just because 'there is a lot to do'."

"Why are you making a fuss about this?" Amelia asked, her eyes narrowing slightly. "I can start asking questions, and you can examine the contents of the chest. Everything would get done much faster."

"Why the hurry?" He looked around quickly, then gave her a serious look. "Acting hastily without all of the information gets people hurt, Amelia. Go back to your hovel of a boarding house. Tomorrow, we can start afresh."

She folded her arms and peered up at him. "Are you under the misguided delusion that I am a delicate woman with fragile sensibilities who cannot handle herself in a place like London?"

Gabe reared back a little. "Well, I…"

"Because I've seen the underside of this city, Rogue," she overrode, stepping closer to him, her chin lifting with a stubborn jerk. "I was raised in it. I've seen worse and come through stronger. I know where to avoid and what to say, and I can take care of myself. Or didn't you wonder what happened to the man who lied to me when I tried to find you?"

She shrugged his hand off her arm and quirked her brows, then turned and continued on her way.

Gabe stood there, voices and sounds and smells of the London evening surrounding him, reminding him of all the reasons why he should go after her. Protect her. Not let her do anything so foolish.

If he had a conscience.

Which he did not.

He turned on his heel, started towards the carriage, and then stopped after three steps, wincing with a hiss.

No. No, he was a hardened man without gentlemanly tendencies. He had work to do. Serious spycraft involving some very dangerous men and potential national security matters and seeing to them was long overdue. Why, the Crown could be in danger, and it was his duty to investigate those concerns, and if Amelia Berger or whatever her name was wanted to get herself killed…

His hands became fists at his sides, and he exhaled sharply. "Taylor, take the carriage back and put that chest in my office."

"Aye, sir." The grizzled man tapped the brim of his hat and flicked the reins.

Gabe nodded, turned around, and jogged back to Amelia. "Let me do all the talking," he grumbled. "I've been at this a lot longer, and who knows what you'll say."

She smirked up at him and clasped her hands behind her back. "Yes, Rogue."

"And stop looking at me like that. This is business."

"Yes, Rogue."

"You look like the wrong side of hell."

Gabe jerked as he hung up his coat on a peg. No one ought to have been in the office. It was too early for the clerks to be in, Rook was on assignment, and Cap was with his children. Which left only one feasible option.

He blearily stared down the grinning man leaning against the doorway of one of the offices. He wore his usual common clothes, same as the rest of them, and a cap sat almost jauntily atop his dark hair, tilted back and making him look much younger than he was. Which was nearly as maddening as the grin he bore. "Is there a right side of hell, Gent?"

Impossibly, the grin spread. "Well, of course. The side we are on."

"That's debatable." He stepped forward to shake his friend's hand and then moved past him into his office. The worn chest sat on his desk, just where he'd instructed Taylor to put it. He blinked hard, trying to find the motivation.

"Don't tell me you've been out all night," Gent said as he followed him into the office. "You're too old for that."

He really was, but he wasn't about to admit just how much his back and neck were aching. Not to mention his feet. Amelia had been relentless in her energy and enthusiasm, and they had quite literally been investigating all night. He'd only just convinced her that she ought to get some rest to be fully prepared for the mysteries of the chest they must sift through, not to mention the answers Taylor would have from the landlord.

Truth be told, Gabe wasn't sure they would get much out of either compared with what their full night of work had done, but aside from telling her that he was desperate for five minutes without her yammering on so he could shut his eyes, he couldn't think of what else to do.

The worst part of it was that, exhausted beyond measure as he was, he'd actually enjoyed his night.

With her.

Oh, *hell.*

"Yes, I am," Gabe grunted, shoving the thoughts away. He sank into his seat and emptied his pockets. "And I already regret it, so shove off."

"What were you doing all night?" Gent asked, ignoring his command.

"Working."

Gent hummed in disbelief and took a seat. "Docks?"

"No."

"Gamblers?"

"No."

"French?"

"I wish."

"I'll keep guessing."

Gabe put his head into his hands on his desk. "Please don't."

"Your aunt?"

"I will shoot you."

"Tell me, then."

"Fine," he snapped. "It was a woman."

The utter silence of the room would have been comical had he been coherent enough to process it properly. He picked his head up and looked at Gent, curiosity getting the better of him.

His friend stared at him with wide eyes, his jaw slack. "A… woman?"

Gabe sat back slowly, smiling a little. "Yes. A female. You know the sort? You just married one."

Gent blinked slowly, not seeming to hear him. "You… don't like women."

"Not true."

"I've heard you disparage them."

"That is true."

"You can't stand them."

"Also true."

"Yet you willingly spent the night with one?" Gent's voice cracked a little with the force of his questioning. It was astonishing how pale he had gone, considering his customary tan. His exotic travels with his bride had only enhanced that, yet he looked rather sickly at present.

Gabe held up a finger immediately. "Clarification is required. I passed the night with one. I did not spend the night with one."

His friend's dark brow lowered. "I see. So, this is not… romantic?"

Gabe hooted a hoarse laugh and crossed himself, which wouldn't mean much coming from him, but he'd always heard that God was merciful. "Absolutely not," he choked out. "I've not fallen that far. She's a client."

Gent's relief was evident, but it was short-lived as suspicion set in. "A client you passed the entire night with? Un-romantically?"

Gabe did not like Gent's tone, and he averted his eyes, turning to the chest on the desk.

"She's the worst sort of termagant that ever existed. Demanding, rude, reckless… She thinks she is above something as insignificantly mortal as death, as evidenced by the fact that she had us traipsing all over London in the dead of night and would have gone by herself if I'd let her. She's been through hell, I'll grant her that, but that's no excuse for possibly killing an informant or lying to a family about being a relative. Who knows, maybe the story she told me is a complete fabrication because I'm not entirely certain she won't kill me as soon as I let my guard down. I'm really starting to hope that she is a French spy just to get rid of her. She is the most unladylike, irritating, maddening, scheming, unpredictable woman I have ever met."

"Pretty, too, I'd wager."

"Oh, she's beautiful, and it just makes…" He trailed off, frowned, and looked up at his friend in horror.

Gent was smiling far too smugly, crossing one leg over the other and drumming his fingers together. He raised a taunting brow, tilting his head slightly.

Damn.

Gabe swore, which made Gent chuckle quietly. "I despise you," Gabe muttered, rubbing his tired eyes.

"I know," Gent sighed, sounding far too pleased about it.

"Don't you have a wife at home to make passionate love to or something?" Gabe determinedly avoided looking at his no-doubt smirking friend as he opened the chest and started through the papers within.

"I do. And I did."

Gabe paused for only a moment, as the words sunk in. Then he shuddered for effect and resumed his shuffling, not really seeing any of it. "And she's had enough of you already? I know your obsession is too great for you to be so easily satisfied."

He heard Gent shuffle slightly in his chair. "She is visiting friends today and asked me to get back to work and stop distracting her."

Gabe snorted his disbelief and pulled the stack of journals out of the chest.

"Besides," Gent continued, leaning forward, "I wanted an update on everything, considering the mess I left behind."

"It wasn't that bad," Gabe assured him, finally looking up. "Everything's been pretty quiet. Rook took over your monitoring, and he says they've been meeting less and less. Looks like they'll have to find someone else to fund the operations. I don't have time to take care of my assets and contacts, thanks to this bloody cover. Your maggots have reported in regularly, but I left most of those to Cap."

Gent snorted and picked up one of the journals before Gabe could stop him. "Figures. You ought to take a few of them for yourself. You'd be amazed at what they can give you."

Gabe made a face. "Children at the docks and in the gambling rings? I thought you liked them."

"I do, very much. But you'd be there, and no doubt your contacts have limits where children are concerned." He flipped open a journal and started to read, dark eyes going wide at once.

"You underestimate humanity in general," Gabe said with a shake of his head. He extended his hand and flexed his fingers. "Give that back, it's not yours."

Gent sniffed and held the book further away. "Never stopped me before. Besides, it's not yours either, unless..." He lowered the journal to give him a sardonic look. "Have you started to catalogue events of your day in the form of a love letter? And to whom would you be writing, I wonder?"

Gabe returned his look with a snarl. "That would be for me to know, and you to find out. Give that back."

Gent considered him for a moment, then handed it back. "My apologies, Rogue. I had no idea you would be so sensitive about the romantic scribbling of a woman currently in her early fifties, if I'm not mistaken."

"My business, not yours." Gabe set the book down and began to flip through it himself.

"Of course." Gent rose and put his hands on the desk, leaning over to read upside down. "Who's Amelia?"

Gabe jerked and covered the pages. "Get out."

"Your client of the night, then. Excellent." He grinned, his nearly perfect white teeth glinting in the morning light. "Which means this is her mother's journal, and several others lay there. If her mother is writing to her dearest love and telling him about Amelia's dealings, I must assume we are looking for Amelia's father. And given that you have an illustration of the mother in your possession, and you have been out all night investigating, I may assume she was from London or spent some time here. If you are going off what you know of the mother, it means we have no information about the father whatsoever, which means Miss Amelia is most likely illegitimate. If all of that is true, I must ask if we suspect the father of being a peer and thus granting her a fortune to which she ought to be entitled, or if you really have simply taken on a wild goose chase because of a pretty face."

Perhaps it was Gabe's sleep deprivation interfering with his ability to process rational thought, or perhaps he had merely forgotten how incredibly astute his colleague was, but he was utterly taken by surprise by the perfect accuracy in Gent's brief assessment of the situation.

All he could manage was to blink and slowly sit back in his chair, watching the subtle play of emotions on Gent's face as he attempted to interpret the underlying working of Gabe's mind.

He would have quite a time of that.

Gabe couldn't even fathom the whole of it, and he was privy to every little detail.

He groaned and waved Gent back into his seat. "Fine, I'll let you in on it, but only because I'm too bloody exhausted to care."

Gent sat down eagerly, elbows on his knees, rubbing his hands together. "This is going to be good."

Gabe threw him a glare. "First of all, it had nothing to do with her face. Pretty or otherwise."

Gent held up his hands in surrender. "My apologies." Then he grinned. "But it *is* a pretty face, yes?"

He debated lying, he truly did.

But Gent would never believe him.

"Yes," he relented reluctantly. "Yes, it is."

Chapter Ten

"*H*ertfordshire? It can't be Hertfordshire. Are you sure? She never spoke of Hertfordshire, she was always talking of London and Surrey. It cannot be Hertfordshire."

Rogue sighed and gave Amelia a pitying look. "I did not close my eyes and point to a random county on a map to fix upon, Amelia. Give me a little credit for doing my job. I really am quite good at it."

She smiled at him and patted his arm. "Of course you are, Rogue." Then she sighed and looked back at the assorted papers filled with notes they had compiled over the last few weeks. "Hertfordshire. So, you've found her family there?"

Rogue nodded, then nudged her with his elbow. "Your family too."

She scoffed a little and shook her head. "Not really. Not yet. Maybe eventually, but I want answers first. Did she run away? Did she get married, and we just haven't found the marriage record yet? Was she a proper lady or not?"

"Careful now," Rogue warned, giving her a scolding look. "You'll start dreaming of more if you get too far ahead."

Amelia rolled her head dramatically to return his look. "My mother changed her name at least once, perhaps even more. She lived in destitute circumstances with no family to call upon. What are the odds that anyone we meet will actually be pleased to see me?"

Rogue shrugged and moved to the other side of the table, sitting down in the chair. "I think you would be surprised at how strong a family connection can be, especially when time has passed, and grievances have lessened."

"Or intensified," she countered, folding her arms and leaning against the table. "Things can fester too. You forget, I've lived with other families."

"Ah, so this makes you an expert?" he asked with a smirk, one hand dangling near his mouth.

She fought against amusement and exasperation. "No," she managed through her teeth, somehow smiling, "but it does make me wary."

He accepted that with a brief nod. "Wariness is warranted, I will grant you that." His eyes took on a faraway look, and his brow furrowed. "Sometimes things aren't as you expect, and all you have are your instincts."

Amelia tilted her head, watching him carefully. In the two weeks since their investigation at the cottage, she and Rogue had developed a different sort of relationship. They prodded and teased each other, tossed insults and jabs, but there was mutual respect between them beneath it all. It had been a wonderful reprieve from being on edge all the time, and they had been very productive.

They'd been able to track her mother's life far more easily now that they had her real name and greater insight into her life. They'd found some of the shops frequented by her during a short stint in Cheapside when Amelia was young, as the journals documented, and though she was not known as Mary Clairbourne to them, Mary Palmer had, at last, become a person. The Clairbourne clue was a bit trickier, as the family was extensive and finding any sort of connection had proven difficult. Some were quite low in station, and some were rather impressively positioned in Society.

Her Clairbournes, however, had been squarely in the middle of everything. Not too high, not too low, without much to recommend them. Her mother had been born in London, christened at St. Mary's in Putney, but the minister there had no recollection of the family, as he had only been at the church for twenty years, and they had not been in the parish in all his time.

It did not help that the names on the christening register had the parents' names as being John and Anne, which seemed to be traditional names for the Clairbournes.

She had begun to wonder about the intelligence of her family predecessors.

Thankfully, Rogue was not put off by the challenge and seemed to relish the idea of a project needing true investigation.

Then they'd gotten a lead, a Clairbourne family with an infant daughter had moved into the Cheapside district, and some of their former servants had remained in the house they'd lived in, though they now worked for the current residents, who were no relation and no connection. But the servants remembered the family as being very fair and proper but thinking 'a mite too high for their station', as they were of no significance in Society. It seemed that Mr. Clairbourne was an unfortunate son of a respectable family and had never quite adjusted to reduced circumstances.

Despite the entertaining stories the servants had told, they did not know much of the family whereabouts after they had left London, only stating that they had gone north into the countryside to retrench.

Rogue had not been put off by that at all. On the contrary, he seemed to think that any Clairbournes out of London were a right sight better than all the Clairbournes in it.

Amelia hadn't understood that one bit, but Rogue had gone off on his own to check some things, and adamantly refused to take her with him. She'd been forced to remain with the clerks and Gent, a new ally who seemed to enjoy any sight of her and Rogue together. She'd given him some real entertainment with a number of their rows, and in Rogue's absence, he'd helped her find some answers in London.

Rogue had been gone a few days, and only just returned with the shocking news of Hertfordshire.

Imagine, a family of her own rusticating in that part of the world.

But she'd had some success herself here in London while he'd been away, and she was going to put it all to excellent use. There was, however, the small problem of informing Rogue of her plan, and she did not think he would approve of it. Which was why she had not told him and might not tell him at all. Why bother venturing into perilous territory when it might prove fruitless? Gent had seemed rather pleased with her plan and vowed to aid her in it, and he was a much more even-tempered fellow.

She was content with that.

She'd lost too much for caution.

And by the look of Rogue's expression at this moment, he had lost a great deal as well, and it seemed to have the reverse effect on him.

"Who did you lose, Rogue?" she murmured softly.

His eyes tracked back to hers, but his face lost none of its gauntness. "Pardon?"

She leveled her eyes at him. "Come on, you know my story. You've lost as well. Tell me."

He watched her steadily for a long moment, then exhaled a little. "Everyone."

Amelia blinked slowly, her mind spinning. "Excuse me?"

He moved his hand and straightened a little. "I've lost everyone," he stated, his gaze fixed on her. "My father when I was too young to care much, through recklessness and greed, which I happened to inherit. My mother to illness when I was a child. I have no siblings, and no cousins remaining. I lived a wasteful life before coming to this, and as I had nothing and no one, I was content to be a waste."

It was chilling to hear his complete lack of emotion about his own life, almost as if it had happened to someone else. No one should sound like that. Even if he had enough control and detachment to avoid the feelings associated with bereavement and loss, which she doubted, he would not be able to discuss it without some sort of bitterness. This was not bitter.

This was rehearsed.

"There's more to that story," she pointed out. "You're hiding something. You avoid forming relationships of substance and intentionally give off an acerbic exterior that no one in their right mind would come near. No one is that callous naturally."

He scoffed almost silently, giving her a patronizing smile. "I happen to be."

Amelia shook her head, smiling herself. "No, you're not. You lost someone who meant a great deal to you. Possibly more than one. I'll say your mother, as you gave the least details about her."

"That's enough, Amelia," he warned, his jaw tightening at the same time his fist did.

She eyed his hand, then raised her eyes to his and turned her smile soft. "Going to hit me, Rogue? Too close to the truth?"

Rogue's brow furrowed, his head cocking to one side. "Why are you looking at me like I am a temperamental child? And speaking to me as the same?"

She laughed and found herself beaming. "Because I understand, Rogue. You don't have to hide any of it from me. I won't pry, I'm not meddlesome."

He clamped down on his lips and raised a taunting brow but said nothing.

Ignoring him, she tossed her head a little. "But I understand. How old were you when your mother passed?"

He settled more fully into his seat and just stared at her, apparently not inclined to share at all.

Amelia stared just as intently back, letting her eyes take in the picture of him. Extended interaction with Rogue had given her a new appreciation for his physicality, the way every emotion of his, no matter what he portrayed, was on display in the rest of his body. He could glower more fiercely than any man she'd ever met, but the set of his shoulders would be relaxed and open. His eyes could be frigid and intimidating, while his jaw would have none of the tension that ought to follow.

He smiled far more often than he thought he did. Oh, it was not a smile by anyone else's standards, but once you knew what to look for, it was impossible to not notice it. He was amused by a great many things and took great pains to hide it. He had a reputation to uphold, after all.

She did not doubt that his cynicism was real, nor that he was hard from the life he had led. But she saw no evidence that he was the blackguard he pretended.

And he had an intriguing sense of fairness.

"You know my secrets," Amelia pointed out gently, willing him to open up even a little. "You know everything about me."

"If only that were true," he replied in a quiet tone, his eyes taking on a new light.

Her breath caught, and she blinked in confusion.

He was always doing that to her, making her heart stop in her chest, suddenly speaking in a tone that made her tingle, or looking at her in a way that made her knees weaken. And he always looked so handsome when he did it.

Insufferable man.

"You aren't going to tell me, are you?" she asked with a heavy sigh, needing this moment to pass and do so quickly.

Rogue only smiled a knowing, crooked smile.

Amelia rolled her eyes and stood. "Fine. Any luck with the landlord in Surrey?" Despite their efforts that day in Surrey, the landlord had been away, so they'd not been able to find out more than a name. It had taken this long merely to track him down and ask questions about the property. One of Rogue's associates, whom Amelia did not dare ask about, had done that bit and was to report back.

"Some," he replied with a shrug, apparently unaffected. "You were right. No one took the cottage after you left, but not for want of offers."

That did not make any sense at all, and she frowned. "So… people wanted to live there, but he turned them down?"

Rogue nodded once. "It does not add up, so I think I will pay him a visit and try to find more specific information." He smiled in a way that made Amelia wonder just what sort of methods he meant to employ to do so.

She smirked at him knowingly. "Do I want to know how you intend to bring this confession about?"

"Probably not." He rose and brushed off his vest, not that it helped the worn article one bit. "Some things, my dear, even you would draw the line at."

Amelia snorted and adjusted her shawl. "I doubt that very much."

His eyes suddenly flashed a little more dangerously than usual. "Don't."

She stilled and stared at him for a long moment. He rarely spoke harshly to her anymore, and when he did it was never unwarranted. This was different.

He shook his head slowly. "You don't know half as much about the world as you think you do, Amelia, no matter what you've experienced. It is darker, crueler, and more savage than you can ever imagine. And you should fear it. For your own sake, be a little less hardened. Don't get jaded. Save whatever remains of your innocence." His throat worked on a swallow, and he shook his head again. "Keep yourself above the rest. Far, far above."

She wanted to say something flippant, something that would bring him back from this almost frantic precipice he was on, but she couldn't deny that his words had taken root, and she felt the severity of their meaning. She couldn't brush this off, as she might have other warnings from him, as she *had* done other warnings. But this was Rogue stripped of his artifice, and the first time she had seen him speak with real sincerity.

It might have been the only thing she could honestly take as real where he was concerned.

So, she simply nodded, keeping her eyes steady on his. "All right."

He swallowed and gave a brisk nod, then eyed the door. "Now, go find something else to do," he said with forced brusqueness as he moved to his desk. "I've got a lot of things to do, and you're distracting me."

Amelia grinned at his back. "Are you calling me a distraction?"

"I believe I just said that." He turned and gave her a look, making a shooing motion with his hands. "Go. Get out."

"What exactly do you find distracting about me, Rogue?" she asked, suddenly feeling rather impish.

A classic Rogue expression of derision appeared, and he lowered his chin a touch to stare at her more directly. "Your neck is absolutely perfect for throttling."

Amelia laughed, one hand going to the aforementioned throat. "Are you tempted by it?"

"Constantly." He inclined his head towards the door. "For your own safety, vacate my office. *S'il vous plaît.*"

He was continually tossing French at her, as he had the first day they'd met, and always with the slightest hint of suspicion. She'd grown used to it, and as she had no reason to explain herself, or to hide that she could understand, she played along. He never said why he did it, and she never asked.

She needed to keep up her French, so it suited her just as well.

So long as he never learned where she learned it, she could be content.

"*Comme vous voulez*," she responded with a playful curtsey.

He rolled his eyes far too dramatically for his nature and shooed her out again.

She turned to exit the door, then paused when Rogue softly called after her. She glanced over her shoulder at him to find him staring at her intently, all former traces of scorn, derision, and teasing gone.

"I was eight," he said softly, his hands spreading a little on the desk surface. "When my mother died."

Amelia's breath caught in her chest, and she fought the temptation to clasp her hand to her heart. So young. Her mother had faded from existence when she was young, but at least she had been alive. "What did you do?"

Rogue's eyes lost some of their focus, and his hands tightened. "Cried a great deal, as I understand it. Then nothing at all. I have distant relations who were charged with my care. They sent me off to school, where I misbehaved every day of my life, and nothing has changed since." His eyes flicked back to hers, and he smiled faintly. "What can I say, I have always been terribly misbehaved."

She returned his smile, touched that he would share a little of his surprisingly painful past with her, though the details left something to be desired, and she was beyond tempted to ask for more. But she knew better; she was fortunate to have received any answer at all. And yet, she knew instinctively that there was so much more to Rogue and his past than this. More that was, perhaps, more painful than this, which would explain his sharing the vague details now. If this was the least painful part, it would be easiest to share.

But what, then, of the rest?

He shook his head with another smile. "No, you do not get to hear any more. Go cry for me somewhere else."

"Cry for you?" Amelia said with a snort. "Hardly. For all I know, you are lying to try and make me trust you more so you can find and expose my secrets and flaws with more accuracy and flourish."

"I never do anything with flourish." He waved at the door and sat down at the desk, rifling through papers and not meeting her eyes again.

She went without a fuss, smiling to herself, not because of Rogue and his continually shifting demeanor, but because she had work to attend to this evening, and the more time she could spend preparing, the better.

Out in the hall, Gent met her with a warm smile. "Amelia, how was our resident dragon today?"

She cocked her head a little. "Him or me?"

Gent tossed his head back on a laugh. "*Touché, mon chère.* I won't even ask if your skirts are singed."

Amelia shrugged and walked with Gent towards the back of the building. "Only as much as ever. We seem to be getting on well these days, which makes me think he is up to something."

"You never know with Rogue." He shook his head and rubbed at some faint smudges on his cheeks. "He can be fairly companionable, when he's of a mind to, which doesn't usually occur more than once or twice every four months."

She snickered and reached for the cloak she'd hung up near the door. Since her adventure in Surrey and that night they'd spent scouring London, she'd been given a sort of unspoken permission to do as she pleased in the office. She never ventured into the private offices without authorization, she was not so bold as that, but the common areas she quite took over when she felt like it. Even Callie and the clerks had stopped moving her things around, and they almost never fought anymore.

Almost.

"Well, he won't suspect anything tonight, will he?" Amelia asked, bringing her mind back to the present and the man beside her, now holding the door.

Gent grinned and shook his head. "Not a bit. He's got as much to do as you have and will be very busy this evening. Whatever you have planned, it will never be noticed."

Amelia nodded, smiled in her excitement, and stepped outside. She slid her gloves on and started walking away.

Crisp steps behind her made her turn, and she gave Gent a surprised look as he followed her. "What are you doing?" she asked with a laugh.

He returned her look with a superior one of his own. "You didn't think I was going to let you venture out on your own, did you?"

"Gent…"

"That is my name," he said with a firm nod, "and also my nature. I don't care where you come from, Miss Berger, or what you think you need. You will never be unescorted while I can help it."

It was sweet, and she was flattered, but it was also the silliest thing she had ever heard. And she could never tell Gent she was touched by it; that would tarnish her image. So, she rolled her eyes and huffed, even with a smile, and continued on her way, Gent whistling jovially behind her.

Eventually, he came up to her side, and they chatted amicably until they reached her intended destination, at which point Gent waved her on and sauntered off into the London streets, no doubt to save other females in his path.

Amelia made her way down the hallways, passed several rooms, then arrived at the place she'd been directed and knocked on the door.

It only took a moment before the door opened, and a tall woman with dark hair and a knowing look answered.

"Tilda," Amelia greeted her with a smile. "Is everything ready?"

Tilda smiled rather mischievously. "Yes, darling, and I may have gone too far, but I won't apologize. Come in, I've got it all sorted, and we haven't much time."

Chapter Eleven

$\mathscr{A}$s it turned out, masquerade balls were just as bad, if not worse, than your everyday run-of-the-mill balls. Especially when the female attendees knew what the token male prey of the evening was wearing. It was bad enough that a masquerade allowed the guests leniency with propriety under the protection of absolute anonymity, but when one is in particular pursuit of another guest in attendance, the behaviors could be downright shocking, even to one as morally dissolute as Gabe.

Why could he not be doing something dangerous and possibly bloody instead?

"So help me," Gabe muttered to the caped man beside him, "if one more girl strokes my leg, I am going to step on her toes, tear her skirt, and break a finger."

The man choked on a sip of his beverage and managed a chuckle. "Come now, my lord. You must be flattered by all the attention you are receiving."

Gabe offered as black a look as he could manage with the silver and blue mask upon his face. It was a far more elaborate mask than he'd wished for, but Geraldine had actually forbidden him to come in costume as many of the other men had done. She had arranged everything about his ensemble for him, down to the exact stockings he wore, so he had no choice. It was this or go exposed as himself, and that was not going to happen.

He felt oddly underdressed in his tails, even with the waistcoat to match his mask, especially considering the elaborateness of some other costumes. Either the Prince of Wales had indeed come to his aunt's ridiculous gathering, or someone wished to imitate his excesses. Also in attendance were King Louis XIV, Marie Antoinette, Queen Elizabeth, Dionysus, and, oddly enough, a statue. Several birds had made their rounds about the room, though one swan looked quite like another, and some poor girls seemed to think canaries were flattering characters for themselves.

Poor fools.

"I'd be more flattered if an assassin showed up," Gabe said with a sigh of longing.

His companion chuckled and adjusted his thick cape around his entirely black ensemble. "Don't behave too badly. Some of the women here might consider that encouragement."

Gabe groaned and scratched at the too-frilly cravat. "I will pay you to stand in for me."

"You don't have any money."

"I will win some."

"I'm married, my lord."

"Is she here?"

"As a matter of fact, she is."

Gabe turned in surprise. "Is she really? Where?"

He received a knowing look. "No. You cannot pester Lady Marlowe instead of doing your duty."

"Lord Marlowe, and his blessed sense of duty, can go stuff it," Gabe grunted, taking another glass from a passing servant, who wore the token white domino of all servants tonight.

Why the servants should need to be masked, he had no idea.

"Actually, I think I will go dance with my wife," Marlowe said with a bit of a smug smirk. "After all, I've jumped through my hoops."

"Noose," Gabe corrected, waving him away. "And don't look so damned happy about it."

"Don't pester Rothchild, either. He doesn't want to deal with you, he only came to see his wife wear a mask, and to see you forced into interacting properly with women for a laugh."

Gabe rolled his eyes and waved him away again. "Rothchild is fortunate he has a wife at all, masked or not, and the day I interact properly is the day I'll ask Rothchild for a waltz."

He heard his friend laugh over the sound of the music, and he felt sourer about it by the second. Rothchild would have been a passable companion through all of this, if only to make Gabe laugh, but when he was with his wife, he was remarkably lovesick, and Gabe did not need that influence tonight.

This whole thing had been positively interminable. Gabe would have been better served by soaking his head in the Thames for three hours than being here for half as long.

If it weren't for that meddling aunt of his…

"Gabriel, don't glower, the women will never approach when you look like that."

"Speak of the devil," he sighed, as he turned to his emerald-encased aunt, wearing a wide, Georgian dress with far too many jewels about her neck, which he suspected to be paste. Her mask bore matching emerald feathers, and her fan flicked rapidly, which probably added little comfort to her ensemble. The towering powdered wig she wore would have overheated anyone, least of all the woman flitting about to manage every detail of the evening. He could see the sweat glistening on her face, despite the faint powder she wore.

Geraldine's fan stopped, and she glared at him. "What devil?" she snapped.

He shrugged nonchalantly and chose not to answer her. "Can I go home now?"

She rapped him on the shoulder hard with the aforementioned fan. "If you didn't glower so, you might enjoy yourself. Change your face, change the evening."

"This is my face, Aunt."

"More's the pity."

"I could wear a bigger mask," he suggested hopefully.

"For the rest of your life? I doubt it."

Gabe groaned and returned to watch the dancing, which was quite comical. Shepherdesses ought not to dance with their crooks. It led to such difficulties.

"Any ladies striking your fancy?" Geraldine asked, leaning close to pretend at whispering.

"Not half as many as are striking my arse," he replied.

Again, he was rapped with her fan. "Gabriel!"

He shrugged, hiding a smile. "What did you expect, Aunt? You know inhibitions disappear when masks and costumes are brought out. It's beginning to scandalize even me."

"Oh, I doubt that very much," she scoffed, resuming her fanning. She waited a long moment, then gave her nephew a curious look. "Have they really been striking your…?"

"Yes," he answered bluntly. "Three swans, two fairies, and two queens have taken such liberties. Most of the others tend to stay with my extremities, but only four have not touched me at all. I was getting quite used to it, so those four might have scared me most."

Geraldine snorted a soft laugh behind her fan.

"It is unseemly to laugh at such matters, Aunt," Gabe said with a faint sniff.

"Call me unseemly all you like," she quipped. "That would not bother me at all."

He gave his aunt a wry look. "And yet you will not let me be such?"

"You are all sorts of things against my wishes," she replied, smiling a little. "Unseemly is in our blood, so you'll never escape it entirely."

Gabe heaved a sigh. "Well, that is a relief. I have lost many sleepless nights to concerns about my mannerisms."

Geraldine rolled her eyes and snapped her fan shut in her hand. "You are impossible."

"I've been trying to explain that to you…"

She turned him slightly and shoved hard. "Go dance with someone. I don't care who."

He looked over his shoulder at her, chuckling a little. "Well, I *was* going to ask you, before you brutalized me."

She looked a little surprised, then her eyes narrowed. "I don't believe you."

Gabe let himself smile fully, which he never did in public, and took the few steps back to her. "Lady Geraldine, would you do me the honor of standing up the next dance with me?" he asked in the most polite voice he had ever pretended in his life, extending his hand to her.

His aunt's mouth dropped open, and she looked between his hand and his face repeatedly.

He bent a little closer to her. "It is generally customary to accept such a polite request, particularly from a peer."

She clamped her lips together, smiled and rolled her eyes. "Oh, Gabriel. What am I going to do with you?"

He shrugged again, smiling. "Accepting my dance request would be an excellent place to start."

Geraldine took his hand, laughing to herself, and let him lead her down to the dance floor. "Oh, why not? It will give me a chance to see who is watching you and push you in that direction afterwards."

Gabe's cheery attitude vanished, and he glared at her. "Don't make me regret this."

Her smile turned conniving, and she tapped her chin with her fan. "You had to know I was not going to give way just because you flattered me with a dance."

He scowled as he bowed. "One can always hope."

True to her word, Geraldine began describing every woman looking at him and speculated on who it might actually be. Gabe stopped listening after he heard the words "dairy maid" and chose instead to focus his thoughts on the details of his investigation, more particularly on Amelia herself. He'd not been able to progress as far as he would have liked with that, as she was continually planting herself in the middle of everything, so he'd been forced to actually investigate her mother and attempt to discover details about her along the way.

So far, he was not doing well.

She was as private as he was, despite her trying to draw him out, and no matter what she said about her name, he knew it wasn't right. Her Clairbourne relatives were on her mother's side, but where had the Palmer name come from? Had her father's last name been Palmer, or had there been another name change in the middle she had not told him about? Had her mother died under yet another name?

What had happened to Amelia between the time her mother died and the time she had moved in with the Bergers?

Where had she learned to speak French so well without a governess or school?

It was a tangled mess of things, and he would never figure it out if he kept letting her get under his skin.

The more he got to know her, the more time he spent with her, the less he wanted to discover her secrets, for among the secrets would be lies.

And he could not abide lies.

That seemed odd, even to him. He, who lied for a living, required honesty from others. What a contradictory thought, and a paradox for his soul.

He snorted. Soul. What? The blackened center of him that could not manage to twitch for morality? As if that added any substance to him.

Perhaps he ought to speak to someone about being re-christened. He doubted the first one was valid anymore.

He glanced down at his aunt, stunned that she was somehow still talking. What had possessed him to be sentimental and ask her to dance with him? He could have had a dance where he ignored his partner this much with quite literally any other female in the room, and without any of the previous expectation of enjoyment.

He groaned as he realized that he'd made the gross miscalculation of standing up with his aunt during a long dance, of all horrid things. Next time he was so stupid as to dance with his aunt, he would ensure it was a quadrille. That would entertain him sufficiently.

A movement to his right caught his attention, and he looked towards it, grateful for the distraction.

Weaving in and out of the several-bodies-deep border of the dance floor was a woman in a white gown, looking to be in her early, perhaps middle-twenties, and her focus was nowhere near the dancing. She was looking at the people, mostly in the distance from her, but she glanced carefully at the ones nearest her as well.

Gabe wouldn't have given her a second thought, but there was something about the way she moved that interested him. There was an ease to her gait, a confidence that belied the presumed nature of young women in Society, and yet she was not haughty or puffed up. She moved with natural grace and poise, but no airs, and not for effect. In fact, despite his looking at her so intently, no one else was doing so. Hardly a single man looked in her direction, and even fewer women did.

A break in the crowd allowed him a better view of her, and his world seemed to shift on its axis. She was dressed as a Grecian goddess, with the loose, yet somehow form-fitting gown of the same style, gathered at her waist with a gold belt, from which vines of braided gold proceeded upwards to the bodice, twisting themselves within and extending up to her shoulders, which shockingly were without sleeves. Her arms were strong and lean, and surprisingly elegant, and the depth of her neckline, though hardly shocking by any stretch, was enough to warrant a double look.

He could not see her face, as she was turned away, displaying a tantalizing turn of her throat, and the long, intricately curled and braided length of blonde hair cascaded from whatever form contained it and hung down her back. She turned away from him altogether, moving towards the rear of the room, and he was more transfixed by her retreating form.

Against the custom of the day, the back of her dress scooped low, her shoulder blades visible, as the fabric drooped beneath them. The cut of the costume was such that it would intentionally put her shoulders and back on display, and hers were quite the sight for anyone fortunate enough to see. From her shoulders and back hung a sheath of fabric, gathering together to form a cape or train, elegantly flowing along behind her, giving her an added regal air that had nothing to do with the golden diadem perched within her blonde curls.

Had Gabe ever noticed so much about one woman at once?

Had he ever cared?

Look back, he thought fiercely, turning as he must with the dance, returning his eyes to the goddess as quickly as he could. For the love of God, look back.

Just then, she stopped, turned slightly to glance down at a bit of her train that had been caught and tugged it loose, then raised her face.

Gabe's heart slammed against his ribs with such force that he grunted softly.

She wore a gold and cream domino mask, and even from this

distance, he could see the lace detailing and small gatherings of gold feathers on each side, blending back into her elaborately-coifed, blonde hair. Her eyes had been heavily lined with kohl, and gold paint dusted the visible skin around her eyes, which were a striking, dusty shade of blue. Her full lips were painted rosy pink, but beyond that and the costume, she appeared to be completely natural.

Gabriel Statler had never had any real interest in a particular woman, finding them to rarely be worth the time or effort. He'd never spent more than three minutes wondering about his future with one or considering any form of courtship, wooing, or pursuit with one.

At this moment, none of that mattered.

As soon as the goddess's eyes had clashed with his, his heart and mind joined forces and emblazoned one word in his thoughts:

Mine.

Why were there so many people in this cursed ballroom?

Amelia tugged her train free of yet another inconsiderate shoe, wondering if she was going to have to take this exquisite, yet troublesome costume back to Tilda so damaged that she would have to pay for it. Tilda hadn't seemed too concerned about it when she'd dressed her earlier, but Amelia wasn't quite sure she trusted her enough to believe it.

She glanced up and across the room, finding the man in dark tails and a crisp white shirt still staring at her fixedly, his blue eyes magnified by the silver and blue mask he wore. He completely ignored the flock of women around him, including one in bright green that seemed to wish for his attention in particular.

He'd been staring at her all night, first in his dance with the green lady, then during two more with others. He had not yet managed to get to her, but she sensed that he would soon. There was something powerful and captivating about him, and it sent a thrill down her spine to have him notice her. She felt her heart stutter a little again, but there wasn't time for fancies.

No matter how curious she was about his attention.

She dipped her chin in an acknowledgement of his notice. His eyes flashed in response and a corner of his mouth lifted, sending her knees shaking and her breath catching.

Oh no, that was *not* what she had intended.

She swallowed and turned quickly, hoping to lose herself in the mass of people. She'd only been here an hour and hadn't managed to find the people she needed to.

Some Clairbournes were in attendance tonight, and she'd bribed no less than three servants to tell her what they were wearing and where to find them.

She'd created the perfect identity for herself. Her mother had been a schoolmate of Mary Clairbourne, and when this venture into London had come about, she had just begged her to try and find her, as they had lost touch. She knew enough of the details of her mother's life to be able to pretend her way through any story, and Amelia had spent years acting a part. She could improvise her way through almost anything, and her ability to read reactions and play off them had not failed her yet.

She was still incredulous that she had managed to scrape together an invitation to this event. Lady Geraldine Rochester was nothing to her, and certainly not a particularly well-known name in Society. At least, that's what the servants of various households had told her during her escapades of late. But talk of this masquerade had been buzzing about. Apparently, costumes and masks were an exciting diversion, and definitely not an event to be missed, but invitations were limited. It was to be a rather exclusive party.

Amelia Berger would never be able to attend such an event.

Her saving grace had been some connection of Gent's, the details of which he had not gone into, and she had not asked.

As she looked around now, she wondered how a party of this magnitude could ever be considered exclusive. It appeared as though the whole of London had turned out for it. How was she ever going to find the Clairbournes here? And despite it being a masquerade, how could she possibly manage to approach them without an introduction?

Were they the sort of people to turn their nose up at such things? None of the servants had been able to give her that much detail, and it was hardly the sort of question one asked if one wished to remain above suspicion.

"Pardon me, miss," a kind male voice said nearby. "I seem to have trod upon your costume."

Amelia turned with a polite smile to find a simply-dressed and simply-masked man by her side, holding part of her train. "It's quite all right," she replied in her perfectly cultured voice, a little higher than her natural tone. "It is quite meddlesome; it has been happening all night."

The man smiled and inclined his head. "But it is a lovely costume. My wife is quite envious and has been telling me so all night."

Amelia laughed and took the train from him gently. "She ought to have a word with me, then. I shall tell her all the faults of it, and she would not feel so jealous after that."

He chuckled and held out his hand. "She would enjoy that very much. Thomas Clairbourne, at your service."

What were the odds of that? Amelia didn't bother to hide her smile. "Alexandra Driscoll," she said with a curtsey. "A pleasure, sir."

He nodded, still smiling. "Might I take you to my wife, Miss Driscoll? And find you some refreshment?"

She released a small sigh. "That would be much appreciated." She gave him a look as he gestured the way. "Do you normally approach women this way and with such introductions, Mr. Clairbourne?"

He shook his head, moving around a crush of individuals. "Not at all. But you looked a trifle lost, and Lucy insisted I save you."

"So, you didn't really tread on my costume."

"Oh, I did, I promise, and not even intentionally."

Amelia smirked and fought the urge to scratch at her wig. It was a glorious part of her costume, but a bit maddening to wear. Still, it masked her identity and suited the ensemble so perfectly. No one would have recognized her, even if they did know her outside of this room. And no one would be able to find her when the masquerade was over.

And that was what mattered.

"Clairbourne," Amelia murmured as if thinking hard. "My mother knew a Clairbourne at school, she was only just speaking of her before I came down to London."

"Truly?" Mr. Clairbourne responded with surprise. "Any idea who? There are a few of us, after all."

"Mariah?" Amelia suggested with a frown. "No, Mary, I believe. Imaginative girl, always scribbling something and had her nose in a book, but very pretty. That was how Mother described her, at least."

Mr. Clairbourne frowned a little, brow furrowed. "I don't know of any Marys in my direct family, but I'm not the most informed with the line. I'll turn you over to Lucy and go find my aunt, she's milling about somewhere, and she knows all the cousins and all the gossip." He rolled his eyes a little, making Amelia smile.

"If you like," she replied with a small smile. "It is no matter, though it would be delightful to write to Mother about her old friend, if I could."

Mr. Clairbourne was as good as his word. Once Amelia had been introduced to Mrs. Clairbourne, who was somewhat more reserved than she had expected, and therefore not inclined to conversation, he presented his aunt, Mrs. Armenia Brimley. There was no restraint with this woman, and soon Amelia was privy to all the details of that particular branch of the Clairbourne family. It took quite some time, but eventually, she heard the name Mary, and she stopped the older woman at once.

"Tell me more about Mary," Amelia said as kindly as she could while wishing this would all end quickly.

"The Hertfordshire cousins," Mrs. Brimley wheezed, her expansive girth making the chair she sat in creak with every breath. "Strange lot. My second cousins. Mary, Dottie, and Frank. Dottie married a barrister, you know, and while I never think very well of barristers, I think Mr. Chapman might be all right. Frank married some chit from Bristol; a love match, as I understand it. Not a particularly good match, but considering Mary, they were pleased by it."

Amelia's stomach clenched. "What happened to Mary?"

Mrs. Brimley clucked her tongue, shaking her massively powdered wig and sending bits of it falling into Amelia's lap. "Poor Mary. John and Anne were so distraught. She was determined to marry for her heart, and the man was a merchant, of all things.

Completely unsuitable, and she had to visit him in prison at one point. She was cut off, you know. But she was of age, and so she married him. It was dreadful; nobody came to the wedding, and the man left straightaway for a shipment. Lord knows what became of Mary after that. She was never welcomed back to Hertfordshire."

Thoughts and feelings were filtering through Amelia's head so fast she could hardly keep up. Rage at her mother's family for cutting her off. Dismay at her mother for wedding a criminal. Relief at a marriage at all. Confusion… Curiosity… Too much, and yet too little. What could she ask? What could she say?

"Poor thing," she settled on, trying to sound sympathetic. "Did anyone in the family hear of her?"

"Dottie might have done," Mrs. Brimley said with a huff. "The sisters were close, there is no denying it. You could try her. They're in Cheapside, now Parliament is in session. Mr. Chapman enjoys that sort of thing." The older woman rolled her eyes and fanned herself. "Good heavens, it's warm. Where is my nephew? He must fetch me punch."

Sensing she would not get any more out of the woman, nor her relations, Amelia excused herself and moved towards the terrace, wishing for the night air and some peace. The room was too hot and the music too loud, and the perfume of several ladies was so excessive that breathing was becoming difficult. A few moments of refreshment, and then she could slip away unnoticed and return to her boarding house to search for clues in her mother's diaries.

Rogue had let her take them for a time, as he had gone through them and analyzed what he could from them, though apparently there was too much sentimentality for him to stomach.

Served him right.

Someone else trod upon her train, jerking her to a stop. She turned to tug the fabric free and found a man dressed in a turban and foreign costume staring at her back as she did so.

"Might I help you, sir?" she asked stiffly, still keeping her voice high.

"I rather think you might," he slurred, weaving a little where he stood.

Amelia rolled her eyes a little. "Well, remove yourself from my costume, and perhaps you will get it."

He shuffled back, and Amelia tugged herself free, then turned in the opposite direction, away from her drunken admirer.

She moved between several people and started towards the doors when the masked man from before stepped into her path, his lips quirking into a smile. "Not yet, goddess."

His voice was low, and it sent a tingling sensation into her fingers and toes. "Not yet what, sir?"

He shook his head slowly, his blue and white mask making his eyes shimmer dangerously. "You cannot leave yet. Not without meeting me. Especially with how you've been avoiding me all night."

Amelia smiled slyly, enjoying the playful nature that was somehow without any sort of dark intent. The man was charming and undoubtedly attractive, but she felt that somehow the power was hers. "And who are you that I should be so inclined to stay?"

He stilled and tilted his head a little, seeming curious. "You don't know who I am?"

She shrugged one shoulder. "Should I?"

"It should be obvious."

Amelia smirked a little, wondering why that should be the case. "And yet, I am without the answer. Are you supposed to be important?"

He smiled at her then, a full, beaming smile that no sensible woman would have been unmoved by. She nearly swooned where she stood. Good heavens, what a smile!

"Now you must dance with me. That is the most wonderful thing I have heard all night."

She put a finger to her chin and tapped. "Am I permitted to dance with a stranger?"

"That all depends," he said with a wry smile. "Which goddess are you?"

She dropped her hand and dipped her chin to look at him more directly. "Whichever one induces you to behave, sir."

He chuckled and extended his hand to her, his eyes crinkling at the corners. "Dance with me, goddess, I beg of you. And save me from everyone here that is not you."

Well, what was the harm in dancing with an attractive man with a smile like that and words that made her sigh? It was only a dance, only this night, and she was no one at all.

She placed her hand in his and shivered at the contact. "Consider yourself saved, then."

He squeezed her hand gently. "You have no idea."

Chapter Twelve

$\mathcal{O}$ne dance turned into three, and what was not dancing was shameless flirtation and fun. Amelia wasn't sure she had ever laughed so much in her entire life, and as it was a masquerade where the usual proprieties were undoubtedly looser, she felt quite free to monopolize her mystery man as much as she liked.

And he was certainly content.

He had not looked anywhere else since they'd met, and while that ought to have disturbed her, it was instead rather tantalizing.

Who he was had been as much of a mystery as anything she had portrayed tonight. He'd not asked her name, always calling her 'goddess', and she'd never asked him his. Names made everything real, and this was anything but. She wanted to live in this fantasy where a wealthy man with manners and charm wished to flirt and spend time with her, while never taking liberties of any sort.

They'd walked the ballroom twice, her arm politely linked through his, all the while smirking and laughing about the more ridiculous costumes of the evening. He'd comment on the dance, she'd reply with some sort of dry humor, and then he'd whisk her into the silly dance they had just criticized. She was hardly skilled in the dance, but he made up for her ineptitude with his grace and good humor. And he never commented on it, so perhaps he did not notice.

She found that idea hard to fathom, as he seemed to notice everything.

They were out on the terrace now, at last getting some fresh air and a reprieve from the oppressive ballroom. Amelia took a moment to study the man that had taken up so much of her evening so unexpectedly.

He was taller than she was, but not overly so, which was to be expected. She was a little tall for a woman, as she had often been told. He wore his hair combed back, but she could see where the almost too-long strands curled at the ends. Would his hair have been filled with curls if not for the style of the evening? He was clean-shaven, almost brutally so, but he would need to shave again soon; she could see the dark shadow along his cheeks and jaw. It was a strong jaw with chiseled features, just as a man ought to look, in her opinion.

And his body… well, perfectly tailored clothes were designed to make a man look his best, and he was no exception. But he did seem to fit the cut exceptionally well, and Amelia could undoubtedly appreciate a strong, broad set of shoulders. All in all, the man appeared to be perfectly ideal.

Then there were his eyes…

Generally, Amelia preferred dark eyes, much like the Gent had. All three of the men she had favored in the past had possessed dark eyes, and it had been her favorite feature on each one. They always seemed to be warm and inviting, and one could get lost in the dark swirls therein.

Yet his eyes were a most potent blue. And nothing in the world had captivated her like they had. A strange fire had begun to burn within her the moment those eyes had found her, and it had only intensified in heat and sensation as the night had gone on. He could see through her disguise into the depths of her soul, and never had such vulnerability felt so very freeing.

"Tell me two things that are true," he said after a moment, holding one of her hands, as they leaned against the railing of the terrace beneath the stars, "and one thing that is a lie."

Amelia grinned and played with the fingers she held. "Oh, where to begin?"

"Anywhere you like. Quite literally anywhere. I will accept any insight you give me."

She chuckled and leaned against him a little. "I can ride a horse astride and sidesaddle but cannot drive a team to save my life."

"Then let us hope you never have to save your life by driving a team."

"Indeed. Then some dashing fellow will have to save me."

"I volunteer myself to your service, madam."

"I accept."

He smiled at her a bit wickedly and brought her hand to his lips, lingering too long for propriety and not long enough for her satisfaction, but certainly long enough to distract her.

"I… I shouldn't be here," she managed, her words shaking as much as her kneecaps.

"And there is your lie," he scolded with a knowing look. "For you most certainly should."

Amelia needed to find her composure, her control, some sort of protection against herself. This was too dangerous, and she was slipping on this somewhat precarious slope. She was never so unsteady, and the unfamiliarity of it all frightened her.

And despite his correction, that wasn't her lie.

"I have never been to London before this," she said at last, ducking her face as though she would blush.

He squeezed her hand gently, chuckling. "No need to be embarrassed about that. I wondered that myself, having never seen you before."

She glanced at him as much as her mask would allow. "Are you certain of that?"

She could almost see a brow rise, his smile turning crooked. "Are you saying that you have seen me?"

Amelia shrugged one shoulder, her braided strap inching closer to her neck. "I might have done. One never knows."

"I would know."

"How fortunate for you to live with such certainty."

"I am certain about everything and nothing where you are concerned."

She had to smile at that, desperate to ask what he meant, and just as eager to avoid the very same. "What honesty, sir," she praised, turning her smile to him. "Will you be as honest with your truths?"

He nodded, smiling crookedly, entwining his fingers with hers. "I will always be perfectly honest with you."

Well now, *that* was a bold thing to proclaim.

Amelia chose to say absolutely nothing to that. Best to not

remember such things, as they would never live longer than the breath they were spoken on.

"I hate balls," her companion said with no reluctance. "Can't abide them in general."

She let out a laugh and shook her head. "That is no surprise. I saw your expression before you came over to me at last. You were having a miserable time." She laughed again at the memory.

"I will admit to such freely," he agreed, smiling at her laugh. "It was all wrong before you."

There he went again, setting her thoughts and senses askew. She bit down on her lip and looked away, no longer feeling the need to laugh.

"I do not care for dessert," he announced as if his last words were not painfully sweet to her ears.

She jerked and looked at him in surprise. "You don't?"

He shrugged. "Perhaps I will never properly appreciate the sweeter things in life." He heaved a dramatic sigh, then smirked in her direction.

Amelia giggled at his playfulness, and then adopted a somber expression. "Perhaps not. But too many sweets have undoubtedly led to many a downfall, so you are quite right to avoid them."

"I am glad you approve." He looked back towards the ballroom and chuckled softly. "I've never really thought about my future. In fact, I think I've been running from it."

"Is it so dreadful a prospect?" she asked, studying his profile, loving the way the shadows of the night played across his features.

"I don't know," he admitted. "I never trusted myself enough to look towards it. Never thought I would have much of one. Never made plans." He exhaled slowly, then looked at her very directly.

She reared back a little. "What?"

"You make me want to plan."

Her eyes widened, and it was all she could do to manage a very faint "Oh."

He studied her for a second, then smiled a little. "Which shows what a disastrous state I am in, to be sure."

Amelia swallowed hastily, wanting to shake her head free of the fog currently surrounding it. "Yes, indeed," she said with an attempt at a laugh. "You know absolutely nothing about me save for what you see, and I make you want to plan? It is fortunate I have no idea who you are, or I should be quite shocked, I am sure."

He snorted. "If you knew who I was, you would not be surprised in the slightest by that. It is quite commonly expected of me."

She couldn't help smiling as she watched him, wondering who he was, how he could admit so much to her, and why in the world he was spending his evening out here with her when there were so many others he could choose. And why he seemed to be everything she had never thought a man would be. It was all too perfect.

"Why are you smiling?" he asked in a low voice, touching the corner of her mouth.

Amelia felt her smile spread, taking his finger with it. "I don't know," she replied easily. "You make me smile."

He shook his head, sliding his finger down to touch her chin. "Not possible. I don't make anyone smile."

"Then I must be an exception."

His eyes darkened as he met her gaze. "That you certainly are, goddess." His finger stroked under her chin slowly, unintentionally stoking the fire that grew within her.

She sighed at the contact and closed her eyes, her fingers fluttering against his hold. She'd never felt sensations like this before, never felt so much in so short a time, never known these feelings existed.

Which was why it must all be a fantasy. Amelia was dreaming, and oh, how painful would be the waking.

"Who are you, goddess?" he whispered, his breath dancing across her skin.

"I can't tell you," she breathed, leaning her head back, feeling the hair of her wig dance against the bare skin of her back.

"Why?"

"I can't tell you."

"What if I ask nicely?"

She smiled and sighed as his fingers wandered down her neck a little. "You are."

"I can ask more nicely."

"Don't. I can't bear it."

His hand was on her chin again, this time tipping it down, and Amelia managed to open her drowsy eyes to meet his heated gaze.

"Please," he whispered, his thumb pressing just below her bottom lip, parting her lips easily.

"No," Amelia sighed, her breath racing past her lips.

He leaned forward and pressed his lips to hers gently, tenderly molding them in a medley of caresses and grazes. His hands moved to cup her face as he kissed her again and again, each kiss teasing and searing, gently wringing exquisite delight from every tingling part of her.

"Please," he whispered against her lips, between each touch, each breathless moment weakening her further and further.

She couldn't stand this, didn't understand it. She'd never felt anything like this, and the onslaught was heady and overwhelming and wonderful. She had never dreamed she could feel this way, so alive and wild, so insecure and filled with light. She had spent so long feeling nothing, and now she was infused with more emotions than she could bear to comprehend. This man had torn down her walls, stripped away layer by layer, and turned her into a creature she barely recognized, yet she had never felt more herself in her entire life.

The heat was unbearable, the tenderness too sweet, and the sensations too real. Amelia broke off and pressed her face into his shoulder, fighting for control, gripping the back of his coat tightly. Her breathing was frantic, unsteady, and her legs shook beneath her.

"I'm sorry," he whispered, his arms reaching around her to pull her in, hands gently smoothing along her back. "I didn't mean to…"

She shook her head against him. "Don't apologize for that," she scolded between breaths. "I've never… that is, I did not know…"

"I know, goddess." He kissed her cheek quickly. "I know. Settle yourself, we have all night."

But they didn't have all night. They had almost no time at all.

"Lord Wharton."

Amelia felt him stiffen at the servant's voice, then growl a bit of a sigh. "Yes?"

"Lady Geraldine wishes to know if you intend to return to the gathering at all."

He did growl this time, and Amelia pulled back a little from him, smiling at the frown he wore.

"Tell her I might, but I make no promises," he said firmly.

The servant bowed, then returned to the ballroom.

Amelia continued to smile, feeling more at ease. "Will she accept that reply?"

"She's my aunt," he muttered with a shake of his head. "She certainly ought to by now." He sighed and looked at her with a slight smile. "Well, now you know who I am, I suppose."

She pursed her lips and shrugged one shoulder again. "I suppose. Technically, at any rate."

"Technically?" That seemed to amuse him. "Explain."

"Well, if I knew anything about Lord Wharton, or who he was, or why it should be significant that you are Lord Wharton, then yes, I should say that I know you." She smiled with as much of a mischievous air as she could manage with her mask on. "But as I know none of that, and only your name, it is only technically that I know you, my lord."

Lord Wharton stared at her, his blue eyes wide behind his mask, his lips barely parted. He slowly reached out and took her hand once more, then encased it in both of his. "I did not think," he said slowly, his voice a low rumble, "that it was possible to find you any more perfect." He laughed a little breathlessly. "And yet…"

Amelia smiled in delight, tossing her hair behind her and turning to look at the garden behind them, which would have been quite exquisite by the light of day. "I am not at all perfect, my lord. Not even close to it."

"I did not say you *were* perfect," he murmured, his thumbs rubbing across the top of her hand. "I said I find you perfect. There is a marked difference there."

She closed her eyes on an exhale, shaking her head slightly. "You really must stop saying such lovely things to me, my lord. I might begin to believe them."

His grip on her hand tightened. "You should believe them. You should believe everything I say to you and everything you feel with me."

"I don't know what I feel," she whispered harshly. "I don't know what I believe. I don't know what I want."

Her voice caught on the last words as she unexpectedly found tears forming, and she dropped her head, fighting for control.

"Oh, goddess," Lord Wharton soothed, kissing her hand again. "Don't cry."

She laughed softly despite her tears. "I don't think it stops with your order."

"I cannot command your tears?"

She shook her head, laughing again. "I cannot even command them, and I have no title or authority."

"You may command me."

She opened her eyes and turned to look at him, so earnest and tender, so much of what she would have wished for if this had been her reality. He really was quite ideal, and were she anyone else, she would have fought hard for him.

"May I?" she whispered almost to herself.

He heard it and smiled a little. "Please."

The strains of music from the ballroom reached her ears, and she looked towards it with longing. But she did not want to return to the crowd, to everything else, to her investigation. She wanted to remain here with this man, in this moment.

"I've never waltzed," she admitted as she watched couples prepare within. "And I've always wanted to."

"Ask me."

His voice warmed her from head to toe, sent a shiver down her spine, and drew a sigh from her. She felt more alive than she had in her life and more herself than with anyone else. She looked over at him, smiling, "May I have this waltz, my lord?"

He grinned and drew her hand to his lips. "You may have them all, goddess."

He tugged her gently to the middle of the terrace and set her hand in position, then took her waist in his hand, and swept her into the movement easily, in perfect time with the dancers within.

She'd never waltzed in her life, and until now, she had never known why.

Now, she understood. She was meant to waltz with him.

It was perfection embodied and nothing less. They glided effortlessly together, as if the steps had been prepared for them and practiced for hours in advance. They moved with more grace and poise than Amelia had ever managed in her entire life, let alone with someone else. Lord Wharton guided her expertly, spun her in his arms, drew her close to him, and never shifted his gaze away from her face.

Amelia felt her blood begin to pound in her ears even as her steps became lighter, as she melted into his embrace in the dance. This was no mere waltz, no simple dance between strangers. This was so much more, a promise and a conversation, and every word went straight to her heart. She felt carried away, swirling in the sky among the clouds and the stars, yet she felt her heart was quite soundly here with his, beating in time with the music, and drawing her breath from her.

Closer and closer they moved, and although it was not proper waltz form, it was the most natural thing in the world in this moment. There was no leader and no follower anymore. They only moved, always together, as one, and where she ended and he began was impossible to say. It was breathtaking and poignant and beyond her ability to describe or imagine.

So, it was only natural that with a particularly evocative swell of music, he should pull her flush against him, take her face in his hands, and kiss her with all the passion in the world, as if he could reach for her soul. She responded without thought, tangling her fingers in his hair and pouring her sudden longing and desperation into her kiss, wishing she could draw herself into him, become part of him, and only exist as his.

His lips seared her, branded her, and she yearned to do the same to him. To make him want her and only her, to erase the memory of any other woman from his mind and his body. If she could give her heart to a man after only a few hours of association, she had done so now, and she would not be the only one to do so. She wanted his heart and everything that came along with it.

She sighed against his mouth, loving the feel of his hands on her face, clenching as if they would never let go. Then one hand moved and wrapped around her, hauling her up against him for a somehow even deeper kiss, and she was lost.

Except...

She wasn't a goddess. She wasn't Alexandra Driscoll. She didn't belong here. She didn't belong in the arms of Lord Wharton, or anyone of that station. She had a past that would horrify any member of the gentry and scandalize anyone who knew her.

She could not do this.

Fantasies were not realities.

And she had a job to finish.

With a gasp and a cry that seemed to wrench her heart from her chest, Amelia tore away from Lord Wharton's embrace with such force that he stumbled. She raced into the ballroom and around various guests in varying levels of sobriety, ignoring any and all cries, least of all any in a particularly lovely voice. She was grateful for the ease with which she could move in her costume, even with the troublesome train, and that she had taken time to examine the particulars of the room earlier. She knew exactly where to go, and there was nothing to hinder her.

She darted out the main door, past the footmen who looked curiously at her, then out of the house itself. She had stashed her thick cloak a few blocks away, and only when she was safely ensconced in that alley did she pause. She pulled the wig off and stuffed it into a satchel, not caring if she ruined the exquisite piece. Tilda could curse at her for years, and still, she wouldn't care.

She changed her shoes, put a larger, plain colored dress over her costume, and wrapped the cloak around her, drawing the hood up over her disheveled hair.

Then, and only then, could she proceed at a more sedate, sneaking pace.

And let her burning tears fall.

Gabe stared down the street in front of his aunt's home, confused, disappointed, and flat-out angry.

If it weren't for all those inane guests in the ballroom, he would have been able to catch her. But the sight of Lord Wharton alone was enough to end the blessed reprieve his goddess had given him from the rest, and when he had managed to extricate himself from them, there was no sign of her.

Why had she left? Had he been overwhelming her? That was possible, he was feeling quite overwhelmed himself, but why then run without a word?

And he'd heard the pain in her cry when she pushed herself away from him. He'd felt how tightly she was clinging to him, and she was not so skilled an actress that she could pretend such reactions to him. She had been perfectly present with him in their time together, and he most definitely had not been alone in what he was feeling.

He was simply astonished he had been feeling it at all.

In his entire life, with all that he had been through, he'd never felt anything like what he had experienced with that woman.

Was that what it was supposed to be like?

If so, why wasn't the entire male species doing everything in its power to secure it for themselves?

If not, what was the bloody point?

He stared down the road with a dark glower. Whatever had made her run, it would not be enough. He would find her and find a way to make her his in truth. He had endless resources at his disposal and more motivation than he had ever had for any task assigned to him. London was his territory, and there were not that many places to hide from someone who knew London as well as he did.

For her, he would turn the city upside down.

He would restore Whitleigh and live there for the rest of his days, if she wished it. She was everything he had never known he wanted, as bewildering as the thought was.

And she kissed as though it was the breath of life.

Which it very well might have been.

Three men were suddenly beside him, and he barely glanced at them.

"Trouble?" the cold, clipped voice of Cap said.

"Not for you," Gabe grunted, turning back for the house.

"What's going on?" Weaver asked, flanking him on one side.

"Nothing."

"Wharton…" Gent murmured.

"No."

"My lord, those answers will not..." Cap began, his voice straining for politeness.

"It's personal, Monty," Gabe barked, allowing himself to use Cap's lesser-known name.

Despite the mask, he could see Cap's astonishment, and the look he exchanged with Gent was telling.

"Go back to your wife," Cap gently ordered Gent, returning his eyes to Gabe. "And for pity's sake, keep Pratt from snooping."

Gent nodded and left without a word to any of them.

The less time they spent together, the better. It would not be unusual for men of their station to associate or even be friends, and at a masquerade there was even less chance it would be an issue. But old habits were hard to break, and they almost never met socially.

Cap folded his arms and stared at Gabe hard. "Personal," he said at last.

Gabe only nodded, his jaw tightening.

"A woman?"

He looked away, unable to answer.

Cap grunted, shaking his head. "That's surprising, considering... Well, makes no difference. Do you know who she is?"

"No," he admitted with a wince.

Cap and Weaver exchanged looks. "Ah ha," Weaver said slowly. "And how serious is this?"

Gabe took a moment to gather himself, then looked directly at his superiors in both position and title. "I understand Gent's situation now. I would do exactly as he did, only I would not have been so obedient."

Cap nodded slowly, his mouth tightening. "I see. I know better than to tell you what is at stake, and I will not give you orders."

"Nor I," Weaver said, though he looked more amused than Cap.

"Thank you," Gabe said with a snort.

"But I will say this," Cap continued without stopping, his eyes serious. "Control yourself. Use your instincts, but exercise caution. And don't give up."

"Absolutely don't give up," Weaver added, grinning now.

That surprised him, and Gabe tilted his head in an unspoken question.

Cap smiled just a little. "Any woman who can turn you into knots is worth hanging on to. I look forward to meeting her." He clapped Gabe on the shoulder and started away.

Gabe stared after him for a moment, then shook himself. "Monty."

Cap turned, looking like the polite earl he really was.

"What are you doing at a masquerade like this?" he asked with a hint of a laugh.

The smile turned slightly bitter. "I'm a widower, Wharton. Children need a mother." He dipped his chin in a nod and swept away.

Cap was looking for a new wife? That was more shocking than almost anything else that had occurred that night. Gent would never believe it, not after how fiercely Cap had mourned his first wife. Gabe looked at Weaver in shock, though Weaver did not seem nearly as surprised. He quirked his brows at Gabe and turned back for the house.

That was all they had to say? Cap encouraged him, Weaver echoed the sentiment, and neither seemed concerned by his desire to pursue his lost goddess?

Gabe hadn't been looking for permission to be given, but now that it had been, his goddess was going to have to watch herself.

He was coming after her.

A satisfied smirk lit his features, and he strode back into his aunt's ballroom, not seeing anything or anyone else.

The chase was about to begin.

Chapter Thirteen

$\mathcal{I}$t was astounding how unhelpful a person could be when they put their mind to it.

Amelia would swear up and down on any religious relic that Rogue was intentionally making things difficult for her in the days that followed the ball. Whatever progress he had thought the Hertfordshire connection would bring seemed to stall completely, and he was always too busy for more investigating about London. Too busy with what, he would not say, and he was biting her head off far more than before, even more than when they had first met.

She had not even managed to tell him what she had learned at the ball, though she had created a perfect cover story, so he would never suspect she had breached the societal barrier. He likely wouldn't approve of that, so it really was better that she keep her impersonation abilities to herself. She might need them later.

She'd thought to present him with the clues as evidence of her usefulness, but when she'd come to his office, he'd glared at her as if she were the very devil and said, "Unless you are producing the man who sired you, I don't bloody care what you have."

"But it could still help," she'd said with a smile. "I've been rather industrious."

His expression hadn't changed. "Then why are you still here?" He'd snorted to himself, shaken his head, and gone back to whatever he'd been working on.

And that had been one of his more polite moments of late. At any given time, he was surly, he was cross, and he was rude.

Which ought to have been normal by now.

Except they had been passed this.

He was avoiding her like the plague, and when he did see her, there was a sneer etched into his features. It wasn't fair, and it wasn't anything she could explain. As far as she knew, she'd not done anything to upset him. She'd actually become more biddable and docile in recent weeks. He could quite freely order her about these days, and she wouldn't even snap at him. But instead, he was sharp without warrant and absent most of the time, only leaving instructions for tasks and no word explaining anything he was doing.

It was as disheartening as it was irritating.

Even Gent had no answers for her. He'd only shrugged and said it was probably something personal, and he would be moody until he figured out what to do about whatever it was.

That was not helpful.

For pity's sake, Amelia was in agony over how she had left Lord Wharton and could not close her eyes without feeling his lips upon her again, and she needed work and distraction to keep herself from going mad! If she thought about it for too long, she would begin to cry, and she absolutely could not cry at the offices. One and Two would see, and they would start to fuss, and then Callie would start fighting with them while trying to help Amelia feel better, and either Rogue or Gent would show up demanding to know what the fuss was about.

And beyond all that, it would be a terrible display of emotion, which she simply refused to succumb to.

Not in front of him.

Then again, if he were never around, she could do whatever she pleased and pay no consideration to him whatsoever. He would never know how she carried on when he was not present.

One day, she wore trousers she'd nicked from the boarding house laundry, and while One and Two nearly burst with anxiety, no one else even noticed.

What was the point in being shocking if the person you wished to shock did not notice?

After a full week of this, Amelia decided she'd had enough. No more avoiding Rogue's office for fear he would lash out at her, no more going to Gent to circumvent him, and no more being biddable.

What had that ever done for her? She was Amelia Eloise Tribbett, and she was a force to be reckoned with.

Now, she was in charge.

She rose from the desk she'd been sharing with Two, brushed off her faded calico and took a deep breath.

"What are you doing?" Two asked hesitantly.

She gave him a hard look. "What I should have done days ago."

"That sounds ominous," One said, shifting his spectacles.

She turned to scowl at the slight man. "Are you as bored as I am?"

He shrugged. "Probably. But I, at least, have other things to work on. You're not the only client, you know."

Amelia frowned a little at him. "I realize that. But we had been making progress, and now nothing? What else am I supposed to do? Wait for him to decide to work my case again?"

One shrugged again, as he tended to do. "You've got brains. Find a way to make him."

"That sounds like a horrible idea," Two protested, shaking his head vigorously.

"I like it," Callie announced, sticking her head into the room.

Two scowled at her. "No one asked you."

The blonde woman snorted. "Like that matters."

"It ought to," he muttered under his breath.

Amelia looked at Callie a little speculatively, her mind whirling.

Callie met her eyes, then narrowed her own. "What's in your head, Amelia?"

"Ideas…" she said slowly, gesturing for Callie to come fully into the room.

Callie did so, looking at the clerks in confusion.

Amelia tapped her chin with a finger, circling Callie carefully. They were of a size, and had similar features, aside from Callie's eyes being green. Why, if Amelia had the blonde hair she'd worn the other night, the two could quite easily pass as sisters. Provided they both cleaned up a little and dressed properly.

It was a thought.

"Well?" Callie asked, putting her hands on her hips.

Amelia beamed at the maid. "Nothing, for now. But I might have need of you for a special project in a few days."

Callie returned her smile. "That sounds promising. Why not today?"

Why not indeed.

Amelia had tossed the idea of seeking out her supposed aunt, Dottie Chapman, ever since she'd learned of her existence. But there was a vast difference between talking *of* one's relations and talking *to* one's relations. This was her mother's sister, and she did not think she dared to face her yet.

As frantic as she was for answers, perhaps she was not prepared enough to cope with the consequences of them.

She only meant to find her father, not dredge up painful memories of her mother, and with all of that, she'd just found more questions, more confusion, and more heartache. She could not venture further into that while she still ached herself.

She'd always pitied her mother for loving someone so violently as to die from it, and when she'd found her diaries and read them, she'd wondered why in the world she would continue to write to someone who was obviously never going to return to her. What use was there in pining in such a way? Why cling to such agony?

That was before she had experienced those intense feelings herself, the closest to love she had ever come, and perhaps had found, as fanciful as it sounded. And she understood her mother in a small way, now. Why, she'd even begun her own diaries to him, never addressing him directly for the sake of privacy and propriety, but as her mother had done.

Dearest love.

It helped to pass the days, to not hurt so much, imagining someone else reading the passages of her day and her feelings. Eventually, the tears would fade, and the ache would lessen, but she did not want to forget.

She couldn't.

Her eyes suddenly burning, Amelia sniffed loudly and avoided eye contact with the others. "I'll just go have a word with Rogue, then," she said, her voice rough. "Surely he has something for me to do by now."

"Watch out for the flames," Two called. "He's been right foul all morning."

Amelia stopped and glared at the young man. "So have I."

Without checking for a reaction, she marched out of the room, desperate to control her breathing and force the impending tears away.

She refused to cry in front of Rogue.

He would only snap at her, and in this state, she might cry more because of it.

On the other hand...

She shook her head, smiling in spite of herself. That was a ridiculous idea, and it might not even work. Rogue did not act according to the pattern of other men. He might not care that she was crying.

The Rogue who took her to Surrey would have. The Rogue in this office would not even blink.

She straightened her shoulders, exhaled slowly, and then barged into the room without knocking, as she always did.

Such a grand entrance ought to have received an equally grand reaction. Alas, in this instance, it failed.

Rogue was asleep.

On his desk.

Such a chance did not come every day. Amelia smiled with all the impish delight she could conjure and tiptoed around to get a better look at him, and to assess just what sort of trouble she could cause.

She frowned as she approached, Rogue's features becoming clearer.

There were dark circles under his eyes that were an almost ghastly purple. He was slightly pale and very drawn, lines on his face making creases that ought not to be there. His shirt was wrinkled and limp, and he had not shaved in days. His hair, while usually wild, was utterly disheveled.

He looked somehow very young and very old at the same time.

But there was not anything amusing in this.

Amelia bit her lip and reached out to shake his arm. "Rogue."

He mumbled something unintelligible, groaned a little, and squeezed his eyes more tightly shut.

She looked heavenward with a sigh. If she were ever to have any saintly acts to her name, ignoring the perfect opportunity to do something childish and quite rude to Rogue would be chief among them. She shook him harder. "Rogue!"

He jerked awake with a cry and sent a few papers flying in his agitation, looking around the room wildly. "What? What is it?"

Amelia backed up hastily, raising her hands. "Nothing, Rogue. It's all right."

His chest heaved as he stared at her, his eyes still slightly wild. Then, at her nod, he inhaled sharply and sat back in his chair. "Thank you," he said roughly, looking away. "I hadn't realized I'd drifted off."

Somehow, he looked even worse awake than he had asleep, and Amelia found herself quite concerned. Perhaps it was the contrast between the pale color of his eyes and the darkness of the circles. Perhaps it was the lack of vibrancy in his countenance. Perhaps it was the strain that had returned to his features. Whatever it was, she was not immune to the sight, and no amount of anger towards him could displace her sympathy.

Her silence must have been suspicious, for he turned to look at her, eyes narrowed. "What did you do?"

"I beg your pardon?"

He rubbed at his eyes and looked around carefully. "You came into my office and found me asleep. I would hardly expect to survive the experience or come out unscathed. Is there a guillotine about to fall upon me?"

Amelia managed a faint smile but could not find the humor. "Rogue..."

"Or perhaps a bucket of ashes?" he suggested, looking towards his door as if the bucket would rest upon it.

"It is a thought," she murmured, not following his gaze.

He craned his neck, then grabbed the back of it with a wince. "Or perhaps you are just going to let me live in a sort of suspended terror for a few days by admitting nothing."

"That would be more my fashion."

Rogue sighed, then looked over at her, eyes clear at last. "Why are you staring at me like that?"

"You look terrible," she said bluntly, forgoing sympathy in favor of honesty.

He blinked at her slowly, then his brow furrowed. "You woke me up to insult me? That's low, even for you."

She scoffed quietly. "It's no worse than your treatment of me the last few days. I could say far worse without any twinge of guilt."

"That's because you don't feel guilt."

Recognizing his tactics as diversionary, Amelia folded her arms and leaned against the bookshelf behind her. "Rogue. How long as it been since you've slept?"

"Three minutes or so."

Now she had to smile, but she kept her gaze fixed on him. "You know what I mean."

He shook his head, sitting up and turning back to his desk. "It's nothing," he said too quickly, rifling through papers aimlessly.

"For pity's sake, Rogue," Amelia snapped, "you look like someone has wrung you out and hung you out to dry. You're the worst version of yourself that I have ever seen, and I did not think that was possible after these weeks. I am not in the mood to be sparred out of genuine concern just because you don't feel like admitting something is wrong. Stop being so damned proud and stubborn and tell me what is going on!"

He stared at her in surprise, and she could see his mind whirling as he tried to find some way out of doing precisely what she asked. Then he exhaled, and she could see the weariness more clearly. "It's been a few days," he told her with a sort of rawness that spoke volumes, "since I've slept."

Somehow Amelia managed to keep her relief in check and only nodded slowly. "Do you want to talk about it?"

He hesitated, then shook his head. "I can't."

"A case?" she prodded, watching him closely, waiting for some sign she could adequately interpret one way or the other.

"Yes," he said slowly, drawing out the word. "A case."

She didn't believe him for a second, but she would never claim to know everything that Rogue did, and she freely admitted that it was possible she was wrong. But he was hiding something, and she would figure it out.

"Like mine?" she suggested.

Rogue exhaled roughly and rubbed his hands over his face. "No. Not at all like yours."

She chewed her lip, fearing that he was nearing the end of his patience, and not knowing quite how to proceed.

"Someone is missing," he went on, which surprised her, "and it is important that I find them."

"Someone you know," Amelia added, sensing there was much more to the story. "This isn't just business; it's personal."

He nodded, his throat working. "Yes."

Something in her heart, and she wasn't sure exactly what, started to hurt a little. Rogue seemed far more tormented than he would ever admit, and for someone like him, that was astonishing. "Trouble?" she asked quietly.

"I don't know. I'm trying not to think about that." He shook his head quickly. "There's no reason to think that, I just can't seem to…"

"To find them," she finished, sighing a little. "All the extremes are going through your mind, even if they are not logical."

He nodded to himself. "I know how the process goes, and I have all the connections. I have told clients time and time again not to think the worst and to let me do my job, but…"

"But there's no one to tell you that. No one to be you. Very well, let me try." She cleared her throat. "Stop worrying like a ninny. You don't know anything. They will be found, they will be safe, and this will be nothing. Stop interfering in the investigation and let me do my job, or you can find someone else with fewer skills, less contact, and a higher price to make a hash of the whole thing." She cocked her head and lifted a brow. "Fair enough?"

He laughed a little. "That almost sounded like me. You forgot to curse, though."

Amelia shrugged without concern. "It was implied." She quirked a grin and then let it fade almost at once. "Did it work?"

Rogue exhaled loudly. "Maybe. I don't know. We will see, I suppose."

She did not care for his defeated tone and decided another tactic might work better. "So, you've been working yourself into the ground trying to do your job, and worrying yourself halfway to the grave, and snapping the heads off of everyone around you, because it isn't working."

He looked up at her with an inscrutable expression. "True," he finally said.

"And because it's personal, you can't talk about it."

"Also true."

"Because anything personal makes you break out into hives."

"That's hardly fair," he protested with a hint of a smile.

"And this means you can't work on my case because yours comes before mine."

He scowled now. "Amelia."

She shrugged, a little pleased that she'd managed to goad him out of his mood even a little. "It makes perfect sense. So, while you go on your merry chase, I will take matters into my own hands."

Now Rogue shook his head fiercely. "No, that is a terrible idea, and I refuse."

"Refuse." She snorted. "Weren't you the one who told me it was my case and reminded me that *I* hired *you*? You're so tied up in knots and half asleep, I could take control and solve the whole thing before you realized you were clueless."

He lifted a thick brow at her. "Clueless? Really?"

"You've been at a stalemate all week," she reminded him. "What else can I presume?"

"I have been a trifle busy!" he protested, his eyes starting to flash a little.

"I would *like* to have been busy," Amelia retorted while flinging her arms out. "I've done nothing but sit around here waiting for you to tell me what we were doing next and having the very great pleasure of you bellowing at me like I took whomever you're looking for, and neither of those things was a particularly pleasant experience."

Rogue pushed up from his seat and leaned across the desk. "You are not the only priority here!" he barked. "You have no idea!"

"Then give me something to do so I can move us in one direction or another, because right now you are stuck in the middle and going nowhere at a breakneck pace." She folded her arms again, trying not to smile.

It was odd, but Rogue in a rage was the most encouraging thing she had seen all week. There was a fire in him now, which had been gone for too long. His behavior of late had been a different sort of temper, darker than before and more heartless. There was nothing he cared about and an odd mania about everything he did. But without life or heart.

This anger was much more like it.

Rogue's jaw tightened, and for a moment, she thought he might lash out again. But then he turned and went to the chest that remained in his office. The diaries she had, but everything else in the chest had remained.

He returned with a sheet of paper and thrust it at her. "There. You can go to these places."

She read over the names quickly, then looked up at him. "These are shops on the east side."

He almost rolled his eyes, she could tell. "Very good, your royal genius."

Amelia clamped down on her lip as she scanned it again. "Dressmaker, mercantile, milliner..." She jerked her head up to look at him. "Why here?"

"Because I thought you might want a hat," Rogue snapped. "I analyzed the diaries and did some digging in the chest, and I believe your mother spent more time in London than we thought. But not in Cheapside. She might have worked as a seamstress for some of these shops."

"How did you think of that?" she asked, folding up the paper and clenching it in her hand.

He gave her a patient look. "Because the lists in her chest were not shopping lists, but tasks. And the mending was skilled, so I made a logical leap. Pity her daughter did not inherit those skills," he added, pulling at a stray thread near her shoulder.

Amelia slapped his hand away with a playful scowl. "You're letting me go out into London alone?" He had been so adamantly opposed before, it seemed odd now.

"Did you want an escort?" he asked with his customary snide smirk. "I'll see if Two is free, but it's not the Seven Dials or the docks. Even you should be able to keep out of trouble there."

Biting back a squeal of excitement, Amelia whirled from the room. "Thank you, Rogue!"

"For getting you out of my hair? Any time."

She ignored him as she skipped out of the office and grabbed her bonnet, smirking at the astonished clerks on her way out. Once outside, she inhaled deeply and sighed, then looked at the little girl with wide, dark eyes near the front step.

"Come along, Daisy," she said with a smile. "You'll want to be able to give a full report after this, and if you keep up, I may give you sweets."

Daisy grinned and fell into place beside her, chattering away about the sorts of sweets she liked best, and Amelia was content to hear all about it.

Freedom and progress were excellent distractions, and hope began to burn once more.

Chapter Fourteen

"*I*'m good at this. I am. I'm a spy, dammit. I'm the best bloody investigator in England."

"If you say so."

Gabe glared at Rook, who leaned in the doorway of his office. "Shove off, peacock."

Rook smirked easily, striding into the room and closing the door behind him. He was dressed less finely than usual, which always was appreciated in these offices, as finery had no place here. And it was easy to forget that Rook was just as impressively skilled as the rest of them, and possibly more so when he was all frills and airs.

It didn't make Gabe any more pleased to see him, but it did bear remembering.

"What's the trouble?" Rook asked, taking a seat without invitation.

Gabe hesitated, unwilling to let anyone else in on his hunt for the goddess, and embarrassed that he was struggling with what ought to have been a simple enough task for him. And then there was the fact that it was completely unrelated to any of his professional interests, either for the Crown or otherwise, and he was not supposed to have a personal life.

Besides all of that, it was Rook. There was no way in hell he would tell him anything remotely personal about himself. Or the woman he wanted.

No way.

"Rogue, I'm not about to intrude upon your privacy or make you divulge secrets," Rook announced with a snort of indifference. He crossed a muddy boot over his knee and gave him a wry look. "You've been a right bear these last few days and now that Gent's back, I've lost my traitors. I'm bored out of my mind, and nothing is happening in my finer circles. Give me an occupation, I beg you. Or I'll be reduced to going to Weaver for suggestions, and I hate begging."

Gabe scoffed and sat back in his chair, feeling himself relax a little. "Boredom is not something we are accustomed to here."

Rook smiled without humor. "I am not accustomed to it at all. Not in my nature."

"Nor mine."

There was a long pause that felt oddly companionable, and then Rook spoke again. "It's too quiet, Rogue."

He nodded once. "I know."

"I don't like quiet."

"Nor do I."

Rook drummed his fingers against the fabric of his trousers, his brow furrowed in thought. "Why the quiet?" he asked carefully. "We hardly thwarted their grand scheme by removing Castleton's source of funds, yet everything has gone silent since then."

Gabe shook his head, an odd shiver starting down his spine. "I honestly don't know. My contacts have not had new intelligence for ages, and there doesn't seem to be any movement in any other quarter. It doesn't make sense, but we only ever had a small glimpse into various pieces of their plans." He sighed and rubbed his brow hard. "And it doesn't help that my life is getting ever more complicated. I cannot go undercover as I have done before, and it drives me mad."

That drew a chuckle from Rook, who slung an arm over the back of the chair. "Well, I am very good with complications." He gestured faintly at the papers under Gabe's arms. "Something in there I can assist with?"

"Not this, no," Gabe replied at once, shaking his head. "But perhaps…" He glanced towards the door of his office, mercifully still closed from Rook's entrance. "Something else."

Rook sat forward, suddenly looking eager. "Do tell."

Gabe smirked a little. "Would you prefer dockside or high

Society?"

"Either." Rook grinned when Gabe raised a brow. "Believe it or not, cravats are not as fun as one might expect."

"I believe it." Gabe nodded thoughtfully, then said, "But I'm afraid it is cravats for you for now. I need you to take a drawing around to some of your more discreet associates there and see what you can drum up."

"What are we looking for?" Rook asked, not looking disappointed in the least.

"Anything," Gabe told him, handing the picture of Amelia over. "Quite literally, anything."

Rook took the picture in hand, and his brows shot up. "You're not serious…" He looked up at Gabe for confirmation, all traces of humor gone.

Gabe felt the need to wince but avoided doing so. "Nothing adds up," he admitted reluctantly. "Why seek me out specifically? Why hide things when she claims she has nothing to hide? Why the desperation? Why…?"

"Why does she speak French better than I do?" Rook murmured, a knowing look entering his eyes. "Especially when she has no reason to."

"Exactly."

The two shared a look, and Rook nodded somberly. "I'll see to it." He rose fluidly, turning towards the door. "You know, I like Amelia. Quite a lot. I hope I find nothing."

"So do I," Gabe replied quietly, belatedly realizing how the words could be taken. He glanced up at Rook, who was suspiciously composed.

Rook tilted his head slightly. "Did you know she knows all of the good French curses? Some that even I had never heard of."

Gabe snorted. "That does not surprise me in the least."

"That she knows them or that I don't?"

"Both."

Rook sneered and gave a mocking bow as a farewell, then left the office as silently as he had entered.

Gabe stared at the doorway for a long moment, wondering if there might be more to Rook than he'd considered before as well.

But that might be nothing, and it was best not to get carried away with ideas.

"Rogue!"

Gabe groaned and put his head down on his desk. Amelia had been blessedly absent from the offices for two days seeing to the shops he'd listed. They were viable places to investigate, granted, but he'd handed those off merely to be rid of her for a time, and he highly doubted anybody would be able to give them anything of use. It would have been more than twenty years ago since Mary worked there, and the odds of anyone remembering her were low.

He was hoping Amelia would have gotten distracted or stalled in the efforts, and knowing her stubbornness, she would have continued to work at it without involving him until she could give him some progress.

Gabe shuffled the papers on his desk so that her affairs were on top and leaned back in his chair just as she burst through the door, beaming like a bloody ray of sunshine.

Perfect.

"You'll never guess what I found!" she chirped, flinging off her bonnet and starting on the buttons of her coat.

"I know what I hope you found," he muttered, pretending to make notes on the paper before him. Honestly, how was he supposed to manage to find the goddess with all these cursed interruptions?

Amelia ignored him completely and perched herself on the small table against the wall. "I found three people who knew my mother."

Gabe paused his pretend marking and glanced up at her. That was unexpected. "Did you, now?" he asked, keeping his voice even.

She nodded rapidly, her smile somehow spreading further still. "Mr. Clark at the mercantile did not recall her, but said his father might have done, and asked me to return today, which I did, and we had a lovely afternoon tea while he told me all about her. It seemed she worked with him while she waited for her intended to establish a home for them so that they could wed."

Gabe raised a brow at her. "Why not just marry her straight away? There's plenty of cheap housing for a couple in need, and I presume they were both working…"

Amelia scowled at him playfully. "I will have you know my

mother was cut off by her family, and working was difficult for her at first."

"Poor thing," Gabe said with absolutely no sympathy whatsoever. "Perhaps she should have chosen better."

That earned him a dramatic eye rolling. "One cannot choose where one plants one's affections, Rogue."

"One most certainly can," he protested, "and it sounds as though your mother chose poorly. At any rate, continue."

It might have been better for her to ramble on than actually to engage in conversation.

He could ignore rambling.

"She was still Mary Clairbourne, the elder Mr. Clark said," Amelia went on, swinging her legs like a child. "I found that odd. Why would she not change her name when she had been cut off?"

Gabe thought that was a stupid question, as it gave her some answers, and who would know the Clairbournes in that part of London? But he kept his mouth shut and continued to look busy.

"He was simply lovely," Amelia was saying, sighing a little. "Much kinder than I would have expected. And I suspect he was the first one to hire Mother, which would have been shocking, considering she had no practical skills. But he said she was good with numbers, so…"

Gabe stopped listening for the sake of his sanity. He really did not care what skills her mother possessed or did not possess. He needed clues as to the man her mother married if they wished to get anywhere in this investigation. And as nothing Amelia was saying had any validity there, he could ignore her to his content.

It was interesting, however, how different her voice sounded when she was pleased. He had grown so used to her sniping at him, to their heated discussions, or to her matter-of-fact recitations, that this particular tone was virtually unknown. It was almost musical in quality, and not grating or tinny like others he had heard. It was quite a pleasant voice, not that he would ever admit that or compliment her in any way.

Heaven only knew what that might do to her.

"Mrs. Folsom at the milliners, however," Amelia said suddenly, raising her voice with some agitation, "was of the opinion that my mother was a perfect waste of space." She broke off with a snort. "I don't know why she hired her to help if she was so useless."

Neither did Gabe, but it seemed to fit. A young miss from a decent family working in that part of the city? She would have been dreadful at anything.

Amazingly, Amelia was still talking. "Her interview was terribly short. No loss to me, I'd rather move on myself. I showed the picture to nearly every shop up and down that street and the two beyond, so I got quite a good idea of the area. Many of the others said the picture looked familiar, but could not give me any details, as I expected."

Gabe pushed himself out of his chair and moved to the bookshelf as if looking for some reference to aid him. In truth, he would rather have used one of the dusty tomes to bash himself in the head and end this. He could yell at her, he supposed, but it took so much effort, and she was more easily dealt with if not being attacked. And besides, he liked this musical voice, if only he could tune out the words themselves.

"And then I went to the dressmaker's," Amelia gushed, "and Mrs. Talbot and her aunt were kindness itself. The aunt worked with my mother, and said the sweetest things…"

Oh, this was worse than being tortured, and he knew that from experience. He closed his eyes as he stood there, hoping to drift off at some point. Musical voice or not, it was wearing on him. If he were asleep, it would be only music and no lyrics.

"But, and this is interesting, she was Mary *Cole* when she worked there, and though the aunt could not place a year on when Mother worked for her, she did say that she had to give up her position when she was too great with child to help." Amelia made an amused sound that seemed half a sigh, half a laugh. "I could have talked with them all day, Rogue. It was like having Mother back with me, only she was happy."

There was something about her voice that he could not grasp, something about those warm tones that took him to another place entirely. The more she spoke in that way, reminiscing and inviting, the more torment he felt. If he imagined it enough, if he let go of his reality enough, he could almost find himself back out on that terrace, with a tempting and sweet creature born out of his most secret desires. She was speaking to him in her soft lilt, light as a breath and twice as entrancing, and he was just as captivated. He could almost feel her hand on his again, could smell that faint floral scent that followed her, and his heart pounded thunderously in his chest and ears.

He had to have her. He had to.

Blindly, he turned to his goddess and took her face in his hands, feverishly pressing his lips to hers in a maddening frenzy he could not help, could not control. He could not let her go, his hands tightening against her face as his desperation heightened. He could not. He *would* not.

Scant seconds later, with the stiffening of the goddess in his arms, sense and reason returned to him, and Gabe realized with horror that he was not holding the goddess.

Just Amelia.

He flung himself away with a curse, barely acknowledging her widened eyes and bewildered expression. How could he have done something so foolish? How had he completely lost himself in his own thoughts and daydreams, enough to push him into madness and embrace Amelia instead?

Embrace. He thought back faintly and cringed. He had practically assaulted her in his energy and enthusiasm.

"I am... so sorry," he panted, pressing his fists against the nearest wall and lowering his head. "So very sorry. I cannot..."

Amelia said nothing, but he could hear her breathing, hard and unsteady.

He clenched his eyes shut, every muscle in his body tightening. "Amelia, I cannot apologize enough. I never meant to..." He forced himself to push away from the wall and look at her.

She stared at him, blinking slowly, utterly inscrutable even for him.

Gabe forced his arms to remain at his sides and unclenched his hands. "Amelia, I am so sorry. Please forgive me."

Her throat worked on a swallow, and she wet her lips carefully. "For kissing me? Or for thinking I was someone else?"

Impossibly, he could not find the words to answer her straightaway. In a bizarre twist of fates, the moment her tongue had touched her lips, his attention had gone there as well. And now the only thought crossing his mind was the mad idea to kiss her again.

Except it seemed the furthest thing from mad he'd ever thought.

Which was, of course, entirely mad.

"I don't... normally," he began unsteadily, trying to keep his thoughts in line, "just kiss a woman."

Amelia exhaled roughly, shaking her head, pressing a hand to her chest. "Could have fooled me. You seemed keen enough."

He took two hasty steps in her direction. "It wasn't..."

"Me?" she interrupted with a tilt of her head. "I know. It's whomever she is in your head. The one you can't find. You'd rather be kissing her than helping me, and considering your response just now, I can see why." She chuckled a little roughly, smiling at him. "If she can make you forget yourself, and who you are with, she must be quite a woman. You don't even like me, and you nearly hauled me off."

Gabe ran a hand through his hair, trying not to smile as he scoffed. "I did not."

"Close enough," Amelia retorted with a snort.

He gave her a frank look, letting his mouth curve a little. "I like you well enough."

Another snort. "High praise."

Now he exhaled with some irritation, the madness passing. "Look, can we move past this? I'd rather just forget..."

"Forget you kissed me?" Amelia quipped, quirking a brow. She shook her head quite firmly. "Not likely. It was quite a kiss. I'd love to see what it's like when you actually mean it."

She was teasing, he could see it. She was on the verge of laughing. But he wasn't.

He was so very far from laughing it was almost laughable.

Could he? She was pretty enough; he'd already admitted that, and he liked her well enough. Why not? His heart pounded harder at the thought, curious and willing, and wondering.

Willingly kiss Amelia?

"It's a thought," he murmured, considering her carefully.

Her eyes widened again, and she reared back a little. "What is?"

He allowed his lips to curve more fully. "Kissing you."

Amelia gasped faintly, her body going completely still. "How…" she finally managed, her voice breaking. "How much of a thought?"

He was already moving towards her as she finished. "This much," he whispered as he took her face gently in his hands and kissed her much more carefully than before.

She did not stiffen this time, but she did not respond for several heartbeats. He was undeterred, and gently brushed his lips against hers, grazing and teasing until she relaxed in his hold. And he was startled to find that he enjoyed kissing her. Quite a lot, as a matter of fact.

Her hand eventually slid up to gently rest on the back of his neck, and he rather enjoyed having it there, toying a little with the curls at his nape. She was very sweet, he decided. Sweet and soft, and while not particularly responsive, she was rather indulgent of his innocent display. He kept it all very controlled, very contained. He did not want to get carried away again, or Amelia would get the wrong impression.

What exactly that impression would be, or what the current impression or intention was, he could not have honestly said. All he knew was that he wanted to kiss her and keep kissing her.

What a startling thought.

Gabe broke off gently, leaving his hands fixed along her jaw and in her hair, touching his forehead to hers. He noticed, with a small grunt of appreciation, that her breathing was just as rough as his.

Ah, so she was responsive after all.

Excellent.

"What was that for?" Amelia whispered, eyes still closed, trying to find her breath.

Gabe chuckled and brushed his nose against hers. "You asked."

"Did not."

"Did too."

She shuddered a little and sighed. "Well… Rogue…"

"Gabe," he said before he could stop himself.

She opened her eyes and pulled back just a little. "Excuse me?"

He considered her for a long moment, wondering if he dared to repeat himself. He'd never told anyone his real name. He was far too private and protective of his identity. He didn't even know if he trusted this woman, or her story, or anything about her. But he could not find the suspicions he once had. He could think of a thousand reasons not to tell her. But none of those reasons seemed to find their way to the front of his mind.

He *wanted* her to call him by his real name.

And it scared him senseless.

But he was trained to move forward under the influence of fear. And the feeling of this woman between his hands and this close to him was more than he could withstand.

"Call me Gabe," he murmured, brushing his lips over hers gently. "When it's just us, I'm Gabe."

Amelia smiled and drummed her fingers along the back of his neck. "Gabe," she repeated as if testing it out. "I like the sound of that."

"I like it when you say it," he admitted, slightly embarrassed by the absolutely maudlin nature of his answer. But it was true. He did like it, in a very odd, possessive sort of way.

She tilted her head at him, eyes narrowing. "Are you complimenting me?"

"Never," he insisted, relinquishing his hold on her and stepping back a little. "I would never do something so ridiculous."

"I didn't think so," Amelia replied, sliding her hand down from his neck, and making a pointed effort to dance her fingers along his shoulder and arm as she did so. "But then, I didn't think you would ever kiss me, either."

He seized her hand as it reached his and turned it over. "I like surprising people," he growled. "Get used to it." He brought her palm to his lips and chuckled at the way she jumped.

"The kissing or the surprising?" she asked faintly.

Gabe took great delight in the wolfish grin he cast at her as he let her hand go. "Both."

Amelia pretended to swoon and grabbed onto the table behind her for balance. "Oh, lord."

He smirked in her general direction as he rounded the desk and sat down again. "Thank you."

Her brows snapped down, and she glared at him. "That wasn't a compliment, either."

"Sounded complimentary to me." He shrugged and leaned back

in his chair. "I just kissed you senseless after all."

"I am not senseless!" she protested, putting her hands on her hips.

"I didn't say you *were* senseless," he pointed out. "I said I kissed you senseless."

"And I say you did not!"

He gave her a knowing look. "Yes. I did."

She dipped her chin and smiled a tight smile. "No. You didn't. And I would like to see you try and accomplish *that.*"

He shrugged and started to rise, only for her to thrust up her hands defensively. "No!" she ordered, eyes wide, a hint of panic in her voice. "That was *not* an invitation. Or a challenge."

Gabe eyed her up and down in one slow motion. "Pity, that."

Amelia rolled her eyes and sat back down on her table. "Get a hold of yourself. One kiss and you're a schoolboy."

"I can assure you, I was much worse as a schoolboy."

She hooted a laugh, leaning back. "Now that, I believe." She smiled at him warmly, then frowned.

"What?" he asked, not entirely sure he wanted to know.

"If that is going to happen again," she started slowly.

"It just might," he interjected, surprising himself with the ease of admitting it.

"...then I am assuming," she continued with a flash of a smile at his words, "that we are keeping this to ourselves? Particularly here?"

Gabe blanched in horror and looked at the door. "Damn... Absolutely. No one can know."

Amelia was already nodding. "Absolutely. One and Two would never recover from the shock."

"Rook and Gent would never let me hear the end of it," he added with a shudder. He looked at her with doleful eyes. "You wouldn't want me to regret kissing you, would you?"

Amelia could not have looked any more superior in response. "That, my dear Rogue, would be presuming you would find regret in kissing me at all."

He opened his mouth to respond but found nothing except a mischievous smile and the desire to kiss her again. But he would remain where he was and smirk instead. "Outside of this room, we are to bicker as much as we did before."

"I believe I can manage that," she replied, folding her arms.

"I never doubted you."

They smiled at each other a little, and Gabe replayed the last few minutes back in his mind for good measure. Then he sat up, his amusement fading. "Wait a moment, did you say your mother was Mary *Cole* for some of the time?"

Amelia looked surprised, then derisive. "You weren't listening, were you?"

"Not a bit," he replied without shame. "Tell me again. Spare me the sentimentality. Just the facts."

"You think that's significant?" she asked, all teasing gone.

He nodded slowly, satisfaction and a hint of excitement filling him. "I think it could be something." He pulled out a fresh sheet of paper and gestured to her. "Come over here and tell me again. I want to get this down."

Chapter Fifteen

$\mathcal{T}$here was no doubt in Amelia's mind anymore about why he was named the Rogue.

None whatsoever.

In fact, he was the most entertaining sort of rogue she had ever come across in her entire life. Which only proved that first impressions were not always correct.

But sometimes they were.

When he chose to be, he could be playful, teasing, engaging, or even romantic. He'd been all those things in a very short time, and her mind spun with the effort to keep up with him. And he was a troublemaker. Oh, he very much enjoyed that and took great pains to be so. And, if she were forced to admit it, she rather enjoyed it as well.

She'd honestly believed that after he'd thought their kiss over, after reliving it, he would have decided that it was a horrible idea, and he had no interest in it further. After all, he was vocally dismissive of women in general, no matter how well he might treat them personally. It would only follow that he would have some serious regrets about developing any sort of personal relationship with her.

Not that a kiss or two would necessarily indicate an actual relationship of any personal nature to follow. She was intelligent enough to know very well that one could kiss anyone for any reason.

But Rogue... Gabe, she reminded herself yet again... had been mischievous and teasing the day after he'd kissed her. He'd been just as ruthless with his barbs and expressions before all the rest, but the moment they had entered his office and had a moment alone, he had again taken her face in hand and kissed her quite soundly.

She was woman enough to be dazed, and he'd loved that. He'd smirked proudly and tapped her cheek. "I like putting that expression there," he'd said in a low voice that made her toes curl, and then he'd gone back to his desk as right as rain and gotten straight to business.

Except nothing was strictly business anymore.

Amelia was always staring a little too long, and he was always smiling just a little too much. But surprisingly, they weren't embarrassed about it. She'd told him time and again to be himself, and he'd scold her for gawking, and they would laugh about it.

They laughed all the time now. Teasing and playing, gadding about London in whatever costumes Tilda drummed up for them, staging brilliant fights for the clerks and other investigators, and generally making whatever mischief they could. And when they were alone, things were more comfortable. Safer. And he'd started to hold her hand when they were close enough, and his kisses... well, she was getting quite used to them, and it was surprising how gentle such a rough man could be.

And they were accomplishing a great deal together, despite their newfound affinity for kissing each other. He'd made her recite everything she remembered about her interview with Mrs. Folsom, and then they'd gone around speaking to more people about her mother and this new last name of Cole. No one seemed to know if Mary Cole was married or not, as she did not wear a ring, and she never spoke of her fellow.

But everyone agreed that she had one.

Which did not help at all.

Amelia found herself growing more and more frustrated with their efforts, but Gabe, surprisingly, was not. He was only becoming more determined and gaining more confidence. He adamantly refused to let her get discouraged with the process, and it meant a great deal to her that he cared enough to do so.

But it wasn't enough.

She needed proof, she needed answers, and she needed them now.

Gabe had given her what information he could about the landlord for the cottage in Surrey but said he'd not been able to question him yet. He'd skirted around the issue with some rather weak excuses, but Amelia knew the trouble.

It was the woman in his head.

She cursed whoever she was for distracting Gabe from her case, but she also found herself a little pleased to know she existed. It made her hope. If Gabe could care for that woman, whoever she was, so deeply, want her so passionately, then he was not as indifferent to the world as he pretended to be. And if that were true, then perhaps... well, she was growing rather fond of the irritating man who kissed so well.

But that would stay her little secret. For now.

As would her escapades tonight. Heaven only knew what he would say if he found out what she was up to.

She'd given nothing away this afternoon while they'd finished up their rounds of the boarding houses in the area they presumed her mother had lived in. Gabe had believed her tired and perhaps discouraged, as she had intended, and not commented on it when she announced she would be returning home for the evening. It was a risk, as he tended to be suspicious of everyone and everything, and especially wary of her, even in fun. Even with little Daisy following her, she'd not felt any urgency.

When she'd seen Daisy leave her post, as she usually did in the early evening, Amelia dressed quickly in the rough clothing she'd nicked from the laundry a few days ago. Worn men's clothing would hardly go missing, and the dark colors were perfect for what she needed. She'd gone about London at night before, but not for this purpose.

Well, not in some time, at least.

And she was being followed these days.

Not that Daisy was a particular hindrance. The child was delightful and adorable, and, once Amelia had assured her she would not be in trouble for being made, was content to share many stories with her about her day, her life, and the other children Gent had working for him around London. It was an odd thought to be tracked by a child, but she saw the wisdom in it for their purposes. No one notices a child, while a child notices everything. It would be quite useful for any investigation and notification of trouble.

What Amelia did not know was if another person were assigned to her when it was too dangerous for a child. Someone, perhaps, less friendly, less inclined to befriend her, and more able to hinder her movements.

Hence her disguise.

She tied her hair back tightly and tucked it into a cap, which she pulled down low over her eyes, and checked her appearance in the small mirror on one wall.

A rather dirty and young-looking boy looked back at her, and she smiled with satisfaction. She'd never pass for a man, but she did not look at all feminine either. And with the dark clothing, she could blend in as well as she needed to in the streets at night.

Slipping out of the room quietly so as not to disturb any of her neighbors, she made her way down the hall and turned to the servants' stair, which she'd found the other day and paid a maid to show her the way out. She'd paid her again today to leave the servants' entrance unlocked until after she had verified Amelia's return.

It was quite a luxury to have funds at hand.

Granted, she did not have much, and all she used for her stay here and the venture itself consisted of all that she had. When all of this was over, she would be starting from the beginning again.

She shook her head as she quietly exited the building and started down the rapidly darkening street. Amelia could not think about what was going to happen after this. She needed to find her father, and that was everything. After she accomplished that, she could manage anything.

Amelia Tribbett was a survivor, and she would find a way to do so again.

She nodded firmly to herself and ducked into an alley to cut across a few streets without the trouble of hacks and foot traffic. She felt herself smiling, inhaling the unusual fragrance of London's darker side, and finding it as welcoming as any smell in the world.

London had been her home for far longer than anyone would have guessed and meant far more than she had ever let on. It was not without its evils, and she shuddered at the faint memories she had spent years overcoming, but she had also found herself here. This was where she had truly become Amelia Tribbett, though her name had been hers since the days of the poorhouse.

She'd been trained in mimicry and fighting, pickpocketing and finery, stealth and intimidation. And she'd learned French from the sort of Frenchman that did not bother with schoolroom lessons.

Oh, yes, London had been an education for her. She'd found her thirst for vengeance in its undersides, and those who knew her had fueled her fury. They knew she was better than her surroundings, that she had been cheated of a better life, that someone must pay.

And someone would.

But tonight, she only needed answers that nobody else seemed interested in or willing to obtain. She had no reservations about what she was about to do and was so out of practice, she was actually looking forward to it.

Stealing the address of the landlord at his London address had been only too easy, now that Gabe was a bit more easily distracted. Once she'd had that, she copied it down for herself and then returned the original before he'd ever noticed anything amiss. And conveniently enough, she knew precisely where the address was, how to get there, and, more importantly, how to leave the place without raising any suspicions.

The dark and filthy edifice of the building was suddenly before her, looming its imposing nature over all below, and no doubt causing many to turn to find some more welcoming place for their evening's entertainment or residence.

Amelia, however, felt her excitement rise and pressed forward with a confidence she had not felt in quite a long time.

London was a very different place at night. Darker, deadlier, and while the bustle of the day was gone, its pace was just as swift.

It was only a trifle harder to see it.

And it happened in almost complete silence.

Gabe shoved his hands into his trouser pockets, ambling down the dark and winding streets of London's dockside quarters with all the ease that Gent or Rook might have wandered Mayfair. He never quite fit in those areas, title or no. He was meant for lesser things, for darker places, and for more treacherous realms.

Then again, Society had its own sort of treachery, and its effects were just as deadly.

He shuddered to himself and craned his neck. That was no place for him.

This was his world, and he was welcomed in it.

Various individuals greeted him as he passed them, keeping their voices down in an almost reverent tone. He'd earned quite a reputation down here, and it was not the sort of thing one discussed outside of these streets. He enjoyed being feared, and he enjoyed being left alone.

His thoughts were company enough tonight.

Amelia was on his mind more often than he cared to admit. Kissing Amelia was on his mind far more often than it ought to have been. And finding answers to Amelia's case... well, that was somewhere in his mind, but the other two topics were more prevalent. She was the brightest part of his day, and he could say such without feeling remotely sentimental. It wasn't saying much, considering the way he lived and what his days consisted of.

Still, she had proven herself to be much more than he'd thought she would be, and she was one of the wittiest people of his acquaintance, male or female. She was quick-minded, sharp-tongued, and could turn him absolutely mad with rage. But then, in a second, she could have him grinning and teasing, sneaking kisses as though he were some ridiculous puppy chasing after a high Society miss.

Except they were not in Society, so they could behave without any of the niceties there.

What a delicious thought.

He found himself chuckling, wondering what she would say if she knew what he was thinking. Though he embarrassed her as often as he could in the privacy of his office, he had always been careful and gentle where his attentions were concerned. He had no intention of making her his mistress or any ridiculous notion of the kind. He enjoyed being able to confer with her on clues and information gathered, be his usual cynical self, and be able to kiss her at will or display any sort of attention, without any expectation.

It was odd, but when she was close, he found himself wanting to touch her. To hold her. He'd even found himself toying with her fingers on occasion without ever realizing he had taken her hand.

But it was working.

His desperation over the goddess was fading.

Oh, he had not forgotten her. He could not. He searched for her at every opportunity, had some of his more trusted sources investigating when he could not, and still dreamt of her some nights. But the madness was subsiding. He could sleep at night. He had focus in all his work, no matter which part.

He supposed he could say that Amelia had stabilized his teetering ship in the storm of his own emotions. She had set him to rights.

Gabe snorted to himself. Rights? The woman was infuriating, entertaining, and downright absurd. But heaven help him, he loved the madness she provided.

Which was not to say that he loved her.

He was not *that* mad.

Love was not an emotion he was capable of. He had loved his mother, he was sure, and he certainly felt great affection and loyalty for his aunt, when she did not plague him, but those were familial bonds and quite a different sort. He was not a man who would give himself up for a woman, nor the kind to sacrifice himself for anyone but himself and his own interest.

Oh, all right, and for the kingdom, country, and crown. And perhaps his brothers-in-arms, if he was feeling generous.

Maybe not Rook, but the others, surely.

But that was all. His heart was not that big, and he rather wished it would continue its purpose within him rather than be taken by some female with no notion of what to do with it.

Then again…

His chest tightened at the thought of a white gown draped perfectly over a trim form, moving elegantly through a crowded ballroom, a gold mask obscuring her features, but not her grace, not her essence. Not her passion.

A crash nearby took him out of his thoughts and back into the present, and his instincts reared to life. He shoved the goddess back into the lockbox of his mind, focusing on his task at present.

He'd had enough with the politeness of his day-to-day office life. Amelia certainly livened it up, but he had not been a spy for so long that his life felt tedious, even with her spirit. He needed to feel alive again, he needed to feel the thrill of danger at his fingertips, needed to whet the skills that had made him who he was.

He'd saved this particular errand for a time when he felt the thirst for action rising within him, and tonight was it.

It was a rather insignificant task, considering his usual fare, but given the utter silence of his more critical challenges, he would take what he could get.

A landlord mistreating his tenants when one of them was a woman he was coming to hold in high regard was an excellent excuse to become the Rogue again in truth.

The damp cobblestone added a fine chorus to his steps as horses and other members of the nightlife trod upon it, and soon enough, the address he sought was before him.

He couldn't believe Amelia hadn't asked about this again, and, in fact, *did* not believe it. He suspected she was going mad underneath her relatively calm exterior. After that day he'd looked so terrible in her estimation, she'd made a concentrated effort not to plague him, and it was a refreshing change.

She would be delighted with the information he could present to her in the morning.

With that thought, he pushed open the door to the building and made his way up the creaking stairs, examining the crooked and leaning walls as he did so. Why would someone with holdings in the country live in a place like this, he wondered. Even when he had been nothing more than a wastrel without means and morals, he'd chosen better furnishings.

No matter, it would make this interview far more suited to its task.

When he reached the proper apartments, Gabe tested the doorknob and, finding it most unwisely unlocked, shoved his way into the room without knocking.

It was dark, dank, and sparse, even for a cheap apartment like this, and it smelled quite oddly of almonds and starch. There was no sound but the weak crackling of a fire in the hearth, and a strange, muffled noise from the room beyond.

Gabe made a face and rolled his eyes as he moved in that direction, hoping against hope that he would not find anything more unpleasant than vermin in here. On cue, his boot kicked something small and soft that squeaked, and he stepped quickly to his left, not even bothering to glance down.

The sitting room of the apartments was in complete disarray, furniture overturned, and one leg of a chair cracked and splintered. The bottom of the drapes on one side had been jaggedly cut, and the fabric was not found in the surrounding area. Two candles flickered on an untouched table in the corner, and a series of small, dark stains on the floor led into the bedchamber, where more faint light flickered.

He forced his breathing to slow even as his heart quickened. Quietly and efficiently, he scanned the room for whoever had caused this chaos. Finding no one hiding there, Gabe slowly and stealthily continued forward, his boots making no sound on the worn floorboards. Pressing his back against the door, he inched his way into the room, scanning it quickly with his eyes.

He felt a sharp jab of disappointment when he found a portly man in a bloodstained linen shirt and button-less waistcoat moaning on the floor, his mouth gagged with the drapery fabric. The man looked up at him with pleading eyes, one of which was swelling and darkening, which did nothing for Gabe's mood, and flailed his tightly bound hands in distress. His arms had been skillfully pinioned to his sides, and his nose was swollen and caked in the same blood currently taking up space on his clothing and on the floor.

"Dammit," Gabe muttered as he completed his search of the bedchamber. Finding no one hiding here, either, he pursed his lips and stared at the pathetic man. "Please don't tell me you're Alderson."

The man nodded, making another muffled sound of distress.

Gabe frowned at him. "Shut up. It's not as though I can understand you."

The man's brow furrowed, and he attempted to heave himself to a sitting position but could not manage to do so.

Gabe watched with amusement as he continued to try. "Maybe if you rolled to one side," he suggested mildly.

That did not go over well with Alderson, who ceased his

ridiculous wriggling and lay still on the floor, gazing up at the ceiling, still fuming.

"I'm not going to play nursemaid," Gabe told him as he strode more fully into the room and sat in a sturdy chair by the fire. He rocked to the back legs and folded his arms. "I was coming to do roughly the same thing. Only I would have broken a few fingers, and you wouldn't be conscious at this moment."

Alderson jerked to look at him, eyes as wide as they could go, which was not far for the left.

Gabe nodded in confirmation. "Yes, and a rather pleasant sleep you would have had, but you would have paid for it with a raging headache tomorrow. Although…" He sniffed and glanced around the room, then snorted at the impressive collection of bottles in the corner. "You were already destined to have one. And that would explain your rather unfortunate girth."

Alderson made some noise of protest, but Gabe silenced him with a look.

"Now," Gabe continued, rocking his chair a little, "I am going to remove your gag, *only* the gag, and then I will ask you some questions. You are going to answer the questions honestly and completely but without being annoyingly longwinded, and we will proceed accordingly. If you fail these simple instructions, I will take care of that other eye, your kneecaps, and possibly some internal organs."

He saw the bulky throat work several times and allowed himself to smirk a little.

"Are we agreed?" he asked as congenially as Rook might have done.

Alderson nodded so rapidly his head thumped against the floor.

"Steady on," Gabe scolded, righting his chair and going over to the great lump. "No one is that excited to see me. I have a reputation to maintain." He grabbed at the wad of fabric and tugged it free.

Alderson gasped and choked, gagged a few times, and indulged in some very dramatic breathing, as well as some rather colorful attempts at curses, which were slurred, either from drink or the swelling and bleeding lip he sported.

Gabe sighed and gave the man a look. "Are you quite finished?"

Alderson groaned and twisted to his side. "Help me up, then. Choking on my own blood is a beastly business."

The cultured tone of the man's voice surprised him, even if it was rough and low in timbre. That was an interesting paradox. Gabe hauled the man to a sitting position and waited for him to adjust himself back against the foot of the bed.

"There, now," Alderson said with a sigh, closing his eyes. "That's better. How can I be of assistance, sir?"

Gabe smiled at the faintly patronizing tone in the man's voice. "You own and manage properties in Surrey," he said, returning to his chair. "More specifically in Elmbridge."

Alderson looked at him with a darkly furrowed brow. "What d'you want in Elmbridge?"

Gabe raised a brow. There went the cultured tone, and, as he suspected, the man was a great pretender and nothing more. "I want to talk about a cottage on the road to Finley, about seven miles from Cobham."

Alderson made an irritated noise and leaned his head back against the bed. "Oh, blimey, no' again. No' twice in one night."

Gabe frowned at him. "Again? Who else asked about it?"

"Few weeks back, some bloke took a shining to it," Alderson said, sniffling loudly. "Asked all sorts o' questions. Seemed to think I'd done something wrong."

"That was my man," Gabe interrupted shortly, leaning forward in his chair and folding his hands together. "I don't care about that. What about tonight?"

Alderson gave him a bleary look. "I already answered the lady's questions about the cottage near Finley and Cobham."

Gabe stilled and stared at the man for longer than he normally would have, but a sheen of red suddenly obscured his vision. He blinked twice but could not clear it. "A lady?" he repeated in a cold, stiff tone, the hairs on the back of his neck standing at attention. "What lady?"

Alderson must have been more intelligent than Gabe gave him credit for. He looked bloody terrified, and with good reason, and he sat up straighter. "No more than fifteen minutes ago, sir. Lady came in dressed as a bloke in dark clothing, snuck up on me as I was 'aving a drink, walloped me over the head, and when I came to, I was tied to the chair in the sitting room."

Gabe closed his eyes and fought for control, his temper raging and running rampant through him. "Tell me," he managed through clenched teeth, "what she looked like."

"Tall," Alderson said quickly, his voice rising in pitch, "big eyes, strong jaw, and stronger than she seems. Hair was in a cap a' firs', but she took it off, and it was brown, and she wore it tied back. She... she knew her way 'round a knife, sir. And throws a punch like any street fighter I ever saw. Smart-mouthed, too. Cheeky as a devil. If I weren't scared she'd gut me, I'd have taken a shine to her."

Gabe's head snapped up, and he favored Mr. Alderson with a seething look that he felt to his toes. His heart was pounding in his chest with anger, with indignation, and, he would admit, with a good deal of fear.

Amelia had come here to find this man, who was at least twice her size and ask him questions in the middle of the night. She had the situation sorted, obviously, but the evidence of her efforts only made him shake further still. He should have known she wasn't as complacent as she'd appeared. He ought to have seen her plan before she'd ever set foot out tonight. And he would most certainly be having a word with whoever the hell was supposed to be tailing her when Daisy went home. She ought to have been protected. She should never have made it halfway to the building tonight. She should... well, she would hear all about what she should and should not have done when his hands found her smooth little neck in the morning.

In the meantime, he had a job to do.

He shoved out of his seat and went over to Alderson, lowering himself to meet him at eye level. "You will tell me everything you told her," he ordered in his most dangerous tone, surprising even himself. "Every single detail."

Alderson began to protest at once. "I already answered her..."

Gabe slammed his fist into the side of the man's massive head and gripped his greasy hair to turn his face back to him. "I said every detail," he growled. "Even the insignificant ones. You will tell me what she said, what she did, in every detail. Do you understand me?"

The wide eyes widened further, and he tried to nod.

"If," Gabe continued in the same manner, "there is anything else I want to know, you will oblige me by answering those questions. And when we've finished our little interview, if you have done well, I will cut the ropes around you, kindly ignoring the fact that you were quite thoroughly bested and thrashed by a woman half your size and age. Then, I will leave you to your bleeding peace and drink. Do you understand me?"

Alderson nodded frantically, his head lolling against the mattress.

"Answer me," Gabe barked, fury rolling off him in great waves.

"Yes, sir!" Alderson chirped, his voice nearly squeaking.

Gabe sat back on his haunches, exhaled slowly, and fixed his gaze on his victim. "Very good. Start at the beginning, if you would be so kind."

Chapter Sixteen

$\mathcal{S}$he was late.

It irritated him that she was late.

If she'd had the evening of a woman who behaved herself, as she was supposed to have done, she would not have been late. She would have had a quite pleasant night's sleep and not been so fatigued that the rising would have been difficult. Then he would not have been pacing his office like a madman waiting for her to arrive, so he could throttle her, yell at her, hold her, then throttle her again.

Or maybe he would yell and then throttle. Or berate.

Any of the alternatives sounded appealing at this point.

At three in the morning, he'd considered abducting her from the boarding house and interrogating her about her idiocy, but he'd decided, halfway into changing his clothes, that waiting until he had some rationality would be a better choice. Let her think she was safe in her anonymity for the moment. Let her be quite proud of herself for the time being.

Hell would rain down on her shortly.

He was not anywhere near rational at the moment, but he'd had several hours to concoct a scathing rant that made him feel quite proud. There would probably be tears on her part, a good deal of defensive yelling, and she would probably shake with sobs and humiliation.

Perhaps he would hold her at that point, but he might just ignore her tears altogether.

Killing was preferable to kissing in his mind at present.

But murder tended to be frowned upon even in his station,

particularly when the reason had nothing to do with national security or endangered British citizens.

One particular British citizen was in very great danger at this moment. He wondered, faintly, if that counted.

He heard the outer door of the office open and found himself smiling with satisfaction. He moved to the front of his desk and leaned against it, folding his arms.

The seconds ticked by, and he could hear the low murmur of voices from the front. His instructions to the others had been clear, so it was only a matter of time.

At that moment, his office door opened. Amelia was staring back into the front office in confusion as she untied the ribbons of her bonnet.

"Did something happen?" she asked by way of greeting as she entered. "One and Two hardly said a word, and they looked quite uneasy."

"Shut the door," Gabe replied simply, keeping his voice as even as possible.

Amelia looked at him at once, eyes wide, her hands freezing in the action. "What's wrong?"

He gestured with his head. "The door."

She turned to close it instantly, then yanked off her bonnet and went to work on her spencer. "What is going on, Gabe? You're frightening me."

"Good." His voice was clipped and sharp, and he did not care. He let the fury that had been simmering beneath the surface rise again and enjoyed the way it seemed to ripple across his body.

Amelia shed her jacket and put her hands on her hips, staring at him intently. "What is going on?"

"You tell me."

Her eyes widened, and she gestured incredulously with one hand. "Tell you what?"

"First," he drawled coldly, "you can tell me what the hell you were thinking last night."

She stiffened at once, and her hand dropped to her side. Gabe watched as her eyes shifted from curious and worried to denying and defensive, then finally, to cold and vacant, her expression suddenly a mask. "You know," she said in a hard, lifeless tone.

He smirked a little. "Would you like to know how I know?"

She scoffed and folded her own arms, averting her eyes. "Probably some oaf you had tailing me."

"No," he barked at once, shoving up from his desk. "The oaf I had tailing you *should* have told me, but he didn't notice anything, which I'm sure was your plan all along. If he had done his duty, you would never have made it ten paces outside your door, because he would have forced you back and guarded the bloody door all night long." He barely restrained the snarl he felt rising within him. "He is no longer tailing you. That apparently impossible task now belongs to someone who really does have better things to do that are fairly significant, but since you are determined to be reckless and idiotic, he is now all yours. And you will absolutely be prevented from these nighttime adventures in the future, should you decide to be so foolish ever again. Congratulations, I hope you are satisfied."

Amelia's jaw tightened, but she did not move from where she stood. "Hardly," she muttered.

It took all his strength and restraint not to go over and shake her. Instead, he skewered her with a look. "I beg your pardon?"

She shook her head quickly, then asked, "So, how did you find out, if I may be so impertinent as to ask?"

Damn, she was impudent, and if he weren't so furious, he would have been markedly impressed. And amused enough to want to kiss her.

But he *was* furious.

And he wasn't.

For his own sake, he ignored her tone and offered a placating smile. "Because Mr. Alderson told me."

Amelia's fair eyes went wide as saucers, and she faltered back a step. "You...?" She swallowed, and her cheeks flushed slightly. "You were there?"

He continued to smile, now quite tightly, and nodded at her. "Indeed. Apparently shortly after you, as he was still bleeding, and he had quite a good memory for detail once I convinced him to share."

Amelia turned away and raised a shaking hand to her brow, the other still planted on her hip. "What did he tell you?" she asked unsteadily.

"Everything," Gabe replied with clear emphasis. "All that you said, all that he said, everything you did, every perfect detail down to the ill-fitted boots you wore that were somehow worn in the toe even though they were obviously too large for you." He smiled thinly. "Who did you steal those from?"

She jerked her neck around to glare at him. "Excuse me for not having the proper attire in which to interrogate someone. I'm a bit out of practice."

"Dammit, Amelia!" he barked, his control snapping. "Do you have any idea what it was like to find out that *you* had been the one to get there before me? Any…" He trailed off, shaking his head. He moved around his desk, shoving his hands into his hair, turning away from her.

"Did I wound your pride, Gabe?" Amelia snapped, and he could hear the sneer she undoubtedly wore. "Take all the fun out of your night? I had everything sorted, and I am not some pale and swooning miss who needs a nanny to cross the street. I was raised in the gutters, Gabe. I know far more than you think."

He clenched his hands at his sides and lowered his head. He could not relive last night, could not bear to think what might have happened, but he could not let her think this was about him. That his reputation or pride somehow took precedence over…

"You went into a situation," he tried, keeping his voice low and as controlled as he could manage, though it shook a little, "without knowing any of the facts. You didn't know how big Alderson was or if he had been drinking. You didn't know what I knew about him. You were entirely unprepared…"

"Not entirely," she protested hotly. "I told you I knew…"

"…unprepared," he said again, his voice rising sharply. "Unprepared and untrained for anything you would find. You showed you could accomplish the task you went to do, I grant you, but just because you *can*, Amelia, does not mean that you *should*." He swore with a hiss, his fists balling up again. "It was rash; it was reckless; it was bloody dangerous; and…"

"You were worried."

Her tone had completely changed, soft and clear, no longer

defensive but full of wonder.

He shook his head immediately. "Don't be ridiculous."

"You were worried," she said again, this time with confidence, still keeping her voice soft, and it pierced his heart as surely as any bullet or blade had ever pierced him.

He forced out a weak chuckle, knowing it was pointless to deny it any further. "Worried? I was bloody terrified!" He forced his eyes open and released a long sigh, looking up at the ceiling. "And the worst of it was that you'd already done it. I couldn't even see straight, and that man just sat there, waiting for me to get on with it, while I imagined every twisted scenario with you in it. Everything that could have gone wrong, every injury you could have sustained, every…" He exhaled sharply and shook his head. "Damn you, Amelia!"

"You were worried?" This time it was a question, and it sounded far too sentimental for his taste.

He looked over his shoulder at her, almost annoyed that she was smiling. "Don't read anything into that."

Amelia was moving instantly, her intent clear. "Oh, Gabe…"

He backed up hastily and held out a hand in warning. "Don't come over here. I've more than half a mind to throttle you for being a bleeding idiot. I can't promise anything."

Her smile was placating as she reached him. "I'll take my chances," she murmured as she slid her arms around his waist and laid her head against his chest.

For a few moments, he didn't do anything. How could he? His internal battle between punishing and embracing her had never been stronger, and he had never been a demonstrative man. Well, in the pleasant sense, at any rate.

He was enthusiastically demonstrative in other ways.

But as Amelia clung to him, as her warmth permeated him, he felt himself soften, sigh, and then, before he knew what he was doing, he was hauling her tightly against him. He buried his face in her hair as a few shudders racked his frame, the feeling of Amelia the only thing keeping him grounded. He was clutching at her, possibly painfully so, but he couldn't help it.

He needed her to be safe, to be secure, and to be here. With him.

"Gabe," she said softly, running her hands gently along his back.

"It's all right. It's all right."

"Never again," he growled, gripping her hair tightly in his hand. "Do you hear me?"

He felt her nod against him, and the sensation shot all the way down to his toes. It gripped him fiercely as he held her, clenching at his heart, a gnawing possessiveness suddenly coursing through his veins. He tugged her head back a little so that she could meet his eyes.

"I mean it," he growled, his voice rough. "No more. I can't..."

She nodded, smiling a little and laid a hand on his cheek. "It's all right. My case, but your investigation, all right?"

He searched her eyes for a long moment, then turned his face to kiss her palm. "Right," he murmured against the skin. He moved his hand down to her chin and tipped her face up for a kiss, which soon became a gentle, teasing sequence of kisses that did nothing to settle him, but they did force his fear back into the shadows.

Amelia gripped the back of his neck with both hands and broke the kisses, pressing her forehead against his. "I'm sorry," she whispered. "Forgive me?"

He exhaled roughly and shook his head against her. "It's going to take me a little time. I will forgive you, I have no doubt, but right now..."

She nodded, leaning back a little in his hold. "I understand. It's too soon, too fresh."

He swallowed with more difficulty than he'd ever done. "Are you... injured? At all?" He scanned her face carefully but could not see much of anything. He tried to recall how she'd entered, if there were any indications of pain or discomfort, but he'd been too focused on other things to pay much attention.

"No," she said softly. "I'm perfectly well, I promise." She gave him a little smile. "You don't have to worry about me so much, you know."

"I didn't know I *did* worry about you so much," he admitted, not bothering to hide his surprise. "It never occurred to me until suddenly I was in the throes of it."

Her smile grew and hit him somewhere in the middle of his chest. "That's so sweet."

Gabe groaned and stepped back, dropping his hands and shaking his head. "Don't say that. There isn't anything more emasculating than sweet."

Amelia hummed and moved to a chair, sitting quite properly. "What about endearing?"

He snorted and sat in his own chair, propping his feet up on the desk. "What am I, an aged busybody relative who says all the wrong things?"

"Precious?"

"Not a fluffy dog."

"Attractive?"

"Well…" He paused, considering that. "I like that one." He flashed her a brief grin. "Any more like that?"

Amelia laughed and reached for her reticule. "Maybe later, if you behave."

"I shall attempt to do so," he replied, nodding obediently. He watched her rummage in the small bag and then snorted softly. "What are you looking for, Amelia?"

"My notes," she grunted, sounding rather disgruntled. "I could have sworn I put them… Ah! Found it." She produced the folded sheet of paper and waved it.

His fleeting amusement faded a little. "From last night?"

She nodded once. "Pretend I didn't do something so offensive last night and compare notes with me."

It wasn't a bad idea, considering the events. He couldn't guarantee that Alderson had truly remembered everything, especially when he could not accurately say how long Amelia had been there. If she were any other operative, he would have done so.

But she wasn't an operative.

She was… well, she was something else entirely.

If he were not careful, she would become even more of something else, simply because it was becoming increasingly difficult to find reasons not to. And he found that being with Amelia was far better than being without Amelia.

Whatever that said about anything.

But for now, he could put his personal concerns, and emotions, aside and focus on the task at hand. Because dwelling on the rest was far less comfortable.

He nodded firmly and swung his legs off the desk. "Very well, then." He leaned forward, rested his arms on the desk, and looked at Amelia with what was hopefully a clear expression. "What do we know?"

That had been far too close for comfort.

Amelia let herself breathe a sigh of relief when Gabe had asked her to leave so he could see to other cases. He'd given her plenty to work on, including discovering details of her family in Hertfordshire using what he had found in his preliminary investigations, and she was content with that.

She leaned against the wall outside of his door and closed her eyes.

If only he hadn't been the one to discover she'd been to see Alderson. Anyone else could have done it and never quite put all the pieces together. Even if word had trickled back to Gabe that she had done it, he might not believe someone else's account. Surely someone like her could never have done the sort of damage to a man like Alderson that she had done, and she would never have been able to get the kind of answers from him that people claimed.

At least he had no idea that she had more ability than that in her repertoire.

It was far better that he think she was merely willful than know the truth. Then again, he always seemed to know more than she suspected. It was entirely possible that he already knew just what she was capable of.

She frowned as she considered that idea. Surely, after all these years, she was better at hiding things than that; he would never have been able to see anything of the sort.

Had he caught her lack of promise not to venture out again? She'd almost held her breath, expecting him to make her promise not to do it again. But he hadn't. Gabe was so used to having his way that he probably presumed, and wrongly, that his command was sufficient. After all, who would dare go against the edicts of the

Rogue?

Well, if it suited her to do so, she certainly would.

Not that she had plans to at this time, as last night had been quite sufficient. And after seeing Gabe's reaction and feeling the way he had held her, she was not particularly inclined to drive him to that again. Unless she could truly keep it from him.

She smiled to herself a little as she remembered it. It had been quite lovely, though. To know that he cared that much about her and her safety was rather heady. And he'd never held her like that. He'd never really held her at all before this.

She rather liked being held.

And she found that she rather liked Gabe. Quite a lot, actually.

"What are you smiling at?"

Amelia glanced over at Gent, coming out of his own office and smirking at her a little. She shrugged. "We've made some good progress," she said with real honesty.

"Have you indeed?" he asked, smiling with his perfect teeth.

She nodded and waved the papers in her hand at him. "I have leads to follow up on. Things to do. Problems to solve."

Gent had the good sense to at least pretend to be amused by her. "I see. And the sigh before that?"

Amelia gaped at him for a moment, then blushed furiously, averting her eyes at once and suddenly finding the need to tuck an invisible strand of hair behind her ear. "I'm sure I don't know what you are talking about."

She heard his low chuckle and glanced up at him.

He was watching her steadily but smiled with a sort of fondness that did not make any sense to her. Why should her interest in and feelings for Gabe make any difference to him? Or endear her to him in any way? Surely it was a sign of mental disturbance or deathly illness, more a cause for concern than amusement.

Nothing to make him look so pleased.

"Don't you have something better to do?" she muttered.

"Not really," he replied easily.

"Yes, you do," Rook announced as he strode into the room, his eyes dancing with far too much mischief.

Both Amelia and Gent straightened up, looking wary.

"Do I?" Gent asked his comrade, obviously at a loss.

Rook nodded slowly, still smiling. "Something's come for you. Out front."

Gent frowned as he glanced towards the foyer.

"Out there out front," Rook said with a laugh, indicating beyond the room. "Out. She's. Out. Front. Now."

Amelia was surprised to hear Gent groan and watched him move to the front and exit, his pace quick despite the apparent agony. The office door closed and no one in the front made any comments about it.

She looked over at Rook, who seemed to be restraining laughter. "What's so amusing about that?"

Rook leaned against the wall and considered her carefully. "I'm not sure I should tell you," he mused. "You might get the wrong idea."

"I'd have to have any idea to get a wrong one," she pointed out with a dry snort.

He flashed a smile that made her stomach flip, which made her feel guilty, which made her blush, which made her look away.

"Oh ho, what's this?" he asked, tapping her cheek.

She swiped at his hand. "Nothing!"

He made a quiet noise that seemed out of character, and she chanced a look up at him. He was not smiling now, but neither was he displeased. He looked at Gabe's office door intently, as if he could see through it and into the office beyond, and then he looked at Amelia again.

"Do you know what you're doing, Amelia?" he murmured in a serious tone.

Amelia reared back a little, confused by the sudden turn. "I think so…" she replied slowly.

He dipped his chin a little, his gaze becoming more pointed. "You think, or you know?" He shook his head slightly. "Can't be both."

"I have no clue," she admitted softly before she could stop herself.

That made Rook smile a little. "Well, that's all right," he said, pushing away from the wall. He nudged his head towards Gabe's office. "Neither does he."

Amelia's jaw dropped as Rook started to amble back towards his office, wondering how in the world her emotions, and her situation, were so obvious to Gabe's friends when they were trying so hard to hide it.

But if they knew...

"Rook?"

He stopped and turned to face her again. "Amelia?"

She bit her lip, hesitating. "Is it... is it possible? For someone like him to have feelings for... well, for any of it to be real?" She knew she was blushing furiously, but she had to know. "Can any of you have a real life beyond this?"

Rook gave her another too-thorough look, then looked beyond her back towards the front of the office. "He does," he finally answered, nudging his head in the direction Gent had disappeared. Then he looked at her and tilted his head towards Gabe's door. "He might." Then he looked towards Cap's door and exhaled heavily. "He used to."

"And you?"

He glanced at her with a small smile. "Only if I am very lucky, Miss Berger." He nodded at her and moved into his office, leaving her standing there with more questions than answers.

And a small but fervent flame of hope.

He might.

She straightened up and nodded to herself. She had work to do, and Gabe did too, and until they sorted this whole thing out, until they finished her case, there was nothing for her to hope for.

Her heart skittered to a halt as she heard faint whistling from within Gabe's office, making her smile yet again.

Well, perhaps she could hope a little.

Chapter Seventeen

"*But* why would you not tell me?"

"I can't tell you what I don't know."

"Balderdash. I refuse to believe you do not know."

"Would I lie to you?"

"You lie to me all the time!"

Gabe nodded thoughtfully at this accusation. "This is true."

His aunt threw up her hands and strode away from him, shaking her head. "I should have chosen your cousin Thomas as my heir. He was a sensible man."

That was a laughable thought, and Gabe snorted loudly. "Thomas was an imbecile who would have turned your holdings into a weak imitation of last century France without any means of supporting any of it. Your money would have been utterly wasted." He tilted his head with a cheeky smile. "And he was entirely without a sense of humor."

"At this moment, so am I," Geraldine snapped, giving him a cross look.

Gabe sat forward and defied his usual rudeness by pouring a cup of tea, adding two lumps of sugar and a splash of cream. "Well, sit yourself down, and have a cup of tea," he soothed, stirring it gently and holding it out for her. "It will all seem much less dramatic after that."

His aunt considered the cup for a moment, never looking at Gabe, then huffed and took it from him, sitting rather gracefully on the divan, despite her obvious agitation. "How did you know how I take my tea?" she muttered, flicking her eyes in his direction.

"I pay attention," he replied, sitting back easily. "And tea is not that complicated to begin with."

She threw him a scolding look. "You have no idea how complicated tea can get."

He held up his hands in surrender, trying not to smile. "Apologies, Aunt."

She sniffed and sipped her tea softly, then looked him over carefully. "Why do you look more proper this morning?"

Gabe looked down at his ensemble in surprise. "Do I?" He hadn't thought so, but perhaps the addition of a cravat and waistcoat, no matter how plain, did give him a more respectable air. His usual dress was a simple linen shirt and coat, if the coat at all. The nature of his work afforded him the joy of not having to adhere to the fashion edicts of Society.

But today, unintentionally, he had done so.

"Perhaps Houser has discovered a love for the finer things," he suggested, smirking playfully.

"Doubtful." Geraldine still stared at him, eyes narrowed. "What do you want, Gabriel?"

He folded his hands together over his tweed waistcoat. "Now what makes you think I want anything?"

"You called on me," she pointed out, her expression as serious as her tone. "I can count on one hand the number of times you have done that."

"Oh, please, that is completely…" he scoffed, trailing off as her look became more severe.

Dash it all, she was right.

He groaned and looked up at the ceiling. "I need your help," he confessed, each word feeling rather painful to state.

There was no response from his aunt, which was the most terrifying silence in the world, and he shifted his eyes in her direction.

As he suspected, she was gaping at him.

"Well?" he prodded, wincing just a little.

She closed her mouth, seeming to chew on her answer. "You…" she started, blinking as if she could not believe it. "You… need my help?"

Gabe closed his eyes with a rough sigh of regret. "Yes. Please."

"Good heavens. I did not know you knew that word."

He cracked open one eye to glare at her, which caused her to smile. "Are you going to be cruel to a man who has come for help?" he muttered.

Geraldine smiled, shaking her head. "Of course not. But I fully intend to relish the moment."

She picked up her tea to take another quick sip, no doubt to strengthen her constitution, then looked at him with prim soberness. "How can I help you?"

He really ought to forget about this whole thing. Involving his aunt was the worst idea he had ever had in the history of all ideas. But he was growing desperate, and she had the connections he needed. "The woman at the ball," he said at last.

Geraldine's expression changed into a doleful one in an instant. "I asked you about her not three minutes ago, and you said you didn't know who she was. What in the world am I supposed to help you with?"

"I don't know who she is," he said, echoing her tone exactly. He managed a weak smile. "That is the problem."

It was comical to watch Geraldine's face change as his words sunk in. The myriad of emotions ranged from confused, to incredulous, to gleeful, with a dozen others in between. One of her hands shot up to cover her mouth, though her eyes were free of tears or anything remotely sentimental.

"You wish to seek her out?" she asked with a merry squeak. "Oh my goodness, oh heavens, I never thought... I never even *dreamed* that..."

"Do get a hold of yourself, Aunt," Gabe sighed, attempting to feign indifference. "I only want to find her, not propose matrimony."

Geraldine laughed loudly, clapping her hands. "The fact that you want to find her proves that my plan worked. Your wife! Oh, Gabriel, this is divine!"

This was nothing of the sort. He sat forward and held up a warning finger. "She is *not* my wife. I don't know who she is or anything about her but what she told me at the ball. It is entirely possible that she is very poorly situated in life and quite shrewish to boot."

"I can only wish for both of those things," Geraldine replied with a false smile, "for then she would be your perfect match."

There surely were laws against the extermination of one's relations, but perhaps if he made it look as though a dreadful accident had occurred and appeared injured himself in the process…

"Let me fetch my guest list," Geraldine was saying, rising from her seat.

"I have your guest list," Gabe told her with a shake of his head, waving her back down.

She stilled, staring at him with hard eyes. "How did you manage that?"

He shrugged unapologetically. "I bribed a servant shortly after the ball."

"Which one?"

"Not telling."

She frowned and sank back into her chair. "Impertinent man. Why wouldn't you just come to me?"

Gabe smiled at her knowingly. "Would you have come directly to you if you were me? Be honest."

Geraldine pursed her lips, narrowed her eyes, and retrieved her tea again. "So, you have been trying to find her for some time now, and still have not managed it?"

He acknowledged her unspoken agreement with a dip of his chin and crossed his ankle over his knee. "Roughly, yes." He offered his aunt a weak attempt at a smile that he did not feel. "It seems your guest list is not entirely complete."

Geraldine smirked at him with some derision. "Of course, it isn't complete. I let others invite whom they wished."

Gabe stared at her for a long moment, then dropped his head back against the chair, groaning again.

That explained everything. There had been far more people in attendance than what was recorded on the guest list he had procured. It also explained why he had never seen the goddess before, and why no one could seem to help him find her. He had vastly underestimated his aunt's plans for him if she had allowed others to invite guests as well.

"You were that desperate to find me a wife?" he asked, closing his eyes.

"You'll thank me later. Perhaps at your wedding."

He snorted. "I highly doubt that." He rolled his head in her direction, forcing himself to look directly at her. "Who else invited people?"

Geraldine's brow furrowed, and her eyes clouded in thought. "Let me see... Gerrards, obviously... Whitlocks, Rivertons, Rothchilds, Townsends..."

"Good lord," Gabe moaned, sitting forward to put his head in his hands.

It was a list of the most popular names in London, and he was not on any particularly familiar terms with any of them. And he could *not* have word spread about that Lord Wharton was looking for a woman from the masquerade. That would unleash a hellish storm of societal panic and send the misses from that night into a frenzy, and who knows how many others that were not in attendance would have pretended to be her?

"Pardon me, ma'am," the voice of Geraldine's butler suddenly intoned from the doorway, "but there is a caller for you."

Gabe looked at his aunt, knowing how she felt about callers when she was already occupied. Her lips formed a thin line, and she gestured for the tray with the telltale card atop it. Plucking it up, she scanned the lines, then her mouth curved into a thin smile of satisfaction.

"Send her in," she informed her butler, replacing the card and sitting up straight. "And bring a fresh tea tray."

"Very good, ma'am." The butler clicked his heels and bowed, then swept away to do her bidding.

Gabe watched him go, then frowned at his aunt. "Is that how it's supposed to go? Goodness, I'll have to send Houser 'round for lessons."

Geraldine adjusted her black shawl, fidgeted with her blue crepe gown, and rested her hands in her lap at last, still looking a mite too superior.

Something was afoot.

He straightened up and glanced at the door, then back to her. "What is going on? Who is calling?"

"Someone else that I encouraged to invite guests to your masquerade," Geraldine said airily, her smile mischievous now.

"Geraldine..." he warned.

"Lady Raeburn, ma'am," the butler suddenly announced in a grave tone.

Gabe was out of his seat in half of a second and heading for the side door of the room. There was absolutely no way in *hell* that he was going to...

"Geraldine, darling!" gushed the unmistakable tones of the most terrifying, if not influential, member of London's finer Society.

"Tibby!" his aunt cried in delight, rising from her seat. "My nephew was just saying how delighted he was at the prospect of seeing you, isn't that right, Gabriel?"

Gabe turned to face the women, less than five paces from the door he yearned for and fought back a rather blistering curse. "Delighted," he repeated, sounding anything but. "Absolutely."

Lady Raeburn gave him a reproachful look as she embraced his aunt. "Come now, Wharton, you know very well you were fleeing."

"He would *never*..." Geraldine protested, stepping out of the embrace.

"He would," Gabe and Lady Raeburn interrupted as one. They shared a faint smirk, and Lady Raeburn crooked two fingers at him.

He debated for longer than was polite, because, really, it was Lady Raeburn, and while she was widely renowned as a wonderful woman, she was also interfering and eccentric and altogether unpredictable. None of which were Gabe's favorite things.

Geraldine cleared her throat and widened her eyes meaningfully at him.

Barely restraining the urge to roll his eyes, Gabe trudged back over to them, plucked Lady Raeburn's hand up, and gave it a perfunctory kiss.

He was surprised that Lady Raeburn patted his cheek after that. "It's so nice to see you pretend at the niceties, Wharton," she said with a cheeky smile.

He chuckled and inclined his head playfully, forgetting that, when it suited him, he actually liked this vibrant and intimidating woman. She was everything in the extremes, from her flaming red hair, to the rather expensive looking blue silks currently draped around her form, to the feathered monstrosity upon her head, and her long fingers were almost all decorated with brilliantly jeweled rings. One had to appreciate her for what she was, whatever that was.

No one ever quite seemed to know.

"I do try," he informed her, "but sometimes pretending is so tiresome."

She clucked and sat on the divan next to his aunt. "Don't speak to me of things tiresome. They take up at least two-thirds of my day."

"Then may this interview with my aunt be the least tiresome of the lot," he said with false earnestness. He bowed and started towards the front door of the room.

"Gabriel!" Geraldine scolded loudly. "You are to join us."

He turned with a look that quite plainly said, "Must I?" and was rather perturbed at her nod.

He was a grown man with no tendency towards gentlemanly behavior, but it was somehow impossible for him to go against his aunt in any manner whatsoever.

Somehow managing not to grumble, he resumed his seat and took three of the biscuits with the tea service.

"It is fortuitous that you are here, Tibby," Geraldine said, giving Gabe another warning look before turning to her friend. "We are rather in need of your assistance."

"Indeed?" Lady Raeburn asked, looking between them with interest.

Gabe held up his hands and made a face of adamant refusal.

"Gabriel is looking for someone," Geraldine continued without heeding him. "A young lady from the masquerade. And it requires the utmost discretion, you understand."

He could have strangled his aunt if he were sitting closer.

Lady Raeburn looked at him with calculating eyes. "Discretion is my middle name, my dear. Do please go on."

It was safe to say that Gabe was in a foul mood when he returned to the office that afternoon. He'd tugged off his cravat on the walk and removed his jacket when the day became too warm for it. His aunt and Lady Raeburn had been ruthless in their interrogation of him, and their methods would be something he would have to remember when he next had a suspect in his care.

Or perhaps he could refer them to Milliner for her expert use. She was always looking for additional ways to help improve the skills of the young ladies of the Convent who would be future spies.

They could not have had two better teachers.

He hated how exposed he had felt before them. He'd managed to avoid sharing any intimate details, sticking purely to the facts of the situation and refusing to indulge them in their more ridiculous sensibilities. As a result, he was not sure if they believed him in love, indifferent, obsessed, or simply mad.

At this point, he did not care.

He entered his office and tossed his jacket and cravat in the corner, not caring if they became wrinkled or stained. Houser could deal with that if he chose or purchase new ones if he did not. Funds were no longer an issue for him, despite his aunt's desperation to foist more upon him, and he could certainly afford new clothes.

He sank down in the chair behind his desk and waited for someone to descend upon him, whether it be the clerks, Amelia, or Gent. Someone would. They always did.

Being forced to relive those moments with the goddess today had been sheer agony. Even now, weeks later, he wanted her with a desperation that bordered on madness. He had found control over it, but when all his barriers had been torn down, and the heart of the matter was laid bare, the wounds were as fresh as the day she'd caused them.

He was not used to feeling this way, and it unnerved him. He had spent years cultivating his exterior and hardening himself against all things personal and emotional, and he'd done quite an efficient job of it. After the pain of losing his mother, and the poor adolescence he'd endured both with his uncle and at Winchester, it had been far better for him to feel nothing. And then to form so strong a bond with his cousin Alex despite all of that, only to lose him as well.

There was nothing Gabe hated so much as the raw torment of vulnerability.

It made him feel weak and powerless, and he could not abide either.

"Gent! Rogue!"

He jerked, suddenly alert, and was on his feet in a moment, racing out the door. The clerks never called like that unless it was something urgent. His mind raced through every possibility, every scenario. His thoughts seized upon Amelia. What could have happened to Amelia? Or was it something bigger? Something had happened. But what?

Part of him was relieved when he saw Amelia sitting in the corner she had arranged for herself, looking confused, and concerned.

He nodded at her, but moved on, Gent following directly behind.

A man in rough clothing with a rougher countenance stood in the foyer, looking at the two clerks as if they were the stupidest things he had ever seen.

"Can we help you, sir?" Gent asked in a polite voice but keeping his accent very common.

"Yes," the man grunted, tapping his cap, which he did not remove. "I'm looking for Mr. Turner."

It was as if all the air was suddenly sucked out of the room, and Gabe felt the earth shift beneath his feet.

Mr. Turner had been Trace's deep cover name during his dockside investigation. Surely it was a coincidence. No one ought to know that name.

"Mr. Turner," Gent managed to say after a pause that he hoped their visitor missed.

The man nodded, scratching his chin. "Aye. It was a long time ago, but he told me if I ever saw anyfink out of the ordinary down by the east docks, I was to come and tell him. I plum near forgot until the strangest thing happen' t'other night." He shrugged and fumbled in his coat pocket for a dirty handkerchief that he used to wipe his brow. "Right pleased to have 'membered Mr. Turner, an though' he'd like to know."

Gent looked at Gabe with far too much understanding, and

Gabe jerked his chin once.

He would investigate this himself, whatever it was, but Gent would do the questioning. Gabe could not manage it.

It had been Trace, he was sure of it. Alex was always leaving small clues and tips around, trusting that people would remember and give him the information he needed. The most maddening part of it was that it always worked.

And here it was again.

"Follow me, sir, and I will take down your information," Gent said, gesturing towards his office. "Mr. Turner is out on assignment at the moment, but I will relay everything you tell me to him directly."

The man nodded and followed without a word, his shoes making an odd squelching sound on the floor.

Gabe stood there for a moment after they left, clenching and unclenching his hands as his jaw worked.

"Blimey," Two whispered. "What was that about?"

Based on the sound that followed the question, Gabe assumed that One slapped him in the back of the head. He didn't bother to look but returned to his office and closed the door behind him.

He couldn't breathe for the life of him. One of Trace's aliases coming up now, after weeks of nothing? Years after everything had settled, after he had died for his cursed investigation, it was coming up? He wasn't ready for this, couldn't bear remembering how he had been helpless to save his cousin. He would never forget the sounds of that night. A knife piercing flesh ought not to sound so thunderous from across a stretch of water and a dock. He had imagined Alex's face a thousand times in his mind at that moment, as he'd been too far away to see it.

They'd all had their own injuries that night, but none had hurt so painfully as that sound, and the knowledge that it brought.

Gabe exhaled roughly, surprisingly fighting against a rising tide of tears, which he was quick to quell. No matter what Weaver and the other Shopkeepers said, this wasn't over and would never be over for him. He would find out whatever was going on down there at the docks, and whatever Alex's work as the Trace meant to it. He was a spy, and his comrade had died for this cause.

He would see it completed.

A soft knock at his door brought him out of his thoughts, and before he could open his mouth to acknowledge it, the door opened.

Amelia peered in, her expression soft. "What can I do?" she asked quietly.

He shook his head, swallowing with a little difficulty. "Nothing," he told her, his voice hoarse.

She gave him a searching look, then entered the office and closed the door behind her, placing her back against it. "Gabe…"

Something about the tenderness in her voice, the way she said his name, broke whatever resistance he'd thought to have, and he wordlessly held out a hand to her.

She came to him at once, and he pulled her against him, resting his chin against her brow. "I did not need that today," he managed. His words were choked and rough, and he folded his arms around Amelia's shoulders wearily, gratified to find her arms encircling him in return.

"I'm sorry," she whispered, stroking his back. "What can I do?"

He shook his head against her, sighing roughly, his mouth at her hairline. "Stay right here. This is enough."

Amelia nodded and held him tighter.

And for the moment, it was enough.

It was all he needed.

Chapter Eighteen

"Are you quite sure about this, Amelia?"

"Quite. And it's Alexandra, remember."

"Right, sorry."

Amelia rolled her eyes and scratched just above her left ear where the itchy wig bothered her most. "Don't apologize. But when we are in there with Mrs. Chapman, you cannot forget. We're supposed to be sisters."

Callie gave her a sour look. "Who in their right mind would believe that?"

Amelia cocked her head a little. "There's a good look. That's believable."

"Oh, if you only wanted me to treat you poorly, you should have said so," the maid quipped, grinning across the carriage at her.

Amelia rolled her eyes as dramatically as she could. "Well, really, Anna, you would think our mother didn't love you enough."

"If only she had taken me to Paris instead of you," Callie sighed, looking longingly out of the window. "I would have appreciated it so much more. And learned a *proper* French accent."

Amelia released a delightful French curse that Callie would not understand, but she seemed to catch the sentiment and made a face in response.

The easy banter between them was helping to settle Amelia's nerves, which were at an all-time high. They were riding in a hack they had hired to visit her mother's sister, Dottie Chapman, at her Cheapside home. Her aunt. Someone who knew her mother intimately well.

It was enough to terrify her.

She'd sent a note off to Mrs. Chapman only a few days ago, asking if she might have a moment to spare for two girls visiting London whose mother wished for details of her old schoolmate, Mary Clairbourne. She'd been given permission to use an address Gent had given her for a return address, somewhere in Mayfair, oddly enough, and when the response had come, one of Gent's little urchins had delivered it to her. That had been two days ago, and she'd been so delighted by the response that she'd nearly run into Gabe's office to tell him.

But that had been the day that the man had come to ask about Mr. Turner. She had seen how Gabe turned pale, how still and drawn he had been, all of which had shocked her. He looked lost and angry and confused all at the same time, and he'd seemed rather agitated before that.

Her instincts had told her to go to him, and she was very grateful she had done so. He had held her for quite a long time, and while he hadn't confided in her about what had happened or what any of it meant, he'd surprised her by telling her about his childhood. His mother, his father, the relatives he had lived with after their deaths. He told her about the years he'd spent trying to ruin himself, spending his days and his nights intoxicated and gambling, fighting for sport, and anything else he could think of to avoid actually living a life.

Amelia had listened without speaking, stunned that he would share some rather personal and painful memories with her. His life had been one of heartache and struggle, as hers had been, and he had come through it relatively unscathed. Granted, he was still insolent, tactless, insufferable, and bad-tempered at times, but now she could see beneath all of that. She could see the honor that the Rogue had claimed to be without. She could see the man he truly was.

And he had chosen to share a most private part of himself with *her*.

She barely restrained the urge to sigh now as she recollected it. Since then, he had been softer where she was concerned. Not exactly soft in the way that anyone else might have done, but there was a degree of tenderness when he spoke with her. When he looked at her. When he touched her.

He was constantly stealing her breath and making it difficult to not fall completely in love with him.

She very much feared she was already there.

But she adamantly refused to think about that. If she had run away from the most perfect man ever created the night of the masquerade, she did not deserve the reality of a man like Gabe. Both were in possession of portions of her heart, and she did not know who would win out.

Or would there be any winners at all?

There was so much to lose, and she would lose most of all.

"I am starting to wish I had practiced the way I walk," Callie murmured in a hushed tone as she watched people walk along the streets nearby. "She will know I'm a fraud the moment I set foot in there."

Amelia looked over at the fair-haired, pretty woman and smiled to herself. "If you think I know how to walk like a fine lady, you are sadly mistaken. But I don't believe Mrs. Chapman will hold us to the standard of Society misses. She's a woman from modest means, and she lives in Cheapside."

Callie snorted and quirked a brow at her. "Cheapside, and yet not at all cheap. I couldn't afford it." She smiled at Amelia, looking her over. "Do you know that blonde hair suits you? It looks quite nice."

Amelia opened her mouth to answer when the hack pulled to a stop. Her heart was suddenly in her throat, and she had to take a few slow breaths to steady herself.

Callie disembarked and seemed to transform at once into the character of Anna Driscoll, adjusting her gloves and bonnet. She glanced back at Amelia with a smile. "Do come on, Alexandra. Mrs. Chapman will not wish to be kept waiting while you fuss with your lace."

That spurred Amelia into action, and she scowled at her faux sister as she exited as well. "She will not wish for you to be impertinent, either, Anna."

"I am never impertinent," Callie sniffed as they strode forward. "I simply possess a certain degree of cheek."

Amelia bit down on her lip, amused at the perfectly cultured voice that Callie was using. No one would ever suspect her. And here Amelia had thought herself so perfectly superior in the art of imitation and mimicry, when at this moment she was being put through her paces by this cheeky maid.

What a laugh.

They proceeded up the steps and were let into the house without any fuss at all, as if their visit had been just another in a string of calls being received. Once their outerwear had been taken, they were shown into a simply decorated drawing room that suited Amelia's taste perfectly; pale green wallpaper in good condition, various pieces of clean, well-maintained furniture in the Queen Anne style, and plenty of fresh light from the windows facing the street. It was all elegant, but hardly expensive, and surprisingly sensible.

It spoke well of the woman they were to meet, and Amelia found herself more at ease.

She caught sight of a small writing desk in the corner that almost exactly mirrored one they'd had at the cottage near Finley. The same dark wood, the same detailing, the same simplicity in style. It was neatly ordered on top, which was not at all like her mother's desk had been, but all of the necessary supplies for letter-writing were laid out, and it seemed they had been in use already that day.

Who was her aunt writing to, she wondered. Had she cousins? Was she writing to the brother in Hertfordshire that Gabe had found?

Her curious train of thought was cut short by the entrance of the woman herself, and she and Callie rose as one to curtsey.

Amelia looked up at her aunt and was pleased to see that while she could see the family resemblance, it was not striking. She was not sure she could have endured seeing a woman who looked too much like her mother.

Mrs. Chapman was on the petite side, though of a decent enough height. She wore a simple striped muslin and cap with a shawl around her shoulders, and her hair was a soft amber color, very unlike Amelia's mother's, which had been quite dark. She did have the same blue eyes, though, almost the shade of the sky, and the lines near her eyes spoke of both joyous and somber times.

Mrs. Chapman smiled at them both, but it was an almost sad smile, as though it bore a heavy burden. "Welcome to my home, dear girls. I pray you will excuse Mr. Chapman, he was most insistent on being at Parliament today." She looked at them both, then smiled at Amelia. "I am going to guess that you are Alexandra."

Amelia smiled and inclined her head in acknowledgement. "I am, ma'am. This is my younger sister, Anna."

Mrs. Chapman gave Callie a fond smile and a bit of a wink. "I was a younger sister as well, my dear. It is such a trial, is it not?"

Callie nodded soberly, releasing a heavy sigh. "It is indeed, Mrs. Chapman, but I endure it as best I can."

That drew laughter from the older woman, and she indicated that they should sit. "I have called for a tea service, but I thought we could chat a moment first." She looked between the two of them. "You wished to know of my sister Mary?"

"Yes, ma'am," Amelia replied with a modest dip of her chin. "Our mother knew her at school, and when the opportunity came for us to come to London, she asked us to see if we could find out about her friend."

Mrs. Chapman tilted her head slightly, her brow furrowing. "Your mother did not accompany you?"

"There are two other girls at home, ma'am," Callie said, smiling sweetly as she shook her head. "They were not old enough to come, so she remained with them."

That made the woman smile a knowing smile. "Ah, yes. My own younger girls were most put out with their elder sister when she was permitted adventures and they were not."

Callie laughed a little and folded her hands primly in her lap. "Yes, Lucy and Beth will probably not speak to us for some time, but they tend to go through phases of that anyway."

"And Mother only says 'Girls will be girls'," Amelia added, shrugging one shoulder.

"As they will be," Mrs. Chapman agreed. She looked between Amelia and Callie with speculation, her eyes narrowing slightly. "Your mother was Fanny Heywood, wasn't she?"

Callie and Amelia looked at each other with wide eyes, pretending to be utterly astonished, then turned back to her.

"How did you guess?" Callie asked in a perfectly hushed voice.

Mrs. Chapman looked rather pleased with herself. "I met her a handful of times, and she was one of Mary's dearest friends. You both resemble her nicely."

"Thank you," Amelia murmured softly, unsure of how she felt about the praise.

She'd always been told she resembled her mother a great deal, but Mrs. Chapman did not seem to see the resemblance to her sister. Or had Mary and her friend looked so similar that it was an easy mistake to make?

"Father will be so pleased," Callie chirped with a bright smile, taking away from Amelia's sudden melancholy. "He always said he wanted his daughters to look like her."

"Yes," Amelia managed, recovering quickly. "It's a pity you did not also inherit her good sense and grace."

Callie gave her a sour sisterly look that made Mrs. Chapman chuckle.

The tea service was brought in then, and there was a pause while Mrs. Chapman poured for them all. "Well, what would you like to know about my sister?" she asked, handing tea to Amelia. "I have not seen her in many, many years, I am afraid."

"Oh?" Callie asked with innocent curiosity. "That must be very trying for you." She looked at Amelia quickly, then returned her gaze to their hostess. "I may plague my sisters, but I could not imagine being so separated."

Her words made Mrs. Chapman smile fondly at her as she took up her own tea. "That is sweet. I was of a similar mind, but… well, it was just not meant to be. Mary met a man, a trifle older than her, but not shockingly so, despite what our father said about it."

Amelia had to fight the urge to sit forward and listen with excitement. She forced her expression to remain calm and only mildly interested.

Mrs. Chapman shook her head, her lips curving as she sipped her tea. "Mary was so strong-willed. Your mother will remember that well. She always was, you know, but something about this man made her even more so." She shook her head, her delicate earrings dancing slightly. "I never even met him. Father refused to have him in the house or to have anything to do with him."

"Why?" Callie asked rather bluntly, not bothering to feign

politeness.

"Anna," Amelia tried to scold, though she was pleased by the impertinence.

Mrs. Chapman smiled at her sadly. "It's all right, Miss Driscoll. If Mary can be a lesson for you and your sister, I do not mind." She turned her kind eyes back to Callie and exhaled softly. "He was a ship merchant. He dealt in trade with various countries and, as I understand it, even had smuggling interests. The man was even imprisoned for a time, though the charges did not stand. He had absolutely no business with the daughter of a respectable family, no matter how fine his principles were."

The words sounded harsh, yet the tone was anything but. Amelia had the sense that her aunt was reciting the family's arguments more than her own opinions, and yet there was some truth in her expression. She believed it, in part, but the reluctance and hesitation were there.

"What happened, Mrs. Chapman?" Amelia prodded as gently as she could.

She looked at Amelia with eyes that suddenly seemed much older. "She married him anyway. She was cut off financially once the news of the engagement broke. She refused to take back her promise, though it would be a year, at least, before they could marry. Mr. Cole had no real money to provide for her, you see, so they would have to wait."

"Mr. Cole?" Amelia blurted before she could stop herself.

Thankfully, her eagerness was not noticed.

"Daniel Cole," Mrs. Chapman told her, no longer looking at her. She sipped her tea quietly. "Mary told me several times that she loved him quite madly. She said that all of her dreams were coming true, and she didn't care what anybody said." She smiled a little bitterly, blinking rapidly. "Not even me. I was no match for Mr. Cole, either."

Amelia felt her own eyes beginning to burn, and she had to lower them quickly. She forced her breathing to be steady and focused on her purpose, her act. She could not be emotional; not here, not now.

"How very sad," Callie said with a whimper for good measure. "And no one could persuade her?"

Mrs. Chapman shook her head, seeming to come to herself. "No, and we all tried. Father turned her from the house, and Mary moved to London. After a few weeks, Father sent my brother Frank to London to find her. I suspect he thought Mary would realize the mistake she made when she went to London without the benefit of Society or funds." Now she smiled in earnest, her eyes softening. "But Frank said that Mary was perfectly content, and that the wedding would go on. We were permitted letters for a time after that, and she wrote to me faithfully for a year. Mr. Cole was gone frequently with his ships, so Mary had time to do so. She found employment for a time, which did not surprise me. She was a determined girl who grew into an industrious woman. When she put her mind to something, it was accomplished."

Hearing this account, Amelia felt as if she was being introduced to her mother for the first time. Her mother had been sad for most of Amelia's life, and she could not recall her ever being markedly determined or willful. She had been reserved and unhappy, though even Amelia could not deny her industriousness. She had come from a well-bred family, despite her meager means, and yet had made a life for herself in their cottage after London. She had raised Amelia in circumstances far less than what she had been brought up in and worked hard every day of her life.

"Did she have any children, Mrs. Chapman?" Callie asked with all the sweet-temperedness of a younger sister.

"She was expecting a child when I last heard from her," Mrs. Chapman said with a nod and a smile. "A very active one, she told me. And she said Mr. Cole was so pleased with the prospect." Her smile faded, and she slowly shook her head. "I don't know what happened after that. I never heard from her again."

"Did you try to find them?" Callie persisted, far too engaged in the story for Amelia's taste.

"Anna," Amelia murmured, laying a hand over hers.

Callie looked at her with a question in her eyes.

Amelia shook her head a little, giving her a firm smile.

"Oh, Anna," Mrs. Chapman murmured, her voice a little choked.

Both girls turned to look at her with interest.

A pair of tears made their way down Mrs. Chapman's cheeks, but she did not seem to feel them. "I couldn't search for her. I wanted to. She was my sister, and I loved her. But I could not disobey my father. I needed to make a good match if we were to redeem ourselves from Mary's fall, and our brother Frank needed to marry well, too. We couldn't…" She broke off with a sniffle and looked away.

"I'm sorry," Amelia said quickly, fishing for a handkerchief. "She did not mean to pry."

"Not at all!" Callie echoed, sounding a trifle panicked. "Please, Mrs. Chapman…"

Mrs. Chapman wiped at her eyes and laughed a watery laugh. "No, no, forgive me girls. It is quite all right. I have not spoken of Mary in so long, and it is a relief to do so." She smiled at them with genuine affection. "I know your mother will not think less of Mary for her actions, and now you know the whole truth."

Amelia and Callie shook their heads as one, and Amelia found her heart pounding a little unsteadily. There was real affection here, despite the treatment of her mother by her family. Amelia could not pretend to understand the decision to cut her off, nor of the siblings for clinging to the family, but she did not feel angry or bitter about it. Not now that she saw the feelings that still lingered despite the years of separation.

"I named my eldest daughter after her, you know," Mrs. Chapman told them with a much brighter smile. "Mary. We called her Molly, as it would have caused Mother pain to hear her called by my sister's name. And my Molly has all the energy of her Aunt Mary, I can promise you that."

Amelia could barely blink, couldn't find her breath. Her cousin… Named for her mother. She had a cousin named for her mother.

"That's lovely!" Callie fairly gushed, sipping at her tea. "How sweet. I declare, I don't know that I could name my daughter Alexandra, much as my elder sister would delight in it." She nudged Amelia lightly, grinning at her.

Amelia managed to return it and shook off the emotions swelling within her. "Well, that is as it should be, as I'm quite sure I could never have an Anna of my own."

"But neither of us could have Lucy or Elizabeth," Callie assured Mrs. Chapman with a wink. "They would lord over us for *ages*."

Mrs. Chapman smiled and nodded her understanding. "My sister and I were either the best of friends or the worst of enemies. And we got into some terrible scrapes as girls, I can assure you."

She started to tell the stories, one after the other, and Amelia steeled herself against them all, praying she could keep her act in place.

But she felt more and more hollow as the stories continued.

Callie hadn't said a word on the drive back to Tilda's, and Amelia hadn't bothered to keep up the pretense. She'd tugged off her wig when they were safely away and let down her natural hair, leaving it loose and unbound. They hadn't said a word as they returned the costumes, and Callie had only linked her arm with Amelia's as they'd walked back to the offices after all of that. There were no words for the revelations that had been unearthed today, for the details that had surprised her, for the sheer volume of emotions that now coursed through her.

They'd parted ways at the offices, Callie squeezing her hand before going to her duties there.

Amelia sank onto the bench where she had first waited for the Rogue that day, gripping onto the wall behind her as if it could give her the balance she so desperately required.

How had she thought that she could endure any of this? Had she overestimated her own strength? Not anticipated the still-lingering emotions? Whatever it was, she had been entirely unprepared for what she had encountered there.

Perhaps Gabe was right. She was not nearly as skilled, or as qualified, or as hardened as she thought herself.

She clutched at the wall with her fingernails, thinking back on all she had learned in recent days and weeks. Her father, whoever he was, was at the root of everything. Her mother was partially to blame for marrying such a worthless creature, but if she had loved him as wildly as her aunt had said, could she really be blamed for such folly? Mr. Cole should have known better. He ought to have been honest enough to steer Mary away from him, knowing he could never provide for a family.

And what had happened to make them uproot from London and move to Surrey without him? She knew he had never come there, she never remembered any man giving her mother pleasure with his presence. And why had they changed their name to Palmer? Why had they then become Tribbetts upon leaving the cottage? Why all the secrecy?

Why hadn't he loved them enough to be with them through all they endured?

Why?

She was lost and flailing, and suddenly nothing was certain anymore.

"Amelia?"

Slowly, painfully, she looked up into the icy blue eyes of Gabe, staring down at her with furrowed brow and questioning gaze.

She swallowed with difficulty, her mouth and throat dry and raw. "I met my aunt today," she croaked, her voice breaking a little. Suddenly, everything was too much, too close to the surface, and she hiccupped with the rising tide.

Gabe grabbed her arm and pulled her into his office without any resistance from her, closing the door soundly behind him. He slid his grip to her hand and squeezed hard.

She squeezed back, unable to raise her eyes to his again. "I found out her name some time ago, but I couldn't go to her, not until I was ready. And then Callie and I went today. I concocted a story, and she accepted it." She swallowed back a lump, nearly choking in the effort. "She... she told us... everything." Her voice broke again, and she felt herself being drawn closer to Gabe, his arms wrapping gently around her, cradling her head against him. "Every... everything about my mother I wanted to know, I now know." She slid her hands up to latch around Gabe's neck, her body shaking with the forthcoming tears. "I have an aunt. I have cousins. And I couldn't tell her who I was. I lied to her, and she is my..."

The words died on a sob, and she lost all resistance to the forces within her. She sobbed in agony, her cries loud and unrestrained, burying her face against Gabe, whose hold on her tightened. It was as if her heart were breaking in pieces, incinerating in the flames swirling in her chest, singeing every other part of her in the process. She felt as though her mother had died all over again, and she was mourning her loss twice over.

She'd never cried over losing her the first time.

Would it have hurt this much if she had?

Her cries became more and more panicked as confusion swirled, as her world fell into chaos, and everything she knew was suddenly thrown into the unknown.

Gabe murmured soothing words that she could not hear, and when that did not help, he scooped her up in his arms and carried her to the chair behind his desk. He sat down gingerly and held Amelia tightly in his lap, her legs tucked between him and the chair, his arms still holding her close to him.

His lips dusted across her hair and her brow, and she could feel him speaking to her, could hear the low hum of his voice, the sound soothing away her shudders. Minutes passed as she cried, as he held her, as he attempted to comfort the woman in his hold and the girl within her.

"It's all right, love," she finally made out as his mouth traced her ear lightly. "It's all right."

Amelia pressed her face into his neck as the cries began to fade, clinging tightly to him. Her breath was unsteady, and she suddenly felt weak, depleted of all energy and strength after such an outburst. She craved the warmth that he provided, adored the soothing strokes of his arms sweeping along her spine, and breathed in the scent of him as a balm to her soul.

"There you are," he praised when she finally stopped shaking. "There's my girl."

She smiled against his skin and kissed his neck gently, nestling in a little. *His girl.* It was a lovely thought, and she certainly felt like his at this moment, held in this way.

"Sorry," she whispered, one hand sliding down to play with the edge of his collar.

"For what?" he asked in a rather mild tone, nuzzling against her and entwining one hand with hers. "I'm quite content. This is the brightest part of my day, I can assure you."

Amelia snickered and leaned her head back enough to take his face in her hands and kiss him, taking quite a long time to do so, toying with his lips as much as she dared. Then she sighed and laid her head on his shoulder, wondering if she could stay like this forever.

"So," Gabe began in a serious tone, taking her hand again, "your aunt."

She nodded against him, absently playing with his fingers.

"Does she keep house as poorly as your mother did? Or did she learn better skills?"

Amelia snorted and slapped his shoulder with her free hand. "She has servants, Gabe."

He shrugged a little, pulling her closer with the hand still about her back. "That doesn't mean a thing. We have a servant here, and it isn't any cleaner."

"Don't let Callie hear you say that," Amelia warned, smiling a little. "She'll have your head."

"Did your aunt take her tea properly?" he asked with mild interest. "I couldn't bear it if she only had one lump of sugar. That would put her squarely on the wrong side of Society, and you cannot be related to the wrong side."

Amelia bit her lip to keep from laughing. "She took no sugar."

He groaned dramatically and leaned his head back against his chair. "It's worse than I thought. Outrage! Heathen!"

"She was very nice," Amelia insisted, now laughing in earnest.

"But her teeth were horrid, yes? Stained? Crooked?" He gave Amelia a suspicious look. "Did she have warts?"

Amelia shook her head and kissed the ridiculous man again, loving him for making her laugh when she felt so horrid. And loving him for holding her. And for simply being him.

She loved him.

And her broken heart began to mend. "You are the most charming man I know," she told him with a smile.

He gave her a crooked grin in return and kissed her nose. "Then you are sadly lacking experience with charming men, my dear. But I'll let you have your delusions, so long as you tell me your aunt has a peg leg, a tone-deaf canary, and only one working eye."

Chapter Nineteen

$\mathcal{T}$here wasn't anything quite like the seedy side of London.

One might assume that they knew what to expect, and how dark and vile such places could be.

There were many unpleasant places in London where one could find the dark and vile. But until someone had ventured into the truly criminal heart of its underside, the scope of London would be positively radiant by comparison.

Gabe had been there before. He had been a pillar of its society and a member of significance to its depravity.

And that was before he had been known as the Rogue.

Tonight, he was back into character, and it felt as familiar to him as breathing, and twice as refreshing. He was starting to forget who he really was and how he really behaved.

But that wasn't his fault.

It was Amelia's.

She was uprooting his life and destroying any sense of sanity he had left. What's worse was that he was so damned delighted by it. She amused him to no end, and he was always wondering where she was, what she was doing, what she was thinking, and how to make her laugh. How to tease her. What fresh insult to lay out, wondering with great interest what she would reply with.

Their banter was something he had come to crave, and they were so good at it; the process invigorated him.

He'd been unmanned by her tears the other day, so heartbroken by meeting her aunt that she had sobbed in his arms. He'd been helpless, and utterly clueless, and only thought to hold her and prayed it would be enough. It had seemed to work, and he'd set about restoring her smiles, but the experience had shaken him.

A female and her tears had never meant anything to him before. Quite simply, he did not care. Never had and had never seen a reason to do so.

With Amelia, however, it was all different. Her tears were the death of him, and nothing in this world had tormented him like that.

Not even the goddess.

He shook his head now as he headed towards the docks. An entire lifetime of feeling nothing but derision for women, and now two of them had him so tied up in knots he could barely see straight. It was quite simply bewildering, and he began to wonder if he had entirely lost his senses.

It didn't help that Rook had come to him only hours ago with the report that no one in his finer circles recognized Amelia's picture, even the traitor circle he had managed to infiltrate. No ties to their investigation, no social connections of any certain rank, and no explanation for anything. He'd thought to ask Rook if he was sure they were truthful, but that was Rook's specialty. He could always spot a lie, no matter how cleverly the liar tried to hide it.

Apparently, his early interrogations had been quite the sight, if Weaver and Tailor's reports were correct. Pity he hadn't known him then. Gabe always appreciated the skills of interrogation.

But he was grateful to get away from all of that tonight. Gent had given him all the information he'd gathered from the man who'd come to their offices, and now it was up to Gabe to investigate them.

He'd pored over all the notes Trace had left, which had been minimal at best, and all the notes that any of them had made over the years as they'd tried to pick up where he had left off. Gabe himself had dedicated the entire year after Trace's death to the investigation, practically living dockside and turning more into the man he had once been than had been comfortable for some of the leadership. Until Weaver had pulled him out, physically and officially, he had been obsessed by his work there.

But it had given him purpose and closure, and some minor successes as well.

It was now time to see what had changed and find what had been missing.

He loved the docks, as twisted as that sounded. He loved the creaking of the ships in port, the whistles of shipmates to each other, the bawdy language, the brawling, the gambling. He enjoyed the rough atmosphere in general. It felt more genuine to him than any other place he had ever been. No one on the docks was ever trying to be something they were not.

Except for him, he thought with a faint smirk.

Even then, he belonged.

He inhaled deeply as he neared the wharves, a few of the custom houses and warehouses still lit, despite the late hour. The scent of the Thames and its vessels was also something that would never become stagnant to him. It almost smelled of home.

A movement to his left caught his attention, and he slowed his step, angling himself into the shadows of the crates near him.

Someone was sneaking along the back wall of a warehouse nearby and doing a rather impressive job, moving in silence and with ease. It was obvious that the lad did not wish to be observed, and the dark clothing would allow him a good deal of freedom down here.

Gabe smiled. It was clear that he was quite young. What sort of nefarious work would he get himself into? The docks were a wealth of criminal activity at any given time, despite the security measures taken by the companies running them, and there was very little regulation over them.

As an employee of His Majesty's service, Gabe supposed it was technically his duty to prevent such things, but he felt no compulsion to do so. He was more curious than anything else. Besides, it was entirely possible that this could be tied to what he himself was looking for.

He waited for the lad to choose a direction, and then silently followed behind when he did so.

Amelia crept along the London docks as quietly as she could, smiling to herself at how familiar it felt. It had been years since she had come here, having escaped them when she could, and her friends down there helping her to do so. She would never forget their kindness to her, despite everything, and now that she was in need, it was to them she would turn.

After all, they each owed her their lives at least once.

Surely this was a small favor by comparison.

In the few days following her interview with her aunt, whom she still thought of as Mrs. Chapman, as it was too familiar to think of her as "Aunt Dottie", she'd found a sort of calm and clarity. Gabe had been instrumental in that, keeping her from melancholy and reminding her of the investigation at hand. He'd teased her through her dark times and made her smile, made her laugh, made her love him even more than she had before.

Once she'd found her emotions in control again, she had told him of her interview with Mrs. Chapman, every detail she could recall, and all the information she had unearthed. Gabe had listened carefully and made notes, as surely as he would have done with any witness or client, but he'd held her hand the entire time, and that contact had sustained her. They discussed how they might proceed, speculated on what might have occurred, and how any of this related to what they already knew. There was no saying what else they might find, and she saw the question in his eyes when he looked at her.

He did not know if she could bear any more of this.

If she were perfectly honest with herself, she would admit to feeling the same questions hourly, but she would never tell him that. Even if this entire venture wracked her soul and shredded what remained of her heart, she would see it through.

She had to know the truth.

No matter the cost.

Her father, presumably this Mr. Cole, if her mother had not engaged in less than savory deeds, had been a merchant with ties to smuggling. He had been gone frequently enough not to be known to her mother's employers. He had been imprisoned.

She knew the sorts of men who lived such lives and engaged in such activities.

They had saved *her* life and given her an identity.

If they knew her father, they would tell her. If they knew he was one of their own, they would ask for a piece of him. She was not inclined to give any part of him up to anyone else's vendetta or vengeance, but it was an amusing thought.

Amelia darted between crates and wagons, all abandoned for the night while their owners depraved themselves in whatever sin they chose. There was something for everyone down here, if one knew where to look. Closer to the East India docks, one could find a brothel. By the West Indies dock, a fighting club with limited rules and high stakes.

But by the London docks, there was a gambling club.

One she knew all too well.

She had dressed in her men's clothing again, as any skirt would have made her a target for unwanted attention. No one would look for her here, so she was not assured of any protection, should the need arise. She'd managed without it before, several times, but she was out of practice.

She had no idea if the man supposedly tailing her on Gabe's orders had managed to spot her or keep up with her tonight, but she'd not been stopped.

Something began to tingle along the back of her neck, and she looked behind her warily, knowing she was a prime candidate for a mugging, being small and out alone. And it made no difference that she had nothing of value on her.

There was nothing behind her, no one in sight, and only the sounds of the ships and the river met her ears.

Amelia smirked in derision at herself. She was so out of practice that now her mind concocted all sorts of things, scaring herself with imaginary dangers. It was childish and silly, and if Gabe knew, he would laugh at her.

That sent a cold chill down her spine.

If Gabe knew…

Well, he would be justifiably furious with her for going against his wishes, but if he understood, if he knew…

She'd never know what would happen, because he would never know. She would make certain of it.

She approached the back door of the customs house and knocked three times in rapid succession.

The door swung open, and an aged sailor with multiple scars and a graying beard that hung to his chest poked his head out.

"*Mot de passé*," he growled, towering above her.

"*Tu pues de chien*, Jean," she replied with a smile, tilting her head back to grin up at him.

His dark eyes widened, and he stepped back, looking her over. "*Sacre bleu!* Tribbie?"

She nodded and put her hands on her hips. "In the flesh, *mon ami.*"

He stuck his head out further, scanning the surrounding area. "You should not be here," he told her in his heavy accent. "It is not safe for a woman."

Amelia gave him a look and frowned. "You know very well I am not that sort of woman."

"*Oui*," he sighed heavily, shaking his head. "And you would only get into trouble if I sent you away." He reached out an arm and pulled her in for a tight hug, which surprised her. Jean Valerie was not the sort of man to hug anyone, even her. His vest was old and worn, which left it soft against her skin, and it smelled of cigars and whisky, just as he always had.

He made a choking sort of noise and stepped back. "I think you will find it is *you* who stinks of dog, Tribbie. What have you been doing?"

"Well, I couldn't very well have people following me, now could I?" She cocked her hip and grinned cheekily.

"Who is using their nose to follow you?" he asked with interest as he ushered her into the building. Though she knew the way, he led her along the darkened hallways, which desperately needed new rugs, and the curling wallpaper and cobwebs made her smile.

It had always looked this miserable in here, and nothing had ever changed.

Jean had a small office, merely four walls and a desk outside of the main door to the club, and on several occasions, she had spied him taking naps in the old chair behind it. He led her to his desk, which was dust-covered, as usual, and offered her the chair while he leaned against the wall.

Amelia looked towards the entrance to the club, stationed

behind the legitimate front of the customs works in the building, and then up at Jean. "Not taking me into the club tonight?"

Jean shook his head firmly. "No. There are men in there that I would not wish you to meet, or for them to lay eyes on you."

"Even dressed like this?" she asked, gesturing to herself dubiously.

A heavy chuckle and a mocking smirk preceded his answer. "Who do you think you are fooling dressed like that?"

"It's a perfect disguise!" she gasped in outrage.

"It's a terrible disguise," he assured her before she could finish. "Anyone with eyes or sense would see that you are a woman, and dressed as you are, it would not stop them."

Amelia snorted and folded her arms over her chest. "You assume any of them are sober."

"They are never sober. It would not change a thing." He studied her for a long moment, then tilted his head to consider her differently. "You are, ah, much changed since last I saw you. Perhaps next time I may suggest, ah, binding, and perhaps padding of…" He gestured the form of her waist with a puzzled expression, searching for the word.

"Thank you," Amelia said a little too loudly, her cheeks heating. Really, she did not need to hear about her figure, and how it hindered her abilities, from him, of all people.

He smiled easily and shrugged. "Or perhaps you should jus' get fat."

She barked a laugh and leaned her elbow on the desk. "Would that help?"

"It would not hurt. Might I suggest drinking more? It seems to do the job around here." He gestured faintly to the club and the docks in general.

"I'll take that into consideration," Amelia muttered, taking her cap off and shrugging out her hair. She braided it quickly and tied a strip of fabric from her pocket around it. She flung that over her shoulder and sighed, looking back up at Jean. "I need your help, Jean."

"Name it, *mon chère*," he replied at once, leaning closer. "You need somebody killed?"

She smiled, forgetting how much she loved being around Jean. He always thought someone needed to be killed, and he was more than willing to do it. As far as she knew, no one had taken him up on it.

Yet.

"Not right now," she replied, shaking her head. "I need information."

He instantly looked wary. "You should be talking to Dubois or Skips, Tribbie. I am not a man of information."

Amelia offered him a pitying look, watching his discomfort with interest. "I will ask Dubois and Skips. But I am also asking you."

He shifted against the wall, averting his eyes. "I will help you if I can. But some things, you understand, I cannot speak of."

"I don't care if you are smuggling the wives of Russian aristocrats into the country to be the new girls at Madame Rosemary's," she snapped, drumming her fingers on the table.

He looked slightly offended and more than a little surprised. "How do you know about Madame Rosemary's?"

She waved her free hand dismissively. "The point is, Jean, that I need you to tell me everything you can about whatever you know."

Jean stared at her for a moment longer than she was comfortable with, but then he heaved a sigh and folded his arms. "Very well. What is this about?"

"My father."

The large man jerked and slid slightly on the wall, his eyes wide. "*Ton père?*" he coughed, readjusting his position.

Amelia nodded slowly. "I have a name, Jean. At least, I believe I do. And he was a merchant, perhaps even a smuggler."

He swore rather vibrantly in French, and even Amelia with her high tolerance for vulgarity, had to raise a brow in surprise.

Jean shook his head. "Give me the name, Tribbie. I will find him, and I will gut him like the disgusting pig that he is."

"I will give you the name," Amelia told him, sitting up more fully in her chair, but keeping her gaze firm, "but you will do nothing of the sort. He is mine, do you understand? Mine."

"He is yours, *mon chère*," Jean repeated, though his expression was dark and dangerous. "But if you think that I will not take my revenge on him for what you endured…" He growled and shook his head again. "No. Not after what I saw. Not after… No."

She understood his fury, his emotions at the recollection, and she had the same. There had been some horrible things in her past that should have been avoided, that she ought to have been protected from, and only Jean knew every detail of those incidents. But it could have been so much worse, and they both knew it.

All things considered, Amelia had been lucky.

"So, who is the *scélérat?*" he grunted, taking her lack of response as acquiescence.

Amelia looked up with steady eyes and steadier hands. "Daniel Cole."

She waited for a reaction, any kind of response, and she knew how to watch for the smallest indication of recognition, any trace of hesitation. She would know if he was hiding something; she was sure of it.

She saw no sign.

He blinked at her, then furrowed his brow, obviously lost in thought. Then, with great disappointment, shook his head slowly. "I do not know that name, Tribbie."

That couldn't be possible. Jean had been here for years; he knew everything and everyone that came through all the docks, not just the London docks. If Daniel Cole had been the merchant he claimed, he would have been known here.

"You have to," Amelia insisted, fisting her hands. "You *have* to."

He gave her a pitying look. "I do not. I told you, I am not the sort to trade in information."

This, at least, was true. Jean had always been the guard, the muscle, the intimidation factor. He was the doorman and enforcer of the club when it suited him and had never met with a challenge there he could not manage. His former life as a fighter had given him ample time to understand the perfect ways to injure with minimal effort, which had made him a most capable tutor for Amelia in her hour of need.

He was one of the most well-respected men on the docks, and when he was not working as the foreman for one of the most impressive merchants in London, he was here, keeping the disreputable in line however he could.

Information was not something that he would have access to in these circles unless he overheard its sharing during his rounds, or if he was told directly. As foreman of the docks, he would have more opportunity to hear of it, but she understood him to run a tight ship there. If he did not know Mr. Cole personally in his time, it would be difficult for him to know anything about him.

"*Pardonne-moi, mon chère,*" he said softly. "I do not mean to disappoint you."

Amelia smiled at him as much as she was able, given her upset. "You could never disappoint me, Jean. You merely offer another piece to the puzzle."

Jean smiled at her with real fondness. "You were always very clever with the puzzles."

She laughed a little and ran her fingers over the tarnished candelabra on the corner of his desk, the wax of one candle starting to drip down the sides. "Mr. Banes loved giving me new ones."

"He did," Jean agreed, shoving his hands into his pockets. "He always said you were more clever than half the men in the club. It was why he let you work here, you know."

"I didn't know that," she murmured, looking away. "I never understood why. But I was grateful."

It had never made sense for a grizzled gambling club owner, who only served the riffraff and dockworkers, to hire a young woman with a stubborn will and no skills to work in his club. She'd been a maid, a serving girl, a runner, and had even helped Dubois, the factotum, with some of his tasks. Jean had been her protector and guardian, and the one who had arranged for her living quarters. Mr. Banes had seen Amelia take an interest in the games in the club and had surprised everyone by permitting her to be taught in them all.

Dubois, Jean, Skips, and various other employees had delighted in teaching her the rules, and how to cheat, and it was not long before Amelia had been doing far more when she'd wandered the club. She'd caught at least a dozen cheaters in her time and helped some worthy fellows to earn more than they should have. It was an exciting time in her life, and surprisingly rewarding.

But even then, she had known it was only a stopping point on her journey, and when she had saved enough from her scarce wages, she'd moved on.

She looked up at Jean with a small smile. "Is Mr. Banes still here?"

"Not tonight," he replied, scratching his beard. "But Dubois and Skips are around. I'll fetch one of them, and you can interrogate them."

Amelia's smile turned devious, and she drummed her fingers slowly. "You know how I interrogate, Jean. Mr. Partridge taught me before Bow Street got him."

The older man pushed off the wall with a clearing of his throat. "*Oui*, and that is why I have never done anything suspicious where you are concerned."

He turned to go into the club, and only paused when he heard Amelia come up behind him. He scowled at her, but she just shrugged.

"Who is going to bother me with you nearby?" she quipped, putting her hands in her coat pockets. "Besides, I want to see the place. I'll wager you a half a crown I catch a cheat."

"*J'accepte*," he grunted, shaking her hand like a man. "But stay close all the same, eh?"

Gabe leaned against the wall of the customs house, fuming and furious, but not altogether unsurprised.

Amelia had gone out again. And worst of all, she had come to the docks, the one place he would have quite literally dragged her away from, by the hair if necessary.

That picture was growing more and more appealing the longer he stood here.

But what had surprised him had been her familiarity with it, and with the club itself. It was not a well-known establishment, even in the world of dock life, yet she had been friendly with the doorman, by all accounts one of the most terrifying Frenchmen that Gabe had ever come across.

Granted, Jean had been one of Trace's contacts and, when needed, was also a contact of his. One of his best, in fact. However, that did not explain how Amelia knew him well enough for the man to embrace her warmly.

That embrace had been the only reason Gabe hadn't followed the mad woman into the building. Any other time, he would have tossed her over his shoulder and returned her to a more appropriate place. However, if Jean had her in his protection and took the obvious care with her that he appeared to, she was in the safest place she could have been, all things considered. No one would dare approach her or even tease her inappropriately with Jean by her side.

He wished he'd known it was her earlier, so he could have prevented this at all. It hadn't occurred to him until her form had become clearer, and then he'd caught sight of Knutt, his operative that had been tailing Amelia, following at a safe but mindful distance.

Knutt had seen him at once, of course, and gestured the question.

Gabe hadn't even hesitated. *He* would take over the task of tailing Amelia tonight, and Knutt could wait in the shadows.

It was for the best, really. Amelia required a different sort of suspicion, and Gabe could not let anyone else know just what that was. She might not be a traitor to the British crown or a French sympathizer, but there was certainly something unnerving about this whole affair.

And he would discover it.

His plans for the evening's investigations had been obliterated in the face of her actions, but another investigation had taken its place.

Who was Amelia Berger? And why was Jean Valerie a close friend?

And why did he call her Tribbie?

Had Trace known her while he was undercover here? If so, why hadn't he ever mentioned her?

Gabe decided he would question Jean later.

A movement caught his attention and he watched Amelia exit the building some time after she'd entered, cap situated properly once more. Right now, he needed to follow this maddening, frustrating, confusing woman back to her rented establishment, prevent her from getting killed, or killing anyone herself, and decide how best to act with her from here on out.

He would not be holding her in his arms in relief this time.

But he did not feel the same need to throttle her either.

Now that he knew what she was capable of and who she knew, all he felt was an overwhelming curiosity.

And the instinctive desire to hunt for the answers.

Chapter Twenty

$\mathscr{A}$melia fairly skipped along the cobblestone to the offices the next morning, her optimism only surpassed by the brightness of the day and the chirping of the birds that darted between the buildings.

Her evening had been productive beyond anything, despite having less information than she had wished for. Reconnecting with her old friends at the docks had given her a new sense of purpose and drive, and Dubois had recalled the name of Daniel Cole, and had even given her a potential merchant company. Dawes & Pope, he had said, though the company was no longer in operating business, and all assets had been sold to various other shipping groups.

He had given her some possible associates to track down, and she was anxious to share the information with Gabe.

How she would accomplish that without confessing what she had done, she had not decided, but all the information was now available to them, with the additional notes she had made. She hoped that proof of her success would be enough to dissuade him from attempted murder.

If she were most fortunate, he would even be a little proud of her.

But that might be hoping for too much.

It really wouldn't make much difference either way, for she had a direction and clarity of purpose now. She could track down these men and find answers about her father. She could avenge her mother and finally set herself free of the pain and bitterness of all those years.

What a liberating thought that was!

Amelia looked behind her and saw Daisy walking several paces behind, studiously kicking a pebble with her right foot with every step. The girl was a miniature of Amelia herself, dark eyes aside, and everything from the scabs on the ankles to the patches on her dress brought Amelia back to her childhood. She'd never learned anything about Daisy's personal life, despite her best efforts, but she suspected the child led a life even worse than Amelia had. No matter what she might say about her life, Amelia had always had the love of her mother, and that had left an impression.

She very much doubted Daisy had that.

"Daisy," she called with a wave of her hand. "Come up here and hold my hand, will you?"

Daisy surveyed her with uncertainty, biting her lip with her crooked and gapped teeth. "Dunno, miss. Rogue won' like that."

Amelia shrugged and held out a hand. "We won't tell him, then. Come on, I need a skipping partner."

There was a moment's hesitation, and then the girl broke into a toothy grin and ran for her, seizing her hand, her toy pebble forgotten.

The two of them skipped and laughed all the way back to the offices, and then Daisy surprised Amelia by giving her a tight hug around her middle before darting around to the back of the building.

Amelia stared after her, wondering where the child slept at night, who took care of her, and why she was working for Gabe if Gent was the one who had the children in his network.

It was all very curious. Could it be that the recalcitrant Gabe, who secretly had a soft and honorable spot for women, felt the same way about children despite his vocal aversions?

She'd have to ask him once they got underway with the investigation today. She wasn't sure she wanted him to be fond of children, it would only make him more attractive and give him more power over her heart. Maybe it was not all children, and Daisy was an exception.

That might be even worse.

A shout of a distant street hawker broke Amelia's reverie, and she shook herself, exhaling noisily and forcing her mind back to where it belonged.

Her father. The shipping company. Possible associates.

She nodded to herself and marched into the offices as she would have done any other day. One and Two were scribbling away at their desks and greeted her without ceremony, as per usual. Callie was dusting, oddly enough, and winked at her with a quick smile that Amelia returned. She'd asked her the other day when they could play sisters again, as she had enjoyed herself a great deal.

While she couldn't see the need to do so, she might concoct a reason.

Or perhaps she and Callie ought to just be themselves and gallivant about London together.

It was an entertaining thought. Amelia had never really had friends, particularly ones that were female, for one reason or another. But she thought she could truly become friends with Callie, and more than that, she thought she would actually enjoy it.

The day was getting better by the moment!

She removed her bonnet and long coat, dropping them on the bench outside Gabe's office, and then pushed in without knocking, fixing a bright smile on her face.

Gabe didn't even look up. He was shuffling through documents on his desk in obvious agitation, making notes on another paper with a sort of frantic energy that spoke of desperation. His hair was in disarray, his clothing, though clean, was untidy, and he was muttering to himself as he worked.

Amelia frowned at the sight. Had he found something that could lead them to more answers? He'd said nothing of the sort yesterday, and they'd spent quite a long time together. Surely he would have told her if there was some promising lead.

"What are you doing?" she asked carefully, wondering if he would startle easily.

"Following up a lead," he replied without looking at her, digging through the papers.

There hadn't been that many papers on his desk yesterday, and she knew there weren't that many notes on her case, unless he'd written more after she'd left.

"What lead?" she prodded as she moved toward the desk.

Gabe shook his head quickly as his finger traced down a page. "Not your case."

That drew her up short, and she felt her brow crinkle further still. "Not my case? What are you working on?"

"The other one." His answer was short and clipped, leaving no doubt in her mind where his priorities were at the moment.

Her priorities, however, were not going to be swept aside. "Your missing lady friend?" she demanded, her voice rising in pitch and timbre.

Finally, he glanced up at her, his eyes not nearly as wild as his behavior would have suggested. "I never said it was a lady."

Amelia rolled her eyes and snorted. "Please, anybody could have drawn that conclusion. Why are you so frantically focusing on this today?"

"As I said," he told her, indicating his desk, "a new lead. I need to move quickly."

"Is she in danger?"

"I don't know."

"Do you have a reason to think she will be?"

"No."

"Then maybe you should listen to the new lead I have on *my* case," she snapped, planting a fist on one hip. "Or don't you care about that anymore?"

He gave her a derisive look as he began to stack some of the papers into the corner of his desk. "Of course I care. But this is here now, and you know how important this is to me."

"And you know how important this is to me!" she cried. "Don't you even want to know what I have?"

"Of course I do." He shoved some blank pieces of paper in her direction. "Write it all down, and we can go over it after I finish this."

Amelia gaped at him, her breathing unsteady in her chest. "Write it down... Are you serious, Gabe? Write it down? So you can add it to your pile of work and put it squarely on the bottom, so it comes after your wandering miss?"

His brow snapped down, and he looked irritated for the first time this morning. "Now see here, Amelia..."

"No," she overrode loudly. "No, I will not see here! Do you even know where I was last night?"

He snorted softly and went back to his messy desk. "Of course

I do. You were down at the docks." He paused to give her a scolding look, then went back to his work. "Knutt followed you, and I happened to be down there myself, so I took over and followed you back. I was surprised at your route, there are more direct paths to the boarding house than the one you chose."

"I know that," she barked, folding her arms tightly. "So, you knew I was down there, and you still don't want to know what I have? Or get angry with me for going against your orders?"

"I want to know," he said simply, either not caring or simply not reacting to her obvious distress, "and I am upset with you. But you were tailed, you were protected, and you obviously knew what you were doing. And we will work your lead, just not right now."

Amelia was already shaking her head before he finished. "I'm not waiting for you to get your personal life resolved before my case can be looked at again! Your lady will still be just as missing tomorrow as she is today, and I have information on *my* case now! Just because I know what I am doing, Gabe, does not mean that you can bow out because you have other things to do!"

"I'm just putting it aside for the moment…"

"No!" she bellowed, slamming her hand down on his desk. "No, you will *not* be putting it aside! This is your priority, Gabe. I am paying you for this, remember? This is what you are working on right now. Not her, me."

Gabe sat back in his chair, looking at her speculatively and a trifle amused. "Amelia…" he said slowly, his eyes glittering with a knowing light. "Are you jealous?"

The question stole the breath from Amelia's lungs, and she could only stare back at him, her mouth working absently.

Of all the ridiculous… That wasn't even close to… How could he…?

She wasn't jealous. She wasn't.

This was business.

She glared at him coldly, ignoring the heat in her cheeks, the burning in her eyes, and how her heart twisted at the thought of him looking for another woman with such fervor. For a long moment, all she could do was stare.

"I hired you to do a job," she finally hissed. "Do it. The faster you get it done, the faster I'll be out of your hair, and you can go on your mad hunt for your ladybird."

Gabe's expression never altered, but she saw a different light in his eyes. Something defiant and hard. "What are you going to do when you find your father, Amelia? Knowing what I do, what will you do?"

Amelia dipped her chin down a little, leveling him the coldest glare she could muster. "That is not your concern."

"Amelia."

She shook her head slowly, then swept away, her kneecaps shaking under her fury and the power of his gaze. "Do your job, Rogue."

She wished she could have seen his face when she called him by his code name, but only for the pure, vindictive delight it would give her. If he were not going to feel the same way about her as she felt about him, it would only be too perfect for him to feel the sting of her cold, dismissive distance. She needed to remove her heart from the situation.

If that was even possible.

She picked up her coat and bonnet and left the offices without a word to the others. If Gabe was not going to help her, she would finish this on her own.

Gabe stared at the closed office door for a long moment, chewing his lip in thought. Something wasn't right about this whole situation. Amelia's coldness, her avoidance of his pointed question, and her fury at his lack of focus all made him wonder what lay beneath the surface. What drove her with such madness?

Granted, he probably could have handled the situation with more delicacy. But he'd received a note from Lady Raeburn that a Mrs. Brimley could have some information about the goddess, as she had been seen speaking with her. He'd never even heard of Mrs. Brimley, so he'd immediately set about trying to find out everything he could about her; her family, her position, her temperament...

anything that could help him in dealing with her, or anything that presented a way in which he could approach her.

And then there were always the usual methods of interrogation; blackmail, threats, espionage…

He tried to avoid those when working with members of Society, as he needed to avoid making a questionable name for himself in those circles. And it would undoubtedly be better if Lady Raeburn kept her moderately good opinion of him. She was rather terrifying, and he had repeatedly thought that if she were born within the last two decades, she would be a perfect candidate for the Convent.

There was much to do, and he was anxious to do it.

All of that would now suddenly have to wait, despite his previous words. Mrs. Brimley was not going anywhere, and neither was her memory, if Lady Raeburn's account of her was correct. And Amelia was right, the goddess wasn't going to be any less missing in the coming days.

But Amelia Berger could disappear with her mysterious agenda at a moment's notice.

And that was something he was not willing to risk.

He would work her case, but first, he needed information. About her. He needed to know everything about who she was, who she *really* was, and what sort of secrets she might have kept from him. She would not share these details with him, and he did not have the time to patiently wait for her to decide to trust him enough to do so. Given their relationship, he could eventually have gotten her there, but after her behavior, and his just now, that was suddenly in question.

If last night had taught him anything, it was that Amelia was a dangerous woman. Not because of her skills or her maddening inability to feel fear, but because of those secrets she held. Even now, after weeks of knowing her, observing her, studying her, he had to admit that even he, with all his experience, had no idea what to expect from her or what she was capable of.

And, in the interest of full disclosure, he had to admit that she meant a great deal more to him than he'd ever imagined.

He had to know.

He pushed up out of his desk and shrugged into the worn and faded jacket he wore when he needed to especially blend into his surroundings. He glanced at the clock nearby and nodded to himself.

It was early enough that he could go down to the docks without disturbing their legitimate work. Most of them would be hungover, which was a delightful way to carry on an interrogation, as everyone was always so much more cooperative.

But he knew these men well, and they knew his methods well. It would not take much prodding on his part.

The question was whether their loyalty to Amelia outweighed their loyalty to him.

Gabe stewed in his own questions as he made his way down to the London Docks, this time not being greeted by any of the usual suspects, who were all no doubt asleep or at work, if they were the ambitious sort. He made no attempt to hide his intent or his direction, keeping his focus fixed on the customs house, and the long walk felt good after such a short and restless night's sleep. He was used to working and wandering at all hours, but Amelia and her case were affecting him more than his usual fare, even in the spy world.

Despite what he had said about his hunt for the goddess, this was personal, too.

He approached the customs house with a forced appearance of dejection and bone-deep weariness that he had seen on various faces all over London's poorer streets.

A middle-aged man in simple clothing sat at a desk just within the plain building and looked up at him with a bored expression. "Can I help you?"

Gabe removed his cap swiftly and began mangling it nervously in his hand. "I was told to ask for Mr. Valerie," Gabe near-stammered in a coarse accent, intentionally butchering the last name, as a common Londoner in his situation might have done with a French name. "'e said 'e might 'ave a job for me."

The man looked him over in assessment. "Dock work or ship staff?"

"Docks," Gabe answered with a firm nod. "I retch somefink awful on the water. Can't even swim."

His answer was a grunt that indicated the man could not have cared less. "Stand there, I'll fetch Mr. Valerie." He started to go, then looked back. "Don't sit. You'll get dirt everywhere."

"Yes, sir," Gabe replied obediently. "Sorry, sir."

When he was alone, Gabe rolled his eyes and eased his stance. That man was rather high in the instep for someone working at a customs house on the docks. The office was in even worse shape than his, and that was saying quite a lot. But there was no sense in having anything finer. This was sufficient, and no doubt did the job well.

Besides, Gabe had seen it look worse.

"Here you are, sir," the clerk's voice came from behind him.

Gabe turned to face them and saw Jean's eyes widen. But the Frenchman only grunted and sniffed once. "Better come to my office, Mr. Clark, and we will discuss where we might put you." He gestured for Gabe to follow, giving him a hard look.

"Yes, sir," Gabe said with an awkward half-bow, following with a shuffling step.

Jean's office was just around the corner, and surprisingly well kept, given the man's usual state of dress. But then, Gabe did not have a particularly orderly office either. Or a well-kept state of dress. And he was in the aristocracy. Sort of.

Jean closed the door, then turned to face him, his eyes narrowed.

Gabe tossed his cap into a chair, folded his arms, and stared right back at the man, no longer pretending at any sort of timidity or insecurity.

"Impossible as it sounds, I think you have gotten uglier since the last time we met," Jean commented with a grunt.

Gabe sniffed in amusement. "Funny, I was thinking the same thing about you."

"That is not what your woman says."

"Yes, it is."

Jean chuckled a little, shaking his head and pushing off the wall. "Ah, *mon ami*, it has been a long time. Please, have a seat."

They both sat, and Gabe forced a bland smile.

"What can I do for you, Rogue?" Jean asked with a slight sweep of his hand.

"I need to talk with you, Jean," he replied in a too-kind tone.

Jean scoffed and ran a hand through his beard. "Well, I did not think you came for my cognac. What do you need to talk about?"

"A woman."

"Ah, advice?" Jean shook his head with a laugh. "I knew it was only a matter of time."

Gabe took care to bestow as much derision into his look as possible. "If I wanted to know how to bore her and make her leave, yes, I would come see you."

Jean stilled in his chair, his eyes narrowed once more. "You are as ignorant as you are unsightly."

Gabe inclined his head rather thoughtfully, smiling a little. "You are too kind, as always. Must be those impeccable French manners."

He saw the Frenchman's beard twitch as if he would laugh, but then he only heaved a noisy sigh. "Very well, who is the trollop you must ask about?"

Gabe barely avoided laughing. If Jean knew just whom he would be questioned about, he would never have called her anything remotely resembling a trollop. "Someone you know well," Gabe assured him, crossing an ankle over his knee. He offered the man a cold smirk. "I believe you call her Tribbie. But I know her as Amelia Berger."

Jean's eyes widened perceptibly, his jaw going slack. "I don't…"

"Do not lie to me, Jean," Gabe sighed, shaking his head. "I'd hate the mess of slitting your throat, and you'd be more wine than blood. The stench would sour me from French wine ever again."

The Frenchman's chest rose and fell in great bursts of air, and his jaw tightened. His expression was positively murderous, and his eyes were full of a defiance that Gabe had never seen in his ally before.

Again, Gabe slowly shook his head. "Don't test me."

"Why do you want to know?" Jean grunted, shifting in his chair.

He considered adopting his usual derision and dismissiveness, insisting on asking all the questions and giving no answers, giving up nothing of himself or his knowledge. He did not owe anybody anything. There was no reason for him to answer the question. He never answered their questions. He never behaved as anything but controlling, disrespectful, and markedly efficient.

But for Amelia it was different.

Everything was.

"I need to know who she is," he confessed, keeping his tone as moderate as he could. "I am helping her with an investigation, and she is keeping things from me. I must know the truth about her if I am to help her succeed."

Jean nodded slowly, his eyes steady on Gabe. "You are helping her find her father."

"I am."

"Do you know what she intends to do?"

"No."

A small smile lit Jean's mouth. "But you know it is not good."

Gabe resisted the urge to sigh, suddenly uncomfortable. "Yes," he admitted. "I know that much."

Jean tilted his head slightly, considering Gabe from a new light. "This is, ah, personal for you. In some way."

He stilled, staring at this man for a long moment. He could not answer, could not bring himself to open up to such an extent with a bloody dock-working contact who could very well be aiding Amelia in whatever she had planned. But he could not deny it. Not when it could mean everything.

And not when it was true.

Gabe swallowed, then allowed himself to merely nod. Just once.

That seemed to satisfy Jean, and he pulled two cigars out of his desk, clipped the ends, and offered one to Gabe. "You will need this, Rogue. It is a long story."

Gabe took it and lit it with the candelabra. "I have remarkable endurance. Go on."

"First of all," Jean said with a sigh as he sat back, taking a long draw from his cigar, "her name is Amelia Tribbett. But to me, she will always be jus' Tribbie."

The story then unfolded, and Gabe could barely retain a hold on his cigar as he listened.

Amelia had met Jean when she was fourteen, and she'd been a starving girl with only her stubbornness and determination to survive on. She'd taken him by surprise with her courage and wit, and he'd decided to hire her on, despite every single one of his co-workers being opposed to the idea. He knew what an ugly place London could be, and it would have been no place for a girl like her on her own. Even the docks were treacherous, but at least there, Jean and the others could protect her.

She had become a universal servant for the club by night and Jean's assistant during the day. She had been used to deliver notices, to root out cheaters, to eavesdrop on conversations, and to serve drinks, on occasion. She had apparently been of great use to both the legitimate shipping interests of the company as well as the less legitimate smuggling one. Mr. Banes had found her to be intelligent and capable, which was the only reason he'd agreed to add her to the payroll.

According to Jean, Amelia had always been set on finding her father. It was the only thing that drove her. She was also incredibly self-sufficient, which did not surprise anyone who had heard her story. She did not want to depend on anyone or anything. Everyone who worked with her knew her past, and they would have moved heaven and earth to help her if they could.

When she started to get older and the attention she attracted changed, they pulled her back into a more hidden service, fearing that even their intimidation would not be enough to protect her.

Then had come the first assault attempt.

According to Jean, there had been at least three while she worked with them.

The first time, she had just turned sixteen, and she had not yet become the strong fighter she was now. She had been on a notice delivery at night, and a drunken worker had attempted to force himself on her. She was still small and lacked strength at that time, and it would have been only too easy. But thankfully, a stranger stepped in and saved her, beating her assailant to within an inch of his life.

Gabe rather wished it had been beyond his life, but the point was irrelevant now.

"Who was it?" he growled, hardly able to breathe, his cigar cold in his hand. "Who saved her?"

Jean shrugged, averting his eyes. "She never knew. She ran away before she saw what happened."

"But you know." It was not a question, and Gabe watched his companion, waiting.

Jean looked back at him and exhaled slowly. "It was Trace."

Gabe closed his eyes and pinched the bridge of his nose. Of course it was. Who else would have been a guardian angel for her but his own bloody cousin? His chest seized with pride and pain, and an overwhelming sense of relief. He looked back at Jean. "How do you know that?"

"He recognized her from the few times he had been to the club," Jean told him, keeping his voice low. "He came to me the day after and asked me how she was. She'd never told me about it. If I had not confronted her, I would never have known." He shook his head and scratched his jaw. "She does not like to appear weak."

"I know," Gabe murmured, putting his head in his hands. Damn, what else had Amelia endured without telling anyone? She became a young woman on the docks of London, quite literally in the gutters, surrounded by ruffians, thieves, and scoundrels. The fact that she was not a prostitute or dead was astonishing.

"And the other times?" he asked faintly, not sure he could bear hearing.

"I know none of those details," Jean admitted, sounding disappointed. "But after the firs' time, Trace suggested that, if we meant to keep her, she needed to learn to protect herself. So, I had Benjamin teach her to fight." He chuckled darkly, and Gabe looked up to find the man grinning. "You shoul' have seen his face the day Tribbie bested him. She is a quick one, and he was our best."

"I remember," Gabe murmured. Benjamin had been a fierce contender and rarely lost in the underground ring. Gabe had bested him twice, but Gabe did not fight fairly. He rubbed his hands over his face, then looked over at Jean. "When did she leave?"

Jean tipped his head back in thought. "Four years? Perhaps five. She had earned enough to satisfy her and wanted to find her father. I cannot say what she has done for work since then, I did not see her again until last night." He shook his head slowly. "I worried about her, despite knowing her strength and her character. This part of London is too dangerous."

Gabe nodded slowly, pressing his hands together before his face. Amelia was an amazing creature. She knew perfectly how ugly the world was, how cruel it could be, and it explained much about his first impression of her. How she had survived was beyond him. He'd thought his life a challenge to overcome, but hers? It was unspeakable. And yet she had done it. She had overcome it all and was now a pillar of strength, yet somehow capable of such intuition and tenderness…

This new knowledge of her made him love her more than he had before.

And he hadn't even known he'd loved her then.

But now…

He found it hard to swallow and sat back in his seat, trying for his usual hard persona. "Tell me what happened last night, Jean," he said roughly, his voice almost betraying him. "Every detail."

Chapter Twenty-One

Sleep had no meaning. Food was a waste of energy. Anything except work was out of the question.

Oddly enough, it was invigorating.

Once he had wrung Jean dry of all information, which had been a surprising amount, he had hauled himself at breakneck speed back to Finley in Surrey. He'd spent an entire day interviewing everyone in the village that he could find, and any outlying cottages like the one Amelia had lived in. Luck had been with him, for he'd found the family that they had moved in with when forced out of their home, though they were still known by the surname of Palmer at that time.

It had not been a pleasant interview.

The family had taken them in and allowed them there for nearly four years. They described Mary as being frail and unhappy, and Amelia had been energetic and bright at first, but as time wore on, she became more serious, more defensive, and more obedient to her mother. She was always trying to please her, to draw a smile from her, taking care of her.

"It was the oddest thing," the woman said, shaking her head. "A child taking care of her mother. She had no real childhood, you know. None at all."

That, at least, Gabe could relate to.

They told him about Amelia's working in the village for her mother, but despite the efforts of the townspeople, they could not make Amelia as efficient as her mother had been.

Nor could they pay her enough.

And then Mary got worse.

"We couldn't afford them after that," they told him. "Without wages to pay for the extra food, we couldn't keep them on. They went to the poorhouse in Cobham."

So, Gabe went there also, prepared to hear the worst. Mary and Amelia Tribbett, as they were then, were on record in the poorhouse for three months. Amelia was twelve upon her arrival, and her mother was an invalid. The caretaking staff was lax at best even now, and all who were able, even children, were required to work. Amelia had made an impression on one of the matrons for working her long shift and then tending to her mother all night. She would read to her, talk to her, feed her, anything at all to try and get her mother to recognize her or to find a will to live.

Nothing worked.

"It was eerie," the older woman said, once Gabe had bribed her with a drink. "I've never seen a gel mourn with less emotion. She simply went blank when her mam died. No tears, no cries, no screams. Nothing." She shivered and took a long swig from her tankard. "Unnatural, it was."

Gabe didn't doubt it. But he also understood.

Emotions were costly, and it was so much easier to feel nothing. He'd done that his entire life up to this point. Hell, he still didn't have many emotions. The ones he did have were wrapped up in Amelia so tightly there wasn't room for anything else.

Piecing together the bits of her life was only increasing the intensity of his feelings. He found her to be the most singular woman he'd ever known, and every story he heard of her became harder and harder to hear. It was as if his heart were suddenly awakening, only to be squeezed and crushed and bruised. It pained him to know how she had suffered, what she had endured. He wanted, quite desperately, to hold her in his lap, to wrap his arms around her and keep her safe.

It only followed that he should be more assured of his love for her. It was more than admiration, more than respect, more than need or desire or interest. He loved her. How she could smile and laugh despite her past, how sharp her wit could be and how beautifully she flushed, the way she could see beyond the surface of anyone and know what they were thinking. He even loved that she could thrash a man so thoroughly and without fear. He loved that she was willful and strong, that she did not depend on anyone, and that she scared him out of his mind with her lack of fear.

The woman who drove him mad was the woman who drove him now. And if he had ever done any good in his entire life, he would make things right with her. And for her.

He couldn't begin to understand how he had come to love her, or why, or what had possessed him to do so, but the more he thought it over, the better the idea sounded and the freer he felt. She was the ideal woman for him, and that was a phrase he did not use lightly.

And he had wounded her by seeking after another.

Gabe shook his head as he rode back to London, just as furiously as he had done before. The goddess was a fantasy, an illusion, and might always be so. Amelia was real. She was the most real thing in his life, and she was just as broken as he was. But she was slowly putting him back together, and if he could do half as much for her, he would find himself satisfied.

But how to apologize for not seeing it? For putting her life's pursuit aside, even for a moment?

He couldn't have gone to her that day and mumbled out the words, it would not be nearly enough. He needed to prove to her that she was important. That he was choosing her above all others, not just in her case, but in his life. In her life.

He chose her.

Gads, but they were perfect for each other. The farthest thing from perfect individually, but together, it made a bizarre sort of sense. They would always challenge each other, and with a blinding fierceness. They would cherish each other with the same.

What sort of fate had protected Amelia that night on the docks? To have Alex be present to prevent the horrors at her door? It sent a chill down Gabe's spine, and he tossed up a rare prayer of gratitude for his cousin. It was too much, and it grieved him that Alex would never know how much that would come to mean.

Alex would have loved Amelia. And he would have loved that Gabe loved Amelia.

He would have laughed in Gabe's face, but he would have loved it.

Gabe couldn't tell her how he felt; not yet. There was too much to do. He needed to help her solve this case. He needed to find the closure that she needed. He understood her perfectly now, and he could see almost the entirety of her plan laid out before them. She could never be completely happy until this was over, and Gabe knew that the hatred in her heart would drive her to vengeance. She would never be satisfied with less, but she would lose herself if she succumbed to it. Gabe had been in the darkest place of humanity and had only been spared the loss of his soul by the opportunity to serve a greater purpose.

Amelia needed to find one. She needed to have hope, she needed to let go. And she could only do that with answers.

Gabe would find them. He would give them to her, no matter what it cost. Everything else could wait. National security, personal interests, other clients. He didn't care. Amelia's answers came first.

And if that did not testify to the depth of his feelings for her, nothing would.

He could have bloody skipped his way down to the boarding house. He was working on less sleep than he ever had in his entire life, but he was so energized at the moment that he doubted he could have slept if he was given the opportunity. His body ached, his feet were throbbing, and he looked like a dock worker without having to try for the appearance. He'd been tearing his investigation apart piece by piece, wondering why he hadn't been giving it his full attention before. Was he really such a heartless scoundrel? Could he not see how vital it was?

He knew the truth. Of course, he was not that heartless, despite what he'd spent years believing. He'd just been working with incomplete information and dedicated to his actual work, neither of which were things Amelia could have been blamed for. But now that his eyes were opened, and he saw the truth of the matter, he'd found his skills enhanced and heightened, finding clues he'd missed before, making connections that he had been unable to before.

None of his investigations had ever had this sort of proficiency. Which made him wonder what the hell he had been doing all these years.

Gabe grinned to himself as he neared the boarding house. He'd simply lacked the proper motivation.

It was astonishing to him that he'd managed such single-mindedness when he had been so absorbed in thinking about Amelia, but instead of distracting him, she had given him focus. Hours and hours of work, his own and as many of his contacts as he could manage to send out, and at long last, he had some answers. He could have taken the leads they'd uncovered and possibly solved the entire case, but it was Amelia's case. She deserved to see the end of it.

So instead of following his former instincts, he'd left the office, which had seemed too quiet and too empty without Amelia and headed out to fetch her.

Dawes & Pope, the merchant company that had hired Daniel Cole, had dissolved years ago, but its foreman worked on the West India docks now, and its owners still had interests in the market. They were only too happy to discuss their glory days with Gabe and his associates, and the name Daniel Cole had brought back memories for each. He had been one of them for a time before starting his own small company, and while none of them could say for certain what his interests had been, they could not deny that he had made quite a profit.

There was no indication of what had happened to him, as each of them had said Mr. Cole had quite simply disappeared one day, as had his ships and business, but they could tell Gabe where Mr. Cole had lived when in London.

And if Gabe knew where he lived, he could identify his parish, and, if he were most fortunate, could find the record of his marriage.

And *that* would get Amelia's attention.

Gabe thundered up the stairs to Amelia's room, having discovered her room number by a simple conversation with Knutt, who continued to stand watch over her.

Amelia had not taken any nightly excursions lately, but she had been busy during the day.

It brought a smile to Gabe's face to wonder what she knew

240

compared to what he did.

For whatever reason, Amelia's door was slightly ajar, and Gabe gently pushed it open, feeling grateful that the door swung open silently.

Amelia stood by the window in her room brushing her hair in long, fluid strokes. She swayed slightly as she hummed to herself and the light of the window gave her skin a glow that transfixed him. She looked almost serene in her reverie, and he felt as though he were suddenly an intruder in something very intimate.

He leaned against the doorjamb and watched her, his chest tightening almost painfully. He had seen Amelia many, many times, had noticed her beauty, had scowled at the sensations looking at her had given him, but this was entirely different.

It was inexplicable, but somehow, looking at the woman he loved now that he knew of his love was far more powerful, far more potent, and far more stirring. He could barely breathe, and he could honestly say it had little enough to do with her beauty. It was quite simply and quite profoundly just the sight of her.

And dammit, he didn't want to feel any other way.

Ever.

He swallowed with difficulty and listened to her absent humming, wondering what songs she knew, and if she was at all musical.

A cold chill settled on him as he realized that the song she hummed was the very same song he and the goddess had waltzed to.

He straightened up a little, staring at her with more intensity. Could it be? Could she...?

He gauged her height, the size of her frame, the shape of her face. It was eerily similar, and he did not believe in coincidences. The goddess had been blonde, but a woman with resources could have access to wigs of quality.

Tilda.

He felt himself snarl silently at the thought. His own people had had a hand in this, whether they knew it or not.

Amelia continued to sway and hum, a dreamy look on her face as she moved in an almost waltzing fashion by herself. Her voice rose in pitch, and suddenly perfectly matched the voice of the goddess in his memory.

There was nothing for it then.

"It was you," he interrupted her at last.

She whirled and looked at him, eyes wide. "Gabe? What are you...?"

He marched over to her, grabbed her arm with one hand while the other tangled itself in her hair, and before she could finish her question, he kissed her; angrily, insistent, and hard. She responded instinctively, though he could feel her confusion as he devoured her lips, nothing gentle or tender in his ministrations.

How could she...? *How* could she...?

He growled and drew her closer, unable to stop himself from his mad frenzy, from the searing confusion and desire and fury that drove him.

Amelia shoved off him, panting and disheveled, with such force that he staggered unsteadily back. "What the hell is wrong with you?" she barked, her eyes wild with confusion and irritation, and some desire as well.

Gabe exhaled hard, shaking his head at her. "You. You are what is wrong with me. Why the hell didn't you tell me?"

"Tell you what?" she demanded, flinging her arms out.

"It was you!" he cried. "At the ball! Did you think to mock me in front of the entire world? Just like you plan to do with your father if you find him?"

Amelia looked positively bewildered, none of his words sinking in. "You?" she asked, walking to her toilette to set her brush down. "What does any of it have to do with you?"

Gabe smirked without humor. "Think, goddess. Think hard."

She stopped at once, her fingers still touching the brush handle. Slowly, she turned to look at him, her eyes wide, and her hand shakily rose to her lips. "Oh, good lord..." she whispered, horrified.

His smirk drew to a sneer. "Didn't recognize me without the mask? Perhaps I should introduce myself. Gabriel Statler, Lord Wharton," he scoffed with a bow, "at your service."

"I had no idea," Amelia stammered, fumbling for the furniture behind her. "I didn't even... I went to find information, to track down what I could, I didn't think I'd get access at all, and then...

You're Lord Wharton?"

"Tell anyone that and you'll find yourself silenced," he snarled, feeling more vicious than he'd ever felt in his entire life.

Amelia blinked slowly. "You're threatening me?"

She was not supposed to sound hurt and betrayed. She was supposed to be defensive and riled, something that would make his fury appropriate. But instead, it rushed out of him in a harsh exhale, and he ran a hand through his hair. "At the moment, I'd rather throttle you."

"Try it. Go ahead and try it," she told him, finally a hint of defensiveness entering her voice.

Gabe swallowed, and slowly shook his head. "No."

Now it was Amelia who sneered. "Why not? You just said you want to."

"Because I can't," he admitted, turning away from her. "You know I can't."

"Do I?"

Gabe closed his eyes, exhaling silently, fighting to remain in control of the flurry of emotions swirling within him. "That night…" he began, his voice low and hoarse. "I have to know. Was it an act? What were you thinking when you…?"

"It wasn't an act," Amelia interrupted, suddenly gentle. "None of it was."

He turned to look at her, letting his anguish and confusion show. "How could I not know it was you?"

Her eyes suddenly shone with a suspicious sheen, and she swallowed hard. "I was wearing a mask. I could be whomever I wanted. And with you… I wanted to be myself. I've never felt more myself than when I was with you that night."

He restrained a groan and shook his head, fighting the impulse to draw her into his arms. Instead, he remained a safe distance away.

"I want to believe that. I want…" He suddenly growled and rubbed a hand over his face. "Dammit, I fell in love with you!"

"And you think I didn't feel the same way?" she cried, a pair of tears finding their way down her cheeks. "That I didn't ache in places I didn't know could ache? That I didn't cry for you for weeks? You made me dream of a different life for myself, something I never thought I could have, and I wanted it so much. So very much."

He had to ignore the break in her voice, the pain he could hear that mirrored his own. "And then to have to go on with life, and see you… To really see you… And I fell in love with *you*…"

She gasped softly. "Oh, Gabe…"

He ignored that as well. "And now, after weeks of tormenting myself, I find that it was you all along. You at the ball, and you as you are." He laughed without any hint of humor. "I find that I love both versions of you."

"I wish I'd known," Amelia murmured. "I'd have told you how I felt. Gabe, I've been in love with you for ages. It was far more believable than Lord Wharton. I could never have him."

He gave her a resigned look. "I *am* Lord Wharton."

She smiled bitterly. "And just as far from me as ever. Out of reach and beyond my sight. Serves me right for daring to hope." She shrugged and sighed wearily. "Well, at least there are no more secrets between us."

No more secrets? He could have laughed. There were so many secrets between them.

Gabe shook his head slowly, smiling maliciously. "Oh, but there are, Miss Tribbett."

Amelia's gaze shot to his, her expression changing to one of affront and disbelief. "You investigated me?"

"I had to know with whom I was dealing," he said with an easy shrug.

She was shaking her head rapidly and held up a warning finger. "That was not part of the contract."

"To hell with the contract!" he yelled with a slash of his hand. "I refuse to be kept in the dark anymore, Amelia! Why do you need to find your father? You hate him. You don't want to meet him, you just want his identity, his location even. What do you have in mind? Blackmail? Murder? Some other form of vengeance? What are you up to?"

Amelia stared at him without speaking, her hands clenching and unclenching at her sides, her entire frame coiled with visible tension. "You know what?" she said tightly. "Contract is over. I don't want your help anymore."

Gabe gaped without speaking for a number of heartbeats. "Excuse me?" he managed.

"You're too involved," she told him with a careless shrug. She shook her head. "I need distance and anonymity, and you just ruined that."

"You aren't blameless!" he reminded her, his head spinning.

She returned to her bitter smile and folded her arms. "I know. If I'd known who you were, this would never have happened. That is my fault. I was careless. One more reason to cut you out. So, take the money I gave you and consider yourself freed from commitment."

"What if I don't want to be freed?" he demanded, taking two steps towards her. "What if I refuse?"

Her eyes turned colder, and her expression became utterly devoid of emotion. "You don't have a choice. Get out, or I will do to you what I did to the informant who lied to me."

"You are threatening *me* now?" he asked in disbelief. "You know what I am capable of."

"And you know what I am capable of," she replied with a tilt of her head. "So, are you truly without honor, Rogue? Or will you leave?"

Gabe stared at her, wondering how he had come crashing down so far so fast. Of course he couldn't fight her, would never even dream of hurting her. But leave?

How could he leave?

"Well?" she demanded indicating the door with her head.

He straightened up to his full height, considering her coolly. "Good day, Miss Tribbett," he heard himself say as he offered a short bow. "I sincerely hope you find whatever it is you seek."

He could see her jaw quivering, but he could not bring himself to say or do anything except wrench his gaze away and leave the room, as she requested.

But he was not about to give up the investigation.

Not for her or anyone.

The door closed behind Gabe with an almost thunderous slam, despite the lack of force with which it closed.

It didn't matter.

Amelia gasped sharply at the sound, her heart threatening to pound itself out of her chest, and she suddenly could not find breath in her lungs. She paced about the room in agitation, rubbing her chest and grinding her teeth.

How *dare* he come here and tell her he loved her in one breath while confessing to investigating her in the next! How could he have invaded her privacy so completely? Who knew what lengths he had gone to, and when he was supposed to be working her case, no less! The object was her father, not herself!

He was Lord Wharton? It was too far-fetched, and yet she knew it had to be true. She should have seen it. The same charm, despite Gabe's inclination to hide it; the same eyes, so piercing and captivating; the same smile, so infrequently seen in the day-to-day, but a sight to behold. The very same warmth in his embrace. The passion in his kiss.

The love in his eyes.

Oh, how could she not have seen it?

And how could he betray her like this?

She grabbed onto her bedpost with a screech of distress, finding herself shaking with fury and aching for the man she had just sent from her room, and possibly her life.

She had to focus on finding her father. She had to finish this.

But her heart was breaking into pieces, and she sank onto her bed, still clinging to the bedpost, unable to stand any longer.

Gabe…

She exhaled roughly and found a hint of a panicked sob in its sound. She shook her head quickly, desperate to maintain control, to rid herself of the unwanted emotions. She could not give in, could not be weak, could not let herself be so vulnerable as to succumb to the tide within her.

The harder she fought, the more they resisted, and when she could bear it no longer, she closed her eyes, dropped her head, and let the rising tears fall.

Chapter Twenty-Two

$\mathcal{T}$here were times in Gabe's life when his instincts outweighed his logic, despite evidence to the contrary and against all odds.

This was one of those times.

There was no way in hell that this was a coincidence.

He'd been in a quiet, dogged mindset in the few days following his fight with Amelia, tracking down the leads he'd uncovered, while also receiving updates from Knutt and Daisy on Amelia's actions, which had thankfully been remarkably quiet. He couldn't bear to contemplate why she was so quiet these days, it would make the endless hours excruciating. He'd kept to his investigation, determined to find the answers Amelia so desperately sought.

He wanted her to have them. He wanted her to have the truth. Even if he could never have her for himself, he needed to know that she could be happy. It was, without a doubt, the most sentimental, maudlin, ridiculous idea he'd ever had in his entire life, but he could not shake himself out of it. And if he were the one controlling answers and monitoring her activities, he could ensure that she would not throw her life away for her own agenda.

She deserved better.

He snorted to himself as he drew his cap further over his brow. She deserved a lot better than him, that was for sure, but she wouldn't find that if she wound up in Newgate, or worse.

Would it be too much to ask that her father had already met his Maker? That would solve everything.

After a stroke of luck, he'd managed to find the church where Daniel Cole and Mary Clairbourne had been married. It ought to have been much simpler, but parish lines had been redrawn a decade ago, and a stodgy clergyman had balked at the idea of letting a man of Gabe's appearance peruse the precious archived records. Thankfully, working for the Crown enabled one to exert a certain amount of authority, and once that had been explained in no uncertain terms, the clergyman had been quite accommodating.

It ought to have been very simple. A look in the register for the marriage between Daniel Cole and Mary Clairbourne, roughly twenty-five years earlier, establish the date, interrogate the man on any information on the persons in question, and then he could move on.

What he had not counted on had been the name of the male witness of the marriage.

Richard Keele.

To any other person looking at the record, it would have meant nothing.

But Gabe had felt a memory of his earliest days as a spy when he'd had to engage in operations accompanied by a more experienced spy for his training. A particular trainer of his had used that exact name as his alias.

And that man had been the one they called Tailor, one of the Shopkeepers who ran England, who also happened to be the grand spymaster. In his regular life, he was one of the most influential members of the peerage that ever lived a quiet and overlooked existence.

There was no reason for his alias to have appeared on a marriage record unless one of the wedded couple had ties to his work, and the idea that one of Amelia's parents could have worked for the Crown, or still might, was the single most unnerving thought he'd had in some time.

But there was no possible way he could approach Tailor with this, not even with the exact copy of the license clenched in his hands.

So, he was going to his next best source: Weaver.

He'd been to Weaver's home time and time again for various complaints and situations and knew the way well. He knew better than to use the front door when he was dealing with something of this sensitivity. Instead, he knocked at the servant's entrance, as odd as that may have seemed to the clearly bewildered maid who answered.

"Get your master," he'd instructed her. "Tell him the Rogue is here to see him. He'll know what you mean."

She hadn't looked convinced, but at his quiet nod, she'd bobbed a sort of curtsey and left, closing the door behind her.

Gabe leaned against the stone of the house, tilting his head back as he waited.

If this all became more complicated than it already was, he was likely to go mad.

Gent and Rook had been curious about his work and had tried to ask him about it, as well as what had happened with Amelia, but he had rebuffed every attempt to get the information. Until Gent had sat down with him and stated, "I think you're in love with Amelia, and I think you're terrified of what that means."

"You're not wrong," Gabe had muttered, not even bothering to look up.

It had taken Gent a moment to recover his shock, but then he'd proceeded with a gentle, "How much?"

It was at that moment that Gabe realized precisely the depth and breadth of his feelings, and how to accurately convey them to his colleague and friend. He looked Gent squarely in the eyes. "She is my Margaret," he'd told him without blinking.

Gent had barely moved for so long that Gabe returned to his work. "What can I do?" Gent had asked in a surprisingly rough voice.

Gabe had put his friend to work, and he would no doubt use him again when this interview ended.

The door beside him opened and Gabe shoved off the wall to face the tall man standing within, who had clearly been in the process of preparing for bed.

"Rogue," he greeted simply, folding his arms. "This is unexpected."

"Weaver," Gabe replied with a nod. He swallowed and held out the copy of the marriage license in his hand, pointing directly at the witness line. "What is this?"

Weaver took the paper and tilted it towards the light from the candles within. His eyes widened, and Gabe saw him fight for a controlled expression. He prayed he would not ask any sort of inane question such as where it came from or how he got it, as those should have been obvious. He wouldn't put it past Weaver to try to divert him from the line of questions, despite their years of friendship and professional association, and he would not take kindly to that.

Thankfully, Weaver looked up at him with a bit of a drawn expression. "You'd better come in, Rogue. There's a lot to explain."

The taproom was no place for a woman, but that made little difference to Amelia these days. It was the best place to spend her evenings, tucked away in a corner where no one disturbed her. She could drink to her heart's content without disapproving glances or any drunken sot coming to try his luck with her. Her fellow tenants knew her well enough to ward others off, and they seemed to sense that she was even less agreeable than usual lately.

Her determination had not lessened in her desire for answers, but she could not seem to manage the connections and intelligence she once had. Her investigation was as fruitless now as it had been in her early days of attempting it.

The days before Gabe.

She scowled as she drew her fresh glass of gin to her mouth and faintly wondered if it was her second, third, or fourth. It was so hard to remember these things, particularly when her days seemed to be running together in a monotonous sort of drudgery. And really, she was imbibing so often these days that the drinks were all slurring together as well. Surely this was only her second. She did not feel out of sorts at all.

Her head was beginning to feel a little fuzzy, though. But it was the end of a rather long day, and even the smallest amount of gin could enhance such fatigue.

She took another drink, and this time she tasted something different. Rather than the sharp potency of gin, there was a bitter overtone than tingled her tongue. She pushed her drink slightly away, staring at it.

She knew that taste.

She tried to focus on it, licked her lips and forced herself to remember where she had tasted it before.

Her head became worse, and her limbs felt heavy and strange. She shook her head with difficulty and pushed herself out of her chair, barely remembering to toss some coins onto the table, though if their drinks were this bad, they did not deserve her payment. She staggered out of the taproom to the stairs, fumbling her way up and tripping repeatedly.

What was this? What was happening to her? This was no mere matter of alcohol. This was…

Opium.

Amelia tried to nod to herself at the answer, but she could not manage to bring her head back up to its proper position once it dipped to touch her chest.

Who would have given her opium? She would have to investigate the staff of the boarding house after she slept. She would have to sleep for a while; she was feeling quite terrible at the moment. Sleep would help, and she could sleep on the floor if she had to. The bed was so far away from the door.

She tried three times to manage the doorknob, and finally shoved her way into her room, hardly able to keep herself upright.

Sleep… That was all she needed.

She started to crumple as she found the bed, her hands barely able to grip the counterpane.

Suddenly, arms wrapped tightly around her, and her mouth was covered.

Amelia screamed and thrashed, the sound muffled but her motions frantic enough to throw her captor off balance. Her eyes refused to open, and each move she made exhausted her more, but she was not about to be taken without a fight. She thrashed from side to side, tossing her head back to attempt to make contact with whoever it was, with no success. She managed to slip an arm free and slammed her elbow up and back, grunting with satisfaction as she connected with his head. She faintly registered his pained growl, but her head was growing fuzzier and fuzzier, and she could not fight anymore.

A gag was suddenly forced into her mouth, and rather than resist,

Amelia relaxed and slumped in her captor's hold. What was the point? At least now she could sleep.

She wished her head would explode as it was threatening to. It would be much more of a relief than sitting here with this agonizing throbbing that pulsed against every part of her skull.

Amelia winced as she became more aware of herself and her surroundings. Her body hurt absolutely everywhere, and her arms...

She frowned. Her arms were behind her, bound with rope, if the scratching against her skin were any indication. Her shoulders were aching from their position, but she'd been in worse. Her arms weren't the only things bound; her legs were strapped to the chair she sat in, her body was tied to it, and her mouth...

Hmm. The gag was gone. She licked her parched lips and winced at the disgusting taste.

Opium was dreadful stuff, and she probably had taken in a good amount, given how quickly she'd lost consciousness, and the strength of the taste.

Amelia forced her eyes open and winced at the light, though it was faint. She was in a warehouse of some kind, with crates and boxes filling up half of the spacious room. Up at the top of the thick walls were small windows letting in the faintest amount of light. So, it was morning, then.

Or close to it, at least.

"Good, you're awake."

Amelia stopped scanning the room and slowly brought her eyes to a man standing in the shadows next to the only door.

She knew that voice.

"You," she croaked, her stomach and her throat clenching in unison.

Gabe stepped forward into the light, his eyes steady on hers. "Hello, Amelia."

She ground her teeth at the sight of him, obviously unmoved by her situation, and only the sight of bruising just under his right eye made her feel any better.

"That looks like it hurts," she said with a snarl.

His expression didn't change. "I've had worse."

She didn't doubt that, but it still gave her satisfaction that she'd inflicted pain upon him.

"What did you give me?" she groaned, craning her neck as her head throbbed.

"Opium."

She glared at him as much as she was able. "I had figured that for myself, thank you."

His mouth tightened into an almost-smile. "Laudanum. In your gin. I paid the maid to do so."

"Lovely," she muttered, wishing she knew a foul enough curse for that. She straightened as much she was able and tried to look superior despite her ropes. "Would you care to explain to me why I am here in this building with these ropes restraining me?"

Gabe folded his arms, his gaze never wavering. "I found your father."

There was no air in the room or in her lungs, and nothing else he could have said would have taken her fury at Gabe to an entirely different level. "You... you kept investigating?"

He nodded once.

"Even when I told you not to?" she asked, her voice rising in pitch. "I told you the contract was done!"

"Yes, well," he replied easily, not at all concerned with her distress, "I have never reacted well to orders or commands."

She jerked her gaze away, wishing it did not hurt her so much to see him, to hear his cynicism on full display once more.

Her father... He had found her father...

He had.

Not her.

She raised her eyes to his with all the obstinacy she could muster. "So, if you have found my father, as you claim, why am I sitting here tied to a chair instead of going after him?"

"Because I know him."

Amelia stared at him for a long moment, his words echoing through her mind with every beat of her heart. He wasn't saying that he knew who he was. He *knew* her father.

"You lying piece of filth," she spat, tugging at her restraints. "How long have you known who he was? The entire time? Have you been mocking me since the beginning?"

He was shaking his head slowly before she finished. "No, Amelia, I've only known for a day. I give you my word."

"Your word," she repeated with a snort. "What is your word worth?"

"About two pennies."

She ignored his impertinence. "Tell me who he is."

"No."

She barely avoided growling. "Let me out of here," she demanded, pulling against the ropes again.

He shook his head. "No, Amelia."

"Why not?"

"Because I know you," he said calmly. "You'll vanish and try to find him on your own, and I can't let you do that."

"Why not?" she asked again, glaring at him despite her pounding head. "Why the hell can't I find my own father and finish this?"

Gabe didn't answer for a long moment. He just watched her, expression unreadable. "Because the man that is your father is a man I respect and admire greatly."

"You traitor!" she barked, straining against her ropes. "You lying, cheating…"

"And he is more of a father to me than any man on this planet," Gabe continued, overriding her, "and I cannot let you hurt him."

Amelia was seething, her breathing short and unsteady, and her vision was beginning to blur at the edges. "Then why am I here at all?" she asked through clenched teeth.

He went to the door and knocked softly. "Because you deserve to know."

The door swung open, and an older man with silver hair and a dark brow stepped through. He was taller than Gabe, but they were dressed similarly in their plain linen shirts and simple waistcoats, and they shook hands as the older man entered.

"Rogue," he said quietly, his voice deeper and more cultured than Amelia would have expected.

"Eagle," Gabe replied with a nod, stepping back.

The man turned to face her, and Amelia took a good, hard look at him.

His face was lined, and there were a few small scars there. His eyes were dark and hooded, thanks in part to his heavy brow, which was currently furrowed as he surveyed her. Unfortunately, Amelia could see a resemblance between them, and that angered her almost as much as Gabe's betrayal.

Her father stared at her, not saying a word, and she saw his throat work several times on a swallow. "You look so much like your mother," he told her, his low voice somehow lower and choked with emotion.

Amelia didn't want to hear anything about her mother from this man, but she couldn't manage to unclench her teeth long enough to give any answer at all.

"Why is she tied up?" he suddenly asked, as if only just realizing she was bound. "Untie her."

Gabe shook his head. "No."

The man whirled to face him. "Untie her now!"

"No," he said again, continuing to shake his head.

"Why not?" Amelia and her father demanded at the same time, the inflections nearly identical.

Gabe fought a smile, which Amelia did not appreciate at all, but then he was back to being somber. "Because until I have Amelia's word of honor that she will not try to attack you, sir, I'm not inclined to give her enough freedom to sneeze." He looked at her with a raised brow, daring her to comment.

She gaped at him for a moment, wondering how she had ever thought herself in love with him. He was the most irritating, insufferable, and infuriating man she had ever met, and she could not bear to look at him.

Except she had to.

"Honor," she snorted. "What do you know of honor?"

His gaze intensified on her. "Not a damn thing," he replied. "I'm asking for yours."

That caught her off-guard, and she found she did not have a response for him. She gnawed the inside of her lip for a moment, weighing her options. She did not have to agree to anything. He didn't have to know that her honor only extended as far as her arm or that her knife was closer at hand than he would ever think. She didn't have to kill the man now. She could do it any time after this.

She clenched her teeth again and nodded just once.

Gabe nodded in response and came over to her, flashing his own knife which seemed to appear from out of nowhere. He crouched to slash the ropes at her legs, then moved to her sides.

"I hate you," she hissed, turning her head to say it directly to his face.

"I'll have to live with that," he replied as he worked at the ropes.

She shook her head, ashamed of the tears that were beginning to form. "I don't know how I ever trusted you. Or how I thought you had any honor at all."

He met her eyes then, and somehow, she had no idea if her words meant anything to him. "I warned you against both of those things. You should have known better."

"I wish I'd never met you. I don't ever want to see you again," Amelia managed, wishing her voice didn't sound quite so emotional.

Gabe smirked slightly as he turned to cut the ropes at her wrist. "Don't worry. After this, you won't."

The ropes at her wrists loosened, but before she could feel relief, Gabe's fingers suddenly gripped the small handle of the knife she had tucked into her corset at the neckline. She stiffened as he drew it out and dangled it before her eyes.

"I know you, Amelia," he murmured too close to her ear. "And you won't get the chance." He straightened up and tossed the knife into a far corner of the room as he strode from it, not looking back at either of them as he closed the door.

Amelia stared at the door for a long moment, then shifted her gaze to the man dragging a chair over to sit in front of her, still a safe enough distance away. He sat down in the chair and leaned his elbows on his thighs, staring at her without a word.

She stared back without speaking. He had much to answer for. She did not.

"You undoubtedly have many questions for me," he said at last, having the good sense not to smile.

Amelia folded her arms and barely avoided rolling her eyes. "You could say that."

Her clipped tone apparently had no effect on him, and he nodded slowly. "You may ask me anything you like, Amelia." He smiled a little, and she was bothered by the fact that it was a kind smile. "I will tell you whatever you wish to know."

Well, that was hardly an opportunity she would give up, particularly since she would like answers before she killed the man.

"We could start with your name," she said with a sneer, "and where the hell you've been my entire life."

"My name is James Martin," he replied in his cultured tones. "Or at least it is now. I was born Daniel Cole."

Amelia raised her brows in an attempt at surprise. "So, your marriage to my mother was legitimate."

He nodded with a smile. "In every way. I insisted. My superiors were less than pleased."

"In the merchant company?"

He grinned rather proudly. "You did do the thing properly, didn't you?"

"I do try," she replied. "Though I had help."

James nodded his head, still smiling. "No, not with the merchant company. I did work for Dawes & Pope for a time, but it was a cover. You see, Amelia, I am a spy."

Amelia blinked at him in confusion. "A spy?"

Again came his slow nod. "For the Crown. Normally, I don't tell people that so early in our association, but I need you to understand, and I don't want to hide anything from you."

She hadn't expected that, and she couldn't deny that it had taken some of her indignation away in favor of curiosity. Not entirely, granted, but enough that she didn't have to restrain herself from striking him.

"So, Gabe and Rook and Gent and Cap…" she said slowly, sitting back a little.

He gave her a tight smile. "You'd better draw your own conclusions there, Amelia. I can reveal my own status, and that is all."

She supposed it didn't matter when it all came down to it, but it would certainly explain a lot; their street names, their secrecy, how

Gabe could easily pass as both Lord Wharton and as the Rogue when either was called for. She could easily see the connection, and she could understand why she had not been given such information.

"Why would you trust me with that knowledge?" she asked, narrowing her eyes. "Knowing I would be less than pleased to meet you, why?"

James' smile grew genuine once more. "Because you are your mother's daughter, Amelia, and trust and honor are innate in you."

At the mention of her mother in such warm tones, Amelia's eyes began to burn. "Did you love her?" she asked, before she could think of something else.

He looked surprised by the question, and then she saw him swallow. "Yes," he answered hoarsely, nodding, "Very much. She was the light of my life. I had never known a woman like her, with her spirit and character, and I never have since. She brought purpose to my life, and I hadn't known I was missing it."

Amelia found swallowing rather difficult in the face of his emotions. "Did she know?"

"She knew," he admitted, rubbing his hands together absently. "She would never have actually married a criminal, no matter what her father thought. Mary was far too clever for that, and she would have had my head."

That made Amelia chuckle against her will, and she stopped herself at once. She faced the older man squarely and remembered every painful moment of her mother's life, and hers. "If you loved her so much, why were you gone? We suffered so much, she endured so much, and she died calling for you!"

James groaned and clutched at his hair, his frame shaking. "Lord, forgive me my sins…" he moaned in agony.

"I doubt it works that quickly," Amelia muttered, shifting uncomfortably.

He looked back up at her without a hint of recrimination. "We were betrayed by one in our ranks. Covers were exposed, and all operatives in the field had to go into hiding immediately. I was in France at the time, and one of my colleagues was keeping an eye on you and your mother. When we were in danger, all families of the operatives had to be moved and had their names changed. There weren't that many with families at the time, but I was one of them."

"You weren't in hiding forever," Amelia pointed out, forgetting to insert anger into her words. "What happened?"

"My colleague died," James said with a weary sigh, showing his age for the first time. "We were so worried about what information had been compromised that nothing was documented, and most of our records were destroyed. When I came back to England, I could not find you or your mother. I had no record of your location or your names, and no one knew what had happened to you." He shook his head, his eyes gentle. "I looked for you for years. I would never have given up if there was the slightest hint that you might be alive."

Amelia felt a tear trickle down her cheek, and she swiped it away. "I hated you," she whispered. "I didn't understand why I didn't have you around, why we had to live the way we did. I blamed you..."

"I blame myself," he assured her with a soft interruption. "I will blame myself for the rest of my life. I can explain circumstances and situations for eternity, Amelia, but it will not change the fact that I should have been there. I know it, and you know it."

She nodded, the tightness in her chest easing ever so slightly. "What do you want, James?"

One side of his mouth lifted in a half smile. "A chance. That's all. I want to get to know the daughter I only knew a short while. I want you to have a chance to know me. I won't tempt fate with my further wishes than that, because I have much to make up for. But you have a father, Amelia, and I hope that one day you will be able to see me that way."

Impossibly, she wanted to believe him. She was angry with him, she wasn't sure she believed everything he said, but she believed his emotions, and she could see his genuine concern. She would find it very hard to kill this man sitting before her, now that she knew him and had listened to his side of the story.

She wasn't sure she wanted to even injure him, let alone claim her vengeance. But further than that, she would not speculate on.

A chance to have a father? Was it too late for such a thing?

She didn't know. But if he was willing to try...

"Very well," she heard herself say as if from a distance. "A chance it is."

Chapter Twenty-Three

"What do you mean he's gone?"

"Amelia…"

"No, don't you 'Amelia' me, James." She winced and shook her head. "Sorry. Father."

Her father chuckled and waved it off. "It's fine, Amelia. You may call me whatever suits you."

"If you don't tell me what I want to know, I might call you something else," she muttered under her breath.

He laughed again and came around his desk towards her. "Amelia, he is not gone forever. He's only working, and it may take some time."

"Working," she repeated, pleased that she didn't cringe when he put a hand on her arm.

It hadn't been easy, but the last two weeks had been eye-opening. Her father appeared to be everything she'd ever wanted her father to be, though it was so many years late. Their relationship had become something she was beginning to enjoy. He was witty, he was considerate, he listened with earnestness, and he had a fighting ring in the cellar where he trained daily. He preferred staffs, which Amelia had not understood until he'd shown her.

Now she trained with him every day.

He'd asked her to move into his townhouse, and she had yet to do so, but she was considering it. And not just for the training ring.

As odd as it sounded, and odder to feel, she trusted him. More than that, she liked him.

She hadn't told him yet, but she was also considering changing her last name to his. He was ready to claim her officially, he'd told her that much, and initially, she hadn't thought anything of it. But now…

She shook herself out of her reverie and tilted her head at her father. "Working as in…"

He smiled gently. "You know I can't tell you."

Amelia glowered, which made him chuckle again. "You know, a *real* father would tell his daughter what she wanted to know."

He patted her arm and winked. "Forgive me. I haven't been a father very long; five months when you were an infant plus the past two weeks. Don't worry. I am sure I will figure it out with practice."

She smirked playfully and turned from the room. "I'm going out."

"Take a servant."

She looked over her shoulder with a sardonic grin. "Why? You're having me followed anyway."

He waved her off, smiling in amusement.

Amelia let her smile fade as she went out, grateful her father lived in Cheapside instead of Mayfair. He had plenty of funds to do so, but he preferred the simpler lifestyle, and she was far more comfortable there herself. She would never have enjoyed moving into high Society after everything she had been through.

But even with all of that, she was anxious to see Gabe again. To apologize, to explain, to find out if… well, she couldn't hope that he would forgive her, she doubted he was the forgiving kind, even for her. Especially for her, given all that she had said and done. But she had to try.

If nothing else, she needed to see his face once more.

Two weeks and not a sight of him. Of any of them. Amelia was positive her father was their superior, but he adamantly refused to tell her anything about it. She'd been down to the offices several times, but Gabe was never there. The only thing anyone would say was that he was on assignment, whatever that meant, and that he would be back whenever he finished.

Apparently, he was not finished yet, which led her to believe it was a dangerous assignment.

Had he thrown himself into something treacherous on purpose? Did their last encounter have anything to do with it? Did she?

She could not bear the thought that she had driven him to it.

One thing she could say for her father was that he told her everything else he could of Gabe aside from his specific duties or assignments in their ranks. He told her of his early days with Gabe and how low he had sunk. He told her how reckless Gabe was, how skilled, how he had changed from the man he had been since joining them.

How could she have ever called him a traitor? Or without honor? How had she ever accused him of anything less than respectable and loyal behavior? He might have been irascible, and annoying, and beyond impertinent, but God help her, she adored him. She didn't deserve him, but she loved him all the same. And she had to believe that he had truly loved her.

Which made her betrayal far worse than his had been.

Had his been a betrayal at all?

"Good morning, Miss," came a cheery voice suddenly by her side.

Amelia looked up and saw Gent next to her, dressed in his usual common clothes, cap tipped back, dark stubble on his jaw. She scowled playfully up at him. "Are you on guard duty for me today?"

He barked a laugh and clasped his hands behind his back. "Heavens, no. I leave that for Knutt." He inclined his head behind them and grinned. "He's very bored."

Amelia glanced behind her but saw nothing. She looked up at Gent again. "I am a very boring woman now."

"I doubt that," he said with a chuckle. "But I do congratulate you on having a fine father."

"Yes, so I am learning." She sighed and rubbed her brow. "Gent, is there any word from him?"

He shook his head. "No, but there wouldn't be. He is in very deep right now, and to send word would be dangerous. But Skips will give a signal if anything needs to be done."

Amelia turned to him in surprise. "Skips is one of you?"

That made Gent grin outright. "Oh, my dear Amelia, you would be quite surprised how many people are one of us."

"There's a comforting thought," she muttered, shaking her head. "I can't trust anyone."

"Not really," he told her shrugging. "But you most certainly can't trust Rook."

"I knew that a long time ago," she assured him, adjusting the sleeves of her jacket, pressing down the fraying threads there.

Gent caught it, though. "Hmm," he mused with a sad shake of his head.

"What?" she demanded, daring him to comment further.

"We cannot have Eagle's daughter looking so shabby," he tsked. "It would look badly on the entire network."

Amelia rolled her eyes and scoffed loudly, drawing a look from passing people. "Oh, please, not that again. I can't keep going to Tilda, she'll start to charge me."

Gent smiled and took her arm in his. "Not Tilda, my dear. You're about to turn respectable, once your father officially claims you. There's a reputation to uphold, so you must do the thing properly."

"What, because I have a father with funds I must use them?" she asked with as much sarcasm as she could muster, which was a great deal.

He surprised her by nodding. "Indeed, yes. It is the way of things. But I will start you off easily enough. I'll have my wife call upon you when you are settled in with your father."

Amelia lifted a brow. "How do you know I am going to?"

He returned her look. "Aren't you?"

She opened her mouth to refute it but couldn't find the words to do so. Suddenly, she knew that was precisely what she was going to do. But she scowled up at Gent for good measure. "I hate you," she grumbled.

"It won't last," he promised, leading her down another street.

She thought about what he'd said, then jerked in his hold, looking back up at him. "Wait, you have a wife?"

He inclined his head. "Aye, I do. And she is most anxious to meet you, I can promise you that. She's tried to come by once or twice, but for obvious reasons, I don't allow her to. Dangerous area and wandering woman alone, secrets and intrigue… you know how it is."

"So that day that Rook was looking all smug and smarmy…" she prodded with a smile.

"Which time?" he asked, looking confused, but smiling.

"Gent…" Amelia groaned dramatically.

He chuckled. "Yes, that was because Margaret showed up, and he knew how it would irritate me." He sighed and shook his head. "I love my wife beyond anything, Amelia, but I do believe she will be the death of me. Do try to talk some sense into her, won't you?"

Now Amelia laughed, throwing her head back and pulling herself closer to his side. "What in the world makes you think that I have any sense to give her?"

"One can hope," he replied with a shrug. "Here we are."

They had arrived at Lord Wharton's townhouse, which Amelia had found within a day of realizing that Gabe had been right, and she had been horribly wrong.

She looked up at Gent suspiciously. "How did you know where I was going?"

He winked at her. "Lucky guess." He led her up the stairs and knocked on the door loudly. The scowling butler appeared, looking at Amelia with the same irritation he always did, but taking in Gent with mild interest. "Is your master at home, Houser?"

Houser shook his head. "No, sir, Gent. No' yet."

A scampering sound and a loud screech of delight from within made Houser sigh, and he turned around. "Will you keep yer bleeding mischief down? 'Ow can a man be a proper butler?"

"You're not one!" came a young voice that Amelia knew well.

"Daisy?" she almost whispered.

The little girl appeared and waved at her cheerily.

Houser made an odd hissing noise, and Daisy grinned at him, then dashed away.

Daisy was here? Gabe, who claimed to despise children and sentiment and all things soft, had the child living with him? And she was happy, looking well, and teasing the servants. Gabe was taking care of her.

Amelia could barely breathe, couldn't manage a single word, and barely heard Gent make their farewells to Houser. He took her arm and led her back the way they had come. She couldn't bear this, it was too much.

"She's not his," Gent said when Amelia could breathe again. "He just takes an interest. She stays with Tilda sometimes, but more often of late, she's been staying here. At his insistence."

"Oh, Gent," Amelia managed, tears rising and her chest constricting. "He's better than I ever knew, and I loved him already."

Gent took her hand and rubbed it gently. "I know, pet. Don't tell anybody, though. He likes to be the wicked one."

She laughed despite her tears. An idea had begun to form, and she looked up at Gabe's colleague and friend. "Gent, will you help me with something?"

He grinned crookedly. "Aye, Miss, anything you say."

"It is good to have you back, sir."

Gabe blearily looked at Houser over his breakfast, wishing he had another three days to sleep, as the one night he'd just passed at home hardly seemed sufficient. "Don't get soft on me now, Houser."

The large man grunted. "I would never. But it is good to have you all the same." The servant bowed, actually quite well, and turned from the dining room.

Gabe watched him go with a furrowed brow. He'd been gone a month, all told, and it had been the most grueling month of his life. He'd been so thoroughly into his character he had nearly forgotten who he was. It was quite a satisfying feeling to have the reprieve, but more satisfying to know he'd never truly forgotten his mission.

And to be a spy again had been a pleasant relief.

But he was also bloody exhausted by it, which only went to show he was out of practice.

Still, he'd managed to discover a well-concealed smuggling operation. Weapons and munitions were being sent to their irritating French faction from yet another set of English supporters. Granted, at least half of those supporters were only interested in the reward that such actions would bring them, but treason was treason all the same.

He'd not been able to discover anything about Alex, but it was not for want of trying. He could only assume that, for one reason or another, that particular band of smugglers was no longer working out of London.

It was suspicious, as London was a lucrative location for anyone looking to turn a profit, but if they had known who Alex was…

He had to doubt that. No one knew anything about Trace, it was part of his intrigue. It was the most valuable skill he possessed.

Had possessed.

Gabe sighed and rubbed his eyes, wishing his full-bodied weariness away. He'd returned home very late the night before after reporting in to Weaver and Cap. They had questioned him on everything he'd uncovered, only stopping when he'd almost fallen asleep on the floor of Weaver's office. Then he'd had other reports to attend to at his home, some of which he had managed to take in before finally collapsing into bed. He could only remember one of them.

Amelia.

He pushed up out of the chair with a groan and strode from the room, determined to banish her from his thoughts with distractions of work. When he had moments of clarity, recollecting himself, his thoughts were most often of her, and it drove him mad. The look in her eyes at their last meeting, the venom in her words, the betrayal etched in every line of her lovely face, they were all before him.

He tried to satisfy himself that he had done right by his conscience, and certainly by his mentor, but what about her? He had injured she to whom his heart belonged. Could he be absolved of that great crime by the greater right of truth and best intentions of his actions?

He left the house without a word, ignoring the few people that milled about the streets. The day was one of clouds and gloom, and he was grateful for it. He could not bear to think of light or warmth at present and might not for some time. But to endure association with Gent, who lived in a continual glow of love and fidelity, and with Cap, who had lost his great love and had never recovered, or, heaven forbid, with Eagle, whose life had been brightened by the very woman Gabe himself loved, any of them would have made his day infinitely worse.

Which left only the clerks and Rook whom he could safely

endure.

God help him.

"My Lord Wharton?"

Gabe stopped in his tracks closing his eyes at the soft voice behind him. He was not ready for this. He could not...

He found himself turning towards her with a perfectly blank, yet hopefully polite expression. "Miss Martin."

Amelia looked at him with uncertainty, her smile tentative, her fingers wringing themselves together with a desperation that betrayed her outward calm. She was better dressed than he had ever seen her, and she looked all the better for it. She could have easily passed as a well-born lady with a proper dowry and family, which, he supposed, she was now, and it suited her well. Her features were a little drawn, if he were to be severe, but he did not think he had ever seen a more beautiful sight. Or a more excruciating one.

The swift pain slashing across his midsection was a testament to that.

"So," Amelia began with a slight waver in the simple word, "you are returned."

He inclined his head. "As you see."

Her smile spread just a little. "I had a watch on your house. To inform me when you had arrived. The Gent helped me set it up, and it worked perfectly. Last night, I received word of you, and I was half-tempted to come straightaway, but it hardly seemed appropriate to barge in on you in the middle of the night. But you've been away so long, and no one would tell me anything, so I knew it had to be dangerous..."

She was rambling, and he had learned long ago that she only rambled when she was nervous, which was rare indeed. He couldn't bear the sight and sound of it and had to put an end to it. "To what point and purpose did you have my house watched, Miss Martin?" he interrupted politely. "I do not object, I only ask your reasons."

"I..." She paused and shook her head slightly, forcing her fingers to settle. "I wanted to thank you."

Gabe hadn't expected that. He forced his hands to clasp behind his back to steady himself. He wanted to prod her on, to hear more, and he also wanted her to stop. He couldn't bear her gratitude, not when he wanted so much more. Torn in his extremes, he said nothing.

"Your actions, your dedication to our dealings…" She swallowed, and he was grateful she didn't expound on the specifics. They were in public, after all. She looked up at him with another faint smile. "Even when I could not see it, you always did the right thing. You've restored me to my family, and I am so grateful to you."

He would not bear this. He shook his head, smiling as kindly as he could manage. "It was nothing. I am pleased you have found each other. Your gratitude is unnecessary."

Amelia's brow furrowed in surprise at his formal, polite tone. "It is not nothing! You know how I felt about him, and you knew him, and it's because of you that I have come to know him and love him myself. Without you, I… I would never…" She broke off with a choked sound, and the sheen of tears in her eyes weakened his knees. She managed a watery smile. "He's my father, Gabe. He's my father."

Impossibly, he found swallowing difficult, and he no longer had to pretend at his gentle smile. "I know. And I know what that means."

She nodded, her lashes fluttering over the tears.

Gabe shook his head slowly, still smiling. "But you don't need to thank me. Truly. I am glad you are happy. Good day, Miss Martin." He bowed and turned away, hoping against hope that he could get enough distance to escape the crushing pain in his chest. He strode away in careful, controlled paces, resisting the urge to bolt in order to escape all the faster.

"Gabe?" Amelia called, her voice shrill and filled with such agony that he was forced to stop. "Did I ruin my chances? Has my pride and thirst for revenge made you hate me?"

Gabe's hands clenched at his sides, and he glanced behind him. "I could never hate you," he replied, not entirely certain she would hear him.

"Then look at me!" she cried, the sound of tears evident. "Look at me and tell me if you could ever love me again."

Slowly, Gabe turned to face her, and the sight of tears on her perfect face, vulnerability and distress in her eyes, broke something within him, and he exhaled heavily, shaking his head. "I never stopped loving you, Amelia."

Her eyes widened, and then Amelia suddenly sobbed and took an unsteady step towards him, one hand reaching out, the other clutching at her chest.

Gabe released his own moan of distress and marched to her quickly, gathering her up in his arms and kissing her with all the passion and longing he had borne in the last few weeks. His hands stroked her face, tangled in her hair, clung to her desperately as his lips claimed her for himself, no matter what followed. Amelia gripped his coat and sobbed against his mouth, the taste of her tears softening his kisses.

He pulled back, keeping her face in his hands, and pushed back the hair from her face. She smiled with quivering lips, which his thumb smoothed, while a few stray tears fell, and he kissed those away. "You called me a liar," he reminded her gently, smiling to attempt to lessen the sting. "A traitor, a man with no honor, and who knows what else behind my back. You said you didn't know how you could trust me. You said you hated me. And yet I still love you. I am still wholly and completely in love with you. My time away from you has only intensified that. So, the question that remains, my dear Amelia, is if you could ever love me again."

"Yes," Amelia gasped, nodding over and over again in his hold. "Yes, yes, yes."

Gabe drew her to him, sighing with relief and pressing her face against his shoulder, her hands still clenched on his lapels. He wrapped his arms around her and touched his lips to her ear. "You're going to have to say it, love," he murmured with a hint of a chuckle. "You know me, I need proof."

She laughed against him and lifted her head, her smile dazzling him with its brilliance. "I love you, Gabriel Fitzgerald Oliver Statler. As Lord Wharton, as the Rogue, and as the biggest pain the arse I have ever met."

"Shut up, woman," he groaned, grinning madly like he was someone else entirely.

He leaned down and brought his lips to hers, loving the feel of them and the way they molded perfectly to his. Amelia tugged him closer, and he followed with a faint hum of approval, tenderly ravaging her mouth, giving each aspect its due consideration. There

269

was no hint of the frenzy from before, everything slow and languorous, and very, very thorough.

He could have kissed her until the end of time.

And if he had any say in the matter, he would.

Gabe gently broke the kiss, nuzzled her softly, then gruffly asked, "Who the bloody hell told you my full name?"

Amelia's delighted laughter echoed off the buildings around them and within the walls of his heart, which he'd almost entirely forgotten that he had.

The Rogue with a heart? No one would ever believe that.

But the secret would be safe with her.

As would he.

Epilogue

$\mathcal{T}$he house was dark, as it ought to have been, with no sign of life from within. The grounds were still, and the only sounds were those of his footsteps, which were faint at best.

It was perfect for his plans.

Gabe skirted around the outside of the house, grateful that even the moon had complied with his wishes tonight by rising late and in a cloud-riddled sky. With no light to expose him, he could move even more stealthily than he otherwise might have done.

He kept his back to the wall, measuring his breath against the paces he took, counting silently as he progressed. He reached an almost hidden door and tried the handle, but it was locked.

He smirked at that. For the truly skilled, a locked door was more of an invitation than a hindrance, and he was very skilled. He reached into his coat pocket and pulled out his tools, deftly picking the lock with only the softest clicks of distress from it. The door opened almost silently at his next attempt, and he slipped into the building, closing the door with his back.

Alone in the dark, he waited for his eyes to adjust, not at all concerned about time, as he was earlier than he had planned as it was. For once, he did not need to do his task expeditiously. This was one thing he must do with caution, patience, and absolute precision.

He'd learned that after all this time.

He pushed forward in the darkness, feeling along the wall lightly. He knew the paces in this hallway, but one could never be too careful, particularly when things might have changed in his absence. The structure of the building would not have altered, but obstacles were always a risk, and he must take care.

When he felt the break in the wall, he grinned to himself and stepped up into the small, darkened staircase. No obstacles, then. What a relief.

It was convenient indeed to have nothing to stop him, and no further delays in the completion of his mission.

He almost snorted to himself. Since when was coming home part of a mission?

Though, if he considered it properly, at times getting himself home was a greater mission than whatever he had been assigned. The more complicated things became in the world, let alone in London, the more challenging his life grew.

Least of all because leaving home was no longer an easy matter for him.

He smiled to himself as he went into the first room he reached, silently as he had ever done. It looked exactly as he had left it a week ago, as he'd hoped it would be. One never knew these days, and he missed so much when he was away.

And he was away far too often.

Gabe approached the bed quietly, its occupant very much asleep, and, given prior history, in no danger of awakening for quite some time.

The dark hair was in complete and utter disarray, as usual, and that would unfortunately probably remain its natural state. It was the same hair as his father, and that had never been tamed. Tightly held in a small fist was a toy soldier, the paint worn in places due to age and excessive activity. That, too, had been his father's, and all that remained of what had once been a grand set of soldiers. But the boy adored that lone soldier, and it was rarely out of his sight.

Contrary to his usual inclination against demonstration of affection, which was rapidly becoming less and less of his usual inclination, he reached out and brushed the boy's hair from his brow. He didn't stir, except to exhale heavily and settle more fully against his pillow.

Gabe smiled and let his hand drop, then turned from the room. Tomorrow, he would take his son for a ride, no matter the protests of anyone else, considering the boy loved it and begged for it whenever he could. Then they would play Army out in the woods, wherein Gabe would be a very insubordinate soldier, as he usually was, with a very demanding, if only just barely coherent, superior officer.

The next room kept him a little longer, if only because he still could not believe the delicate porcelain doll of a creature was his. A son he had been ready for, prepared for, understood how to behave and what was needed. But a daughter…

She left him more terrified than most of his covert missions did.

Never mind that she was still an infant, she was already such a beautiful girl that it drew comment, and he was half tempted to arrange a marriage with one of Cap's sons just to ensure that she had a good husband who would be far too intelligent to behave in any respect not deemed perfect.

Gent had sons, but they were not coming anywhere near her, or any future daughters he might have.

If, God forbid, Rook should have sons, Gabe would ensure his daughter was never informed of their existence.

He exhaled slowly, reaching out a finger to stroke the plump cheek of his dark-haired daughter, who had his curls but her mother's coloring. She was a curious one, always crawling about into seemingly impossible places, and she embarked on each of her adventures with a beaming grin that would probably be the death of him one day.

She was the happiest child he had ever seen in his entire life, which made him wonder if he was doing something wrong. He could only count a handful of times where she had genuinely been distressed, which undoubtedly was indicative that his daughter was not well.

Except she was absolutely perfect in every way.

So he, as her father, must only take care not to make any mistakes with her.

Which was a ridiculous thing, since he'd already made roughly two hundred in her life.

And it did not help that her honorary godmothers, his aunt, Geraldine, and her mother's aunt, Dottie, and her designated godmother, Lady Marlowe, spoiled her excessively and enjoyed pointing out Gabe's flaws.

She would see them for herself soon enough; she did not need their assistance there.

Gabe shook his head and stroked her cheek one last time, then turned out of that room as well, finally feeling the fatigue of his journey and the relief of returning home.

A smile formed on his face thinking of Whitleigh as home. A place he had hated for the majority of his life was now the only place he wanted to be. Not because of the grandeur of its façade or the improvements they had made with Geraldine's money, as she had decided he was worthy of it even before her death, or the fond memories he had made here with the family he never thought he'd have.

His family was here. That was what made it home.

And his favorite of all homecomings was the one he was about to have.

He slipped into the room down at the end of the hall, closing the door without a sound, and moved to the window, taking a moment to sink down into the chair near it to remove his boots. Then he rose and turned to the window itself. The curtains were not completely drawn, and he took a moment to stare out at the grounds, now that the moon was out. They were still not what they ought to have been, but considering where they had come from, the change was almost miraculous.

Rather like the change in him.

He turned to face the bed, where the woman who had given him everything that mattered in his life slept, her back to him, the way she usually slept. When he was gone, she took up the entire bed, and it amused him to think that she did not miss him as much as he missed her. She would viciously argue the point every time and say that her expansion on the mattress was evidence of her love and pain at his absence, that she was trying to be where he was supposed to be, but he doubted that. Not her love or her pain at his absence, he could never doubt her there.

He was only convinced she rather liked having the bed to herself at times.

Which was really too bad for her tonight.

Gabe took off the rest of his outerwear and stockings, then

pulled back the coverlet and slid into bed, settling himself directly behind his wife and wrapping his arms around her, pulling her against his chest.

She stirred sleepily and sighed as he rubbed his hands across her swollen abdomen. "You're back," she murmured.

He kissed the back of her neck through the long mane of her hair. "What gave me away?"

Amelia laughed throatily, which always stirred him, and pressed back against him a little. "Lucky guess. Did you sneak into the house again?"

"Of course," he said with a soft snort. "How else am I to test our weaknesses?"

"Even though you have half of the League's contacts scattered about the area to keep watch and that half of our household are trained operatives to protect us?" she asked dryly.

Gabe nuzzled against her hair roughly. "You've never complained before. And I might remind you that you enjoy a great amount of safety and security despite being married to me."

She made a soft sound of amusement. "I do beg your pardon. How long did it take you with the lock this time?"

He chuckled and pulled her closer, moving his hands gently over their unborn third child. "Twenty-three seconds."

"My, my," Amelia commented with a disapproving sound. "So hasty. Why the rush?"

"No idea," he replied, sighing deeply. "But I am much relieved to be in a proper bed again."

A swift elbow jab into his stomach had him wheezing for a moment, and he laughed with difficulty, twining his legs with hers. "Did you check on the children?" Amelia asked softly.

He nodded against her, the desire to sleep starting to wear on him. "Of course. I think Alex has grown since I left."

Amelia scoffed and rubbed her hands over his. "He has not. But he has gained two scratches, one bruise, and someone has taught him some inappropriate French words."

"I don't know anything about that," Gabe said at once. "Must be that unruly grandfather of his, he is always causing problems. Or Cook, you know how she gets on baking day."

"Yes, I shall have to interrogate both of them," Amelia muttered. "They are obviously the most likely."

"Obviously." He let his breathing deepen and settled against her comfortably.

"How did it go?" Amelia asked quietly just as he was nearing sleep.

Gabe hummed a little in thought, wondering how to answer. He wanted to be truthful, but not give her cause to worry. "Well enough," he eventually answered. "Not quite what we had hoped for, but it could have been worse."

She made a noncommittal noise that told him nothing. "Did you lose anyone?"

"Not this time, no."

"Do you miss having Father in charge?"

He could hear the smile in her question, and it made him smile too. "Every bloody day. Cap is insufferable in his new command. I blame you for giving Eagle a reason to leave us."

Amelia snickered and drew one of his hands up to kiss it.

"What did I miss?" he asked, shifting his mouth so it was near her ear.

She turned to face him a little but kept his arms tightly around her. "Mary tried to walk for Margaret. She's nearly there, it should only be a few days. But I told her she had to wait for Papa."

Gabe grinned down at her and stroked her face softly. "Thank you, love."

She reached her hand up to his cheek, brushing her fingers over his features before reaching around to cup the back of his head. "Alex wants to show you a rabbit's den he found. Says you both must investigate."

He chuckled and tilted his head. "Can he actually say 'investigate' yet?"

Amelia shook her head from side to side. "Not yet."

Gabe rubbed his hand over her stomach and paused for a thumping he had come to crave. "And this little one?"

"This one," Amelia said with a crooked grin, "is probably your fighter. I've never had one like this, and I'm blaming you if it gets worse."

"I'll take it," he murmured, suddenly overcome with a sense of contentment and joy that had become a companion of his lately.

He was filled with love for this woman in his arms, for their children in the rooms beyond, and the one yet to be born, and for the future before them all. He had never been a giddy man, but at this moment, he suspected that's what this was.

Amelia cocked her head at him. "Gabe?"

He leaned down to gently kiss her, lingering and lavishing upon her all the tenderness he was suddenly feeling. "I missed you," he whispered against her lips.

"I missed you, too." She pressed her lips back to his, wringing more from him than he'd thought he could bear in his current state.

"Why is it," he rasped, drawing back to look at her, "that I love you more and more with every passing day?"

"I have that effect on people," she replied, smiling softly, her fingers toying with his hair.

Gabe laughed and nudged her with his nose. "Impertinent woman."

"I love you," Amelia suddenly whispered, her eyes misting over. "So much. And I'm so glad you're home."

He shook his head. "So am I, love. So am I." He leaned down and kissed her again, taking quite a long time to do so.

"You know," Amelia said, breaking off the kiss abruptly, "you are making it rather difficult for a woman in my condition to sleep. Shame on you."

He gave her a singularly wicked look. "Well, they do call me the Rogue."

She lifted a brow at him. "Do they?"

He nodded, leaning down to nibble along her jaw. "They most certainly do."

"And are you?" she asked, arching her neck towards him.

"Indeed, madam. A rogue without honor."

"You keep telling me that," Amelia murmured, her eyelashes fluttering, "but I'm beginning to doubt your claims. All I have ever seen is a man with honor that runs so deep, it is the essence of him. He may be a little bit wicked, slightly disreputable, but honor is something he does not lack."

Gabe groaned and drew himself up onto one elbow to shake his head at her. "You must keep that a secret, my love. My reputation will be quite ruined. Whoever heard of a rogue with honor?"

Amelia nodded somberly. "Oh, indeed. It shall be my secret. What a rare conquest I have made."

He touched her lips with a finger, tracing the contours of their fullness as they spread into a smile. "And continue to make, you know. Every single day."

That seemed to surprise her a little, and her fingers stroked his hair as she smiled fondly. "Why, you are most romantic, Rogue…"

Gabe grinned down at his wife, feeling rather roguish indeed at the moment. "Now that, you may feel free to spread far and wide." And then he kissed his wife again, and neither of them had anything else to say for quite some time.

But then, after all, he was a rogue.

Coming Soon

The London League
Book Three

"Not your average cap..."

by

Rebecca Connolly

CPSIA information can be obtained
at www.ICGtesting.com
Printed in the USA
LVHW012146230120
644554LV00004B/59